MOONRISE

"You don't scare me," Pascale said, maddeningly.

"That's the second time you've said that to me." Jack's voice was a low rumble in his throat.

She squared her shoulders. "You cannot stop me from trying to recover my property."

With one hand under Pascale's haughty little chin, he raised her eyes to his. "It's not yours."

"Let go of me. You brute!"

With one hand holding the candle, he had only one arm free to subdue her. Jack hauled her to him with one quick jerk.

"Bête!"

"A beast, am I?" Goaded beyond measure, Jack lowered his head and kissed her.

Pascale's lips, parted slightly with her gasp of outrage, were warm and soft under his own. Sudden passion bolted through him like lightning. Driven by an age-old impulse, he softened the punishing kiss, and molded his lips gently to hers.

MOONRISE

ROBERTA GAYLE

PINNACLE BOOKS
KENSINGTON PUBLISHING CORP.

PINNACLE BOOKS are published by

Kensington Publishing Corp.
850 Third Avenue
New York, NY 10022

First Printing: May, 1996
10 9 8 7 6 5 4 3 2 1

Printed in the United States of America

This book is dedicated to Ollie and Rhona.
Thank you for your support and encouragement.
Know that I love you, always.

One

Paris, 1865

Like most Frenchwomen, Pascale de Ravenault was born with a very practical side to her nature—this was unfortunately the bane of her existence. However, it did serve a useful purpose. Without that wide streak of practicality, neither Pascale nor her father would have been in Paris attending one of the grandest balls of the spring "season." Instead they would have been enjoying a cozy evening at their home in Beaune. Paul de Ravenault, an artist, could only be truly happy in his studio and he would never have thought to leave it. It was due purely to Pascale's ambition that her adored papa was one of the honored guests of a hostess as distinguished as the Princess Mathilde, distant cousin of the Emperor Napoleon III.

"Hold still, Papa," Pascale begged as she rearranged the fall of lace at his cuff.

"I'll do it, Pascale," Paul de Ravenault said pettishly trying to pull his wrist from his daughter's grasp.

"It's easier for me, I've got two hands to work with." She pulled the last little fold of the intricate Spanish lace from beneath his jacket sleeve and gasped. Bright specks of vermilion marred the white perfection.

"Oh, Papa," she said, looking up at him reproachfully.

He avoided her eyes, examining the mess he'd made. "Look at that," he offered. "It's dried already." He dabbed at the spots, awkwardly trying to flick them off. "It's not so bad, is it?" he asked. "It was a little accident, that's all."

"You looked so fine," she said mournfully, batting his hand away and surveying the damage. Oil paint. It would be impossible to remove.

There was nothing to be done now. The carriage was rolling up to the imperial residence of Princess Mathilde.

"It's too late to go home and change it," Pascale said, hastily tucking the offending fold back out of view. "As you well know, you old rogue."

"That's all right," her fond parent said sympathetically. "No one will notice, I'm sure."

As they descended from the carriage, Pascale checked Paul de Ravenault's appearance one last time. Her father looked elegant and distinguished in his formal clothing. His features were clearly inherited from his African forebears, his skin a shade darker than *café au lait*. His high forehead and thin face gave him the deceptive appearance of an ascetic. His newly acquired glasses and close-cropped gray-streaked beard masked the wide unfocused eyes and slightly petulant mouth that gave away his *true* nature, that of an irresponsible child.

He turned to help her from the carriage, ignoring the footman who stood waiting to perform that office. Pascale took his hand and was rewarded with a flash of his familiar wide smile.

"That creamy color you're wearing makes you look quite delicious, *mignon*," he said.

"Thank you, *mon père*." Pascale, too, thought the dress of eggshell satin, with its wide tiered skirt and bodice adorned with scallops of cream lace looked quite good on her. It complemented her cocoa-colored skin. "You chose it," she reminded him.

"So I did," he said, well pleased with himself.

She took his arm and they walked slowly together up the brightly lit walk to the front door. Those impressive bastions were flanked on each side by a liveried servant, who swung them open as they gained the top step.

Pascale had timed their arrival carefully to be neither unfashionably early nor too fashionably late, as befit their status as two of the many guests of honor. The princess had not yet wandered far from her receiving chair at the entryway when they were announced.

"Monsieur de Ravenault," she greeted them. *"Mademoiselle.* I am so pleased to see you both."

"The pleasure is entirely ours." Paul de Ravenault bowed over her hand; quite gracefully, Pascale thought.

The announcement of new arrivals caught the princess's attention. "I must go and greet my guests, but I will come and find you later when we will have time for a little chat," she promised before bustling away.

"Whatever we do, we must avoid that woman," Papa said, grinning conspiratorially at Pascale. She shushed him, looking after their buxom blonde hostess who was, thankfully, too far away to have heard. She couldn't help smiling a little at his irreverence, though, as he led her through the salons and into the ballroom. There the *haut monde* awaited them, resplendent in their satins and silks. The crowd shimmered in the light of hundreds of candles suspended in the crystal chandeliers above.

It was an amazing sight. It was also an intimidating one. Papa halted at the top of the stairs leading down to the ballroom. Pascale gave his hand a reassuring pat and they moved forward together. This soiree was timed to coincide with the Salon; the official exhibition of the Royal Academy of Arts and Sciences. Accordingly, and in keeping with the atmosphere of artistic enlightenment, artists (whether noble and wellheeled, or untitled and impoverished) were invited to this social event. It was an opportunity Pascale had been determined to exploit. It was even grander than she'd imagined. Pascale recognized among the guests not only French royalty, but heads of state from all over the continent, statesmen and great orators, famous authors, and, of course, some of the most important artists in the world. Pascale had used every resource at her disposal to gain an invitation to these hallowed halls and she refused to be daunted now.

She swallowed and rearranged her silken scarf about her shoulders. These influential gentlemen and ladies possessed the power to raise her father's work to the height of fashion, or to cast it into the depths of obscurity. With one well-timed bon mot, they secured their positions as arbiters of art and fashion. Despite her very natural impatience at having to fawn over, flirt with and flatter every supposed art lover she was introduced to, she was accustomed to her role.

Pascale wended her way through the bedecked, bejeweled assemblage that thronged the ballroom.

"How will we ever find anyone?" Papa asked nervously. "I'm supposed to meet François and Guillaume."

"We'll find them, or they'll find us. Just nod and smile, at everyone," she reminded him. It did not matter that most of these scions of society had neither taste nor discernment. What was important was that they accepted the de Ravenault family, regardless of their brown skin, their lack of title or wealth, and her father's unfortunate occupation. Tonight's invitation proved that Pascale's efforts on her father's behalf had not been in vain. She should have been dancing on air, but instead she felt restless and slightly uncomfortable.

She held on to Papa's arm as they threaded their way toward the dance floor. Little as she might like to encourage the pretensions of these shallow-minded people, the de Ravenault family *had* to cater to the foolish vanity of arrogant men with too much money, and silly women who accepted elite society's dicta as their laws. This was how she and Papa earned their daily bread. It would all be worth it, she would make sure of that.

Since the Revolution nearly eighty years before, certain privileges were no longer held by the nobility; art and culture were still, however, the province of those with money and leisure enough to collect and appreciate it. And, of course, official authority over the arts was maintained by the French government, as it was by the ruling powers of every nation. If, as Pascale believed, Napoleon III and the Empress Eugénie were only superficially interested in the arts and artists, that was only to be expected from those who were concerned with governing the entire nation. Others among the nobility had no such excuse, and Pascale had little patience with their posturing. However, she did have friends in every strata of society, true art lovers whom she both liked and admired and who had gained her an invitation to this ball.

To have one of the imperials as an admirer of her father's works was beyond even Pascale's lofty ambitions. But the appearance of official sanction was of paramount importance to any artist who hoped to sell his work, and sell it well. To be acknowledged by the Académie and its supporters was to have a brilliant future. However, for a man like Paul de Ravenault, who had studied with no recognized master, but had trained himself, it was virtually impossible to gain any attention at all from art critics or buyers. Therefore, Pascale arranged that they attend the princess's grand ball.

Princess Mathilde, herself, was a painter of some merit. The jury had awarded one of her paintings, in the Salon of 1861, an honorable mention. One of her paintings had been accepted for the current Salon of 1865. Pascale did not suppose this was entirely due to the position of her lover, Count Nieuwerkerke, who had been appointed minister of fine arts, as well as director general of museums, imperial court chamberlain, a member of the Institute, and commander of the Legion of Honor. Pascale had seen Nieuwerkerke on her way into the room, talking with Monsieur Ingles, the director of the Académie. If they were lucky, he was one of the people they might meet tonight.

Mathilde liked to gather Paris's greatest writers, painters, and composers around her. Pascale did not dare to think the de Ravenaults, father or daughter, would actually join that illustrious circle, but she had set certain goals for herself. If her father's paintings could not command the prices of a Monet or a Renoir, she could still support her household with his more modest sales. Pascale's aim was to increase the number of commissions Paul de Ravenault received. There was even a slight possibility that, with the right introductions, he might find a wealthy patron. As if he read her thoughts, Nieuwerkerke suddenly materialized before them. His secretary, who introduced himself as Monsieur Serratt, apologized charmingly for the lack of formality.

"I'd been hoping to meet you at some point, *monsieur,*" Nieuwerkerke said to Papa. "Princess Mathilde has been very complimentary of your work."

"We're honored," Pascale answered, squeezing her father's arm before he could make any untoward remarks about the princess.

"Indeed honored," Papa echoed.

Nieuwerkerke nodded, then waved at someone behind them.

"Excuse us," Monsieur Serratt said. "The minister promised to speak with Señor Otero tonight." He leaned closer to Papa. "One cannot escape these Mexican émigrés, even at a party."

Pascale watched the two men walk away in dazed delight.

"Who was that fellow?" Papa asked. "And why did you pinch me like that?"

"That," said Pascale triumphantly, "was the minister of fine arts."

"Fine, fine," he said. "That's all right, then. I think I see . . ." The rest of his sentence was lost as he turned and walked through an opening in the shifting throng of people around them. It closed up behind him before Pascale could follow. She looked after him, then shrugged. She couldn't watch him every minute. She didn't think it would cause any harm if he wandered around by himself for a little bit. They had already met one of the most influential men in the art world. She would find Papa soon. Meanwhile, she could bask in the glow created by their unexpected good fortune.

She turned her attention to the splendid scene around her. The ladies' brightly colored gowns caught the light as they swayed and swirled to the music. The jeweled heels of their dancing slippers glinted as they twirled in the arms of elegantly dressed gentlemen. Pascale was caught up in the sight. The music came to a close, and she was forced to a standstill as couples who had been dancing joined the humming mill of people who surrounded her.

She felt almost invisible as she was buffeted by the fine ladies and gentlemen. As usual, when she was nervous, her tongue darted out to wet dry lips. She'd forgotten that in honor of this occasion she'd agreed to let Odelle add some red color to her lips and cheeks. She felt very self-conscious as she clamped her mouth shut again. Her hand went to her hair. As was the fashion, her short locks had been tortured into a mass of curls that ringed her face, and long strands of black curls had been added to fall over her bare back and shoulders. The cream-colored silk dress she had had made for this soiree molded itself to her hourglass figure like a second skin, and outlined her waist and hips before billowing out over her knees and feet. The style suited her. Short of stature, the fashionably long train gave her the impression of height, while the close-fitting bodice enhanced her feminine charms. She had enjoyed the *oohs* and *ahhs* of her loving household, but half-welcomed her anonymity among these strangers.

A debonair aristocrat caught Pascale's eye as he led his very young, very beautiful partner from the floor. She recognized the boy as one of her father's less talented students. She watched him as he returned the ravishing young girl who had been his partner to her mama's side, and relinquished her hand with a graceful bow. The orchestra struck up again and the young gentleman retired. Immediately a crowd of *ingenues* in dresses of white and palest pastels gathered around the lucky girl. Pascale's mind wandered to how she would paint the child, if she still painted.

"He was so charming, so suave. Fancy, the marquis said he'd like to paint a portrait of me in this gown." This naive remark elicited ecstatic sighs from the group of envious young women. "He said it brought out the blue of my eyes," she said, blissful.

"What did you say?" asked one of the debutantes.

"I couldn't think what to say."

"Mama?"

"We will discuss it later, *ma petite*." Mama noticed Pascale watching them, and recognition dawned in her eyes. "Mademoiselle de Ravenault? I believe we met at the ballet."

"Yes, *madame*. It's a pleasure to see you again." Pascale was introduced by the proud mama to the other chaperones. The younger women were still talking of the marquis.

"It wouldn't be proper, would it?" one shocked innocent asked. "I'm certain *Maman* would never let a gentleman paint me."

"We had a portrait painted of the whole family five or six years ago." The beauty looked imploringly toward her mama. Pascale exchanged an amused glance with the girl's mama. Though she was closer in age to the child than to the parent, she felt more of a kinship with the older women who hovered near their young charges.

"You had better put him off. I don't think he could do you justice. Yet." Pascale smiled in an effort to soften her words. "The marquis is still learning." Several pairs of inquiring young eyes turned to Pascale. The young ladies had been so intent on discovering what it was like to dance with a single young gentleman, they had barely noticed her arrival, but her personal knowledge of the young marquis gained their undivided attention.

"It would not do to have a bad portrait painted, you know," Pascale joked gently. The girls giggled, and their chaperones relaxed, just as she had hoped. Pascale knew exactly what to say to put them at ease. It was second nature to slip into the role of mediator between the passionate youngster and the wary mother. She was accustomed to it. She had a family to feed.

If occasionally she wished that she could be as free and

easy as these young girls, rather than a responsible, more mature influence on them, she would console herself with the thought of the portraits that would certainly be commissioned as a result of this daring foray into society, and the monies they would earn.

"The marquis has quite an eye for color, though," Pascale continued. "That blue does become you remarkably well."

The proud mother of the child added her thanks to her daughter's. "Perhaps you'd like to consider having a portrait painted in that gown," Pascale said to both women. "By someone who is rather more experienced, of course." She exchanged a speaking glance with the debutante's *maman* and was satisfied with the glow of approval she saw in that lady's eyes.

Pascale was quite familiar with the challenge of trying to steer an innocent through these dangerous shoals—her father was as apt as these babes to commit a monstrous faux pas. It was left to Pascale to mend fences as best she could when he delivered some unpardonable insult, such as pointing out a prospective client's unusually pointy chin (as he'd done once at an "artistic salon" one of their patrons had invited them to). Pascale scanned the room for the incorrigible scamp, hoping that he was behaving himself.

She finally spotted the thin, overly tall figure talking to two of his oldest friends, and sent up a silent prayer of thanks. He was safe in the company of Guillaume Pelotte and François Elizabeth. As always, the sight of her distinguished parent brought a smile to her lips. It was worth it, all of it, to see Papa surrounded by his admirers in the newly renovated grand ballroom of one of Paris's most elite residents. She could picture his bemused expression. He had hunched up into a stoop-shouldered stance that made him look like a turtle trying to retreat into his shell. She recognized that distinct pose as easily as she could the brush strokes that characterized his work. In this setting, he was easy to spot. Often, at these gatherings, the de Ravenaults had the only black faces in the crowd.

He was dressed, in the current fashion, in black velvet, the white of his cuffs and cravat emphasized his dark complexion. His skin, though lighter than her own, was still several shades darker than anyone else's. His tall gangly frame somehow seemed artistic, rather than overgrown, and his thinness emphasized his unusual height.

She watched, smiling, as some other guests tried to join the little group. The retiring, socially inept artist was one of the most sought-after guests at the party. It had been risky, but Pascale had started a rumor that Paul de Ravenault's abstracted air was caused by his ennui with all things social. She'd managed to imply that actually engaging Papa in conversation was possible only if one were to startle him out of his boredom. It was a challenge that had been picked up by some of the patrons of the arts.

She knew she had no need to worry that her father would give her away. If he didn't insult someone outright (by saying, as he had at a party they'd attended the previous year, that one woman *could* not be painted in a flattering light), her maneuvering should cover up any lapses in the artist's memory. If Paul de Ravenault called anyone he should have known by the wrong name tonight, the insult wouldn't be greeted with outrage. The offended party would merely work harder to penetrate the fog that surrounded him. And as Pascale well knew, that was an impossible feat. Her father rarely even remembered the subject currently under discussion. She doubted he would even respond to half of the comments that might be made tonight in order to impress him.

Pascale relaxed a little. The conversation among the ladies she had joined had moved away from the marquis and portraiture, and it was no longer of interest to her. She excused herself, with a promise to call on the pretty debutante's mother to discuss having a portrait painted. She made her way over to her father's side. As she slowly made her way through the throng, Guillaume hailed another man. He didn't look familiar. She watched, curious, as he and her father shook hands. Even from this distance she could see that he was darker complexioned than her father, perhaps even as dark as she. As she drew nearer, she saw that his features were indeed African, though his wavy black hair proclaimed some Spanish or Italian blood in his ancestry. Her interest was piqued.

She was sure she would have remembered him had they met. His aristocratic bearing and remarkable figure would certainly have made a lasting impression. His dark skin set him apart from the people that surrounded them. For the second time that evening, her fingers itched to grasp a paintbrush again and capture the astonishing beauty of one who was a stranger to her. His eyes were deep set, dark as mahogany, and, when he glanced at her over her father's shoulder, piercing and intelligent. His lips were perfection, soft and supple. The lines lightly etched at the corners of his mouth emphasized his high cheekbones, and the dimple in his cheek just barely softened that square jawline.

Paul de Ravenault was clearly enthralled. He hadn't even noticed her arrival at his side. It was a moment before her father became aware of her presence. Time enough for Pascale to take the measure of the man. He was, she guessed, English to the core. There was something about the way he held himself that made her think of that indomitable race. And his French, while passable, was quite heavily accented.

"Pascale, *ma chérie,* Guillaume and François have brought Captain John Devlin to the ball just to meet us." The gentleman turned to her and bowed, and she was impressed anew by the elegance of the liquid movement. Beauty and grace were a rare enough combination.

"Enchanté, mademoiselle." His voice, as silky and smooth as hot chocolate, sent a shiver down her spine. Her reaction to his voice was unprecedented.

He kissed her hand, and Pascale lost her breath. The vague desire to paint him was replaced by a stronger one: to touch him.

She was shocked by the depth of her response. Pascale had long since learned to judge people not on the outward face they presented to the world, but to value those qualities that were less apparent, such as the sweetness of spirit possessed by her father's dear friend, Guillaume, or the refreshing intelligence of François. The Ravenault château had been visited by some of the most beautiful artist's models of the decade. Her lifelong association with Paris's most sought-after young models had taught her that a beautiful face, or physique, did not necessarily indicate an equally beautiful soul. She had thought it had inured her to such perfection, but she'd been wrong. This man was temptation itself.

"He is the Englishman that Guillaume has mentioned to us," her father explained. "They import goods to the French and British colonies on their boats."

"Ships," Captain Devlin gently corrected.

Pascale remembered Guillaume saying he had met an Englishman of African descent, and had decided to invest in his company. She didn't think the conversation had gone further than that, since her father had no more interest in shipping than in any other subject aside from art. Luckily, she was only required to nod as Papa went on.

"I would enjoy painting you, monsieur, or perhaps marble would be a better medium to capture such a strong face." The captain looked nonplussed by Paul de Ravenault's baldly stated compliment. Pascale was used to Papa's single-minded pursuit of subjects to paint. She had seen others trapped under that intense gaze. She searched her mind for some subject to distract the artist, but she was not quick enough.

"Your hands are perfect," was her father's next outrageous comment. Guillaume and François were grinning, and Pascale couldn't help but smile, too, at Devlin's surprised expression. "I don't suppose you need padding to broaden those shoulders. They're as wide as any I've ever seen."

Pascale took in the shoulders under discussion and silently agreed. As she raised her eyes to his face again, she saw that Captain Devlin had noticed the direction of her gaze, and she averted her eyes. But she had participated in too many similar discussions over the years to turn missish now. It was of no use to deplore her parent's lack of delicacy in discussing such an improper subject in her presence. Her father simply could not help himself. She had to think of some real objection to her father's bizarre suggestion besides her delicate female sensibilities.

"I suppose oils would be best, to catch the fluid lines of your—"

"Papa," Pascale interrupted abruptly, desperately casting about in her mind for an excuse to halt any further analysis of the gentleman's anatomy.

Suddenly it came to her. "The captain doesn't seem to me the type of man who would be interested in modeling. Do you remember what happened when you tried to sketch the Austrian prince?" The gentle reminder was sufficient to dampen her father's enthusiasm. His brow lowered as he remembered the unpleasant incident.

After a moment's thought, he shook his head. "But, no! I'm convinced this fine gentleman would never behave in such a barbaric manner." To the captain, who was looking a little puzzled, Paul de Ravenault explained, "He broke my easel. But . . . ," he continued the debate with his daughter, "Monsieur Devlin is not royalty, after all. He is a ship's captain and an ex-naval officer as well. There is no need to worry about conduct."

François, who was aware of the incident Pascale had mentioned, interjected at this point, "I clearly remember you saying that it was the Austrian prince's addiction to physical activity that caused the difficulties, and I cannot help but think that Jack's disposition is even more . . . energetic."

"I remember," Guillaume added his piece, "you said you would never work with an amateur again." Her father appeared to be much struck by this argument. Guillaume went on, "The British Navy, while an admirable training ground for many fields, has little use for men who excel at sitting motionless for hours on end."

"In fact, the very traits that are most likely to advance one's career in the Navy are just those that would be untenable in a model," François concluded.

"Exactly," Pascale said. "Remember the major, and Lieutenant Varonne? After those two, you said nothing could induce you to paint another soldier, either."

Pascale could only hope the military man under discussion did not object to being dissected in this fashion. She chanced a quick look at him and he didn't appear to be offended. On the contrary, a small smile played over his lips as he watched her father mull over what had been said.

"You really don't think it will do?" Papa finally asked. Pascale shook her head emphatically and he heaved a sigh of resignation. "I suppose not," he said, not unhappily. "It was not such a good idea, after all. The physique is impressive," the artist said, regretfully surveying the shoulders that had inspired so much excitement, "but I really cannot be expected to work with someone so unprofessional. There is a restlessness about him that does not bode well for the sessions I would require. I am sorry, *monsieur,* but I'm afraid, I really am, that you would squirm. It is not your fault—"

"Papa," Pascale admonished. He ignored her.

"But it is all the same, you know. You will forgive me, I'm sure. I should have thought of it . . . observed you further before I . . . but it is of no matter. You must accept my apologies. I speak too often without thinking."

"I can only be complimented that an artist of your stature was interested, however briefly, in painting my portrait," said Captain Devlin, with another graceful bow.

Paul de Ravenault took the compliment as his due and nodded, almost as gracefully, in acknowledgment, before turning abruptly and walking away without a word. Pascale was embarrassed by her father's uncouth behavior, but was relieved to see that Devlin seemed unperturbed by Papa's rudeness, and stood watching him walk away with the glimmer of a smile in his dark eyes.

François hastily took his leave with a muttered, "Pardon."
He hurried after his old friend.

"Your devoted servant, *mademoiselle*," Guillaume said, with
an apologetic smile. "I will see you back at the hotel, Jack,"
he added, before he followed the other two men.

When Captain Devlin turned to her, Pascale excused her
father's rude departure, saying, in English, "He doesn't go to
parties very often. I imagine you guessed that already." He
nodded, his expression bland, and somehow she found herself
being steered through the crowd toward the salon which
opened into the ballroom. "He may sometimes act . . . improperly, but it is never meanness, for he hasn't a malicious
bone in his body. It is just that he isn't accustomed to watching
his tongue. He doesn't have to, when we're at home."

"He doesn't?" he said, mildly, accepting the change from
French to English without comment.

"No, not at all." She was unable to think, overwhelmed by
his presence. Having reached the salon, he handed her graciously into a seat.

"The two of you often discuss the male physique, then?"
he asked. Pascale thought the question bordered on the imper-
tinent, but when she looked up at him suspiciously, he awaited
her answer with a gaze of innocent inquiry. She obviously
couldn't tell him the truth—that her father and she had been
discussing anatomy, male and female, since she was a small
girl drawing with colored chalk on bits of paper. "No." She
tried to think of a harmless reply. She didn't think it was any
of his affair, but she didn't want to embarrass him again.

"Oh, sir, in my father's heyday talk such as that would not
be looked on as anything out of the ordinary. He says we live
in prudish times, and from some of the stories his friends tell,
I must say I believe him. This evening he just forgot where
he was," she said lightly, hoping that would be an end to it.
It was not for anyone else to disapprove of the old goat. She
alone had that right.

But the gentleman did not seem to be satisfied with her

explanation. "I doubt that such subjects were ever proper topics for conversation between a father and his daughter," the captain said.

Pascale gaped at him. She'd seen his quick glance when her father had been cataloging his charms and physical attributes, and had not thought to either blush or simper, as a maid was supposed to do. Instead she'd met his fleeting glances head-on. He wasn't to know that she'd been trying to think of some remedy for their awkward predicament. Improper as she knew her behavior to have been, Pascale bristled at the thought that this stranger had any right to judge her or Papa. Indignation gradually replaced her surprise as he continued, "In any case, it was not his behavior that surprised me, but your own. I have not met any other young ladies in my travels who . . . employed a tone such as that with their parents." She couldn't believe he *dared* to reprimand her. She was an even-tempered girl, but this was intolerable. None of the cogent retorts that sprang to her lips seemed severe enough. She had been trying to stop her father from embarrassing him! She could hardly have changed the direction of that improper conversation without first entering into it. Who was Captain Devlin to censure her tone of voice?

Pascale had rarely been more incensed. How did he think she could have kept the old man quiet? To enjoin her father to be silent would have been disrespectful and even more improper than the lapse the captain had already accused her of making. With great effort she kept her ire under control and managed to respond lightly, "What none, sir? You must be very nice in your choice of companions. I thought you more adventurous." And more chivalrous than to chide her for a situation he must see as none of her making, she thought, with an inward sigh. She had only tried to divert Papa from his foolhardy notion. Which was just what she had done! And what gratitude did she receive from the handsome oaf she'd rescued? A scolding. He deserved a redressing, but she wouldn't give him the satisfaction of seeing that his disapprobation had annoyed her. "Since I seem to have offended you," she said, in dignified tones, "I'll take my leave. Good night, sir."

And good riddance, she thought as she stalked away. It was a shame that such beauty had been wasted on such a one as Captain Devlin.

Two

Jack watched the little minx flounce off, and ruefully shook his head. He should not have chided the girl, for despite her self-assured demeanor and her managing ways, he guessed she was not nearly as sophisticated as she liked to think. Her flashing eyes had betrayed her anger at his presumption. But he'd been unable to control the impulse.

He'd heard quite a lot about Paul de Ravenault since he'd arrived in Paris. The Salon, the most important artistic event of the year, had been a major topic of conversation. He'd heard a lot about this black artist, not only from François and Guillaume, but also from other artists he had met through the two men. The old man had made a name for himself; despite his color, and his lack of money, much like Jack himself. He was respected by his peers in the art world, and in the business world. Devlin had hoped they'd be friends. He'd expected that de Ravenault would be an interesting character. He'd been completely unprepared to find this paragon was just another foolish artist—his mind entirely consumed by his art.

It didn't make sense, until one met his hardheaded daughter. Devlin would have been willing to wager, after their brief meeting, that it was the daughter who had earned the father his reputation as a shrewd businessman. He knew Pascale acted as chatelaine in her father's house. François and Guillaume had spoken endlessly of their visits to the family château in Burgundy, which she ruled, apparently, with a will of iron.

She had probably been the one to maneuver their attendance

at this ball—presumably to make the acquaintance of likely patrons. She must have shouldered the responsibility of finding the artist his commissions and selling his work. A heavy burden for such a young woman—for she couldn't be a day above twenty-one. How many girls her age had the intelligence, and the presence, to meet such a challenge so well? He'd guessed, solely from François and Guillaume's reports, that Pascale de Ravenault was a managing female, and forward. And she'd been both. But he hadn't expected her to be so beautiful.

From tidbits of conversation that Captain Devlin had overheard, he knew that among the respectable matrons of Paris it was agreed that Paul de Ravenault might not have a shred of common sense, but he did compare favorably with the wild-eyed artists whom they feared to introduce to their impressionable young daughters. He could be trusted implicitly under the aegis of his own quite respectable daughter. By "respectable," Jack had assumed they meant Pascale was a fish-faced prude. They had been so certain that Monsieur de Ravenault would never disgrace any party he attended by arriving with one of his models, or some other undesirable, which was often a danger when one tried to entertain bohemians. Pascale de Ravenault might not turn heads, with her quiet beauty and her air of calm assurance, but she was no prim and proper old maid. She was a sensuous creature, feminine and appealing.

Devlin understood now why François and Guillaume said it was considered advantageous that the de Ravenaults were black. It was impossible to imagine that any young person might think they could conduct a flirtation *à suivre* with either father or daughter. Paul de Ravenault and his daughter might have been handsome indeed, but the two were so easily recognizable that it would have been impossible to undertake any kind of clandestine activity with the de Ravenaults without being discovered.

Monsieur de Ravenault could be welcomed into the best homes without the usual fears that young and impressionable members of the household might embarrass their families.

Bourgeois matrons and nobility alike wished to associate with composers and artists who had money and connections, but it was really not expected that an artist would be the first choice of any matchmaking mother as a suitor for her daughter's hand. It was commonly known that de Ravenault's mother had been an African princess and therefore the family was quite respectable. But Paul de Ravenault and his daughter, with their dark skins, were so clearly ineligible that protective mamas could rest assured when they entrusted their offspring to the tender mercies of the artist.

From the incident he'd been obliged to participate in, he knew the old man didn't make it any easier for her. He had to admire the neat way she'd diverted the old man. That she'd been motivated by a desire for self-preservation in no way lessened his appreciation for the skill she'd demonstrated when she'd prevented her father from embarrassing himself any further.

Jack Devlin was too thick-skinned to care that she wouldn't have lifted a finger for his sake. He could only smile as he thought of the deft way she'd turned the conversation away from him. Padding in his shoulders, indeed! Faith, the old gentleman had been stripping him out of his clothes.

It would be no easy task to control such a heedless old gentleman as Paul de Ravenault. It seemed she'd done quite well. If he had gauged the situation correctly, Paul de Ravenault was no more concerned with the subtle niceties of polite conversation than a mouse. He probably filled his house with all manner of people whom no young lady of quality should ever be obliged to meet. The daughter, he guessed, would think nothing of seeing a nude male model—she'd probably seen dozens of them already. In fact, he'd noticed an appraising look in her eye when her father had introduced them. It made him decidedly uncomfortable to think that Pascale had been imagining his "impressive physique" with exactly the same jaundiced eye as her father.

Jack consoled himself with the thought that, however the sweet young Pascale de Ravenault might imagine he looked when stripped to the skin, she would never actually *know.* Unfortunately, while the thought might ease his mind, it did not quell the very improper physical response he'd suffered ever since he'd realized the artist's unusual daughter might well be imagining the masculine anatomy hidden under his formal attire.

A young page claimed his attention as Pascale disappeared into the crowd. The boy was clothed in the full livery of his house, but his raiment had the appearance of having been hastily donned and his wig sat askew on his head. Devlin perused the brief note he'd been handed as the lad stood gaping at the wonders around him.

"Lead me to him, my boy," he said. The page was clearly disappointed at having to leave so soon, but he nodded and dutifully set off.

"Have you ever been to a ball before?" he asked the boy as they made their way through the crowded ballroom.

"Non, monsieur," the child answered, leading him out of the grand hall and through the salon that led to the main part of the house. A quick glance behind them assured Devlin that no one had noticed their departure. Still, he was surprised when the page, instead of leading him toward the front door, took him around a corner and up a small staircase to the second floor. He followed silently, picking up his pace now that they were out of sight of prying eyes. The boy ushered him into a darkened room, and he went quickly forward as the door closed silently behind him. He, of all people, should have known that his friend could arrange their little meeting wherever he chose. Captain John Devlin was well aware that he could rely upon his newest client to proceed with dispatch, and with total discretion. The government of France, after all, wanted him to carry out a commission for them.

His friend, Richard Trenton, now undersecretary to a rather important government official, came forward to meet him immediately.

"Jack!" he exclaimed, clasping Devlin's hand and shaking

it heartily. At the desk, which had been shrouded in shadow, a taper flared to life.

"Captain John Devlin," the man sitting behind the desk did not introduce himself. "We appreciate your cooperation in a sensitive matter."

Jack turned to his friend. "I thought this was just between you and me," he said.

"I am not acting on my own behalf, Jack. I told you that. You can't blame the department for wanting a look at you. The same Monsieur Serratt will be the only other person, besides you and myself, who knows about your mission. He will explain what's wanted."

"I haven't agreed to anything yet," Jack said.

"You will," said Richard, confidently. His eyes darted to his superior, who smiled and nodded. But, Jack noticed, his smile did not quite reach his eyes.

"How do you know you can trust me?" Jack asked, hoping to shake the mysterious gentleman into betraying nervousness, or any other emotion. He had the strange feeling that he was not facing a man, but a machine—a political automaton.

The gentleman's response was as cool as ever. "We have no reason to distrust you. Should you give us one, of course it would be taken care of. But I feel sure that that will not be necessary. I am confident, thanks to your friend here, that we can rely on you. Totally."

"If I decide to accept your offer, your faith won't be misplaced," Jack assured him.

"There can be no question of your accepting, surely? There's nothing to it for an old sea dog like yourself," Richard said, looking once again to his superior for confirmation. The older gentleman nodded in acknowledgment at the younger man's words. An undercurrent of tension ran between the two men, one a petty government official, the other a seasoned politician. Jack sensed it had little to do with him.

"Why all this nonsense, then?" he asked.

"This cloak-and-dagger stuff may seem silly to you, I daresay. I can imagine what you must have been thinking when you came in. . . ." Richard was babbling. The statesman settled back in his chair.

"Can you?" Jack muttered, wryly. It didn't seem silly to him at all. However, it did seem as though he might have gotten himself tangled up in something that was more danger-ous than he'd been led to believe. The "harmless cargo" his old friend had asked him to deliver appeared to be somewhat important.

"I was used to thinking that these matters should be handled right out in the open and all that," Richard said. "I mean, it's not as if the department is doing something wrong, or anything of that nature. In fact, it's the Mexicans, who—" A quick look from the other man stopped him short. "However, that's neither here nor there. It must look strange to you, my dear fellow, but we are just trying to avoid any unpleasantness or . . . need-less delay." He laughed, but it was forced. "The most ridicu-lous people can kick up all kinds of dust about the most harmless directives. It's a trial to all of us in the government, I swear. It's just easier not to open up certain subjects to public debate."

"Which is where I come in," Jack offered, helpfully.

"Just so," said his friend, with a sigh of relief at his quick understanding. "You shouldn't mind all of this." A wave of a hand took in the darkened room, the man at the desk, and the gathering taking place below stairs. "It's just a precaution."

"It is, as our friend says," the older man confirmed. "This is probably unnecessary, but there are standard procedures to be followed, even in a trifling matter such as the delivery of our communiqué. Relax, my friend, and we'll explain it to you. We did not mean to give you the impression that this task was much out of the ordinary. I believe your friend here was right. You are the man for this mission. Forget all of this and think of us as another—what do you call them—customer." His tone was jovial, but Jack was not about to forget the menace of his earlier threats. On the other hand, a government contract would give him the security he craved. He would not want to work exclusively for the French, but if he could secure employment for his ship and his crew on a regular basis, it would all be worth it. His company was only five years old, and already quite profitable, but it hadn't been easy. He'd gotten this far on sheer force of will.

Five years ago, Jack had won his discharge from the Navy. It had been the only home he'd known since he'd been twelve years old. Despite the prejudices of both crew and officers against his race, he'd been lucky enough to prosper in his dozen years at sea. He'd been fortunate from the beginning, when the captain of the very first ship had chosen to make him his cabin boy because of his height and strength. The captain had found his intelligence and his steady nerves very useful. Diligent study and unswerving loyalty to that hard master had helped him to rise from cabin boy to trusted right hand. Fate had made him navigator on his last voyage—at the age of four and twenty.

In 1860, when he left Her Majesty's navy, he put everything he had into a daring gamble. He convinced a small group of friends and acquaintances to finance the purchase of a slightly aged, but still sound clipper ship, which he offered to captain. He provided the crew, and supplies, and scraped together the monies and credit to buy cargo to sell for a nice profit in the ports of Mexico. The country was divided and unstable, and sailors he'd met who had been there had said that on account of the new democratic government, the old aristocracy, and the Catholic Church, the economy was unstable, and the people were desperate for goods from Europe.

His plan succeeded, and that same year he was able to renegotiate his share of the venture to acquire, with each voyage, a growing share of the ship he skippered. When, during the American Civil War the shipping industry in the eastern states was annexed to serve their country, he added to his route ports on the southeastern coast of the new country, where trade had been interrupted by the war and all its attendant difficulties.

Within one year he owned his first ship and had assumed total control of the company.

When France, in 1861, invaded the independent nation of Mexico, he had already established his connections there. After the installation of the Austrian archduke Maximilian as Emperor of Mexico in 1864, Jack had even more buyers clamoring for the precious goods he brought from England, France, and more exotic locales. They were willing to pay in gold. Captain Devlin was well on his way to becoming a wealthy man. He looked forward with relish to expanding his business. He was already planning the purchase of a second ship to be captained by his first mate. But he was no fool. He knew there might be a high price to pay for his good fortune. He accepted it, but refused to risk his integrity.

"I would not be willing to carry anything in the hold of my ship that my government would not countenance," Jack said firmly.

Richard smiled, relieved, and answered, "No need to worry on that score. England is my country, too, Jack. I still consider myself a patriot. I am sure they would not consider our actions disloyal or traitorous in any way."

"Fine," he said, casting caution to the winds. "All that remains to discuss is my fee."

Jack and his friend returned to the ballroom a little over an hour after he had left it. Richard toasted the success of the night's work, and Jack found himself searching the crowd for a woman with clear dusky skin and unmistakable poise. He felt a slight twinge of disappointment when he realized Pascale and Paul de Ravenault must have already departed. But he swiftly put the unusual family out of his mind and prepared to ferret out from his friend the name of the distinguished gentleman to whom they had just bidden adieu in the library.

It did not take Jack very long to discover from Richard that the third man at their meeting had been a Monsieur Serratt, personal secretary to Count Alfred-Emilien de Nieuwerkerke, who held a number of impressive sounding titles, including

Napoleon's minister of fine arts. Richard seemed surprised that
Jack wasn't more impressed when he discovered whom Serratt
worked for, but Jack was just relieved to discover it was one
of Napoleon's intimates who had hired him; for the cargo he
was to deliver was a message from France's emperor to the
emperor Maximilian of Mexico. It stated, in no uncertain
terms, that Maximilian had and would continue to have the
support of Napoleon Bonaparte III, which was, as Devlin was
aware, the same pledge that Napoleon had made since he had
invaded and wrested the country from its new leader and installed his own distant cousin in the imperial throne. The contents of the communique he was to carry were common
knowledge. The secrecy of the meeting had been, as Trenton
and Serratt had assured him, an unnecessary precaution.

"Does Bonaparte fear some objection will arise to his continued support of Maximilian?" he asked his old friend under
cover of the babble of voices and the music of the orchestra.

Richard had relaxed considerably once removed from beneath the lancet eye of Monsieur Serratt. "No," he answered
glibly, immediately following Jack's train of thought. "From
what I have seen of Monsieur Serratt, I must suppose this
secret palaver was his doing. I've never worked with him before. He's a strange one. I think he enjoys all of this intrigue."
Jack thought that an understatement, but he let it pass without
comment. "Or it might be Nieuwerkerke's *affaire* with Princess
Mathilde that led to this havey cavey business. She has a number of Mexican emigres among her acquaintance."

Jack raised an eyebrow at that. "But I thought the emigres
supported Bonaparte in this."

The displaced Mexican nobility had complained endlessly
about the upstart Juarez and his so-called Constitutionalists.
Upon fleeing their homeland, they had directed all of their
energy to campaigns to raise support against Benito Juarez
and his democratic new government.

"So they say, but . . ." Richard's voice trailed off, as he took
a quick look over his shoulder. "What is voiced abroad, and

what might be said behind closed doors are two very different things."

Empress Eugenie had made friends of these Conservatives, who said they hoped to restore the best of the old, while they maintained the new "equality of the people," just as Emperor Napoleon III had promised to do in France. Jack had met the breed in London and Paris, where they had fled with their titles and much of their wealth. They spent all their time reminiscing about the grand and noble traditions of the past and told sad tales of violence directed toward the church and its clergy by the progressives. Empress Eugenie had made it clear that she wanted to restore the power of the Catholic Church in Mexico and Napoleon Bonaparte III added Mexico to his empire.

Richard shrugged. "Napoleon has made quite public his intentions regarding Mexico. No one would dare to challenge him."

Jack nodded. He, too, thought Bonaparte's position was clear. His first commission for the French was a simple enough task. He could only wish that all of his clientele was as easy to please.

Jack Devlin had not expected to meet either member of the de Ravenault family again. His visit to Paris was to be a short one and he certainly didn't travel in artistic circles except for his budding friendship with François Elizabeth and Guillaume Pelotte. Although Pascale de Ravenault had been a sweet, young morsel, he supposed it was better that he wasn't going to see her again. She was too respectable to set up as a flirt on this brief visit to Paris. In his experience, wooing a girl like Pascale required time and patience. Even if she'd been of a pliable nature, it would not be easy to convince such a well-bred young lady to forego her notions of propriety and accept the idea that a little dalliance never hurt anyone. If he didn't miss his guess, this little minx was also much too strong-willed to be easily tamed.

If he saw much more of her, though, he was sure he'd be tempted. She was too beautiful to resist. And a romance with a girl such as she generally resulted in marriage. He was glad circumstance would keep them apart. So it was with some surprise that he discovered Monsieur de Ravenault had come to call on him at an unfashionably early hour the morning after the princess's ball.

Captain Devlin had arisen early, as was his custom, and so was quite prepared to receive his unexpected visitor. He therefore told his disapproving valet, John Douglas, to show his guest into the room.

Paul de Ravenault sauntered into the room, as though he came calling every day on gentlemen he hardly knew. Jack watched curiously as the older man saluted him with a sketchy bow, and proceeded to wander about the room. He waited for de Ravenault to speak, but it seemed the older gentleman was perfectly content examining the paltry bits and pieces that the hotel had scattered about the room.

"I hadn't thought to see you again, sir, so soon," Jack finally said, quizzically.

"Oh, I'm not political."

Since Jack couldn't think of any polite way to ask what in damnation politics had to do with anything, he just settled back to enjoy his second encounter with the artist. His disappointment from last night had ebbed away. The old gentleman might not be the person Jack had hoped, but he might still be interesting. There was no doubt he was unusual. And his daughter was . . . well, incredible. To meet her again, Jack would cheerfully indulge her scatterbrained father.

"All the better for me," Jack said noncommittally.

"Don't concern myself with it. Or much else according to my daughter. Usually buried out in the country, don't hear much news there. Though Pascale always seems to know something about all those doings. She says it's important," he said, clearly baffled. "Don't see that it makes much difference. I just paint," he stated, somewhat proudly.

Jack felt a twinge of pity, once again, for the woman who spent her days trying to take care of this crazy old man. "Well, she's probably right," he defended Pascale, not sure what he was defending her from.

"I'm sure." Paul de Ravenault turned to him, eyes sparkling. "She's got a good head on her shoulders, my daughter." He tapped a finger against his own forehead. "Don't know where she gets it from. But she reminds me of *ma mère* . . . so that might be it."

Jack had heard a number of stories about the grande dame of the de Ravenault family last night. An African princess, she'd brought her four young children to France when her village had been destroyed in a skirmish between French forces and the natives. She'd also managed to smuggle a small fortune in gold aboard the ship that had brought her to these shores. She'd bought the de Ravenault estate and when she discovered the last of the name had died, she took the name for herself. She had lived in seclusion in the countryside from then on. Only her youngest child, the infant Paul de Ravenault, had survived being transplanted to this continent. She sounded a formidable woman—Jack could imagine her granddaughter took after her. Pascale certainly didn't inherit her ambition from her father.

"Won't you have a seat, *monsieur?* Some coffee, or tea, perhaps?" Jack offered.

"Thank you." He took a seat and looked about him with great interest, as though the room he'd just examined had taken on a whole new appearance from this perspective. Perhaps, in his view, it had.

"Coffee?" Captain Devlin gestured at the silver tray holding his breakfast, which lay on the table between them.

"That would be fine," the artist answered, eyeing the spread of bread, fruit, cheese, and pastry. While Jack poured him a cup of coffee and warm milk, de Ravenault helped himself to

some of the choice morsels before him. Jack had to smile at
the old man's excitement. He was so like a child.

"So, if I may ask, to what do I owe the honor of this visit?"
Jack finally asked.

"Oh, I forgot," Paul said with a nervous glance behind him.
He leaned forward, the pastry in his hand seemingly forgotten.
His voice dropped to a conspiratorial whisper. "I need you to
take something away for me. In one of your ships."

Three

The morning after Princess Mathilde's ball, Pascale awoke in good spirits, if slightly later than usual. As Saturday was her day to shop at the marketplace in Les Halles, Pascale rose and quickly dressed and left the house, without breaking her fast. She made her way through the bustling streets of the metropolis to the market that catered to the finest households in Paris. Pascale kept up her usual practice of stocking the household larder in Paris, just as she did at home in Beaune.

She couldn't help thinking about the previous evening's success. Everything had gone just as planned, with the exception of her meeting with Captain Devlin. Discomfort over that unpleasant incident had kept her awake, tossing and turning, for the better part of an hour after she'd lain down in her comfortable bed. However, the dawn of the new day had almost erased the unfortunate scene from her mind.

Entering the market, she wandered past row upon row of farmers, craftsmen, and tradesmen in their stalls; an assortment of colorful characters. It was, of course, quite different to haggle over the price of chickens and ducks with a strange toothless old woman than to barter their grapes and vegetables with Madame Turain at the village marketplace in the little town of Beaune in the province of Burgundy, where she'd been raised.

Pascale breathed in the wonderful scents of the flowers in a nearby shop while she puzzled once again over why she preferred this bustling marketplace to milliners and dress shops, or even to the balls and parties that appealed so to other

women. It was not something she could explain—not, at least,
to Papa, who was no happier to leave his easel in order to buy
vegetables than he was at the prospect of purchasing rubies
and silks.

True artists, like her father, could not bare to spend time
away from their work for any reason, least of all just to make
sure there was food in the house. If she had been a real artist,
as she'd dreamed when she was younger, she, too, would have
resented the time lost when she left her easel. Instead she enjoyed watching the people around her, and talking with them
about their lives. That was a large part of the reason that she'd
decided not to finish her studies and follow in her father's
footsteps. She could still remember clearly how lonely it had
sometimes been to paint. She was content to make her father's
work possible with her less creative skills. When she surveyed
her purchases, she was satisfied with her morning's work.

She returned home to find Papa had gone out early that
morning. No one knew where he had gone. Her quick perusal
of a letter from home made his disappearance seem even more
suspicious. The news from home confirmed the suspicions that
had been forming since before she and her father had left the
country to come up to the city. The letter was from her old
governess, Madame Pitt, who now helped her manage the de
Ravenaults' small country estate and was in charge of the
house in the family's absence.

Pascale sent the youngest valet to the hotel in which Guillaume Pelotte resided while in town, to request that he visit
her that day. Then she sat down to read the letter more carefully.

Francine Pitt passed along a report that the vineyards had
not suffered any harm from the rains that had plagued the
countryside for the past week and which had finally lifted a
couple of days previously. Madame Pitt also assured her that
she would be well satisfied with the new draperies for the
second guest bedroom.

It was the last bit of news from Pascale's old teacher that

was distressing. Pascale's brow wrinkled as she read. Madame Pitt had been unable to find the painting for which Pascale had bid her search as soon as the family left for town. Francine was convinced that the canvas could not be in the house as she had personally conducted a search of the entire edifice, from cellars to attic, and had even taken a look into the outer buildings in case that wicked old man had hidden The Painting outside the mansion.

If it hadn't been Pascale herself who told her that Paul de Ravenault hid his latest work from his loving and faithful daughter, Madame Pitt wrote, she wouldn't have believed it. What foolishness! Everyone knew Pascale would know better than he what was to be done with it. After all, she continued, Pascale was the one who transacted all the business of the estate, including not only the sale of the wines and various agricultural products that the acreage produced, but also all the dealings involving her father's artistic offerings. Paul de Ravenault did not demonstrate an iota of common sense where monetary matters were concerned, or anything else for that matter.

Pascale well knew that her governess's letter owed its outraged tone to the fact that her father had managed to outsmart them both and hide that painting. She had been listening to Francine Pitt expand on her unflattering description of Paul de Ravenault's character for years. From the moment she'd been hired, Pascale's very respectable governess had tried, in vain, to wrest complete control of her young charge's education from her father. Madame took very seriously her duties, the most important of which was to protect Pascale from her father's wicked practice of exposing her to the kinds of people no proper family would have admitted into the house. Models indeed! Strumpets were what *those* women were. And the men were no better. Monsieur's studio was no place for an impressionable young girl.

Madame did not reiterate all her unkind accusations in the missive she'd sent to Pascale. She just wrote that Paul de Ravenault might be a great genius, indeed she had often heard him described in just those words; however, when it came to supporting his dependents he was, in a word, a wretch. If he hadn't turned the reins of management over to Pascale, heaven knew where they would all be now. He could have starved to death before he even realized anything was amiss in his household. Her letter ended with the sad observation that Paul de Ravenault had never been more disobliging than he was being at this moment. She would not be surprised if this strange fit he'd taken—hiding The Painting from his loyal daughter and staff—was only the first sign that he had finally lost his mind completely.

Pascale's euphoria of a few minutes earlier was deflated by the unexpected knowledge that the canvas hadn't surfaced as she'd expected. Her governess's letter confirmed that Papa had indeed finished The Painting. For that was the only reasonable explanation for a missing canvas—which was what had led to the current investigation. She put the letter down and picked up the sketchbook she'd taken to carrying about with her. It fell open to the picture that had first alerted her, when she'd happened across it, to the possibility that her father had finally completed work on The Painting, the one she had been waiting for all of her life.

Pascale had started searching for The Painting before they left the house in Beaune for their apartments in the city, but hadn't uncovered anything other than a pair of paint-splattered lace cuffs soaked in turpentine stuffed under a sofa cushion. On her departure for Paris, she'd asked Francine to continue looking while her father was safely out of the house, but clearly this was going to be more difficult than Pascale had thought.

The boy brought Guillaume's response to her invitation He said he would visit later that morning, and he'd bring François. Pascale could only hope that her father's two oldest friends could shed some light on the mystery. She'd known these two men for as long as she could remember, they were like family.

Unfortunately, if they were hiding The Painting for him, she didn't think they'd betray Papa. She had to make them understand how important this was to her.

When Guillaume arrived she was waiting in the morning room, a sumptuous repast waiting on a table in front of the sofa, and the sketchbook on the cupboard by the door. François accompanied him.

"Good morning, Guillaume. I see you were able to bring François along." She could not bring herself to smile, or offer her hand, but neither man commented on the coolness of her greeting. That, in itself, was unusual, Pascale thought.

"Yes," Guillaume said nervously, "I thought you might want to see both of us."

Pascale easily interpreted the truth behind this statement. The only sensible explanation for their behavior was that they knew why she'd asked them to come. He'd been afraid to face her alone. Pascale would have been just as happy to question her father's cronies separately, but she was willing to try this first. "Would you like to sit down?"

They came into the room like a pair of schoolboys approaching the headmaster, neither moving ahead of the other. Good, she thought. They feel guilty. And so they should. Pascale could have laughed at the sight of these two men, who'd dangled her on their knees as a baby, nervously avoiding her eyes. Under any other circumstances, it would have been humorous. But what her father had done wasn't funny. And if they had helped him, then they weren't the friends she had imagined.

"I had the cook prepare some of your favorites," she said, without warmth. "Don't be shy. Help yourselves."

They kept their hands on their laps. "We're not really hungry," François said.

"As you please." She stood, watching them, letting the silence drag out between them.

"You've been very busy, so your father says," François finally spoke. Guillaume poked him in the ribs with an elbow.

Pascale pretended not to notice. "Yes. I've had meetings

with some of the antiques dealers and colormen here in Paris who sell Papa's prints. And of course, I met with your banker, Monsieur Barson. I had to explain why the portrait of his wife was delivered so late." Both men looked away. She felt a momentary twinge of guilt at having to treat them like this. It was not completely their fault.

Pascale blamed herself, as well as Papa, for not realizing sooner why her father's latest commission had been produced only after she had badgered him unmercifully for weeks. She should have been more alert. But it was not unusual for her father to delay work on a commissioned portrait to devote himself to the execution of his own internal vision. Or to neglect it to run outside to capture an impression of some scene that could only be captured in the sunlight. But this . . .

Pascale, busily preparing for their annual trip to Paris, had relaxed her guard over him when he'd appeared content to work in his studio. She had not thought there was anything there to distract him. They had no company and she had forbidden any of the servants to model for him. She had assumed he was hard at work on the commissioned portrait for the banker. Even when she had realized that the portrait of Monsieur Barson's wife was not going to be ready in time, she'd not become suspicious. It was only when a canvas she had primed had disappeared that she'd started to wonder.

"Somehow," she said to the tops of their bowed heads, "after closeting himself in his studio for more than enough time to produce both the portrait and another canvas, he still hadn't produced either the portrait or any other painting." Too late she'd realized her father had locked himself into his studio not, as he told her, because the hustle and bustle of preparing for the move to Paris was distracting him, but because he had finally painted his masterwork.

"But I found this." She handed the sketchbook to Guillaume. He barely looked at it before passing it to François.

The red-chalk drawing was complete. This was, as Pascale

well knew, the final stage of preparation for the actual painting itself. It was The Portrait of The Lady. He'd finally done it.

Over the years, Paul de Ravenault had painted this one woman again and again. The woman's pose changed, but she always wore a hat that hid the top half of her face. The delicate jawline and graceful hands of this "vision" of the artist's were as well known to Pascale as her own. Pascale had seen so many bits and pieces of The Painting—her father's strongest and only unrealized vision—that she recognized them at a glance as distinct from the noses, eyes, mouths, and hands that her father tended to sketch or paint on any scrap of paper or canvas that fell within his reach. Now he'd finished the drawing, but it was gone. Unfortunately, she could not identify the woman in the painting from the sketch—it was not detailed enough.

"Has either of you seen anything like this before?"

"Uh . . ." François cleared his throat. "Perhaps your father—"

Guillaume interrupted, giving his friend a warning look. "François, I'm sure Pascale has heard *everything* Paul has to say on the subject."

"True. I'd be curious to know what he might have told you gentlemen, though. For some reason, Papa sometimes acts as though he's almost . . . afraid to tell me things." The catch in her voice was almost real. Both men raised their voices in protest.

"Of you? I'm sure he's not afraid . . ."

"Ma chérie, you must be mistaken . . . ," Guillaume tried to reassure her. "You are his daughter. . . ."

François tried again. "Your father has told us many times that he reposes complete faith in you. He trusts you to handle all of his affairs, I assure you."

"You know that Papa gets nervous whenever he completes a painting. He shares the insecurity of most *artistes* when it comes to his work. He is never satisfied with what he has created."

Paul, like so many others, painted over a section of a canvas, sometimes even a complete painting, again and again, until well after the work was due to be delivered to the patron who had commissioned it. The Lady was supposed to be her father's *pièce de résistance;* it had been his life's work. Pascale was sure that his usual crisis of faith would be many times more extreme upon the completion of this painting. If he had, as she suspected, finished The Painting, he would be afraid to let her look at it, convinced that she would not judge it critically enough and perhaps submit it to the Salon despite its flaws. It would not be the first time the de Ravenault family had been divided by this particular debate. However, if Paul succeeded in hiding The Painting from her, it would be the first time he won. The thought was enough to obliterate the voice of her conscience.

She let her eyes mist over with tears, a trick she'd learned years ago, but rarely used anymore. She raised her head, so they could see her teary eyes. "Lately it seems he's changed his mind about trusting me," she said pitifully.

Guillaume piped in, "He doesn't know what he'd do without you. He never did half so well before you had the idea to sell some of his work here in Paris."

She ignored him. "For example," she said, "I've looked everywhere for this painting, but I cannot find it anywhere, in Beaune, or in Paris. I think it may be quite remarkable."

"Oh?" François tried to feign surprise, but did not fare well to Pascale's critical eye.

"Yes. And I think you must know something about it. I can't imagine where he would hide it but with his two oldest friends."

François's surprised laughter was not convincing. "I think you must be confused, Pascale."

"I don't think so," she answered firmly.

"Why do you think he's . . . hidden this painting from you?" François asked.

She pointed to the sketchbook in his lap. "It's quite clear

to me he's been working on it from this sketch. There's also a canvas missing from his supplies. And you two look as nervous as cats."

"Us? Why, we'd never . . ." Once again, Guillaume's voice trailed off under her penetrating gaze.

"Why is *this* particular painting so important?" François said.

"You know perfectly well that if Papa produces a masterwork that is accepted by the Salon, it will change everything. Already *this* season, we've been lucky enough to have gained introductions to Minister Nieuwerkerke, and Monsieur Ingles, who remembers father, a little, from his younger days in Paris."

"The Director of the Académie des Beaux-Arts is a wonderful contact." François ran his finger under his collar. "Maybe he'd be interested in some of your father's other works."

Pascale ignored the suggestion and asked, "Is it too warm in here for you?"

He shook his head. "No." He cleared his throat again. This time, he reached over and poured himself a cup of coffee. "My throat is dry. But otherwise, I'm fine." He held up the cup and drank deeply and then grimaced. He'd forgotten to add his sugar.

She went on as though their earlier conversation had not been interrupted. "It helps, of course, that our friends and so many others are finally beginning to be recognized by the Académie."

Pascale had started insisting she and Papa travel annually to Paris three years ago when the 1862 protest about the Salon's exclusion of work by men like Courbet and Delacroix had actually resulted in the emperor's mandate of a second exhibition in 1863 called the Salon des Refusés for the works that the Académie didn't accept. Though the de Ravenault's resources were not substantial enough to afford framing and shipping Papa's works to the exhibition, she had felt, even at the tender age of eighteen, that she and her father had to demonstrate their support for their friends. Papa had agreed and now their annual trips were a tradition.

In 1863, the year of the first Salon des Refusés, the Salon de l'Académie relented under the pressure of artists, critics, and art lovers alike. They accepted, in the official exhibition, works done in controversial modern styles. And the following year, in 1864, Pascale's voice had been only one of many raised in praise of Manet's controversial painting *Le Déjeuner sur l'Herbe,* which they'd accepted. For all their friends' complaints, and there were a surprising number, the Salon had opened up.

In the current Salon of 1865, some of the more unconventional works by Manet, Degas, Renoir, Pissarro, Morisot, and others had finally been accepted. "This year, we're seeing many of our friends' works displayed. Next year would be the perfect time to present his masterwork," she finished. "If I can find it."

"Well perhaps your father will return the missing painting, if it exists, before next year," Guillaume suggested.

"Yes," François agreed. "I'm sure he will. If he has painted his masterwork."

She looked from one man to the other. Both were obviously pleased to have thought of this argument to soothe their guilty consciences. Their nervousness abated, they were eyeing the food on the table before them. She sighed. It was all she was going to get out of them today. She felt many years older than the two men, each twice her age, who sat before her.

"May we?" asked Guillaume, gesturing toward the food.

"Of course," Pascale said, defeated.

She took the sketchbook back to the cupboard and set it down, regretfully. Then she rang for some more coffee. She wandered over to the window, which looked out over a small, pleasant garden at the back of the house. Guillaume joined her at the window. This gentle man had been the subject of her very first portrait. His financial problems often led to a need to rusticate in the country for a while. He had been a regular visitor to the château since she had been a young girl. She had adored him.

She remembered, with some sorrow, how excited he'd been when he'd seen her portrait of him. "As good as anything your father could do," he'd assured her. She'd been thirteen years old. Those simple, carefree days had disappeared long ago. She wasn't sure how exactly it had come about that she had been transformed from their delightful little girl into their keeper. But after she took over running the farm, it had seemed to be up to her to make sure that everyone was taken care of. And they had thanked her for it. All of them. At first.

She shook off the memory, and tried to bend her mind to the problem at hand. The fresh pot of coffee arrived, and she had Odelle, the maid, leave it for her to serve. As she emptied the lukewarm liquid from their cups and replaced it with steaming coffee and warm milk, she couldn't resist making one last attempt.

"The missing painting, the one I'm afraid Papa hid, it's . . . it's a portrait he's been working on for a long time." The two men exchanged worried glances.

"I'm sure it will show up," François said. "Perhaps until then you should try and forget it and enjoy Paris."

Pascale couldn't forget about The Painting. But she knew there was nothing more that she could say about it, so she only responded to the last half of his suggestion. "Papa and I always enjoy the trip. Thanks to our friends, we earn more commissions each year. Papa says he may paint some Paris scenes 'en plein air' next year, like Manet, since the landscapes from Beaune always seem to sell quite well."

"That's splendid," said Guillaume.

"He was just saying the other day that coming to the city for the Salon every year was a brilliant idea," François tried to placate her.

"And you are still getting some requests for portraiture, I think?" Guillaume added, when Pascale didn't answer.

Since the bourgeoisie had started to buy paintings them-

selves, a privilege that previously belonged solely to the nobility, Paul's more reasonably priced paintings sold a little. The
dealers were willing to trade him supplies for his paintings,
and he then spent less time on the farm and more in the studio,
which was a much more natural atmosphere for him.

Pascale was happy to let him retreat to his sanctuary. She
had found during the last three years that she preferred handling things in her own way—alone. The farm and their vineyards were a handful, but it was their land and their home.
Her father's work was a different kind of enterprise. The challenge of it appealed to her.

She enjoyed her visits to the metropolis, exhausting as they
were, because each year her father's work increased a little bit
in value. Perhaps he would never receive four or five hundred
francs for a landscape as some of his contemporaries did, but
his advice was more highly regarded as each of his friends
succeeded in selling their paintings for more.

Unfortunately, more successful men than Paul de Ravenault
were hard pressed to pay their bills purely by selling paintings.
De Ravenault couldn't hope to compete with those who had
studied in Paris academies, no matter how talented he was. He
had had to train himself with the help of books, and occasional
comments from some of the great teachers whose studios he'd
had the good fortune to visit over the years.

But all of that could change if Pascale found The Painting.
Her heart had jumped when she'd first seen the final sketch
because this was no eye, hand, or other detail, but the entire
scene, an outline for a portrait of a lady as it was, complete
with dress, shoes, hat, and parasol, with a garden in the back-
ground. Pascale leafed through the pages of the book again,
for the hundredth time, until she came to a very distinctive
sketch of an upturned chin.

"Yes," she finally answered. "But I do hope to negate the
need for some of the smaller commissions eventually. The
petit-bourgeois are never interested in paying much. Of course,
I wouldn't refuse any reasonable offer, until, or unless, some-

thing happened to make Papa's work more valuable, such as having a painting accepted for the Salon. I think Papa may be on the verge of just that."

Guillaume laughed nervously. "Better yet," he said, brightly. "Perhaps you should paint something of your own for the Salon."

Pascale smiled weakly. "You know I can't do that."

"No, I don't." Guillaume had never given up hope that she'd start painting again. "You are so talented. I still have that portrait you did of me. Many people have commented on it. You are a better artist than Berthe Morisot, and her work was accepted this year."

"I *had* some talent. I haven't painted anything in five years." It was some consolation, she supposed, that he had kept that early portrait, even if he had chosen to help Papa over herself.

"It's not something you forget," François asserted. "It's in your blood. That's why you're so obsessed with this painting of Paul's."

Guillaume stuck a pointy elbow into his friend's ribs for a second time. "We should be going," he said.

She showed them out. As they opened the front door, the three of them saw Papa mounting the steps to the entrance.

"François!" he exclaimed. "Guillaume! What are you doing here? Did we have an appointment?"

"No, we've been visiting with Pascale," François said, sending him a meaningful glance. Pascale intercepted the look that passed between the two men and was sure her suspicions were correct. They were in league with him. Unfortunately, there wasn't a thing she could do about it.

F our

Pascale wandeed up to the studio. The light in the room was beautiful, the stark white walls and gently curving moldings gave the room a serene, peaceful feeling. There was nowhere to hide The Painting. But if it had been at home, Pitt would have uncovered it. It had to be here, in Paris, somewhere. Maybe he had sent it to the home of one of his friends. The quiet room calmed her, and Pascale lapsed into thought. If Paul had given his masterpiece to one of his friends for safe-keeping, she didn't know how she would recover it. Monsieur Monet, for example, who was one of Papa's oldest friends, was out of town, probably avoiding the Salon. He wouldn't return until after the end of the month—and she would be back home in their château in Beaune, unable to get an inter-view with him. The friendship between the two artists went back over twenty years, to Papa's first visits to Paris before Pascale was born.

Monet's family had been as averse to his artistic career as Papa's mother had been to his, and the two men had shared the common bond of having no money or support from home. Claude Monet had, Pascale supposed, felt sympathy for the exotic gentleman who had pursued his art single-mindedly de-spite the lack of encouragement and financial support from his family. He had shown him around the city, and Papa had conducted himself well, with the air and bearing inherited from the proud African princess who raised him. When his mother died, de Ravenault tried to run the estate, but he was totally

unsuited to the work. The family had been fortunate. Faithful
retainers, hired by her grandmother who had hired many others
of African descent, kept the vineyards going until Pascale was
old enough to assume control.

The contacts he had made in Paris as a young man, before
Pascale was born, had proven useful over the years. His skills
as a draftsman had been recognized, and his teaching ability
had led many men—even the conservative Couture—to recommend that a young artist could do worse than to emulate
de Ravenault's style. A word or two, here and there, had led
students to his home. Most of his untutored young charges
were as impecunious as he was, but often their families were
so pleased to have them out of the way, and not in the wicked
city of Paris, that some arrangements were made to provide
for some of their food and lodging. Generally the young men,
at Paul's urging, spent these monies on art supplies, allowing
the decaying land and house in Beaune to support their baser
needs.

Paul de Ravenault had not had a lot of contact with his old
friends—he was far too absentminded to think of people he
rarely saw—but his door had always been open to them and
their acquaintances when they passed through Beaune. When
the de Ravenaults came to Paris to support the Salon des Refusés in '63, neither the wholehearted approval of that distinguished gentleman nor his exotic daughter's spirited support
could be ignored, and he was welcomed back as if he had
never left.

While Pascale was happily included in Papa's artistic circle,
she was seen as a youngster, separate from them. Her contri-
bution to her father's career and her support of their friends
was taken for granted. She wasn't an artist, and therefore they
would never take her side over her father's. She had given up
her right to be treated as one of them when she had given up
painting.

Papa came into the room after a short time. He started when
he saw her there.

"Ah, Pascale, did you need me?" he asked, busying himself with his palette.

She watched him, wondering how he could look exactly as he always had. He should have appeared changed somehow, now that he had changed the "rules" that governed their relationship. But he was just himself. She examined him minutely. Papa was tall, over two meters, and painfully thin. His long limbs were like a spider's legs, almost like stilts. His arms were twice as long as hers, extended by his thin beautifully formed hands. He tended to stoop, rounding his shoulders a little, a habit that had grown more pronounced as he'd gotten older.

Papa ignored her, focused solely on mixing his paints on his palette, and she circled around him and studied his face. He was, of all people, the most dear to her. He was her only family. But there was little resemblance between them.

She was short and rounded in all of the places that he was angular and bony. His shoulders were wide across, like a thin fence railing, hers sloped downward in a feminine curve. His Adam's apple jutted out of his sinewy neck, and his chin was just as pointed, but he'd grown a fashionable beard and it masked and softened the hard thin point of his jaw. Her face was an oval. His skin was slightly lighter than hers; *café au lait,* rather than cocoa colored. But his eyes, deep set under bushy gray-streaked eyebrows, were darker than her own—almost black. He was a handsome man, or at least Pascale had always thought so. Now she saw that he could be a liar, and that lined brow looked less wise, and more disingenuous.

"Papa?" He looked up at her quizzically. "Why are you treating me like this?"

"Like what?" he asked, sounding genuinely baffled.

"Like some sort of intruder in your life. A stranger to your business."

"I'm not."

"Papa!" He jumped at her sharp tone. "Tell me the truth! Where is The Painting?"

"What painting?"

Pascale gritted her teeth and modified her voice to ask in dulcet tones, "The Portrait of The Lady. The one you've been trying to paint all these years. The mysterious woman whose face I've been waiting to see for as long as I can remember. *The* Painting."

"Oh that," he said, with a quick look toward her. Pascale caught a glimpse of his eyes, the white flash against copper skin, then he turned his back to her and hunched his shoulder so she couldn't see his face. "I don't know what you mean." It was obviously a blatant lie.

Her anger died away, leaving her feeling only hurt at this unprecedented betrayal. Her father was no longer her greatest ally.

"That's the way it's going to be, is it?" Pascale asked. The question was rhetorical, which was a good thing as her father didn't answer.

The battle lines were drawn. And so it went throughout the following week. Pascale couldn't bring herself to beg Papa to divulge his secret, but neither could she let him get away with hiding The Painting from her.

He'd been clever. She couldn't imagine how he had spirited the canvas out of the house. Now, it appeared, he had sent it all the way to Paris without her knowledge. Pascale was at a loss to know how to deal with her parent in this intractable mood. It was the first time in many years that she hadn't been able to talk him around. Usually, as maddening as her father could be, he agreed with her arguments in the end. This time he was holding fast.

He insisted that she maligned his character when she accused him of hiding something so valuable from his only family. When he remembered the argument, which was only about half the time, he treated her to a show of wounded pride and offended dignity. But Pascale was convinced she was right.

She tried to keep track of his movements, and to spend as much time with him as her busy schedule allowed. But Pascale could only devote a certain amount of time to her search. There were morning calls to be made, and visitors to entertain. There were daily menus to plan, and all of the rest of the housekeeping had to be overseen. There were also meetings with potential patrons to be arranged and attended, and her father to shepherd through near-brushes with catastrophe.

They sometimes walked in the morning. The April days dawned cool and misty, and the streets were abustle before the sun came up with street vendors, shopkeepers, and common folk on their way to work. Huge tracts of the city were being redesigned. One of Napoleon III's great ambitions was to re-create Paris, and his prefect, Baron Haussmann, was tearing down buildings, tearing up roads, and generally creating an air of chaos. Pascale thought the changes and all the building was exciting, and the results of the new plans for the city quite magnificent. But Papa complained Haussmann was demolishing the city.

Although she didn't want to let Papa out of her sight, Pascale couldn't find the time to go with him to all of his friends' studios. She did manage to go with him when he went to Switzerland House, where artists with pockets to let could paint live models cheaply. She had heard many stories over the years of Papa's adventures there when he'd visited Paris as a young man.

The grandmother who had raised Papa had allowed him to paint because in Africa her family had been artists—though they had worked mostly with hardwoods from the forests of Kenya. She had never led him to believe that he might make a living for himself pursuing his art. She was a very practical-minded woman, and even the soft spot she held for her only child did not allow her to lose sight of the important responsibilities she would leave to her only remaining relative upon her death. She expected him to run the farm, but she allowed him his avocation because she could not refuse him. Possibly she had also been swayed by her knowledge of the boy, who seemed to be compelled to create. She might have realized that she couldn't stop him, no matter how absent-minded and malleable Paul de Ravenault might seem.

Pascale was starting to believe that her father had a much stronger will than she'd ever given him credit for. He showed an unexpected ability to turn her from the one topic of conversation that most interested her. Paul de Ravenault had succeeded in totally baffling his daughter.

On Thursday evening Édouard Manet and his wife, Suzanne, hosted a small gathering as they did every week. This gathering was the only one at which the most experimental artists and their less daring counterparts could meet and talk, and both the older and the younger generation were frequent guests. Pascale often accompanied her father to those outings, even though she usually left him to his own devices at night.

At this weekly party, Pascale enjoyed renewing old friendships and sometimes found herself forming new ones. Paris was the heart of the art world, and Manet's "Thursday evenings" were the best opportunity for like-minded artists to meet. Pascale was in her element among the artists and critics, the students and art lovers.

On this particular Thursday night, Pascale was pleased to meet Madame George Sand, whose novels she had always admired. As Pascale made her way over to Madame Sand, Sand waylaid Captain John Devlin, whom Guillaume and François had brought to the informal party.

Pascale reached the little group just as Madame Sand said to the captain, "I suppose if Guillaume plans to try his hand in investing in something more profitable than art, he has chosen the right man. You look like you know what you're about, Captain I have never had a head for business myself. In my experience, art and finance make very poor bedfellows."

Guillaume protested, "But in the end, artists must treat what they do as a business, otherwise they would starve."

"But think of all of the great artists who have died without a penny to their names. Mozart was buried in a pauper's grave. Yet his music lives on."

"You must meet Pascale de Ravenault," François said, drawing her forward. "She has often said much the same thing."

Pascale took Madame's hand with a nervous smile. "Don't mind François, he rarely thinks before he speaks." She glared at her old friend.

"Nonsense. You are the proof for George's argument." He turned to Madame. "Pascale gave up her artistic career to manage her father's finances. She holds that it is impossible for a true artist to treat their work as a business and create at the same time."

"Did you indeed?" Madame Sand sent a piercing look down her long nose at Pascale.

"Not exactly. Some artists can do both. My father has a talent for art, but little for business."

"You, I take it, have a talent for business and little for art?"

Guillaume and François protested, "No, she was very talented."

"For a child," Pascale had to add the caveat.

"An adult's talent, though, I assure you, Madame," Manet said, joining their little group. "I've seen some of her work, done at the age of fifteen or sixteen, I think. She inherited her father's eye and not a little of his ability."

"However, I did not inherit Papa's tolerance for discomfort. We all need to eat, even artists."

"Ah, that's the problem," Madame agreed. "But here with all the talk of art, and exciting displays of art work, don't your fingers ever itch to once again hold a paintbrush. I know I'd love to be able to capture the expression of a child playing in the sunlight."

"Occasionally I miss it. But those moments never last long. I simply go shopping for new dresses for the maids, or send off another print to one of the shopkeepers who now can't keep enough of father's prints on hand."

"And that, I suppose, is the difference between you. Your father would be completely inconsolable could he not paint."

Devlin had been silently listening to this exchange and now

asked, "Do you feel the same, Madame Sand? If you had to give up your writing for some reason, would you be miserable?"

"Sometimes I dream of escaping it. But it would depend on whether I was giving it up for something that offered more . . . ," she drew out the word and shot a flirtatious glance up at him, ". . . money."

Everyone laughed. But Pascale felt her smile waver. She had been miserable, at first, when she had given up her painting at fifteen. But she had recovered. Her career, or rather, her concentration on her father's career, was more profitable than painting would have been, but money wasn't what gave her solace. Her father's successes were worth more than all the money in the world. To some degree, she counted them her own.

"So, it seems you made the right choice, little one," Devlin said. "Why do you look unhappy?" The low-voiced question was obviously meant for her ears alone. Pascale almost ignored him. But she couldn't resist the urge to contradict the smug sea captain. He was so arrogant.

"I am not unhappy," she said.

"Really?" he asked in English.

"You know nothing about it," Pascale answered in French. "If you'll excuse me, I have business to attend to."

"Business?" He looked around the room at the Manets' guests, who were laughing, and talking. Soft music came from the piano on the other side of the room.

"That is why we're here, Captain," Pascale told him.

"I hope it goes well for you, then," he said, bowing.

"It will," she said confidently. "Good evening, sir."

It was true. Business was always enhanced by the contact with their connections in town during their annual visit to Paris. This trip was no different in that respect. But Pascale could not totally immerse herself in her work. There was The Painting to consider. And then the memory of Captain Devlin's mocking voice haunted her at odd moments. Despite the fact that Pascale could have done without meeting him again, the Manets' little soiree did serve one important function. It inspired Pascale to arrange a small reception of her own. It would be just for close friends of the family. The guest list would include only those people her father trusted implicitly.

For once she was thankful that her father didn't concern himself with any of the arrangements. Paul de Ravenault wandered about the house with his head in the clouds, so that the servants hired for the month learned quickly enough that it was the young *mademoiselle,* not the master, who gave the orders. The master was likely to wander off in the middle of any discussion about repairs to the furniture, or dinner menus. Then there was the room at the end of the hall on the second floor, which they weren't allowed to enter at all. *He* sometimes was in there all day and all night, muttering dreadful imprecations, and failing to eat until Pascale went in with his tray to bully him. One night he woke the whole house, with his bellowing about a missing item that had something to do with porcupine quills. Everyone relied on the mistress, for she knew how to handle the old man.

Pascale set the servants to making arrangements for her soiree while she took care of the invitations. When she received the responses from those she had invited, she called the cook in to discuss the menu and check on all of the other arrangements that Louise, the cook, was overseeing.

The house needed very little attention. Pascale was well pleased with the little house she had rented for their month in town. A friend of her father's was the owner, and his studio was almost as pleasant as her father's own, back at home. The bedrooms, modest dining room, and two receiving rooms were all nicely arranged and decorated, and had needed only a few personal items scattered about to give the place a homey feel.

Pascale had adopted the smaller of the two salons for her own use, leaving the larger, more ornate room for receiving their important visitors, and that was where the cook found her two days before her little soiree.

Louise had worked in the de Ravenault household since well before Pascale was born. Pascale had grown up with little knowledge of how other households worked. It was only through her contact with Papa's "students" that she gained some knowledge about how other homes were run. She had left Francine and the schoolroom behind at thirteen, she had taken the knowledge she had gleaned from these boys and tried to create a haven of domestic bliss for Papa, herself, his friends, and his students. She rarely heeded Francine's advice. Her governess was so old-fashioned as to make absurd suggestions such as breakfast should be served in the impersonal formal dining room rather than welcoming everyone into the warm, toasty kitchen for the first meal of the day.

Louise and Pascale had always understood each other. The cook had been the closest thing to a mother that Pascale had ever had, since her own mother had left her when she was an infant. She didn't approve of all of Pascale's domestic arrangements, and she could never understand why Pascale encouraged Papa to invite young artists to live with them.

More often than not, Paul tutored boys who had been turned away from the academies but had money enough to pursue their studies, and were tenacious enough to study with anyone. Louise called them Pascale's pups and treated them much like she would their canine namesakes. But when one of his students showed real promise, and was able to make something of himself in Paris, it brought more recognition of Paul's abilities as a teacher. Pascale thought that was ample recompense for the care and feeding they received at the château. Louise said Pascale let the pups take advantage of her soft heart, but if the young mistress wanted to throw their hard-earned bread away feeding it to the ungrateful whelps, it was not her place to scold. She did have a right to her opinion, though. And she had one on most topics.

She didn't approve of Paul de Ravenault's boundless hospitality, for example. Cook thought it ridiculous that his friends would come to visit, without warning, whenever they pleased.

Pascale once tried to placate her by offering to cook in her place when these awkward situations arose. But that just offended the cook further. She offered to resign her position if her work wasn't satisfactory. It was a threat Pascale had heard often, and the young woman knew it only signified that the discussion was at an end.

The one time Cook had actually packed her bags was when Pascale had suggested she and her father travel to Paris without any of the family retainers.

In 1862, at the tender age of eighteen, Pascale took to heart the democratic tradition that was espoused by the emperor and the radical writers of the day. She decided, with the zeal of youth, that the time had come to fight the academies and the newspapers, and right the wrongs that society perpetuated against talented but penniless artists like her father. The daughter decided that the master had to go to Paris to add his objective opinion, and moral support, to the protesters. It took her a year to convince Papa.

Since Louise had patently disapproved of the scheme from the moment Pascale began to talk about it, she had never even considered asking the cook to go with them. Pascale had briefly toyed with the idea of inviting Madame Pitt along, to act as chaperone, but she had quickly decided against it. Madame disapproved of artists in general, and could not abide female artists. They lived such irregular lives. It was not at all the "thing" for a young woman of consequence to do. She had been known to concede to her harsher critics that it would have been a waste for Pascale to go totally untutored with a father as talented as hers, and Pascale suspected Madame might have been able to reconcile herself to an education that included some instruction in sketching, watercolors, even the rudiments of painting, so that Pascale could draw a credibly pretty bowl of fruit or flowers. But Madame Pitt could not forgive Monsieur de Ravenault for encouraging his daughter to study anatomy, the most egregious of Monsieur's sins in Francine's humble, but oft voiced, opinion.

One might have thought Madame would have been pleased

when, in Pascale's thirteenth year, Paul de Ravenault developed a predilection for painting outdoors. But Francine thought he did it just to spite her. There was no other explanation for it. No proper father would encourage his daughter to "be alone with nature." She didn't care what Monsieur Claude Monet said about the benefits of painting on the scene—everyone knew his family was in trade.

If the master would not forbid his daughter to wander off alone, Francine would. Why, anything could happen to an unprotected girl, alone in the woods. The battle still raged between them. Although Pascale had left the classroom years ago, Francine Pitt was still convinced that Paul de Ravenault would do anything to flout her methods of teaching Pascale to be a proper lady. Only Pascale's very proper renunciation of an artistic career, for which Madame took full credit, enabled her governess to live peacefully with her employer under his own roof.

Louise had no argument with artists. And she could appreciate, even if Francine could not, Papa's role in persuading Pascale to choose to run a household falling to wrack and ruin under the unobservant eye of its distracted master. Pascale could argue with her dying breath that it was her father's example that led her to eschew the life of an artist, but Francine would not believe that her lord and master was anything other than the selfish man who had almost lost the family estate through his negligence.

Louise, on the other hand, had worked for the de Ravenault family since long before Pascale was born. She had lived through those years when the master and his employees struggled just to feed themselves, and had seen that art was Papa's passion. She thought him not quite right in his mind. And she thought herself obligated to care for his only child, since his mother had taken her in when she had nowhere to go, and given her the position of cook when Louise had no references and little experience.

Cook, irascible as she was, was the one person in Pascale's

life who could always be counted on to do what she said she would. Her bitter exterior hid a heart of gold, but Pascale was the only one allowed even a glimpse of it. One of those rare moments had occurred when she had refused to let Pascale go to the city without her on that first trip three years ago. Ever since, she'd shared the housekeeping duties with her young mistress on their annual sojourn in Paris.

All their shared history flitted through Pascale's mind as she looked up at the diminutive bone-thin woman standing before her. Pascale sighed as she caught a glimpse of the martial light shining in Louise's brown eyes.

"Is something wrong?" Pascale asked.

"We've got to have more help if we're to have a party in just two days," Cook said firmly.

"Fine," Pascale said, taking the wind out of her sails.

"Odelle and Philippe can manage, but those two children you hired to work with them don't have the slightest idea what to do."

"There will only be us, and eight or nine others for dinner, Cook, but if we need more staff, I'll hire them."

"Well!" she said, clearly gratified by Pascale's easy acquiescence to her demand. "Well, perhaps we can manage with the servants we have."

"That would be nice," Pascale said.

"But I must say, even though I know you won't listen to me, I don't know why we are suddenly inviting all these people to dine here? We never did before." Cook hated change.

"Perhaps we should have," Pascale said. "We are always invited to so many parties when we are in Paris, and we never have one of our own."

"And why should we? It's just a lot of fuss and bother for nothing, if you ask me," she replied, bristling.

"It's only polite," Pascale said.

"Polite!" Louise snorted. "You feed enough hungry mouths already in that orphanage you call a home. If you start doing that here in Paris, you won't have a feather to fly with."

Five

Nerves were stretched on the day of the de Ravenaults' first party as the fateful hour approached. The youngest housemaid almost upset one of Cook's cooling racks, and had her ears soundly boxed by that demanding lady before Pascale thought to set her to arranging the sideboards in the dining room with the youngest of the serving boys.

Despite the chaos and the growing tension, Pascale had high hopes for the evening. It was the first time she'd hosted a dinner party "at home," and she had been more than satisfied with the enthusiastic response to her invitations. She was also certain that she would unmask whichever of her father's friends was his conspirator in secreting away The Painting, and she looked forward to catching the traitor.

With the arrival of the first guest, Pascale's tightly wound nerves uncoiled. She patted a stray hair into place and assumed her place at her father's side, with a smile for Monsieur Valon, who had been one of the master's first pupils and had remained a friend for many years, though he painted only for pleasure. Pascale had known him since she was a small girl, and she stood on no ceremony with him. As with many of her father's good friends, he was accustomed to treating her just as he had when she was a little girl dangling on his knee.

But tonight he took her hand and kissed it and then stepped back, pursing his lips in a silent whistle of admiration. Pascale's rose-colored gown complemented her cocoa-colored skin. It was cut low at the bodice and billowed out from the cinched-in waist to cascade over her hips.

"In that dress you make me think of a succulent berry dipped in chocolate," said Valon, quite improperly.

"Thank you, I think," Pascale quipped.

He was not done teasing her yet. "So, *mignon,* will we finally see another of your delightful paintings tonight? Or are you still adverse to following in your father's footsteps?"

"How many times must I tell you, Valon," Pascale returned, with a laugh, "I no longer kneel at the feet of the muse, Calliope. . . ." Her words trailed off as she saw Captain John Devlin over Étienne Valon's shoulder. She recovered quickly, "She is too cruel a mistress for me."

"I am the expert at choosing cruel mistresses, as you know, my dear." Though she'd often joked with her friend Étienne Valon and knew him to be a harmless old roué, Pascale felt herself warming under Captain Devlin's scrutiny as he listened with interest to their banter. Étienne's long-suffering wife gave him a tap on the shoulder, reminding him of his surroundings. With a grimace, he moved on, leaving Pascale face-to-face with the devil himself.

Pascale hadn't expected to see Captain Devlin again, and his quite remarkable male beauty again made her breath catch. The familiar glint of disapproval in his eye, however, brought back all the resentment she felt toward him.

"We meet again, *mademoiselle,*" he said.

"Captain, what a pleasant surprise. I hadn't expected to see you here." Guillaume and François must have brought him along with them. He *would* flaunt convention by attending the small party uninvited.

"Did you not?" he asked, looking puzzled, "but I understood from your father that it was you that made up the guest list?"

"My father?" He had stunned her. She must have betrayed her chagrin, because the quizzical look in his eyes was replaced by one of amusement.

"He seemed to think my invitation must have been lost and

was so kind as to extend one in person when last he visited us at the hotel," he explained.

"I see. Well, you're . . . very welcome, of course." Pascale was grateful for the dark skin that hid her blushes as her lips formed the lie. He bowed and walked on, leaving her to greet the rest of her guests with her mind in a whirl. What in the world was her father thinking of, to invite a virtual stranger to the intimate little party? He had mentioned that he would invite anyone they had overlooked if he saw them, but he had never mentioned the sea captain. She had not divulged her true motives for arranging the sociable evening, but he must surely have understood the tone she hoped to set for the evening. The captain would be the only guest who was not immersed in the art world. As the thought struck her, she realized she'd have to change the seating arrangements at the dinner table.

Pascale didn't know where to seat Captain John Devlin at dinner. She cherished no illusions about the captain's interest in artistic endeavors. She had divined at their first meeting that he wasn't exactly impressed at being introduced to a master artisan, and the way he had laughed at her father's offer to paint or sculpt him had left her with no doubt that he thought little of Papa's abilities. She more than suspected he didn't hold artists in high esteem. Their second meeting, at the Manets' house, had reinforced that opinion. The conversation with George Sand had left no doubt in her mind that he thought artists were emotional creatures. Doubtless a man with shoulders as wide as John Devlin's, and legs so muscular that even plain black stockings couldn't disguise their shape, shared the prevailing opinion that artists were poor, weak creatures, playing about with their paints like women, rather than building empires and amassing fortunes as real men did.

Pascale wavered for a moment in her decision to place him between Guillaume and François. As the hostess, she should seat him next to herself and make sure he was entertained with conversation better suited to his interests than discussion of the latest rages in the artistic world. But in the end, she let the arrangement stand, reasoning that Captain Devlin was well acquainted and comfortable with Guillaume. He would no doubt entertain himself quite well with his old friends. Pascale planned to devote herself to asking questions tonight, and she couldn't allow Captain Devlin's unexpected presence to divert her from her task.

The party had grown in size when she rejoined the guests, who were standing about in the larger of the two salons. Papa was talking with Guillaume and Captain Devlin. Madame and Monsieur Valon were happily discussing mutual acquaintances with François. Renoir and Pissarro had arrived, with two young artists whom Pascale had met last year and who had been corresponding irregularly with Papa ever since. The Manets had been unable to attend, due to a previous engagement, but Pascale hadn't really thought Édouard would help her father hide his painting anyway. The man was too sensible for such dramatics. This small group comprised the most likely people to have had a hand in aiding her father in his scheme.

Auguste Renoir was the most likely candidate, as he was a big admirer of her father's work, and had little respect for the Salon. She made her way to his side. He barely took the time to greet her before he requested, "Pascale, help me explain to these idiots. The critics are dependent upon the academies and the Salon for their success, just as we are."

Pissarro explained the reason for the question. "Renoir thinks the critics are only surrendering to the pressure of the academies with their reviews of our work. He thinks they are only giving young artists negative reviews because they think it will raise their credit with Ingles and the Académie members."

Pascale didn't completely agree. "You cannot expect them suddenly to change their views," she said to Renoir. "Especially after years of criticizing anything new or different. Ingles has been the ruling force in the Royal Academy for ten years and he continues to reign supreme. The critics take their cue from him. Until he retires as the director of the Académie, or cedes the point, classicism will always be preferred over the less traditional. Added to that, people are accustomed to seeing that kind of painting. They were raised with it, and they love it. The critics must serve their audience."

"Your friend Zola seems to think it simple enough. He wrote that Manet's *Olympia* was a masterpiece in his article in *L'Événement*," Renoir said.

"Émile is our age, and he has to prove himself. He has ambitions of his own," Pissarro answered.

Dinner was announced, but Renoir couldn't be halted. "But the critics can't really hate Monet's work. Or Degas's. They're too good." Pascale took his arm and turned him toward the door, and still he kept on. "They are crucifying *Olympia*. How can they do that in good conscience?"

"Nothing that is truly different is going to be embraced at first. Manet's *Olympia* is a good case in point. Manet painted a nude, because, he said, that was the only way to get attention these days. He painted her in a classical pose, for the critics. Then he made her a whore—for himself, or for us and our friends, or perhaps because he felt compelled to do so. Whether or not you like the painting, you must see the critics' job here is not easy," Pissarro pointed out.

"But the critics are calling it obscene! That's just ridiculous," Renoir said heatedly.

As they moved toward the dining room, Pascale looked around for Papa, and noticed that he, Guillaume, and the captain had disappeared. They appeared at the door to the dining room just as she was sitting down at the table.

Renoir was awaiting her response. She turned her attention from the three men who were finding their places at the table to respond to him. "None of us would call it obscene, but he might have guessed it would be taken that way. As for Manet, there can be little doubt he is conducting some experiment of his own. I've heard it said that he did it just to paint a nude, and then made her so brazen to thumb his nose at those who 'forced' him to do so." The painting under discussion had been the focus of many a review, and much debate, since the Salon had opened. Everyone had an opinion.

Valon said knowingly, "Manet."

François grimaced. "Here we go again."

"Olympia? But surely everyone here agrees that it is not quite the work of art we'd like to focus on. It was clearly painted just to create a sensation." Valon's wife said.

"Once a critic is established, it is his duty to honestly critique a work of art, rather than pandering to the established schools or playing politics," Renoir insisted.

She couldn't help overhearing Guillaume explaining to Devlin what the conversation was about. "Manet painted the model Victorine Meurent in a classical pose—reclining nude on a couch. Her nudity might have been acceptable if she'd been a classical model; Aphrodite perhaps, or one of Zeus' concubines. But she is clearly just some prostitute displaying her wares, her expression is not lascivious, but impassive. What makes the painting so disturbing, I think, is that she seems to be staring directly at the viewer of the painting. Not only did Monet paint a whore, but anyone who looks on her cannot help but feel she sees *them* as a client," Guillaume opined.

"I saw the painting. It was provocative," Devlin said, "but fascinating."

Pascale personally thought Manet was thumbing his nose at those who were titillated by the nude but wouldn't admit it. *Olympia* was his painting for those who tried to disguise their voyeurism as appreciation of art. But she agreed with Renoir that the critics should not concern themselves with why Manet had painted *Olympia*, but rather with whether or not he had done it well.

The two young artists, Thierry and Louis, took opposing sides on the debate. "What's amazing," Yves said, "is that he's so surprised at the uproar. He must have known it would be unacceptable to make her so obviously a common strumpet."

"But if he'd painted a classical nude, it would have been fine," Louis argued. "It is so hypocritical."

All of the guests ignored dinner etiquette, which demanded they at least pretend interest in speaking with those seated nearest them, and focused instead on the conversation between the four young artists and herself. Pascale needn't have worried that Captain Devlin would be left out of the conversation; he was quite prepared to join in.

"François, you complained when the critics crucified the works in the Salon des Refusés last year that they were pandering to the Salon. Now they are turning their pens on offerings from the Salon. You should be pleased," he was saying when the young men around her finally quieted to concentrate on their dinners. Pascale thought he might be teasing his friend, but François took him seriously.

"But it is not the Salon they are disparaging, but the artists whom the Salon has refused so often in the past. Morisot, Renoir, even Paul Cézanne and Edgar Degas—these are artists who have studied with their own gods!" François said.

"Ah, but the paintings they've submitted are often the unfinished 'impressions' that are considered so raw by the Académie, the educated viewers. If the artists insist on painting their own way, and encourage each other to flout convention by leaving their brush strokes exposed, and painting ordinary men and women rather than the nobility, then they must suffer these slings from the press," the captain argued, reasonably, and, Pascale had to admit, intelligently. Devlin demonstrated to Pascale a much more intimate knowledge of the subject than she'd have thought he would possess. "But even more established critics have been supportive in their evaluation of some of your friends. You read to me that review in the *Gazette des Beaux-Arts* that praised Monet's impression of *The Pointe de la Heve at Low Tide*. I've heard it said the critics are completely prejudiced against these impressions, purely because Ingres, as Director of the Académie, says they're unfinished works. But that review was very positive."

His unemotional argument doused Renoir's fiery passion. The conversation became more general. A few carefully worded queries to Renoir satisfied Pascale's curiosity about his involvement in her father's secret. Madame Valon caught Pascale's attention next, and she was able to ascertain from that lady that her husband hadn't had any contact with Papa in some time. However, she had to spend an inordinate amount of time satisfying that lady's curiosity about where and how she had her dresses made in the country.

"And all in the current mode, too," Madame kept saying. "Remarkable!"

When dinner was finally over, Pascale made her escape. She and Madame joined the men in the garden for brandy and coffee. Pascale was able to slip away while François and Valon debated which region of France produced the best liqueurs.

She sat on a bench shrouded in darkness. She was disappointed that none of her lures concerning her father's artwork were picked up by any of his friends. Unless these men, whom she'd known since she was in short skirts, had acquired much better acting abilities than they had previously possessed, none of them were privy to the existence of The Painting.

Guillaume and Captain Devlin strolled past her hiding place, engrossed in conversation. Devlin's French was quite good. His accent was charming. She sat quietly, listening, hoping that they wouldn't notice her. The bench was set back a few feet from the slate-tiled path, the light of the lamps didn't reach it.

She was not in the proper frame of mind to entertain the captain. His mocking smile was not to be borne tonight.

"We should be leaving in a week, if all goes well," Devlin was saying.

"It was worthwhile, then, to come to Paris."

"Certainly. The Mexican émigrés alone could almost fill the hold with cargo."

"I thought so." Guillaume sounded pleased with himself.

"Although I know there are many Mexican nobles who have taken up residence in England, too."

"Certainly, but I am hoping to buy another ship, and this trip convinces me that expansion is more than possible."

They had passed by her resting spot. They stopped a few feet farther on, where the path ended, but they didn't turn around immediately to start back.

Instead Guillaume asked, "You do not worry that there will be trouble when you arrive in Mexico? I have heard there is unrest under Maximilian's rule."

"Unrest? It is almost rebellion. And Maximilian has not got enough men, or enough money, to quash it. It was only to be expected, once Napoleon installed an Austrian noble as the emperor of Mexico. How he thought to hold the country, I do not know. It is larger than France and half a world away. And, of course, most people support Juarez, who was, after all, elected by them."

"The emperor was persuaded by his empress."

"Does he admit that?" Devlin asked, surprised.

"It is well known. Empress Eugenie and Maximilian's wife, Charlotte, were very public about their sympathies, and their aims. The Church was neglected under the elected government of Juarez, and they wanted to reinforce it. But Napoleon upheld the electoral process."

Pascale must have moved, because Guillaume looked toward where she was sitting. Pascale suddenly felt ridiculous. What was she doing hiding away? Her common sense reasserted itself. Just because Captain John Devlin's handsome face and silky voice made her nervous was no reason to take out her frustration on Guillaume.

"I noticed at Princess Mathilde's party, many of the émigrés were in attendance," Devlin was saying as Pascale stood and walked toward the two men. He didn't seem surprised at her sudden appearance. He must have known she was there all along.

Guillaume nervously smiled in greeting, but answered

Devlin before turning to her. "The émigrés play a very risky game. They play on the women's allegiance to the Church."

"It is not only women who are loyal Catholics," Pascale defended her sex.

"Of course not," Guillaume agreed. "But it was the empress who responded. The emperor would not, I think, have felt it his obligation to support the pope without her urging."

"Once Napoleon chose to act, the imperials were supported, of course, by the French nobility. Eugenie and Mathilde and the others adopted the émigrés. That is why there were so many of them at the princess's ball," Pascale explained to Devlin. "The Mexican nobility miscalculated. I'm sure they didn't expect Napoleon III to install Maximilian as emperor of their country."

"Well, it made sense. Napoleon had his own goals. Now he has a powerful ally in the Americas," Guillaume said, cynically.

"You English do not care to colonize any more of the Americas," Pascale teased, unable to resist the opportunity to tweak him for his very British arrogance.

"We will leave that to you, and wish you joy of it," Devlin responded in kind.

"You are very blasé, Captain. Won't your business suffer if Maximilian is overthrown?"

"My ship can travel to many ports, Mexico is not the only possible destination. And politics have not interfered with my trade thus far."

Guillaume supported him. "Jack has had great success despite all of the upheaval overseas."

"You might even say *because* of that upheaval," Devlin said, with a smirk.

"You cannot be proud of that," Pascale proclaimed. "You trade on the misfortune of others! Not only in Mexico but in the United States where men fight for freedom."

"The War Between the States is not about men, it's about power and money, as wars invariably are." The cocky smile was gone, but his self-confidence was not diminished. He radiated strength and self-assurance. Pascale had never met a man as impassive as the block of ice who stood before her, blandly awaiting her response. She didn't know how to respond. She wished she had his certainty. She didn't envy him, though. Whatever he might say about the American war, Captain John Devlin's major interest in life was clearly his business. She wanted more than that.

Pascale wanted her father to be a successful artist, certainly, but she also wanted that art to be created for its own sake. She was sure the man standing in front of her could never understand that. He was too cold, too caught up in his precious business, to comprehend her father's passion for his art; or her own belief in the artist.

Guillaume looked back and forth between the two of them. "Shall we return to the house?" he asked.

"Yes," Pascale said, hastily. She turned and led the way back, very conscious of Devlin's eyes following her.

"I imagine the others are still discussing Manet," Guillaume said. "He seems to have become a focal point in the Salon. Have you been there yet? People point at *Olympia* and laugh and snicker."

"I can see how that would be more interesting to this gathering than the state of affairs in Mexico. But don't they ever discuss anything else?" Devlin asked.

"When Papa and I entertain, we try to invite guests who share our interests." She tried to disguise her hostility, which had returned in full force at the criticism, but she was afraid she didn't fool him.

"And nothing but art interests you? You sound as obsessed as they are. You said yourself you're not an artist anymore. Yet the Salon consumes you, too."

"Would you prefer everyone discussed business at all times?" Pascale countered acidly.

Devlin had not missed the sarcasm in her tone. "Unlike you, I reserve my evenings purely for the pursuit of pleasure. Pleasant conversation, pleasant company."

"Of course," said Guillaume. "Like this evening."

Pascale remembered the conversation she'd interrupted. "I must have been mistaken, I thought I overheard you discussing your next voyage."

"I think we have touched on every possible topic of conversation, including art, politics, religion, and shipping," Guillaume joked, in an attempt, perhaps, to prevent an argument. They had reached the flower garden behind the house where her other guests stood talking in groups of two and three. Pascale spotted Papa still speaking with the Valons.

She would have gone to his side, but Devlin's next barb stopped her in her tracks.

"I am intrigued. I thought you were more interested in business than in art. Isn't that why you gave up painting?"

He infuriated her. This man with the face of an angel and a body of sculpted marble, was an invincible force of nature. She suspected it was a destructive power that he yielded, and that frightened her. She was drawn to his strength, but she was also repelled by it.

"I live by the one, I love the other. You may find this hard to understand, Captain, but there are more important things in life than finding a profit in the misery of others."

"Pascale!" Guillaume exclaimed. "I have invested in Jack's enterprise. Do you accuse me, too, of such heartless behavior?"

Pascale knew the accusation had been unjust. In the face of Guillaume's embarrassment, she relented. "No, of course not. I'm sorry, Guillaume, Captain Devlin. I'm afraid I have not been a very good hostess tonight. Please accept my apologies."

"Of course," said Guillaume instantly.

"No apology is necessary," Devlin chimed in. Pascale looked into his eyes for some hint that his honeyed voice disguised contempt. But she saw only sympathy and understanding. It left her breathless and slightly flustered.

"Excuse me, gentlemen. It appears the Valons are preparing to depart." Both men bowed as she beat a hasty retreat.

Other than her tiff with Devlin, Pascale thought that the

evening went very well. At the end of the night, a burgeoning friendship seemed to be forming between Devlin and the four younger artists. The other guests, old friends all, were satisfied to have renewed their acquaintance.

Her only clue that Devlin's invitation this evening might have had a devious motive behind it came when Paul de Ravenault insisted on showing the captain out, personally. Her father's unprecedented act of gentlemanly bonhomie left Pascale stunned and, suddenly, suspicious.

Six

A few days later, her suspicions were confirmed. She had yielded to an impulse to take a walk in the Tuileries to a spot that, according to a number of her cosmopolitan friends, afforded a view of both Paris greenery and society's finest. She saw quite a few people of her acquaintance as she strolled through the park, but didn't stop to speak with anyone. When she reached the place she sought, she was unprepared for the sight that greeted her. Her father and Captain John Devlin stood a little removed from a party that included François and Guillaume; Camille Pissarro; Édouard Manet and his model for the controversial painting of *Olympia,* Victorine Meurent; young Émile Zola, the sickly and tortured-looking young critic, and two women Pascale did not know, who were probably models or friends of Victorine's. Papa did not see her approach until Guillaume hailed her, and then he started, guiltily, and tried unsuccessfully to assume an air of innocent pleasure at Pascale's arrival. The captain made no such attempt, but greeted Pascale with smug self-assurance and stood amused, watching her father's antics.

Pascale could cheerfully have killed him at that moment as she realized suddenly that he had allied himself with her father against her. But she managed to control herself and greet him with cold civility, "Good morning, Captain Devlin."

"And to you, *mademoiselle.*" He took the hand she offered him and raised it to his lips. It took monumental self-control not to pull out of his light grasp before he released her. She was irritated by the leap of her pulse at the sight of his male perfection. Despite the annoyance she felt upon seeing his cocksure smile, she felt branded by the warm, strong imprint his hand left on hers.

She turned to the others. "Édouard, I haven't had a chance to congratulate you on your triumph. All Paris is abuzz. One hears of nothing else these days but your *Olympia*." She exchanged smiles with Victorine.

"Thank you, Pascale," Manet said, fidgeting with his beard in his usual manner. "I don't know if I'd call it a triumph exactly."

Pissarro raised an eyebrow. "Our modest friend doesn't much care for his newfound notoriety. He'd rather curry favor with the critics, and keep his dignity."

"What do the critics know? After all, they are usually just frustrated artists and writers themselves." The remark had been aimed at the captain. After his comments on the night of the party, she'd been sure it would annoy him.

However, Zola, whose presence she'd forgotten, was the one to protest. "Writing criticism is writing, *mam'selle*. And it can be very satisfying. I do not personally find it frustrating at all."

She couldn't resist. "Perhaps because you are able to alternate between writing fiction and writing your articles, Émile." The young author stammered something incoherent in response, but Captain Devlin rescued him.

"I read your review of Manet's work. If your fiction is as beautifully written as your prose, I predict your novel will be a great success."

Pascale added her agreement to the chorus of assent, and hid her grudging admiration for Devlin's tact—another addition to the list of things she disliked about him.

Her father stood by the captain's side, his mind obviously elsewhere. She took his hand to draw him closer to her and away from John Devlin, and turned to Pissarro. "Have you heard from our friends Bazille and Monet in Chailly-de-Sur?"

she asked. "Do they regret missing the Salon? Monet's landscapes are very fine."

"I am glad you reminded me. Bazille sent me a letter." His smile invited them to share his amusement as he related its contents. "Apparently, Claude has been surveying everyone he has met in order to compile statistics about sales of paintings hung at the Salon. According to his latest calculations, his work only has a thirty percent chance of selling at the price he is asking." Even the downcast Édouard Manet managed to smile at that. "You know how he is about money. According to Bazille, whenever anyone congratulates him on his favorable reviews, he is thrown into a depression." Pascale chuckled along with everyone else at Monet's mercenary sentiments, but her laughter was forced.

She was positive Captain John Devlin had The Painting, but she was still in a quandary as to how to approach him.

François suggested they walk on, but Manet was descending into a depression at the thought of having to keep *Olympia* forever. The thought had only just occurred to him, inspired by Monet's statistics. Pissarro, Zola, and the women carried him off to have a drink, and only Guillaume, the captain, Papa, and herself strolled along with François.

"Beautiful spot, eh?" her parent offered, smiling nervously as he looked from the captain to his smoldering offspring.

"I didn't expect to find you here, *mon père*," Pascale said. "I thought you said you'd be busy in the studio all morning?"

"Ah, well, it's such a lovely day. I decided to go to the Salon. Met poor Manet trying to defend his *Olympia*." She could tell that he was lying, he couldn't meet her eyes.

She felt very conscious of Devlin's eyes on them both. She could not confront her father in front of his friends. She had more respect for her honor and his than to confront him in such a public place. Though she would have much to discuss with him later. For the moment she wondered how to minimize the damage he might have done. She tried to hold his gaze, but Papa, exasperating man, had lost all interest in the conversation and was wool-gathering as usual.

Pascale, well used to his eccentricities, was easily able to spot the exact moment when he forgot all about his real reason for visiting the park. Therefore, she was not at all surprised when he turned to the captain and joked in his awkward way, "Not at all your kind of place, though, is it, Captain? Never thought to get you out here with us admiring the bounties of Mother Nature."

Pascale would have laughed at the other man's stunned expression if she hadn't been so annoyed with both of them.

He made a quick recover. "Well, sir, François and Guillaume fairly live here. Thought I'd see what all the fuss is about," Devlin extemporized.

"I'm sure you've seen many more beautiful places, *monsieur.* Exotic ports of call spring to mind, of course." Papa pursued the subject. The annoyed look Devlin sent her father when he asked the question convinced Pascale that it was Papa who had arranged this meeting, and chosen the meeting place. Of course, the absentminded artist waited for his answer, completely forgetful of the fact that he had been Devlin's only reason for visiting the park. He probably hadn't even noticed his surroundings until that moment. She bit her lip.

The others, Parisians all, awaited Devlin's response with interest. Narrow eyed, Devlin shot a glance at Pascale, then turned slowly to take in their surroundings again.

"This reminds me of London, in a way. Exotic is all very well, but it is pleasant to be reminded of home."

"London's never as green as this," François protested.

"It can be," Captain Devlin said. "Hyde Park in the spring has just the same young maidens walking with their chaperones, nurses with their babies, and gentlemen and ladies strolling along the paths."

Pascale barely heard the captain's words. Her mind was fully occupied adjusting to this unexpected development, and figuring out what it meant to her own plans. Papa had surely engaged the English sea captain in his little plot, and she was not well regarded by that gentleman. She would have to gain a private interview with him, and that was not going to be a simple task for a woman in her position.

It would not be considered improper if she called with her maid at his hotel, but he would probably be surrounded by his friends there, just as he was here. She couldn't possibly go to the docks, for the only women to be found in that masculine district were doxies and trollops. His ship was off-limits to any woman of breeding, and if she tried to slip in to see him, her actions would surely be noted. The true nature of her mission might go undetected, but the chance that she could manage any kind of clandestine meeting without being recognized was very small—it was nearly impossible to hide her dark skin. There had to be some way to meet with Captain John Devlin without calling too much attention to herself.

As it was, the solution to her dilemma quickly presented itself.

"I must be going," the captain said.

"Where are you off to, Jack?" François asked. "I thought you had the morning free from those plaguey meetings you're always attending."

"I do. I decided to take the day off, and I'm going to visit the Louvre."

"You have not seen enough at the Salon?" François teased him.

"There is supposed to be a wonderful astrolabe on display there. I might be able to convince the director to sell it."

"What is an astrolabe?" Guillaume asked.

"A nautical instrument," the captain explained.

"I've never heard of it."

"Do you collect old nautical instruments, *monsieur?*" Pascale asked.

"Not exactly. But some of them are still more accurate than the devices we use today."

"I've been meaning to visit the museum, myself," Paul de

Ravenault said. "I want to see some Italianate paintings which I have been meaning to reacquaint myself with. I've had enough of this place. It's putting me to sleep. Shall we share a coach?"

No one besides Pascale seemed to notice her father's gaucherie in inviting himself along on the captain's excursion.

"Are you coming?" he asked, holding out his hand to her as though he were the host of the expedition.

"Yes," she agreed, instantly. Devlin was not likely to invite her. For once, she decided, she'd take advantage of her father's rudeness, rather than making excuses for him. Perhaps it would be a good idea for her father and the captain to spend some time together. He could then see that she knew what was best for the de Ravenaults and might help her discover where The Painting had been hidden.

It was worth trying, anyway. She might even get an opportunity to question the captain.

Her impromptu scheme didn't achieve the desired result. It might have been more effective if Papa had been alone with the captain in the coach, but there were six of them. Guillaume and François, of course, Pascale and her father, and Captain Devlin and another gentleman who'd joined them at the entrance into the Tuileries. His name was Mr. Henry Bates and he had been introduced by the captain as his first mate.

Conversation in the carriage was—unfortunately—lively and amusing. François and Guillaume more than made up for her father's shortcomings as a conversationalist. Monsieur Bates did not participate, and after observing him for a short time, Pascale realized he was having trouble understanding them. Whenever anyone lapsed into French, his eyes glazed over. Every once in awhile the captain would translate for him, and he'd nod his understanding, but when François or Guillaume tried to include him in the conversation, he didn't seem to understand a word they said—even when they spoke in English! Pascale had met other people who couldn't understand the heavily accented and slightly out-of-date English that was spoken by her father and his friends, and she watched the sorry exchanges with mixed sympathy and amusement.

Once in the museum, she fell into step beside him, behind the others, while a debate arose over which exhibit they should visit first. Everyone was being marvelously polite, except for her father who was, as usual, oblivious to anyone's desires but his own.

"We should visit your mariner's room, first," Guillaume insisted.

"No, no, it is all the way down at the end, we might as well stop as we pass the art exhibits," Captain Devlin said.

Papa wandered off down the hall, examining the latest architectural wonders of the former palace, and effectively ending the debate for the moment.

"We're all going the same way, at all events," François said, setting off behind him. The rest of the party fell into step in twos, Guillaume and the captain behind François and Papa, and Pascale and Henry Bates bringing up the rear.

"Have you known Captain Devlin long?" she asked in English.

"Aye, lass. We were in the navy together," he said.

The party wandered this way and that through the rooms and halls. Devlin did not seem to mind the rambling path they followed. She turned her attention on his second-in-command.

"That must have been exciting."

"The Navy? Oh, aye," he said, looking at her as if she were daft.

"Did you always want to be a sailor?" Pascale persisted.

"Aye. I always wanted to go to sea. I grew up in a little fishing village. My pa was a fisherman and I was s'posed to be one as well. But *I* wanted to wear a fine uniform and sail in one of the big ships all over the world. I was a foolish lad. Nothing me mum said could change my mind."

"But you did it." Pascale couldn't tell whether he regretted his decision or not. "How is it that Devlin is your captain?

You are older than he is, you must have been in the Navy longer than he was."

"Aye. Forty years. But I never had the captain's way with men." He shot a glance at her, eyes twinkling. "Or women."

Pascale was disconcerted for a moment. He thought that her inquiry was due to some romantic interest in the captain. However, he seemed willing enough to answer her questions, so she supposed his misguided assumption would serve her purpose.

"How did you meet him?" she asked.

"Ah, now, that's a bit of a story."

She nodded encouragingly, slowing her pace so that they fell farther behind the others. He nodded and began his tale.

"My commander had been killed, during a skirmish in the Indies with an illegal slave ship. The ship was lost, and when we survivors were picked up, there were only a handful of us left. They put us with the remainder of three other crews that were in the same case we were, under Devlin's commander, Admiral Yates. That was a strange crew. We were like ghosts, most all of us. It were a miracle we were alive, and every man jack among us knew it. We'd all had the stuffing knocked out of us, seeing so many of our mates die like that.

"And there was Devlin. He was naught but a boy, maybe fourteen years old, but he looked like a full-grown man. It got about that he had saved his captain's life when his ship had gone down, and the crew didn't let him forget it. They teased him about being the captain's pet, though Yates hardly gave the boy any attention at all. Devlin took it all without flinching. He must have wanted to go home to his mama. I sure did, and I was twenty years older'n him. But he never buckled, never broke, no matter what they said or did.

"There were nights when the berths were so full of men screaming and crying you couldn't barely catch a wink of sleep. Big men who could have broke you with a snap of their fingers cried like babies in their sleep. The lad was a good 'un," he shook his head, smiling at the memory. "He'd do what he could for them. The men who were worst to him were the ones from his old crew. I reckon they were embarrassed that he'd had the heart and the strength to save the captain when they'd been diving for cover, or some'ut like that. Anyway, they were outright bastards to him. He was nicer to them even than us. Guess he felt somethin' for them. They'd been his mates since he was naught but a tadpole.

"He'd get them, and all of us, food and drink from the officer's stores. We didn't know if he stole it, or begged for it, and we didn't ask. We just took it. And some of the men asked him, on the sly, to ask the captain for leave for 'em. He did it, too. He knew if we didn't come back, he'd be sure to catch it for our desertion." Bates shook his head again, ruefully. "They didn't thank him. You know how men are. The better he was, the worse they treated him. But I guess that didn't bother Jack none."

"That's incredible," Pascale said when he paused. The story was so sad, and yet his tone of voice was so matter-of-fact. "Have you been together ever since?"

"Mostly," Bates said, nodding. "When the captain left the Navy, I did, too. I went home to marry my girl, thirty years late. And she was waiting for me. When he asked me to be his first mate on the *Aurora,* I left Molly behind with her blessing. She said she'd loved me all those years, she'd keep on doing it. And she'd come accustomed to doing things her own way."

"It sounds like she loves you very much."

Bates smiled, abashed. "She's headstrong, my Molly, but she's grand. Jack taught me to read so I can write to her."

"Captain Devlin?"

"Aye. The old lady his mum worked for made him learn to read and write like a gentleman. He said if he was going to steal me from Molly again, he'd better do something to repay her."

"That was . . . nice." Pascale was overwhelmed. There was a lot more to Captain John Devlin than she'd imagined.

"You don't know the half of it." Bates ran his fingers through his graying hair. "It wasn't no easy thing to drum that stuff into my hard head. We were like to kill each other at first. But I learnt. Forty years old before I ever wrote the alphabet."

"Why didn't he teach you before?"

"I never had no reason to learn. I had no one to write to till Molly."

Pascale was so moved by the first mate's stories she'd almost forgotten the reason for this interrogation. Almost, but not quite. "You like working for him, then."

"What else is there for an old sea dog like myself to do?"

"You're leaving next week? For Mexico?"

"Aye."

"So between now and then, what do you have to do?"

"Me? I don't do nothing. Just write letters to Molly about Paris. The cap'n takes care of all our land dealings." Pascale tried to hide her disappointment as he went on, "He's got a head for it. He'll secure a cargo, then we'll load her up on a barge and take her out to sea."

"The *Aurora* is a barge?"

"No, ma'am, she's a clipper ship. The barge will take the goods from Paris to Rouen, we'll load her up there."

"Does the captain own the barge, too?"

"No, we rent a warehouse down by the docks. When it's all in, the barge picks up the freight there."

"It must be an amazing sight, all of those fine things bound for the other side of the Atlantic."

"Grand enough, I suppose. The clipper doesn't hold as much as some of the bigger ships, but it's a big enough haul, I suppose. But the warehouse is just a big, dirty, old pile of bricks. That's a rough part of town, you know. We don't just leave the goods laying about. We've got armed men on guard. And a scurvier lot you never saw."

"Oh," said Pascale. She chanced a look up at him, and registered a calculating look in his eye. He knew, somehow, that she'd been thinking for a moment of examining Devlin's cargo and he didn't like the idea. That made his warning about the guards somewhat suspect. She'd think about that later.

She said, as though disappointed, "Oh, I thought it would be like a big market, with silks and satins in a big pile."

"No, miss. We've got to pack up the merchandise for the long sea voyage."

"What is it like, at sea?"

"It's hard to say. The cap'n might be able to tell you better. He talks better 'n me 'bout that kind of stuff."

"Do you enjoy visiting all of the different ports on the way?" Pascale didn't think Papa was sending The Painting to Mexico. He didn't know anyone in the Americas.

"Some are okay. The clipper's a fast ship. We've done the crossing in as little as a month, from Portsmouth."

"So you'll be in Mexico in a month?"

"Or less. We're only stopping for water, down south, before we head out into the open sea."

"Where do you stop?"

"Spain, probably. I think the captain's found what he was looking for."

Pascale followed his line of vision to see Devlin looking into a wooden display case. As they had talked they had entered a room at the end of the long hall, where the walls were devoted to paintings of naval importance, and various wood, ivory, brass, and gold objects littered the room.

"What are all of these things?" Pascale asked.

"You'll have to ask the cap'n about that. I don't know much about these things." He walked over to a steering wheel, mounted on a huge wooden block. "Seems odd seein' this here, on land," he said, shaking his head. "Somethin' not quite right about it, if you ask me. I think I'll wait outside. This place gives me a case a' nerves."

"I hope we will meet again," Pascale said honestly.

"So do I," Bates replied. "I just wrote to Molly I hadn't

met any nice French girls. I s'pose I'll have to write her again and tell her different, now."

"Thank you," Pascale said graciously.

"You and her would get on just fine, I reckon. Yer the kind o' girl she likes, one who knows just what she wants and goes after it."

"I'll take that as a compliment, Mr. Bates."

"That's just what it was," he said.

Seven

Jack could feel Pascale's eyes boring into his back. She laughed at something Bates said, and he had to resist the temptation to turn around and look at her.

He had thought her beautiful the first time they met, and the second and third, though she had treated him as though he were no more a man to her than her father—less of one, perhaps. But when he had seen her today in the park, he'd been stunned. She glowed with the gold of the sun. Even now, it took all of his self-control to resist the urge to turn and watch her talking and laughing with his first mate. Her eyes, lit by her fury at seeing her father and himself together, had sparked an answering flame in himself. She was his fantasy woman—the beauty he'd dreamed of for years at sea, the grace of nobility, and intelligence enough to outwit the whole of the ton. How could he have missed it before?

With a supreme effort he focused on the objects housed in the wooden cases in front of him. It only took him a moment to spot the piece he wanted. Beautifully crafted, the ancient golden astrolabe shone up at him from its red velvet nest. He couldn't wait to touch it. This was beauty he could understand. The device had been created by a man who shared his fascination with the precise movements of the heavenly bodies, and the immutability of time and movement. The universe was an incredible, magical place, but when Jack held this intricately crafted tool in his hand, he felt he held the key to that vast mystery.

He held on to the thought that he would be out at sea in a week. Pascale de Ravenault and the emotions she stirred in him would be left behind, and forgotten.

Pascale suddenly materialized at his side. "Monsieur Bates has gone back to the carriage to await our return. The others have gone on to see the painting. What is that?" she asked, pointing at a diptych with an ivory face inscribed in various colors with the major port cities of the world, and of course the seas. He looked around. Apparently, in his reverie, he hadn't noticed the others leaving. She and he were the only people at this end of the hall.

"It's a diptych sundial. There is a compass in the middle there, too," he explained. He only had a few minutes before custom demanded that they go and find the others. He might as well enjoy them.

"What's that for?"

"It's the gnomon. I can attach that string in different places, and the sundial will work in three different latitudes."

She looked thoughtful. "You can read all of that." Pascale gestured at the neatly printed lettering, written on the small face of the works. "Oh, look how they put a 'z' at the end of Paris! This must be very old."

"Yes, at least two hundred years old, I would say," Jack confirmed.

"Do you know how to use all of these devices?" Her gaze traveled around the room at the glass and wood cases that housed navigational charts, octants, traverse boards, and many other tools of his trade.

"Most of them," John said, shrugging. "We rely on charts much more now than they did a hundred years ago. Much more of the seas have been charted."

"And Monsieur Bates? Can he, too, understand what that says?"

"Perhaps not that instrument. However, he can read all of the charts. Many of these tools aren't used anymore. They've been replaced with modern ones, which are more precise."

"And which one are you planning to buy?" she asked saucily, a dimple appearing in one smooth chocolate-brown cheek.

"The gold astrolabe, there." He pointed it out and she leaned over the edge of the table to see. She was tiny, fully a foot shorter than he was. He was tempted to lift her up to look through the glass at his latest find.

"It's a work of art," she said reverently. "Is that still used?"

"Not anymore. It's been replaced by the cross-staff," he looked around until he spotted an example. "Over there." She wasn't interested in the plain wooden device. Pascale wandered toward a water-stained coasting pylot framed against the far wall. He tore his gaze from her and noticed that this copy of the familiar chart had clearly been well used. It was frayed at the edges, but the gilded frame that held it was sturdy. It must have been someone's cherished possession. Pascale read aloud the inscription on the board below.

"Greenville Collins undertook the survey to produce the Great Britain Coasting Pylot of 1693 on his yacht *Merlin,* using only a compass and measuring chain," she read aloud. She turned to him in astonishment. "It says here it took ten years."

He nodded. "The pylot was the first atlas of the area based on personal survey. It was in use for over one hundred years."

"If the British coast took ten years to chart, how did they chart the entire ocean?"

"All atlases are not as detailed as this one." He gestured toward one of the old maps, with a colorful depiction of a dragon to the west.

"Beyond this point reside demons and sea monsters," she read aloud.

Pascale nodded and moved on to a nearby showcase, and he couldn't resist the urge to follow. Jack would have been willing to bet everything he owned that the little minx had little interest in the pylot, or any of the other charts and navigational tools that the Marine Society had collected. If her agile mind wasn't bent on some plan to cozen him into telling her where a certain painting had been hidden, then he wasn't the captain of the clipper ship *Aurora*.

Pascale was engaging, scintillating in fact. Jack didn't doubt her ability to wrap any man around her delicate little finger. Pascale might have looked a fragile beauty, but she'd have no qualms, Jack was sure, about trifling with his heart or anything else he offered in order to bring her father one step closer to success. Tempting as she was, he didn't relax his guard as they made a leisurely circuit of the room. He responded to her conversational gambits carefully—never straying from the point, or giving her an opportunity to bring up the subject he was sure she was dying to raise.

"Were you ever in a battle like this one?" she asked, staring at a large painting of an encounter between two galleons, one had a French flag flying, the other Spanish.

"Mr. Bates told me you own a clipper ship," she said.

"Yes," he assented, smiling. She was so transparent, and adorable.

He waited for her to realize that he wasn't going to give her an opportunity to discuss his next voyage, or any business connected to it—no matter how nearly she was concerned.

Jack had agreed to take de Ravenault's latest painting out of Pascale's reach when he left for the colonies at the end of the week, and had met de Ravenault in the park to receive his final instructions concerning its delivery. He was putting in along the southern coast of Spain in any case, and the painting was no great charge on him, he could deliver it to de Ravenault's friend without any change at all to his schedule. It was none of Pascale's business to try and stop him. But if she were determined, he was game to let her try.

"Do you need to ask the curator, or someone, if you can buy the astrolabe?" she asked as they once again approached the display case.

"No. I will write to the exhibitors and make my interest known."

"Oh," Pascale said, nonplussed.

"Shall we go find the others," he offered.

She sent him an odd look from under her long black eyelashes, before turning away from him to take a quick look about the room, though she must have been as aware as he was that the others had wandered off a good quarter hour before. She managed, without actually touching him, to make him feel that all her attention was suddenly centered on him, the *objets* she'd been so interested in apparently forgotten.

"Before we do, *monsieur*, I must speak with you."

"We can talk as we walk, *mademoiselle*," he said, offering his arm.

She shook her head. Her grave air was such a change from the expression of mild curiosity she'd displayed a moment ago that he couldn't help but smile. A small line appeared across her forehead as she looked up at him.

"This is no laughing matter, sir, I assure you. My father has done a foolish—a very foolish—thing. I think you know what I am talking about."

"Oh?" he prompted. "What would that be?"

"Are you going to deny that you and my father have been discussing something . . . crucial to my family ever since the night you supped at our apartments."

"I don't plan to deny or confirm anything," he answered. "Why should I?"

"You must," she whispered urgently. "I need your help."

"That's funny," he said, holding back a smile as he prepared to dangle the bait in front of her. "That is almost exactly what your father said to me."

As he had expected, Pascale pounced on that statement. "And are you planning to help him?"

"Possibly," Jack answered, drawing the word out. "But I do not see what that could have to do with you."

"Perhaps my father hasn't told you that I am the one who makes all of the arrangements about his work."

"Yes, he mentioned something about that," Jack conceded. "But he didn't sound at all happy about it."

"He didn't?" He had managed to surprise her, but she was not to be deterred for long. "Well, that is something new, and now I come to think of it, I suppose it is to be expected, you see—"

Jack interrupted, "The whole thing seems easy enough to manage to me."

"I don't see how!" Pascale snapped. She took a deep breath. "I'm sorry, but perhaps you don't understand—"

He stopped her again. "Nor do I wish to," he said, simply. "Shall we join the others?"

"Wait!" He raised an eyebrow at her sharpness, but she didn't seem to notice. "You must listen to me."

"Why must I?" Jack asked.

She gaped at him, and then finally seemed to understand that he was being deliberately obtuse. That this was a totally unexpected response was clear in her astonished gaze. "Well, because . . . because . . . ," she spluttered. "I'm trying to explain how important this is to my father as well as myself. You don't know anything about it, but it isn't easy to make a living from an artist's work," she said seriously.

"Nor is it wise," Jack said equally seriously.

"Perhaps not," she answered, shortly, "but we don't have any choice." Jack could see that nothing he could say would divert Pascale from her course. Short of walking away, he had no alternative but to weather the approaching storm. He crossed his arms and waited. "My father is a genius," Pascale began, "but he shares the usual insecurities of artistic men. With each creation he becomes less certain of his abilities. We have been through this many times before. His latest painting is one that has a . . . great deal of importance to him. I'm not sure why, exactly, but this time the crisis has been more severe. I should have expected it, I suppose, because I knew how long this particular painting had tormented him. I am guessing that he has given his latest painting to you, to dispose of, or to hide somewhere. I must have it back." She looked up at him with an expression of such emotion that he felt a jolt throughout his entire body. "Sir, can you help me?"

He almost faltered. He hadn't expected that pleading look, not from this proud, passionate creature. There was something more to this than she was saying. Pascale de Ravenault had personal reasons for wanting her precious portrait returned. He wondered if she'd tell him what they were, if he asked her. He doubted it. When he'd dined with the small party at her house, she'd gone from guest to guest with an anticipatory air, and left each of them with growing bewilderment in her eyes.

It changed nothing. "No. I'm afraid I cannot." He kept his face impassive.

"You have not been listening to me," Pascale said, sadly.

"But I have," Jack assured her. "You are very persuasive, and I can see that this means a great deal to you, but I'm afraid that my answer must be no."

Her crestfallen expression made him long to reach out and comfort her somehow, but she quickly recovered. She stiffened. "Are you playing with me, *monsieur?*" she asked.

"By no means, *mademoiselle.*"

"Then how can you say this? I explained—"

"So you did. And I wish that you had not gone to the trouble of trying to convince me, so that I might have spared you the pain of having to be refused. I did try to dissuade you, but you insisted I listen, and so I have. But there is nothing that you can say that will change my mind." As she started to argue further, he said baldly, "If I did have your father's painting, and I were to help you, as you call it, I would be doing both you and myself a great disservice. It would be no less than theft."

He had managed to shock her. "Theft? To give me my father's painting? That is ridiculous."

"I call it stealing to deliver a cargo *not* to the person for whom it was intended, but to a party whom I have been specifically instructed would attempt to . . . umm . . . wrest it from me."

She spent a moment trying to digest this, only to reject it offhand. "But it is my . . . I mean, our painting."

"No, it belongs to your father. And it is with him that you should be discussing this. I have nothing to do with it. Shall we go and find the others now?" She resisted at first, but after a moment she succumbed to the gentle pressure of his hand on her arm, and turned toward the archway that separated the exhibit from the main hallway.

Then she shook off his hand. "But I told you my father is not capable of making this decision." It was clear to him that she was far from defeated, despite her growing frustration.

He kept walking, forcing her to walk alongside him, or be left behind. "That is immaterial to me. Whether you like it or not, it is neither your place, nor mine, to gainsay him."

Despite the fact that he thought Paul de Ravenault misguided in not just ordering his daughter to leave him and his paintings alone, he had no intention of betraying the man's trust. Though he didn't approve of the artist's methods of dealing with the girl, he realized the overindulgent father would find it difficult, if not impossible, to oppose the headstrong young woman.

"It *is* my place. And if you weren't such a . . . a philistine you'd see that it is *your* place also to protect my father from his folly."

Charming though Pascale was, the traits he'd been prepared to admire in her father—a cool, clear head; a shrewd and calculating mind for business; and an indomitable will to succeed—were not nearly so attractive in a lady. He'd have liked her better if she weren't so intent on this one subject.

"I disagree. He is a full-grown man. However, I do believe it my duty to protect *you*. You really shouldn't plan your life around a painting, you know."

"I don't need your protection. I need your cooperation. You do not know the harm you could cause. My father's reputation is our mainstay. This painting could be the one that cements it in the eyes of the *haut monde* forever." Jack frowned. His aunt, too, had believed that the intrinsic value of great art could support her family . . . and she'd been wrong. Her faith had left his mother and himself destitute.

Pascale continued, "If the painting is as wonderful as I think it is, it is almost guaranteed to do so. By the same token, its loss could ruin us." He knew he couldn't convince Pascale that she and her father should not try to live off the fruits of his artistic labors. He couldn't stop her, but he could force her to think about her situation, her goals.

"I doubt that," Jack responded. She might not think she needed his protection, but he could see disaster looming in the future. It was time he made it perfectly clear that he wouldn't be swayed by any argument she could advance. "And even if that should be the outcome, it might be a very good thing. Your father would be forced then to attend to his patriarchal duties, including finding a suitable husband to occupy your time, and keep you out of affairs that do not concern you." He turned away, and this time she didn't try to stop him.

They walked for a moment without talking. Jack looked down at the top of Pascale's bent head; he almost regretted that their sparring had ended. He almost felt sorry that he couldn't accommodate her. But he knew he helped her more by holding firm. Even if she didn't think so.

As though she could read his thoughts, Pascale said, *"Monsieur,* I will see that painting."

"Certainly," he agreed. "As soon as your father allows it." She quickened her pace, and he followed suit. She was nearly at a run by the time they joined the rest of their party.

After the Louvre he was not at all surprised to learn that Pascale had pumped Mr. Bates for information. His first mate was completely enamored of the beautiful young lady with the "werry fine mind" who had flattered him with her questions about his "exciting" life at sea.

When Jack smiled wryly at the old sailor, the other shook

his head knowingly and laid a finger to the side of his nose. "Course, I knew right off that it was you she was really interested in." Jack could have set him right, but thought it might be best to keep his business with Paul de Ravenault between the de Ravenault family and himself. "But for an old sea dog like me, it's nice to 'ave a gel like that astarin' with those big brown eyes, like I was the most fascinatin' creature she ever met." Henry Bates had decided recently, that his Captain had to find a girl like his own wife, Molly, and nothing Jack said could dissuade his old shipmate. Every pretty black girl his first mate found was paraded before him and her good and bad points analyzed, like a ship presented for his inspection.

"That's not a girl, Bates, that's a shark dressed up to look like a lady," Jack tried to warn his old friend.

"Course she is, Cap'n," Bates said. "They all is. With all those questions she was asking, she's after somethin' more than a tired old sailor." He winked.

"You don't understand, Henry," Jack said. "It's not me she's interested in, but the ship. We're taking aboard precious cargo, and she'd do anything to get her hands on it."

"Are you atellin' me that pretty little package is a thief?"

"Not by her lights, Henry. She feels this . . . item belongs to her."

"I don't believe it, Jack. Damn, I don't know as you've ever lied to me afore, but this beats all. She don't have the look, and I can always spot the dishonest ones. You know I can, too. Happen you made a mistake?"

"Not I, old friend. But it's not that she's lying. She just believes that what she thinks is true is, in fact, the God's honest truth. Many before her have made the same mistake."

"That's a fact, Cap'n."

"She's got more call than most. Her father's pretty much left her to herself all these years, and she's grown accustomed to making all the decisions for both of them."

Bates said, pursing his lips thoughtfully, "Not a good thing for a spirited young filly like that one. Bound to make it difficult to break her to the bridle."

"I'd say you had the right of it," Jack said, much struck.

Henry Bates looked at Jack speculatively. "Not thinking of trying your hand at it, are you, guv?" he asked.

"Lord, no!" Jack said, recoiling. "I just thought I ought to tell you which quarter the wind is blowing from."

Jack took the first opportunity that offered itself to pay a call on Mademoiselle de Ravenault; to issue a warning about interfering with his business. Pascale was alone in the salon where she received her morning visitors, except for a young maid servant who sat by the window contentedly doing her mending. He was shown in directly, and Pascale issued a stiff formal greeting. He saluted her with a brief nod.

Jack had never seen Pascale in her natural element. Despite her air of cold formality, the cozy atmosphere suited her. Her blue cotton morning dress was as becoming to her as her evening silks had been. The room was pleasant and he almost wished he had come on some other errand, so he could join her where she sat. She was tracing out a pattern on some cloth. He couldn't quite see it from where he stood. The peaceful scene was inviting, but that was not why he was here.

She didn't rise from her comfortable chair. Nor did she look up at him, which was fine with Jack as it gave him the opportunity to study her minutely. He wished he knew what it was about this woman that so intrigued him. Her dark hair was pulled back from her forehead, but a few stray tendrils had escaped and they caressed her temples. Longer curls fell down her back just past the round collar of the cotton dress. Her delicate hands moved back and forth over the embroidery silk.

He cleared his throat. "You might not want her to hear what I have to say to you," he said softly, inclining his head toward the young girl on the other side of the room.

She gave him a measuring look and nodded. "Odelle, would you please go ask Cook to send in some of those cakes she's baking?" The girl rose from her chair with ill-disguised enthusiasm. "And get one for yourself while you're there," Pascale added. The maid dropped a curtsy and hurried away. Pascale looked up at Jack challengingly.

"I suppose you think you've been very clever," he started.

"I'm a resourceful woman. I don't think any particular cleverness was needed in this instance." She dropped her nonchalant pose and gestured to the seat facing her. As he came forward he caught a glimpse of her sketch, the pattern she was drawing on the silk. It was magnificent. Flowers and birds twined around the border, and in the center a rose bloomed.

"I see that you still do practice your art a little. That is very good," he said, sitting down reluctantly.

He was surprised to find her examining him earnestly. "Shall we, as you English say, drop the gloves, *monsieur.* I want that painting. I am willing to pay you whatever my father paid you to take it away. Or whatever you think is fair."

Bile rose up in his throat—this little chit thought she could bribe him. She didn't even realize the insult she had just paid him. He reined in his temper by clinging tightly to the self-control he'd developed in his many years at sea. He jumped up and paced rapidly across the room. He returned to find that she wasn't even looking at him, but was busily drawing.

"You are playing with fire, *mademoiselle.* I suggest that you give up this ill-advised scheme before you get burned."

Her head still bent over her handiwork, she responded, "If one of us is to catch fire at this, Captain, I think it is you. I have nothing to lose."

"There you are wrong, miss. With your insulting offer you have just altered the stakes. I will not entertain these ridiculous notions of yours for one moment longer. You, *mademoiselle,* are too headstrong for your own good. I know your father is to blame for this deplorable tendency of yours to act the shrew, but there is a point where you will suffer the consequences of your actions."

That got her attention. "A shrew?" Her hands shook until

she put her charcoal aside, and clenched them in her lap. "You, *monsieur,* are a boor, and a bully. I am merely fighting for what is rightfully mine. If it weren't for your interference, my father's little escapade would have come to its natural conclusion by now."

"Natural? There is nothing 'natural' about a girl who thinks she can order the world about."

"Oh! Only you can do that, eh?" She muttered a Gallic imprecation under her breath, and stood up. "You do not frighten me, *monsieur,* but your ignorance does."

"There is nothing very complicated about this situation. For the first time in her life, a very spoiled child has not gotten her own way, and she indulges in a temper tantrum and some very foolish threats to her betters."

"Do not try to intimidate me, Captain Devlin. It is always the same. If I look pretty and smile and sit back, and let you ruin everything I have worked for, then I am a good little girl who will receive a pat on her head. But I don't behave, you will call me a shrew and threaten me. I will not cater to the whims of egotistical monsters who do not care any more for what I want than they do for the wishes of their pets. Do you hear?"

"Everyone in the house can hear you," Jack answered. Pascale looked at the doorway to find the maid was back, and behind her were the butler, Pierre; the new underbutler; and a couple of serving girls, with their mouths agape.

"Is everything all right, *mademoiselle,*" Pierre asked, glaring at the captain. The butler had worked for her father since before she was born, and she had never before seen him display such emotion. He was clearly prepared to throw their guest out of the house bodily, should she request it.

"No. I mean yes," Pascale corrected herself as he took a step into the room. "Everything is fine. Captain Devlin and I were just . . . I was just going to ring for Odelle, to tell her to forget about the cakes. The captain is leaving."

Pierre waved the others away. "I will escort you to the door, *monsieur.*"

Faced with that severe countenance, there was nothing for Jack to do but to take his leave. *"Mademoiselle,"* he said, bowing.

"Monsieur." Pascale did not offer him her hand to kiss, they were clenched in the folds of her skirt.

"Good day," he said, turning smartly on his heel and going to the door, to be ushered out by the butler. A brief glance back afforded him a sight to soothe his savage emotions: Pascale furtively dabbing at her eyes. Tears of frustration, he thought. Good. Perhaps that little outburst would settle her. Get this ridiculous nonsense out of her system. Somehow he doubted it, though. She was a managing miss. And an obstinate one. But he was leaving in a few days. That wasn't much time. He'd probably never hear from her again.

E ight

Pascale had never been in this part of Paris before. The warehouse where John Devlin received the cargo for his ship, *Aurora*, had a huge square facade that loomed over her menacingly. The street was quiet. The hustle and bustle of this rowdy section of the city was confined to daytime activities. Tonight there wasn't even a tavern door open to spill light on the uneven road.

Pascale didn't know whether to be relieved or worried. After the warnings she'd received, she had only herself to blame if something happened to her in this deserted neighborhood.

The rustling of rats and other nocturnal creatures didn't frighten her. She was a sturdy country girl at heart. Nothing on four feet was threatening to a woman who was capable of chasing hungry predators from the chicken house, armed with nothing more than a simple broom. The creatures of the night that made Pascale nervous walked upright, and could have been lurking in any of the deep dark shadows that surrounded her.

She'd never been exposed to this kind of danger before. As unconventional as her father was, Paul de Ravenault was not completely foolish. He knew as well as Pascale how easy it was for a woman to be insulted, accosted, even attacked if she was left unprotected. Any of these circumstances could have consequences beyond hope of repair. But tonight's adventure was a necessity. By her calculations John Devlin would be moving the merchandise in this warehouse to his ship on the morrow in preparation for his departure. Guillaume had mentioned he'd be leaving Paris in two days. She didn't have any time left.

Pascale crept around the eastern corner of the building, keeping to the shadows while she searched for a side entrance. The front door was off-limits. She knew from her inquiries that if it wasn't heavily bolted, it would be guarded. Security in this district was not as strictly maintained as Bates had implied; however, Pascale had interviewed a policeman the previous day and had been told that the owners of these kinds of strong houses had no need to fear the criminal element. Thieves were too intimidated to transgress against men like Devlin who had at their disposal, not only connections in the highest circles, but also crews of rough, burly seamen who took personally any offense to their master's property.

Pascale couldn't believe she was about to defy a man so powerful that in some circles his very word was law. After asking so many questions of Henry Bates and Guillaume, she'd come to think of him as a captain of industry as well as master of his vessel and his crew. It was not for the fainthearted to cross such a one. Pascale shivered and pulled her cloak closer about her head and shoulders, though she would not be recognized here. This part of Paris was not frequented by any of the elite. Their lives were worth no more in this section of town than those of the rats who scurried about at her feet. She hadn't met a single soul. There was no one to know, nor care, who she was.

The only stumbling block she'd encountered since she'd set out on this evening's foray had come from the driver of the cab she'd hired. A formidable-looking gentleman, whom she'd purposely chosen for his twisted nose and frightening mien, he had accepted the purse she'd offered only after she'd shown him the firearm she carried in her reticule. Pascale was glad that the coachman with the murderous visage had turned out to be the talkative father of three flighty daughters. He had tried his best to convince her not to journey into these deserted streets. She trusted him to await her return.

She drew comfort from the memory of his avuncular tone as he'd said, "Step carefully now, *ma petite,*" when she'd dismounted from his rackety equipage. Surely, nothing too dreadful could happen to her with her new friend only a block away.

In one dark niche in the side of the building, Pascale found what she'd been searching for—a door. The handle turned easily in her grasp, and, straightening her shoulders, she stepped through. Inside the building Pascale didn't even have the faint light of flickering stars to guide her. When her eyes had adjusted to the yawning blackness, she could make out only tall squares that loomed on all sides. She inched cautiously forward. She could see very little about the shrouded shapes, except that they all seemed much too large to house her father's painting. When removed from its backing and rolled, it would have been only a couple of inches in diameter and two to three feet long.

She lifted the heavy burlap that covered the object nearest her, and felt rough-hewn wooden slats. Windows set high up in the walls let in a glow that reflected off the light-colored pine planks that she'd exposed. What she stood facing was a large wooden crate, almost as tall as herself and some three or four feet wide. For the first time since she'd decided to trespass, Pascale despaired. She did not have the strength, or the tools, to open one of these huge boxes, let alone the time to search through all of the stacks. A darker spot on the wood caught her eye. She pulled the burlap covering aside; there was writing on the box. Pascale leaned down, but the murky darkness defied her attempt to decipher the lettering.

Just as she thought her eyes might pierce the shadows, she heard a sound. She tensed. It might have been the same rustlings she'd heard outside, rats and mice foraging for food. Pascale cocked her head, listening intently. It came again, a squeak magnified by the cavernous room where she stood.

Was someone looking for her? If the guard had heard her

enter, he might be crouched in the darkness, listening as intently as she was. Perhaps he was stalking her, thinking she was a thief. Her nerves stretched to the breaking point, but she heard nothing more.

Her eye fell on the words burned into the wood before her. Some trick of light, or perhaps the moon rising higher in the night sky, made the words suddenly decipherable. They read clearly: *Colonie du l'Empire.* Relief flooded through her. Now she knew how to find The Painting.

Pascale's research had made one fact clear. She had discovered that Captain Devlin had only one port of call on this continent before he sailed on to deliver his merchandise to the Americas. Her father had to be sending the Portrait of the Lady to the south of Spain, to an old friend of his who lived there. He knew no one in the Colonies.

Bates had given her the information she'd needed. She'd learned from him that Jack planned to restock with food and take on more water in a port on the southern coast of Spain. The first mate didn't think they'd be delivering any cargo there, but Pascale was certain they would. But the object she was interested in would never be in one of these large crates. She inched her way down the row, checking the inscription burned onto each gargantuan box. Her excitement mounted as she failed, time after time, to find any reference to merchandise bound for Spain. Unfortunately, she still had no idea how she would pry the thing open, should she find the right one. But at least she was sure she could locate it.

"Looking for anything specific?"

Pascale shrieked. Her fear and surprise were quickly replaced with anger and frustration as she recognized Devlin's voice. A taper flared to life, illuminating his sardonic face as he lit some candles. Pascale clamped a hand over her racing heart. Breathing hard and unable to speak, she warily watched his measured approach.

He appeared totally calm and self-possessed. However, as he came nearer, Pascale saw that his eyes were ablaze, his jaw clenched shut. She backed away before that murderous look. "What the bloody hell are you doing here?" he demanded.

"You scared me half to death!" she choked out in French, then in English. Her heart had lodged somewhere near her throat.

"You little fool. You deserve that, and more. I was worried that you might come up with some harebrained scheme, but I thought at worst, all you would do was convince one of those hapless idiots your father employs to venture down and take a look. I never dreamed you'd be so stupid as to come here yourself!"

"There was no other way. I couldn't send any of my servants—how dare you suggest such a thing! I would never send them to do what I would not. The danger to them would be far greater than that to me. No one could mistake me for a thief. Or if he did, I could explain."

"It is unlikely you'd be taken for a thief, it's true." Pascale nodded triumphantly as he ceded her point. "However, by wandering around in this neighborhood at this hour, most men could be forgiven for thinking you a woman of easy virtue."

"What are you implying, *monsieur?*"

"I am not *implying* anything, I'm telling you. By coming here you endangered not only your reputation, but your virtue, and possibly your life. My men shoot first and ask questions later. Which is why I was here." He appeared to be exercising an heroic degree of self-control.

Pascale was not impressed. "Pooh!" She was not frightened any longer. "You are just annoyed because I defied the great and powerful Captain Devlin."

"Annoyed?" Jack had not thought it possible to grow any angrier, but he was incensed. The little baggage stood staring triumphantly up at him, totally unaware of the danger in which she had placed herself. If one of his men had discovered this little morsel wandering about, Pascale would have been fair game, just as she would have been to any miscreant who prowled these darkened streets. They would have made a meal of her.

"*Mademoiselle,* do not push me too far. I am already seriously considering strangling you and putting both of us out of our misery."

"You don't scare me," she said, maddeningly.

"That's the second time you've said that to me." Jack's voice was a low rumble in his throat. Any of his men would have recognized that tone, and gone to hide himself away until the thunderclouds cleared. If Pascale heard the menace in it, she ignored it.

She squared her shoulders. "You cannot stop me from trying to recover my property."

One long stride brought him within arm's reach of her, another forced her back a step, but he wouldn't let her retreat. With one hand under that haughty little chin, he raised her eyes to his. "It's not yours."

"Let go of me." Pascale tried to pull away, and when he didn't let her go, she raised her arms to push him away. "You brute!"

With one hand holding the candle, he had only one arm free to subdue her. Jack hauled her to him with one quick jerk. The movement trapped her arms between their bodies. She continued to struggle.

"*Bête!*"

"A beast, am I?" Goaded beyond measure, Jack lowered his head and kissed her.

Pascale stopped struggling instantly, her indrawn breath betraying her shock at this unexpected assault. Jack registered her reaction with the small part of his brain that was still capable of reasoning. The rest was busy adjusting to his body's response. This was supposed to be a simple demonstration of her powerlessness. But the moment his lips touched hers, everything changed.

Her lips, parted slightly with her gasp of outrage, were warm and soft under his own. They neither opened invitingly, nor closed to deny him entry to the sweetness within. Instead, she tried to pull her head back, at the same time pushing against his chest ineffectually with her elbows. Sudden passion bolted through him like lightning.

He was inordinately pleased by her obvious lack of experience in fending off unwanted advances. He had not supposed her, exposed as she was to all manner of men, to be so innocent. Driven by an age-old impulse, he softened the punishing kiss. He molded his lips gently to hers, ignoring the clamoring of his overheated body to deepen the contact between them. Then he lifted his head slowly.

"That, *mademoiselle,* whatever you may think, is far removed from the brutish behavior you would have been subjected to if someone besides myself caught you here." He was pleased to hear his voice sounding so even and calm. The feelings the simple contact had stirred in him were a shock.

"Let me go, please," she requested through clenched teeth.

"Not yet." Her head jerked up in surprise at his response. "Not before I'm certain that you realize the danger you were in tonight. What if I hadn't been here, Pascale?"

"I would have been spared the insult you just paid me," she shot back at him.

"Need I demonstrate just how much more 'insulted' you could have been?" he asked, bending his head again.

"No!" Pascale exclaimed, with unflattering alacrity. "I understand much worse luck could have befallen me. Cutthroats, thieves, and ruffians might have done more than . . . kiss me," she said. Her tone was doubtful, but it would have to do. He didn't think he could continue to hold her without kissing her again.

"Good," Jack said, releasing his hold on her.

She immediately moved out of his reach, but apparently couldn't resist one last comment. "Of course, they would behave that way because they wouldn't know who I was. You, who have dined at my table, treated me unconscionably despite knowing my name and family, just to punish me for my temerity."

"Your stupidity, more like. But I will not bandy words with you."

"But—" Pascale started.

Jack cut off any further argument. "I am warning you. Do not try my patience any further, *mademoiselle*. Or . . ." He looked at her speculatively. "Would you like me to . . . punish . . . you again?"

Pascale's jaw dropped in surprise. "Never, you conceited, arrogant bully!"

"Never?" he teased. At her look of alarm, he relented. "Well, I probably shan't see you again after we set sail anyway."

He should have thought of this method of controlling the heedless child earlier. For the second time this evening, he had succeeded in disconcerting her, merely with the threat of making love to her. He wondered what it would take to tame the chit. Jack's blood warmed at the thought of the various forms of seduction he might have used to bring the little termagant under his thumb. It was a shame he would never find out.

With a long-suffering sigh, he offered her his arm, saying, "Shall we go?"

"There seems no point in remaining here with you."

She ignored the proffered arm, and turned to the door.

He followed her. "Wait here, I'll have my carriage take you home."

"There is a coachman waiting for me in an alley not far from here," Pascale said. She glanced triumphantly at him.

"I'll send him home, then," he said, blowing out the candle in his hand.

"You'll do no such thing," she retorted, incensed. "Who do you think you are?"

He held the door open for her, but she stood immovable just inside it.

"I am going to make sure you get home safely whether you like it or not."

"I don't need your protection," Pascale almost shouted.

It was too much. He admired her tenacity, even in the face of defeat—after all, he was the same way. He could even applaud her ambition. Silly as her scheme was, he might have done the same thing in her position. But he could not, and would not, stomach this. The little witch had no idea how vulnerable she was . . . how tempting she was. Jack didn't want to admit, even to himself, how dangerous she was.

He stepped toward her, prepared to propel her through the door by force if necessary, and instead found himself pulling her into his arms again. Between the anger she'd unleashed, and the passion she'd inspired, he teetered precariously near the limit of his self-control. He held on to it by a thin thread, and forced himself to let her go.

"Pascale—" Before he could explain once again that she was not safe on these streets alone, she slapped him across the face. The thread broke.

Captain John Devlin, the man who had worked his way up through the ranks of the British Navy from cabin boy to navigator, and who had managed, purely by the sweat of his brow, to become master of the *Aurora* and its crew, could not contain himself in the face of the provocation offered by one young woman. She must have seen the choler in his face, for she turned to run. With lightning-quick reflexes, he caught her hand before she could take a step. He reeled her in, just as he would have recovered a line that slipped free of its mooring on his ship. He pulled her closer, hand over hand, until only the thin barrier of their clothing separated them. He'd captured her wrists, and held both of them behind her back in one of his hands, in a firm but gentle grasp. She was so small, it required no exertion to hold her still. For the first time she looked truly afraid.

He almost took pity on her. But he was caught in the

clutches of an uncontrollable desire to taste more fully the lips that had, so briefly, taunted him with their sweetness.

Slowly, inexorably, he lowered his mouth to hers. She turned her head. His lips brushed her cheek. He caught her chin in his free hand and turned her face back to his.

"Don't," she protested. He took advantage of her open mouth and lightly ran his tongue out to wet her lower lip, before he caught it gently between his teeth. When her teeth clamped shut, he settled his mouth on hers. He teased her with little nibbles at her lips, and when she didn't open up, he pressed his tongue to one corner of her mouth, then the other. She kept her jaw clamped shut, and he moved upward, nuzzling the tender flesh at the corners of her eyes.

He felt the change when she stopped pulling away and let his hand fall from her chin to her shoulder, though he still held her arms loosely cinched in his other hand. She stood motionless and submissive, giving nothing, holding nothing back. Her eyes were shut tightly, but he sensed that she was no longer afraid of him. She waited, barely breathing, and he felt the tide had shifted—she anticipated his next movement with as much curiosity as trepidation. A woman of passion, Pascale's anger, if not forgotten, probably added a frisson of excitement to the physical stimulation of his kisses. He hoped this gentle assault was as torturous for her as it was for him.

"You should not have come here," he said, to remind them both why he was doing this, himself as much as her. A shudder ran through her, but she didn't open her eyes. He couldn't help himself, he hadn't had enough of her yet.

He lowered his head again and felt intense gratification as she raised her lips to meet his. As a reward, he took his time before bringing his lips back to hers again, working his way gently over her cheek to her ear, where he gently nipped the lobe, then followed the line of her jaw back to her lips. When he finally pressed his mouth to hers, her lips parted on a gasp of pleasure. That simple sound sent a wave of sensual pleasure through him. They shared a kiss so long and deep that Jack knew he had to stop, now, or they would never stop.

He lifted his head.

With difficulty he managed to say, "Lesson's over, *princess.*"

Her eyes flew open, passion dimming to be quickly replaced with fury. He had purposely uttered the words most calculated to make her hate him, and it had worked, but he was more disappointed than he would have thought possible.

"May I go now?" Pascale asked, her voice icy.

He had forgotten to let her go. He did so, slowly, hoping she'd mistake his reluctance for a part of the "lesson."

"If you will allow me to escort you home."

She restrained her first impulsive retort with a visible effort and said, after a moment of thought, "I think you will be satisfied with the carriage I hired, if you come and talk to the driver."

"Fine." He would let her find her way home, if satisfied that she would indeed be safe. He was not certain that his own escort was any such guarantee any longer.

It would be pure torture to drive with Pascale in a closed carriage and not make love to her. Jack was sure that he could do it, if necessary, but the toll would be steep. He was already tempted to tell her the kisses they shared had affected him just as deeply as they had affected her. But it was best that she believe he was cold and uncaring, the bully she already thought him. Best he let her think he had merely been toying with her. She could hate him, then.

How could she, young as she was, be expected to react to the truth. He, with his years of experience, could barely handle the knowledge of what she alone did to him. It was better for both of them if she thought he had been unmoved. He was leaving Paris on the morrow, and they would never see each other again.

Nine

The stormy weather that descended on the city the next day perfectly matched Pascale's mood. The normalcy of the household chafed at her nerves, which remained aggravated even after the time appointed for Devlin to leave the city. She thought of Devlin continually, wondering whether he'd arrived yet in Rouen, or whether he'd brought her painting onto his ship. This made her even more angry at him. She knew she was being unreasonable, but Pascale couldn't help feeling he was actively influencing her mind just as, for a minute, he'd overpowered her body. She couldn't stop dwelling upon everything that had happened, though she shied away from reliving that moment when she had almost . . . given in.

Frustrated fury, disappointment, and regret accompanied these thoughts. She was baffled by how every reminder of him inspired so many emotions at once. Her anger and the stomach-churning frustration were easily understandable . . . he had bested her at every turn. She couldn't believe that she couldn't recover The Painting from such a boor.

Despite her regret at the outcome, Pascale couldn't regret the methods she had used. She hadn't had any recourse in her dealings with him—she'd tried to reason with him, bargain with him, and had only resorted to less ethical tactics after he had been impossibly stubborn.

The pervasive sadness that sometimes overcame her had to be for the loss of The Lady. She would never see her now, perhaps never know who she was. She sat in her salon with the sketch on her lap, staring at it, again, as she had so many times in the past weeks. Pascale examined the vague outlines of her father's masterwork minutely. There was a tiny part of her that still hoped. She admitted to herself, for the first time, that she wanted this painting for reasons that had little to do with the noble aspirations and high ideals she'd espoused to John Devlin, and even to her father.

This painting might be of her mother, the woman who had abandoned her and her father less than a year after Pascale was born. She knew nothing about her. No one, not even Louise, seemed to remember her. Papa never spoke of her.

But no matter how she turned the portrait to catch the dull gray light, Pascale couldn't discern any clue to the lady's identity, nor make out the face, anymore than she had in the past. Instead, Captain Devlin's mocking face swam before her eyes; the memory of the heated desire she'd seen in his eyes before he'd kissed her sent the same shiver through her now.

Pascale blinked, and the red chalking in her lap came back into focus. She had begged her father to redo the painting for her, promising him with total sincerity that she wouldn't do anything with it against his wishes. He remained steadfast in refusing the request. She couldn't give up, but she didn't know what more to do. She'd stretched the truth a bit when she faced him: saying that Jack had told her that The Painting did indeed exist and had been given over into his care. She'd hoped he'd finally admit that The Portrait was finished. But he shrugged, not offering excuses or comfort. In fact, just this morning he'd had the nerve to say that he thought she was more upset about losing The Painting to Captain Devlin than about the work itself.

Pascale knew that wasn't true. She hated Devlin, and what he'd done to her. But when she thought of The Painting, the ire inspired by the man faded away, to be replaced by the dull ache of despair. The utter hopelessness she felt was so foreign to her that she didn't know what to do. Pascale had spent so many years working with her father toward this one all-important goal, and now, just as they finally had it within their grasp, he snatched it away. Her father's betrayal left her feeling empty and alone.

A few days after Devlin's departure from Paris, she found herself sitting in her small sitting room, wishing she could return home to Beaune. But the Salon would be closing next week, and she and her father would be able to get out of this city only a week later. Perhaps then the de Ravenault family could return to the way it had been. She couldn't stand this isolation. She longed for the closeness she had always shared with her father. She was desolate without it.

The chiming of the front doorbell brought her out of her reverie. Pascale dabbed at her eyes, but it was unnecessary, for they were dry. She went into the hall to see who had come to call, and found Guillaume handing his wet coat to the butler. The sight of her old friend cheered her immediately. His visit was just what she needed to chase away unpleasant thoughts, of Devlin and The Painting.

"I'll show him in, Pierre," she said. "Will you please have Cook make him a hot drink."

"You are too good, *ma petite,*" Guillaume said gratefully.

"Only to you, *mon cher.*" She took his hand and led him to the larger drawing room, where a fire burned brightly in the hearth. "What brings you calling in such dismal weather?"

He stood by the fire warming his hands and didn't answer her, but asked instead, "How is your father? Is he in?"

"He should be upstairs. But I warn you, he is in no fit state for company. Papa is so disheartened he says he cannot even paint."

"*Paul* said that?"

She nodded. "It is too gray. In the country, the rain washes the earth, and the wind blows through the fields and forest, but even during the worst of it, the soil is black and the sky white, and everything in between is muted and misty but still green. Here in Paris the masonry is gray, the sky is gray, even the people in the street seem lifeless and drab." She knew exactly how Papa felt, for she agreed.

Guillaume shook his head. "Do not try to fool me, my child, I have known you for far too long. I have seen your father, and you for that matter, painting at the break of dawn, and in the middle of the night, complaining about how the shadows change in the lamplight."

"This is different," Pascale said, but she felt uneasy under his searching gaze.

"Nonsense," Guillaume said. "What is it? Is he still going on about that sculpture he wanted to buy?"

"No . . . ," Pascale said slowly.

"Don't let him plague you, *ma petite,*" Guillaume admonished her.

"He seems restless. I thought it was the weather," was her honest answer, but now that she thought about her father's petulant behavior, she could think of only one reason for her father's mood. Could it be that her father was more affected by the harsh words that had passed between them than he let on? The thought lifted her spirits a little.

"Where is he?" Guillaume asked.

"I am sure Pierre sent one of the men to fetch him." The door opened, but it was only Odelle with the tray. "Thank you," Pascale said to the girl, dismissing her. "Will you serve yourself, Guillaume. I will go and fetch Papa. He's been in such a foul mood, he may not answer if anyone else knocks on the door."

Pascale ran up to the studio, her heart lighter than it had been in days. All was not lost. She had only to talk reasonably with her father to . . . to . . . what? Pascale didn't know exactly what she wanted anymore. She didn't know whether she wanted him to send for The Painting. Or to repaint it. Or just to tell her who The Lady was, which had been something she had wanted to know since she was a very young girl. But she did know that she'd been suffering since her dear, sweet papa had started keeping secrets from her, as though she were an enemy rather than the devoted friend she had always been.

Perhaps, in her confused state, she had refined too much on

her father's foolish escapade. She had become too obsessed with the captain and with wresting her property from his grasp. She supposed she might even have been a little jealous. She had always been the first to see her father's work. Pascale smiled at her own foolishness as she went into the studio.

"Papa?"

There was no response. The master bedroom was just down the hall, but she didn't find him there, either. He must have been somewhere else in the house. She couldn't be so rude as to leave Guillaume alone while she searched for him, she'd ask Pierre to find him. She ran back downstairs. She entered the salon only to find her father sitting before the fire conversing with Guillaume. He must have come down the back stairs while she'd gone up the front. When she entered the room, he jumped up as if afraid. She supposed, after her behavior of the past few days, that he had been treading on eggshells all this time, and she'd been too wrapped up in her own roiling emotions to notice it.

"Papa," she said, smiling reassuringly at him. "Guillaume will cheer you up. His visit has done me a world of good."

Paul de Ravenault's nervous smile warmed her full heart further. "Has he told you the, uh, news, then?"

Guillaume rose, suddenly agitated, and said, "No, no. Nothing like that."

"What news?" Pascale inquired. She crossed the room and eased her father back into his seat. She sat beside him and took his hand in hers, raising it to her cheek. Only then did she look up and notice the odd look that passed between the two men. "It cannot be as bad as all that, surely." Papa looked away from her inquiring gaze and gently disengaged his hand from hers. "What is it? Tell me. You are both making me very nervous."

"I am probably making too much of this," Guillaume said. "I mean, after all, I know you don't much like the fellow . . ."

"What?" Pascale's heart sank with foreboding.

"Devlin's ship went down early this morning, just after setting out from le Havre at dawn," he said. When she stared at him uncomprehendingly, he continued, "It was still in sight of the harbor. They think it may have been struck by lightning."

"No," Pascale breathed.

"The survivors have been picked up. Jack didn't . . . wasn't one of them."

She felt nothing, except disbelief. The shock was too great. After a moment she managed to say, "Are they sure? In this weather, the ocean is so turbulent."

"They seem to be." Guillaume was clearly still reeling from the news of his friend's death. His sorrow broke through the curtain of mind-numbing shock that had dropped around her, and she rose and held her arms out to him.

"I'm sorry, *cher ami.*"

He returned her embrace for a moment, then straightened. "I'm sorry, too," he said.

It hit her like a bolt of lightning—The Painting was gone forever. The strangest part was, she hadn't even thought of it until that moment. When Guillaume had uttered those fatal words, she'd thought only of Jack Devlin—of how sad it was to lose such a man. Even now, the precious cargo he'd carried didn't seem as important a loss as the vibrant *élan vital* that had engulfed and enflamed her a few nights ago.

She was confused, that was all. When her thoughts and feelings sorted themselves out, it would be just like any other tragedy that touched their lives but didn't change them. She had known him less than two weeks. The sick feeling in her stomach couldn't be grief for him. It must be the loss of The Painting, which caused the sinking in her chest.

Her father would redo The Portrait of The Lady, and everything would be fine.

"Papa, it will be all right," she said through the tears in her eyes.

"Yes, yes," he agreed. He urged her onto the sofa behind them and sat next to her, handing her his handkerchief.

"And Guillaume, will you . . . will your business be all right? I know you had dealings with . . . Jack."

"I'll be fine," he said. "Really." He sat on the couch beside her, and Pascale wiped her eyes to find both men looking at her solicitously. They were clearly befuddled by her emotional reaction to the news, realization dawning in Guillaume's baffled face.

"I don't know why I'm crying. It's just The Painting, I guess. I did so want to know who . . . I mean . . . I just haven't gotten over losing it, I suppose." Pascale managed a half-hearted laugh to cover her embarrassment. Her father looked much relieved by Pascale's explanation, but Guillaume still regarded her sympathetically, understanding lighting his eyes.

"Of course," said Papa. "You were very upset about The Painting."

"Aren't you?" Guillaume asked his old friend. Pascale thought he looked at Papa suspiciously, but tears filled her eyes again, and she fled the room before they could fall. She couldn't explain her own complicated emotions right now, let alone worry about the strange note in Guillaume's voice.

It was some hours before she had recovered enough to face anyone. That night, dinner was a subdued affair, she and her father were both occupied with their own thoughts. Papa retired directly afterwards to his studio. They had no social engagements scheduled for the evening. Paul de Ravenault had shown no inclination to set foot outside the house today and vowed that he would not venture forth again until the skies cleared.

She retired to her room after dinner and watched the display of lightning through her window. From the second floor, she could see the Seine, which had risen alarmingly. There was even some danger of flooding. In April and May, Paris was usually much more gentle. This year the weather vacillated between gentle rains and mild sunshine, culminating in the unexpected storm that had cost so much. The maelstrom echoed the tumult within her. Pascale could not reconcile herself to Jack's death. How could someone so young, so strong, be gone? And then there was The Painting as well. And her old easy relationship with Papa. She had lost everything.

The Valons were having a little soiree during the following week, and Renoir had planned a picnic. Pascale sighed. It was odd to be in Paris, amidst all their friends, and all the gaiety, and not to feel a rush of excitement.

She had never had any trouble amusing herself during their annual pilgrimage to the mecca of the arts. Usually, a month was not long enough. This year she just hoped to survive it. If anyone had told her a week earlier that anything could mar her enjoyment of her friends' successes, she would have thought them crazy. But with everything that had happened, she couldn't seem to recover her *joie de vivre*.

For days after Guillaume brought the news that Devlin's ship, and everything aboard it, had been lost, she conducted her business for her father and carried out her other self-appointed duties automatically. She kept to her schedule, and found even that didn't quite suffice. She had to make lists of everything she wanted to accomplish, or she forgot to do anything at all.

She had never had to muster up enthusiasm for doing business in Paris. She had first used it to expiate the longing for her easel, which had plagued her since she'd given up her art at the tender age of fifteen. She had immersed herself in the newfound art of managing her father's career, and was content when she found it was no less creative than the painting she had forsworn. But the satisfaction that usually followed her successful business dealings was lacking now.

She tried to disguise her lassitude, but her effort to appear cheerful made her even more weary. The simplest chore seemed onerous. It was fully two days after she received the blow that she finally realized the malaise she suffered was grief, pure and simple. If it had been the loss of The Painting, she could have found the inner strength to rise above her self-ishness. But it was not an inanimate object that her soul cried out for, but a man.

She missed Jack Devlin. Pascale did not know how she could have grown so accustomed to him, even attached to him, in such a short time. She felt his absence as keenly as if it had been her only friend who had died. No matter what she had said in the past, in her heart she had felt they were destined to meet again—perhaps when her father sent for The Painting. Pascale felt fully alive for the first time when she had met him, fought with him. She tried not to think about that. It made her heart ache more to think about what might have been. And it led to regret. Regret for what had been started, and never finished, between them.

She and Papa never spoke of it. For the first time in her life, her father was not privy to her feelings. He might have guessed, but he never introduced the subject of either the captain, or The Painting. She didn't have the energy to confront him. Pascale had learned one thing. She could no longer follow him about with the slavish devotion that had been such a large part of her life.

Amazingly enough, Papa did not seem to have been very deeply affected by the loss of The Painting. Perhaps he was already repainting The Portrait of The Lady. Maybe, as she'd begun to suspect lately, he just didn't care.

Her musings left her drained, dry-eyed and bereft. At night, alone in her bed, she wondered what would have happened if John Devlin hadn't died. Would she have continued to live for her father's comfort? Or would Jack somehow have saved her? No one had ever tried to protect her before, not even from herself. She kept remembering the conversation they'd had in the Louvre, when Devlin had warned her not to rely on her father's work. At the time she had been furious. But now she understood that he'd only been trying to help her. He might have gone about it badly, but he had been trying to be kind. She saw that now—too late.

Ten

Jack dreamed of his last voyage on the *Aurora*. Somehow he knew it was a dream, but he couldn't stop it from unfolding in front of his eyes. His crew had loaded the last of the cargo, brought by barge from the warehouse in Paris, into the hold. From Rouen, where the big ship had been docked, he set sail up to the mouth of the Seine at a good pace, and unfurled the rest of the canvas when they'd hit the English Channel. They'd still been in sight of Le Havre when the problems had begun. The weather had been threatening since dawn. The waters of the Channel were rough before the storm descended; when it broke, the fury of the wind and waves were as bad as any turbulence he'd weathered on the open seas.

It was while they were battening down that the first mishap occurred. One of the lads went over the side with a rope that suddenly came free in his hands. After they'd managed to get the boy back aboard, the first mate bid Jack come see the ends of the rope. It had been cut. Jack set the men to finding any other frayed sections. There were three in all.

He hadn't had time to think about how it might have happened. The ropes had to be replaced, and the ship checked over for other signs of foul play. The bomb must have been in the hold. One minute he'd been standing on the bridge trying to shout his orders over the wind, the next the entire world seemed to split in two. Jack had been thrown down to the main deck by the force of the explosion. He thought at first they'd been hit by lightning, but as he saw fire spewing through the gaping hole in the deck, he recognized the sulfurous odor of gunpowder.

The ship wasn't built to withstand that kind of punishment. If he'd been on his old warship, he might have been able to make a recovery from the damage—or if the storm hadn't conspired against him, he might have been able to rally his men to make the necessary repairs. As it was, he could only quickly assess the damage. The bomb must have been hidden in the cargo, its placement wasn't precise. A few feet closer to the hull, and the ship would have been taking on a lot of water. As it was, the force of the blast had been directed upward, and the explosion had ripped through a section of the flooring. Unfortunately, it had unbased the columns that supported the mainmast.

His men had suffered, too. Three were dead; two injured; and the others half-panicked. They were relieved to hear the command to heave to and bring her around. Land was in sight, and the worst seemed to be over. The wind and rain were ignored as they scuttled about, eager to limp home. They weren't as pleased when he ordered the mainsail brought down—they wanted to reach port quickly, and the *Aurora* could move like the wind under full sail—but they realized quickly enough the danger of putting the pressure of this battering storm on the crippled mast.

Jack had started to feel the pain in his chest by the time he had everyone back under control. It didn't stop him from taking his place with his men to haul the hundred-foot square of canvas down to the deck. One of the ropes in the rigging lost tension and fluttered to the deck on the third pull. Whether it had been cut, or just damaged in the explosion, they would never know. An edge of the mainsail caught in the rigging of the topsail, and suddenly the mast started to topple.

"Clear out!" Jack yelled as the heavy timber came down. "Jump!" He saw two men jump out of the way, but by the time Jack looked around for the third, he'd been caught in the falling debris.

The next thing he knew, Bates was screaming at him, "Move, Captain, move! You bloody slow-foot, move!" It had been difficult to open his eyes, but he'd managed it, to find Bates laboring over him, clearing away wooden planks and the piles of rope that seemed to coil about him. When he tried to sit, a wave of pain and then nausea hit him, and he retched.

Amazingly enough, that made Bates laugh. "That's it, mate. It's about time ye opened yer eyes," his old friend yelled. Jack rolled onto his side and tried to work his way free, but it was useless. His right arm was pinned under a block of the skeletal iron stay that girded the ship beneath the wooden hull. He could see a section of ragged wood and twisted iron, which had been exposed by the force of the explosion. Jack couldn't imagine how this section had come to land on the deck, but a foot farther and it would have caught his head.

He tried to warn Henry, "I'm trapped, go on." But his first mate didn't seem to hear him. By the time Bates had cleared the last of the debris off of him, Jack had realized the futility of trying to convince him to leave, and Bates was now searching for something to use as a lever to raise the heavy metal, something that wouldn't break under the weight. The deck was littered with rope, wood, and canvas, plus an odd assortment of the goods that had been stored below, including bolts of satin, bottles of champagne, and statuary pieces. Craning his head, Jack considered and discarded such items as an Oriental footstool covered with hand-embroidered silk.

The fire in the hold was spreading. He could feel its heat. The rain had failed to put a halt to the destruction it was causing. He could see no sign of his men. He hoped they'd been able to take the boats and that they'd make the shore. He wished Henry Bates had gone with them. He didn't want the first mate's death on his conscience.

Jack couldn't hold on much longer, and the ship was starting to go down. His only other chance was to pray the water rose quickly, before the fire got him. If he didn't drown before the iron sank, the buoyancy of the seawater might save him.

"How 'bout this, Cap'n?" Bates had rolled one of the marble statues over and wedged it next to the chunk of iron that held him captive.

It might just work, he thought. All he could manage for his friend was a weak nod. They still needed a lever and he couldn't think of anything. The ship rolled, taking water over the damaged portion of its side, bringing Jack's attention to the twisted metal skeleton again. That gave him an idea.

"The sledgehammer," he tried to yell, but his voice was as weak as a babe's. He felt around with his left hand and found a champagne bottle within reach. He grasped it around its neck, and took careful aim. He couldn't afford to miss. The effort of lobbing the bottle across the three feet that separated him from Henry was almost more than he could stand, but it got the first mate's attention. "Sledgehammer!" he screamed as loudly as he could. Bates nodded and ran, returning in moments with the heavy steel tool. After putting the hammer in place, Henry Bates put all his weight on the handle. The pressure on Jack's arm eased.

His first attempt to move the broken bloody limb met with total failure, and another wave of nausea. He tried again, pulling on the injured arm with his free hand, and he was loose. Bates let the iron down with a thump and came around to help him up. As they walked toward the railing, Jack sensed, rather than saw, the lightning that hit the exposed iron on the other side of the ship. The last thing he remembered was jumping into the foaming sea.

Jack woke with a start. He was in hell. Yellow light seared his open eyes, but when he closed them, all he could see was blood. He recoiled from the vision, and the red haze burst into showers of golden sparks. His arm was being torn from his body. He opened his mouth to scream, but nothing emerged but a whimper.

"Captain!" John Douglas shouted urgently, somewhere in the distance. His eyelids flew open again to tell him to stop, as the yelling was hurting his head. His valet, John Douglas, bent over him, only inches from his face. His lips moved, but Jack couldn't hear a thing. Somewhere else, someone was saying something about a doctor.

"No," he tried to protest. This time, a grunt came from his raw throat, and with it a wave of excruciating pain. For a moment Jack thought he was going to faint. He swallowed. It was torture. His throat burned, all the way down to his chest. His arms and legs were on fire as well. And his head was pounding, a deep drumbeat.

So this is what death feels like, he thought. God, it hurts! John Douglas's concerned face swam into view once again. "Goodbye, old friend," he wanted to say, but he knew better than to try to speak, or move. Already he was falling away, John Douglas receding in the distance. Just before he let his eyes slide closed, he had an odd vision. Paul de Ravenault whispering something in John Douglas's ear.

It was ironic. If his pain-filled mind was conjuring up pictures of the de Ravenault family, it might have chosen Pascale. The sight of her face would have been a sweet memory to take with him into the darkness.

E leven

Pascale awoke on the third morning, determined to bring an end to this orgy of profitless self-pity. Unfortunately, her heart and her mind seemed to be at odds on this decision. Three days was long enough to mourn a man who had been a virtual stranger to her. What difference if he had kissed her? That was not exactly a momentous event: Men kissed women all of the time. Jack Devlin was gone and she had important business to conduct.

If her spirits still stayed low, Pascale was resolved to ignore it. She made her way to her father's studio. She had not cleaned it in some time, and since the servants were permanently banned from the room, it had to be attended to.

The task was so familiar that Pascale didn't even need to think about what she was doing. She counted and organized Papa's used and unused canvases, taking a mental inventory of supplies he needed such as colors and paintbrushes. She could never seem to convince him that turpentine-soaked cloth was volatile and could cause a fire, and her nagging only caused him to hide the rags in odd places.

As she was scraping a streak of oil paint from a window-pane, Papa came bustling into the room. When he saw her he stopped, looking guiltier than ever. Pascale supposed she should relent. He was much more likely to repaint The Painting if she was kind, rather than punishing. But she couldn't bring herself to do it yet. She felt an unfamiliar urge—to exact revenge for the hurt he'd inflicted.

"You've been cleaning," he said unnecessarily.

"Yes. And it was a good thing I did. You can't just throw your cleaning rags anywhere, Papa. One warm ash from the fire, and the whole house could burn down around our ears."

"I'll try to remember," he promised. His unexpected docility sent a warning to her mind.

"Thank you," Pascale said, wiping the last of the tiny streaks of paint from the glass window.

She watched him as he busied himself at the drawing table, rearranging again the chalk she'd just neatly placed in its box. He was definitely nervous.

He withstood her scrutiny as long as he could, then asked, "Are you almost finished in here?"

"Almost," Pascale answered. "Why?"

"No reason. I was just curious." He stood. "Perhaps I'll return later, when you're done."

She blocked his way to the door. "What are you up to, Papa?"

"Me?" He tried to meet her gaze, but couldn't stop blinking rapidly. "Nothing, *ma fille.*"

"Papa, I thought we agreed. No more secrets."

He drew himself up to his full height and advanced on her. "I know we agreed." Pascale stood her ground. He tried to step around her.

Pascale did not let him by. "You promised. Now out with it! What are you doing?"

"Pascale, this superior attitude you've taken lately is not at all becoming to a dutiful daughter."

Pascale let out a small burst of laughter. "My attitude, as you call it, is fine. You have a guilty conscience, that's all."

"Me?" He tried blustering. "I've done nothing that merits such treatment from my only child."

"You call it nothing to steal one of your own paintings. And then to lose it? When have I ever lost any of your work?"

"Never," he admitted.

"Because I know what I'm doing. That is why we're here in Paris, to sell your work."

"I didn't want The Painting sold," he said adamantly.

"Fine! That's all you had to say."

"Ha!" he shouted.

"What do you mean by that?" Pascale asked, all of the hurt she'd been feeling suddenly rushing back.

"You never listen to me. You always think you know better than I do."

"And don't I? Usually?" she asked.

"Sometimes, perhaps. But that is not the point."

"Then what is it?"

"You would have done whatever you liked with my painting."

"I would never have purposely hurt you." She wanted to add, "As you did me."

"You would wheedle, and reason with me, and make me think you knew best, until I didn't know what I wanted anymore. You didn't trust me to figure out what to do with it. You didn't like it when I gave it to Captain Devlin, a very reliable man. You paid no attention to *my* wishes, and tried to steal it."

"And I was right, wasn't I?" She wanted to hear him say it.

"Maybe. Maybe not."

"How can you say that after all that's happened?"

"You're just upset because he beat you."

"You said that before," Pascale replied, injured. "The captain has nothing to do with it. This is between you and me."

"No it's not," he argued.

Pascale didn't want to get into a childish debate with him. "What are you doing now that's got you all flustered?"

"Nothing. I swear it." He tried to pass her once again, but Pascale stepped into his path. "Fine," he said. "I'll just stay here, then. I have work to do, anyway."

He went back to his drawing table and, opening his sketchbook, he began to draw. Pascale sighed. Once he started to draw, he wouldn't hear a word she said. He was already totally absorbed. She took one last look around the room. She was done here. She crossed the room to stand behind him and watched his sketch take form. It was a picture of Devlin. There was no escaping the sea captain.

"We'll talk later, Papa," she warned.

He didn't answer. She couldn't stay any longer as familiar black eyes took shape beneath her father's deft hand. She took the rubbish she'd collected and left to discard it.

Pascale descended the back stairs only to find that the kitchen was in an uproar. She could not, at first, discern what was causing the commotion as the two men and three women in the room were all rushing about at cross-purposes. Meanwhile Cook flailed about with her rolling pin, nearly bashing it into the head of the footman who was trying to get out of the door with a small uncovered tray of bread and cheese.

"Aha!" Cook was less than five feet tall, and thin as a rail, but the tiny black woman had a lot of strength in those wiry arms and callused hands. So when she took aim at the man's back, Pascale shouted, "Stop!"

The resultant tableau looked quite comical—Louise, frozen with her arms akimbo; the footman scrambling so as not to collide with the girl who had stopped abruptly in his path at Pascale's command; and another woman halted in the midst of sautéing an egg on the stove. The sizzling of hot oil was the only sound in the room as the footman righted himself, and—under Pascale's reproving glare—the others brought their hands to their sides and bowed their heads. "What is going on here?"

Everyone started to speak at once. Louise, the cook, who spoke with her hands as much as her voice, raised the rolling pin again to gesticulate, narrowly missing the head of the youngest maid. Smoke rose from the pan on the stove as the eggs began to burn, and Philippe, the footman, tried to sneak past Pascale and out of the room.

Pascale turned her attention to him. "Wait!" She waved at the woman at the stove. "Do something about that smoke, please." And to Cook she said, "Come here." When the cook and the footman stood in front of her, she crossed her arms in front of her and waited for them to speak.

Cook was the first to explain herself. "They've got no right coming into my kitchen. If the master wants something, they can send a message down, and I'll have one of the maids bring it to them. I will not have these oafs coming into my beautiful kitchen, tracking mud on the floors, and stealing food right out from under my nose."

Philippe tried to defend himself. *"Mademoiselle.* Your father asked me to bring him a little *déjeuner,* and I thought his wishes were more important than that one."

"My father was wrong to bother you with serving food, Philippe. He knows that is not the way to go about it. I will speak with him. But Louise, you cannot attack people for entering the kitchen. You could kill someone with that thing."

She followed the footman up the back stairs. In the kitchen she heard the cook expelling the other servants from her domain with a "Here, I'll do that. Get out!" By the time they reached the top of the stairs, it was quiet below. She told herself she wasn't really angry with her father, for she knew as well as anyone that he never paid any attention to the hierarchy of the servants in the house, and didn't understand the hurt feelings caused when his orders countermanded the intricate structure. She was spoiling for a good fight, however.

"Papa," she called, entering his bedroom in Philippe's wake. But he wasn't there. She looked inquiringly at the footman, but he just shrugged indifferently and put the tray down on a table by the window.

"If you please, *mademoiselle,* I have my regular duties to attend to." She sighed. It would take days to soothe his ruffled dignity. First he'd been asked to fetch a tray, like a common maid, then he'd been forced into an undignified tussle over a loaf of bread with Cook, a woman who would never let him forget it.

"I appreciate your attention to my father's comfort," Pascale said. He unbent enough to give her a slight bow before he huffed his way out of the room.

Paul de Ravenault was not in his dressing room, nor was he in the studio when Pascale checked that chamber. She assumed he'd gone down the front staircase to confer with Pierre about the day's outing, and settled herself on his bed to wait for him. When he hadn't reappeared after fully a quarter of an hour, she stuck her head around the doorjamb and out into the hallway, hoping to see him coming. There was no one in the hall. That was unusual; at this time of the morning, the maids were generally busy cleaning the upstairs, the ground floor having been dusted and polished as soon as the sun rose, in preparation for the arrival of any guests.

Pascale went to the top of the stairway. She heard no activity below, nor, when she leaned over the railing, could she detect any sign of movement. Where was everybody? It was all very curious. For the first time in days, her interest was piqued. She tried to remember if there was a special saint's day or fete that the servants might be preparing to attend. But for the life of her, she could think of nothing to explain the unusual silence, which reigned both above and below stairs.

She climbed the stair to the third floor where the under-servants' rooms were. Louise slept in a room off the kitchen, and Pierre's room was on the first floor as well, but the rest of the staff retired at night to the third floor. Pascale sensed, rather than saw, a flurry of movement as her footsteps were heard on the wooden runners. At the top of the stair stood Pierre. Pascale was amazed. To her knowledge, he never went more than ten feet from the front door without arranging for Philippe to replace him. He slept in a roomy closet with a hidden doorway near the entrance to the small house.

"Is someone ill?" she asked, seizing on the only explanation she could think of for the elderly man to desert his cherished post.

It made her even more nervous when he hesitated before answering, "Yes, miss."

"Well, is it serious? Shall I come and take a look?"

"I don't think so," he answered, hesitantly. He was wearing his most stoic expression, which was usually reserved for very serious infractions of his stiff notions of what was proper.

"Well, then, perhaps I should call the doctor?" He recoiled at that, and she knew there was something very wrong. "Have you seen my father, or better yet, one of the footmen—I'll need to send someone and I don't see anyone about downstairs."

At that moment one of the maids popped out of Philippe's room. When she saw Pascale she blushed and fled into her own room. Pascale was less shocked than intrigued.

Pierre stood, straight and stiff and, she suddenly realized, effectively blocking her way. "I did see your father already this morning. I don't think he would want you to send for a medical man. I believe I can handle the situation without too much assistance. The footmen are here, should I need them, and I believe the girl in the kitchen has been told to answer the door, should anyone ring."

"Perhaps I should talk to Papa myself." She climbed the two remaining steps and came straight up against Pierre's unmoving body. She didn't retreat but waited patiently until he finally stepped back and allowed her to pass. Pascale walked down the narrow, spotlessly clean hallway, which divided the servants' quarters, women on one side, men on the other. She hadn't visited this floor since she'd toured the house upon their arrival. She paused with her hand on the doorknob to Philippe's room, the only private one on this floor.

She hesitated for a moment only, then turned the handle and pushed the door open. A number of people had crowded into the tiny space. Someone was moaning, but the bed was obscured from her view by most of her household staff. The curtains had been drawn and much of the room was in shadow.

Odelle looked up at Pascale as she stood in the doorway, then tried to step out of the way, and nearly fell over the youngest boy who had been wedged between her and the bedpost. A tap on his shoulder finally got his attention, and when he looked up, she handed him the bundle of sheets she held. Stooping, she picked up a basin on the floor and then led him toward Pascale, whom they gave a wide berth on their way out of the room. Neither of them said a word as they beat a hasty retreat.

Slowly Pascale came closer. A stranger was bent over the bed, murmuring soothingly to its occupant. She couldn't see his face in the flickering candlelight. Papa stood across from him, on the left side of the bed, looking down at the patient anxiously, while Philippe and the older servant boy tried to hold the thrashing figure down.

As Pascale drew near, the occupant of the bed grew still and silent. The two men who had been holding him released him slowly and stood back as Pascale reached the foot of the bed. She entered the circle of lamplight and saw the face of the man lying in the bed, Captain John Devlin.

Twelve

The stranger spared her one quick glance, then returned to his ministrations. His big hands were gentle as he held a cloth to the brow of the unconscious man.

"He's burning up with fever," John Douglas said to the room at large. "Mebbe we should send for a doctor, after all." Pascale had forgotten Pierre was standing behind her. She jumped when he spoke.

"I don't think that would be wise. Besides Louise knows more about medicine than any big-city doctor," he said. Pascale stared at him over her shoulder. Pierre usually disparaged the cook's homemade remedies. Pascale stared at Pierre in amazement as he volunteered to go to the kitchen and request Cook's assistance.

"Tell her I said it was urgent," she suggested as he left.

He paused in the doorway. "I think I know how to handle her, *mademoiselle.*"

Pascale moved around the bed to stand beside John Douglas. "How is he?"

"It's too soon to tell, miss. He's broken some ribs and his arm, and you can see what happened to his face. We don't know with all the bruising if he's injured himself internally as well."

Pascale could not believe he was here. Jack was alive! Seeing him in this condition brought tears to her eyes. Her rising joy caused them to spill onto her cheeks.

"What can I do to help?" she asked.

It took the combined efforts of her father and herself to persuade John Douglas to allow Pascale to help with the nursing. He was only finally convinced when they forced him to admit that, since he had not slept in two days, he was more of a burden to them than a help.

Pascale took over immediately. Pierre returned with a potion to help Jack sleep more peacefully, a salve for the bruises he'd sustained, and some evil-smelling medicine that was supposed to reduce his raging fever. Louise didn't visit the patient. She had the knowledge to cure, but not the bedside manner. Pascale applied the salve, with Philippe's help. Jack tossed a little, but one arm had been tied to the bedpost, as well as one of his legs. She thought at first that this was a safety precaution, to keep him from turning over and injuring himself further.

When she tried to give him his medicine, she discovered another good reason for the restraints. She could barely keep him still enough to get the spoon to his lips. He pushed her hand away and turned his head. When she tried to hold him in place, he struck out at her. She stumbled backward at the force of the blow, but she didn't realize until much later that he'd hit her hard enough to blacken her eye. After finally getting a dribble of each of his medicines past his lips, she watched him until the sleeping potion took effect. Then she went down to the kitchen, which was still chaotic.

To complicate matters, Pierre had left his post by the front door to see what the commotion was. "What's all this?" he was asking as Pascale came into the kitchen.

"What are you doing in my kitchen, you old snot?" Louise demanded belligerently. He only stared down his nose at her. "Get yourself back to your own business," she said, in a huff, and turned her back on him.

Pascale caught the butler's eye and she would have sworn he winked at her, if it hadn't been for the fact that in all the years she'd known him he'd never made light of any situation, no matter how ridiculous. She'd rarely even seen him smile. She'd been dumbfounded when he'd suggested that they try

Louise's remedies instead of sending for the doctor. He called Cook's potions "silly, superstitious nonsense." The cook, well aware of her own worth and confident of her healing skills, had her pride, but Pierre's insufferable attitude invariably made her lose her temper. The haughty gray-haired white man was fully a foot taller than the scrappy black woman, but each time her cures worked, Louise confronted him. The household suffered mightily when the two unlikely combatants faced off. Pierre wouldn't argue with those he considered beneath him. Instead the supercilious butler peered down his long straight nose at Louise and offended her further by refusing to be baited by her insults.

Somehow, despite the fact that it was Louise who flung all the wild barbs and unpardonable insults, when the dust cleared, it was she who was the injured party. Every time someone on the farm was taken ill, the cook had to be coaxed, begged, and bullied to render the aid she was actually dying to dispense from her stock of herbs and spices. Pierre, in answer to Pascale's scolds, just sniffed and suggested calling a real doctor, which served the purpose of getting Louise's dander up, and began the cycle again.

Pascale knew she had only to ask Cook to oversee the housekeeping while she was occupied upstairs. Louise and Pierre would put aside their antagonism in order to work together. They'd done it before, many times, at home in Beaune.

So she turned her attention to Odelle and Philippe, who were glaring at each other. They had both come with the family from Beaune, and there had never been any trouble between them. Odelle was quiet and efficient. She sometimes served as Pascale's "dresser," more frequently in Paris than at home in the country, where Pascale did little formal entertaining. But even when she spent hours arranging Mademoiselle's hair just so, she didn't speak about herself.

Pascale knew little about Odelle's past, other than the few salient facts that Cook or the housemaids had passed on to her. Her family lived on a small farm in the same province, and she worked for the de Ravenault family because it was common knowledge that they provided all of their servants with small cottages upon their retirement, even single women. She had come to work in the château ten years ago, at the age of sixteen. Although only five years older than Pascale, they had never become close friends. Odelle didn't have any friends, to Pascale's knowledge.

"That is just stupid," she said to Philippe after trying unsuccessfully to stare him down.

"It is the truth. He needs care, but it's a man's strength that is needed in this situation." Philippe was an uncomplicated fellow of some twenty-odd years. He had grown up on the farm. The young black man had followed his father into service with the family. He had stepped into his current position when the old man retired. There was nothing enigmatic about him.

"That situation is not to be discussed, especially outside this house," Pierre interjected a word of warning into their argument.

"For the moment at least," Pascale declared, seconding the order.

Odelle and Philippe had not noticed her arrival, so intent had they been on their confrontation. They looked toward her when she spoke.

"Pascale," Odelle said, alarmed. "Are you all right?"

"Fine." When Pascale looked at the maid questioningly, Odelle came to her side to look more closely at her face.

"What happened to your eye?" she asked.

"Oh, that. It's nothing." Pascale put a hand to the cheek where Devlin had inadvertently slapped in his struggles. She hadn't noticed before, but it did sting a little.

"Ice," said Louise. "It will keep the swelling down. Go!" she told young Adele, who stood gaping at all the excitement.

"I told you," Philippe said, undiplomatically. "He's too strong for a woman to handle. We even had to tie him down." Odelle shot him a look of scorn.

Pascale sympathized with her, but there was a grain of truth to Philippe's contention. "Don't worry. If I need you, Philippe, I'll call, you may be sure. He was sleeping peacefully when I left him. I came down to make sure Monsieur's man is given anything he needs, including a bath and some of Papa's clothes when he awakens." She turned to Pierre to issue her next order. "Make sure he doesn't come next or nigh to the sickroom until he's bathed and fed, please. I'm sure he's devoted to the captain, but I can take care of him this evening."

"Yes, *mademoiselle,*" Pierre answered.

Papa appeared in the doorway, took one look about the room, and turned to leave.

"Papa!" The sound of Pascale's voice halted him in his tracks. His shoulders hunched over self-protectively, like a child caught stealing a sweet from the pantry. But Pascale was not inclined to make the usual excuses for him.

She didn't dare speak to him in front of the servants, who were trying to appear unaware of the two of them. She joined him at the door, and they walked a few paces down the hallway. Then Pascale turned to look him in the eye.

"How did you think you could sneak a wounded man into my house? And care for him under my roof? You have no more idea of how this house is run than an infant. You had to realize I'd find out eventually."

"I thought he might be gone by then."

"What happened? How did you come to find him in this state? And what on earth made you bring him here? Why not to François or Guillaume?"

"They weren't home. I went to his office here in Paris to find out what I could about the shipwreck and found Monsieur Douglas and Monsieur Bates trying to decide if they could care for him there or get him a hotel room. I didn't think they had very much money so I offered to bring him here. I have not forgotten what it is like to try to pay your bills here in Paris, without friends or family. Hotel rooms are so dear."

"But whatever possessed you?" Pascale said dumbfounded.

Papa looked at her as if she were addlepated. "I just told

you," he said kindly. He patted her gently, on the shoulder. "I suppose the shock has muddled your brain a bit."

Pascale shook her head to clear it. She had to get back to the sickroom and didn't have time to question him further. Besides this was probably the most coherent explanation she would get from her absentminded parent. One question still nagged at her. Knowing it was probably in vain, she couldn't resist asking, *"Why* did you go to his office?"

"Oh . . ." said Papa, waving his hand dismissively, "Just a little business, *ma petite."*

She well knew he referred to The Painting, but there was no point saying anything further about that. It was buried at sea in the wreckage of the *Aurora.* He had to be as disappointed as she was. She held her tongue.

Pascale returned to Jack's bedside.

He was still sleeping peacefully when she came into the room. She sat by his side, and looked down at his poor battered face. His bottom lip was split, and she pressed a damp cloth to the painful-looking cut. His chin was firm and warm beneath her palm.

"The painting," he murmured, shocking her into immobility. "She will give up the painting."

His eyes were closed, but the lids fluttered as he turned his head. Pascale waited breathlessly for him to say more, but as the effect of the sleeping potion wore off, he could only moan in pain.

So it went for the rest of the day. She was afraid to give him too much of the sedative, and in between doses he tossed and struggled, as though to escape the pain.

The only peace they had was the hour right after she gave him the drug. Then he lay still as death, and she memorized the large hand she held in her own, or his face. His black hair waved away from his wide forehead. His deep-set eyes remained closed. His lashes were long, for a man's. His cheekbones might have been further evidence that his ancestry might not be pure African. His nose and mouth were full and round and strong. His square chin gave him that decisive, self-assured look she had found so irritating.

She prayed for his eyes to open. His injuries were extensive, and there was no way of knowing what internal damage he had suffered. She had seen men, who were less battered than he was, die. She was able to hold his face still while she applied the healing salve to his lacerations, but Pascale couldn't apply it to the bruises that covered his chest and abdomen by herself. She had to call Philippe to help her hold him down. The violent jerking of his body when she touched the angry abrasions and black-and-blue marks on his ribs told her more clearly than anything that the marks that discolored his almond skin went far deeper than the surface. She would have cried, if she'd had the time. But his fever rose throughout the day, and she was kept busy bathing him with a cool damp rag, which seemed inadequate to battle the fire that had been kindled deep within.

John Douglas came in at the end of the afternoon.

"I'll take over now, miss," he said, leaning over their patient to lay a hand on his forehead.

"He's feverish," she warned, as he looked down at his friend, concern etched on his drawn face.

"I was expecting he might be. I ordered a bath brought up for 'im. I'll use cool water, if you'll tell that young Philippe to bring it."

When Pascale didn't move, he ushered her out of the room. "I'm sorry about that." He nodded toward her eye. Pascale had forgotten all about it. "But it ain't proper for a woman to be in here while I bathe him and change his bandages. We'll be all right and tidy for the night. You go out and get a breath of air. It's not so fresh in here."

He closed the door firmly behind her. Pascale stood just outside the door until Philippe appeared with the tub.

"He'll need cool water for the bath," she said, then watched the footman go into the sickroom with something close to envy.

Pascale couldn't stand the thought of waiting without anything to do but worry whether Jack Devlin would live or die. She walked slowly down the stairs, turning over in her mind the idea of meeting her father at the café Guerbois in the avenue de Clichy on the edge of Montmartre, where they'd agreed to meet some of their friends.

She went into her room and took off her dress, which smelled of Louise's potions. As she stood looking in her closet, she hesitated. Should she? What if she was needed? She thought of John Douglas's impatient face when he'd pushed her out of the little room on the floor above. He wouldn't be calling on her. Unless Jack . . . Pascale didn't finish the thought, even to herself. Jack wasn't going to die. He couldn't.

She pulled a gray muslin walking dress and its matching coat from the armoire. She couldn't just sit about the house. She stepped into the dress and went to the mirror. The white collar shone slightly in the dusky light filtering through the window behind her. The pearl-gray muslin fit loosely from the hips down, to allow her freedom to move, but still complemented her slight figure. She was surprised to see her cheeks were slightly flushed. She'd expected her reflection to match her gray mood. But the face shining back at her from the mirror looked healthy, and even a bit more animated than usual. She supposed it was nerves. Her brown eyes were dark with worry. All in all, she appeared perfectly normal.

She had held ice to her eye, which had kept it from swelling, but she did have a slight nick and a small bruise right below it. She covered it with a dusting of powder, which didn't completely disguise the mark, but made it undetectable to the casual observer. With one last glance at her overall appearance, she swung the gray wrap about her shoulders and moved quickly toward the door, suddenly eager to get out into the evening air.

She found Papa at the café. She leaned over to whisper in his ear, "John Douglas is watching over Captain Devlin." She presumed her obtuse parent understood the delicacy of the situ-

ation. He didn't even ask how the patient was, but went back
to the conversation about their friends' troubles and triumphs.
Olympia was once again under discussion. Manet was not in
attendance, at least not yet. So Auguste Renoir felt free to
announce with great disgust, "There are many people saying
now that Manet is flaunting his affair with Victorine."

"That is an accusation that has been leveled at every artist
and his model since man first laid paint to rock," her father
assured him. "Suzanne does him great credit, supporting him
as she has since he married her."

"It is a shame he had to wait for his father to die in order
to make their romance public. I think that is a great love affair.
All those years, he had to go to Germany to be with her."
Guillaume, the romantic, was easily diverted from the scandal
of the painting by the thought of Suzanne and Manet's affair.
She had been his piano teacher when he was seventeen and
she eighteen years old. She had returned home to Germany
and borne him a son, but their affair remained a secret until
his father's death twelve years later.

Not so the young Auguste Renoir. "I brought this for
Cézanne," he said, waving a copy of *L'Événement* at the table.
"He only reads Zola's reviews—"

"I went to school with Émile, and I *like* his reviews,"
Cézanne said defensively.

"We all like his reviews, but what about this," Renoir persisted, flipping through the pages like a man possessed. "Here
it is, and includes a quote from no less a man than Gautier.
Ah, no, the part I want comes later . . . ah, here . . . *'Olympia*
can be understood from no point of view, even if you take it
for what it is, a puny model stretched out on a sheet. The color
of the flesh is dirty, the modeling nonexistent. The shadows
are indicated by more of less large smears of blacking . . . ' "
He paused for breath, then hurriedly read on, " 'Here there is
nothing, we are sorry to say, but the desire to attract attention
at any price.' "

Pascale's thoughts were diverted momentarily from the captain lying at death's door by the outrageous criticism. "But the press is doing exactly the same thing they accuse Manet of doing. Milking the situation for all that it is worth."

François shushed them, pointing down the street to where Édouard and Suzanne Manet approached. "Perhaps it would be better to speak of something else," he suggested.

"I agree," said Papa, with unusual tact. "I am sure Suzanne has enough to do with comforting her distraught husband, as it is."

The conversation became more general. The elegant Édouard Manet had recovered enough of his usual aplomb to sit in state, discussing the other artists' work. If he guessed at the conversation that they had been having before his arrival, he gave no hint.

Suzanne exchanged greetings with the others, and then leaned closer to Pascale, the only other woman at the table, to confide, "He is better today. He had written to Baudelaire, who is very sick now, you know, from alcohol and also opium smoking, to tell him of the terrible reviews he's been getting and the way people are laughing at *Olympia*. Baudelaire wrote him a scathing letter. You know how wonderful the poet can be when he is emotional. He said Édouard was being stupid to complain of this criticism. He will not die from it. Others, greater than he, have had worse said of them, and done to them, and they have survived."

Pascale listened sympathetically. It seemed so ironic that she sat in this café watching the lamps being lit on the boulevard, talking of an artist's "surviving" a bad review, when Devlin was fighting to survive his injuries.

"Édouard seems to be taking it well," Pascale said, surveying the dapper blond man sitting across from them, exchanging fulsome compliments with Renoir.

"No, he did not at first," Manet's stolid German *hausfrau* said bluntly. "But today we had news from a mutual friend, and Charles sent a kind message that he should not torment himself, for it will be good for Édouard to suffer these insults.

This injustice, he said, is an excellent thing. Our friend read us a portion of the letter, in which he spoke so kindly of Édouard's talent and ability, that I believe it will carry him through this. Charles has set poor Édouard quite to rights again, thank heavens!"

Pascale noted the contradiction that Charles Baudelaire so easily orchestrated, congratulated her, and they sat up and away from each other again.

She found herself wondering if Jack's fever had broken yet. Or if, God forbid, it had worsened.

Suzanne Manet interrupted her thoughts. "You will be joining us on Thursday night, then?" she asked.

"I think so. I have been so looking forward to it," she answered, distracted. At Suzanne's puzzled look, she added, "You always attract such a pleasant company."

"We are lucky in our friends. They are so clever," Suzanne said happily. "Even those who are hotheaded . . ." She glanced at Renoir, pounding on the table to illustrate his point.

"Or impolite?" Pascale's gaze went to her father, who was staring off into the distance, totally ignoring the conversation around him.

"Or even naughty. They are so charmingly improper."

"I would like to see George Sand again. I only met her recently," Pascale said. "But she is certainly charming when she is . . . irreverent, shall we say?"

"Yes, she's a friend of Charles Baudelaire, too. She shares our concern for him. She seems so unfeeling, but she really has a sweet nature, when she's not playing one of her devilish pranks. And she has introduced me to a number of her musical friends, which is nice." A smile blossomed on the staid woman's face. It chased away her usual peaceful expression, which made her look much like the full-figured housekeeper that she was, despite—or perhaps because of—her marriage to an artist with a touch of genius. Her quiet joy lit up her bland features.

She might not look the perfect wife for a genius fully a year her junior, but Pascale thought Édouard Manet a very lucky man to have found such a wife. She didn't imagine Suzanne was able to share her art, her music, with her husband, as she did his, and yet she seemed so happy to be with him, so at ease. Pascale envied her.

She was tempted to ask her advice about the situation in which she found herself. Pascale's attraction to Jack had not lessened with his return to the land of the living, even though his miraculous survival had left him with only a tenuous foothold on this side of the void between life and death.

Pascale did not believe for a moment that she would lose him again. Her feeling that their meeting had been cut unnaturally short had grown when he'd been given back to her. This man—a shadow of the forceful captain that had haunted her dreams—now struggled with unseen demons under her very own roof, and she both yearned to help him, and dreaded his recovery.

She feared the way he made her feel, even in his current vulnerable state. What would she do after she had nursed him back to health? She doubted that he would be grateful to her. He had already made his opinion very clear—he questioned her manners, her motives, and her morals. He had made her doubt her knowledge of herself. She didn't think she could stand it again. Not now that she had opened herself to him— even if only in her mind and heart. Even if he didn't know it.

The Painting, she finally admitted to herself, had been an excuse for seeking out his company. That was gone. It didn't even seem all that precious, now that the object of her obsession was gone. It had been the man, not the masterpiece, that had filled her thoughts since the storm that had tried to sweep them both away. Suddenly she couldn't wait to return home. She wanted to be there, in the same house, if not in the same room.

Thirteen

Pascale couldn't bring herself to confide in Suzanne Manet. She waited for a lull in the conversation, then bid farewell to those gathered around the table. She felt utterly alone as she returned home, leaving her father planning a night out with his friends. The rented house looked peaceful and familiar. The sun was just setting. The lengthening shadows of the spring evening seemed to follow her inside. The lamps had yet to be lit. She stood alone in the welcoming dark. Her spirit was like the wicks on those candles, waiting for the touch of the flame that would ignite and spread warmth and light to all the cold dark spaces in her soul.

She stood at the window, watching the moon rise slowly in the sky. She could not bear it. She went and knocked lightly at the door of Jack's room.

John Douglas let her in immediately, almost as though he had been waiting for her. "The bath seemed to help. He's still some'ut warm, but not as hot as before."

"That's good," she whispered back. "I'd like to stay with him for a while. Why don't you go stretch your legs?"

"I will at that," he agreed, to her surprise. "I won't be gone above a couple of hours, I don't think, but I've got to go meet Henry Bates."

Pascale nodded, relieved that she wouldn't have to argue with the valet about staying. "Tell him he's welcome here, too."

"I don't think it would be safe to have him wandering in

and out of here. Bad enough I've got to go. But someone's got to find out what's happened." He jerked his head toward the bed. "He'll want to know when he wakes up."

"What happened?" Pascale asked, distracted.

"Don't worry. I'll be back as soon as ever I can," Douglas replied.

Pascale had forgotten about him before he'd even gotten out of the door. "Take care, miss," he said, as he left.

Pascale watched Jack sleep, sometimes peacefully, but more often fitfully. It was as though his soul were in torment. He tossed and turned, tried to sit up and even to stand, which was well beyond the ability of his poor racked frame. Pascale felt completely useless when Jack moaned in fear and in pain as he relived some terrible experience, either of the past week, or of earlier years.

There were times when his terror and sorrow were almost palpable, and she tried to comfort him with her hands and her voice, but he couldn't be consoled. At those times, Pascale was sure he was reliving the moment when his ship went down, and her heart bled for him. He often called out for Bates. And more occasionally, his faithful John Douglas. He even called her name once. When she took his hand and ordered him to "open your eyes, damn it!", he subsided into silence again. The seemingly endless minutes of quiet, when he barely moved and sometimes barely seemed to breathe, were the worst. He slipped away from her then, and there was nothing Pascale could do. At least when he thrashed about, she could hold him down and make sure he didn't hurt himself. She couldn't stand the waiting.

She bent over him, putting her ear to his chest and listening for the telltale thrum of his heart. In the small hours of the morning it grew faint, and she became frantic with anxiety, piling blankets on him. In his delirium he didn't seem to realize that his broken right arm had been trussed to his body, and his fingers would flutter and grasp at the edges of the heavy coverings, as if to push them away. Then he'd subside, and she'd breathe easier for a moment. The worst symptom was his hacking cough, a deep, harsh sound that John Douglas had told her had come from swallowing too much seawater. It made her wince, but at least it meant he was alive, and struggling to hold on to that second chance he'd been given when his men had fished him from the water.

When the dawn broke, she breathed a sigh of relief. John Douglas must have been delayed. Pascale was bone weary. Her exhaustion was caused by the effort of spooning Cook's potions into him hour after hour, but also because she held so tightly to the thread of hope that he would open his eyes. She greeted John Douglas's arrival with as much enthusiasm as she could muster, gave him a report on the events of the night, and stumbled to her bed, where she collapsed.

The second night Jack was quieter, but no calmer. He seemed to have gone further out of the reach of either her or John Douglas. He didn't respond at all to their voices, or their presence at his side. John Douglas stayed for an hour with her, then went on the prowl again.

Jack's murmurings were indistinct and often incoherent, but they did offer a glimpse into his past, and even his childhood. He mentioned The Painting a few times. He said, "She will give up The Painting," in a litany, which was almost a prayer. She assumed it was her Portrait of The Lady that worried him, until, in his delirium, he rid her of that notion. It was in one of his one-sided conversations with "Mama" that it finally became clear that Jack had clashed with a woman over a painting long before he'd met Pascale.

"It will be all right, Mama," he said, in the voice of a young boy echoing what he'd been told. "Everything will be fine. We'll be fine as soon as Aunt Jane sells the paintings." He was obviously soothing himself as much as his mother, and the fearful voice of the young boy he'd once again become was uncertain, and not very hopeful.

"She will give up the painting," he said again.

She became convinced as she listened to him that this was

why he'd acted so strangely. Captain John Devlin had wanted her to give up her painting, just as he'd begged his Aunt Jane to do. She didn't know why it was so important to him; it wasn't clear from the lopsided arguments she listened to that night. It did, however, make her feel better about the arguments they'd had. He had had a reason for his pigheaded behavior. She found out a little more about him from John Douglas.

It quickly became her daily ritual to take a nap in the morning, attend to business in the afternoon and early evening, and to spend her nights trying to pull Jack back from the edge of the abyss. Pascale "took her watch," as John Douglas termed it, at moonrise. The valet had business that was better done after nightfall. She suspected he felt there had been some foul play in the explosion that had sunk the *Aurora*, but he wouldn't talk to her about it. Instead he talked about Jack.

His hair, high cheekbones, and love of the sea must have been inherited from his father. John Douglas told her Jack's father was a Spanish sailor with Irish blood who had fallen in love with a young Carribbean-born barmaid in Portsmouth and married her. She had told him their wedded bliss had not lasted long.

"You know Devlin's mother?" Pascale asked.

"O'course."

"How?" she couldn't resist prying.

"The captain and I were sent to the hospital together. We were both injured five years ago, almost to the day. He was in the bed next to mine, and we got to talkin'. Anything to take my mind off the pain." She'd seen the scars on Jack's back, which she was sure were from gunfire, and the remnant of a particularly ugly wound on his leg. "Is that when you two left the Navy?"

"He did. Yes, miss. I wasn't in the Navy. I was shot during a robbery."

Pascale swallowed as she looked into his impassive face. "By the burglar?"

He smiled, wryly. "By the master o' the house I was robbin'."

"And in the hospital you told Jack?"

"I thought I was dyin'. I told him everything. Every miserable thing I'd done in my life."

"My God. What did he say?"

"He told me things he never told a living soul. He thought he was talking to a dying thief, you see. A man who wouldn't judge him, which I never would. A man who wouldn't confront him with his sins the next day."

"But you didn't die."

"And he offered me a job. My first honest job."

"Because he was afraid you'd tell someone?" Pascale whispered, sadly.

"Who would I tell? He hain't done nothing wrong. He just feels bad about leaving his mother and such like. But all his sins he done because he was a fighting man, a soldier. No call to feel guilty, not a bit of it. He took me home to his mother, and she got us back on our pins again, and then we went to London. He said his mama liked me and that was good enough for him."

"Why did he feel guilty about his mother?"

John Douglas shook his head. "Forget it. I shouldn't have said it."

The set look on his face told Pascale more plainly than words that she'd get no more from him on that score. "What happened to his father?"

"He died on a ship that went down in the China Sea when Jack was a babe. His mother took him inland to live on an estate where she'd gotten work as the companion to a widow woman, 'Aunt Jane.' "

"He talks of them sometimes in his sleep."

John Douglas gave her a knowing look. "I've heard."

They left the subject of Aunt Jane's painting alone. "So what did his mother do?"

"The widow had to go live with her brother. She invited

Mrs. Devlin to come with her, but she couldn't take Jack. He ran away to join the Navy. The rest, you know."

"He left the Navy, bought the *Aurora*, and became a merchant seaman."

John Douglas nodded. "He's made some'ut of himself." He was clearly proud of his employer. "Captain of the *Aurora*." His lips drooped downward, as though he'd tasted something bitter. "I should be going, miss," he said.

Pascale didn't know how many people might know of Jack's survival. But it was clear that John Douglas had contacted someone about his miraculous escape. There had been odd coded messages received and sent during the day. She didn't inquire into the full extent of the clandestine activities. She was sure they were on Jack's behalf.

She asked John Douglas only one question. "Will you be safe?"

He shrugged and said, "Safe enough."

His long, stern face had become haggard with worry and lack of sleep. But Pascale couldn't keep him from doing what he considered his duty—whether it was combing Paris's backstreets and back rooms, to unearth potential threats to his employer; or spending hours on the uncomfortable little stool that stood next to Devlin's bed—any more than she could have kept away from Jack herself.

Her father was no help. Although it had been his idea to sneak Devlin into the house, Paul de Ravenault was not interested in actually spending any time at the bedside of his newest friend. Once Pascale stumbled onto his secret, he was content to let his daughter assume control, as usual. How he had thought he might hide the captain right under her nose, she could not imagine. Whatever had been his original intention, he washed his hands of any further responsibility. Pascale learned more about Jack as she nursed him.

Mesmerized, Pascale listened to his nightmares. She came close to tears, as he coaxed and pleaded with the phantom Aunt Jane to save them. "We have to pay the man, Aunt Jane.

Sell the paintings. You can do it. We need you to be strong, or we're going to lose our house. This is our home. We can't let him take it."

Then, to someone else, he cried, "She doesn't want to live with you!" He cringed as if he'd been struck, and Pascale couldn't stand it anymore. She leaned over him, holding his face in her hands."

"You're safe now, you hear me. No one is going to hurt you. It's over," she repeated, until he subsided with a gusty sigh of relief, or resignation, she didn't know which.

Later on, he relived bloody, senseless battles and the deaths of those around him. She shivered as she listened to horrifying stories of war. The loss of his friends had gone on and on, until finally he seemed to enter another world comprised of nameless, faceless comrades, whose loss he didn't stop to mourn.

"Men!" he'd yell. "Prepare to fire! You! Shore up that port side. We've got to bring her around again."

He hovered in that netherworld for three days and nights before his fever finally broke. Then he lapsed into a deep, quiet sleep. John Douglas came in a little before dawn at the end of her third long vigil, and found her standing by the window, waiting for the sun to rise. When he felt his friend's cool brow, the older man broke down and wept.

"He's going to make it," she said, keeping her eyes averted.

"I never doubted it for a moment," he answered. When she turned to look at him, his wry smile begged indulgence for the blatant lie.

Fourteen

Now that Jack had been returned to her, Pascale had no idea what to do with him. The feelings he evoked in her were totally new. When she thought of his kisses, her knees went weak. When she thought of the arguments they'd had, her ire rose. But she had also seen something in his eyes that had called out to her soul.

She couldn't get rid of the feeling he had tricked her, somehow. She had mourned his death!

It was not his fault. He hadn't planned any of the events that led to this awkward situation, any more than Pascale had. If she was eager to reconstruct her world, he was even more intent on returning his life to its proper course.

At least, Pascale could get out and about. Jack was trapped in one small room. His broken ribs made breathing, sitting up, even laughing a difficult proposition. Not that he had a lot to laugh about. His frustration at being incapacitated was never far from the surface.

Pascale suspected he would not have been a good patient under any circumstance. She was often summoned to beg or bully the recalcitrant invalid into complying with Cook's instructions. At other times the household depended on her simply to amuse him. Only Pascale had the patience—developed over years of dealing with Papa who was also impossibly selfish and demanding when he was ill—to handle him.

Upon awakening, he seemed surprised that she had given

him shelter. He didn't ask any questions, except, "How long have I been here?"

"Four days. Papa brought you. Do you remember?"

"Yes."

John Douglas had been clearly eager to have her gone, so she had waited to make sure he was in no danger of relapsing, then had left. The valet fed him his first few meals, and Pascale assumed he'd explained that she'd discovered his presence soon after Jack's arrival. He never mentioned it at all events.

Pascale was only in and out of the sickroom a few times that first day. In the evening John Douglas had to go out again to meet Henry Bates, so she watched over him, as she had for the past few nights. It was different, now that he was awake. But Jack was still very weak. Pascale fed him broth whenever he'd eat, and then sat with him while he slept, for a while. When John Douglas returned at midnight, she left him to keep the vigil.

The next morning, Jack was more like his old self. He demanded real food, rather than gruel. He cursed Philippe and John Douglas when they tried to make him comfortable.

"Leave me be!" he shouted so loudly that Pascale heard him from her own room. She came up to see if she could help, which elicited only a scornful look, and a request to be left alone, couched in less than polite terms.

"Nonsense," she said, giving Philippe an encouraging nod. "Just grit your teeth for a moment, and these two strong men will have you all set up in no time."

He surrendered, though she suspected it was only because he had no choice. John Douglas thought he'd be better sitting up, so he and the footman slid the tall man's body up in the bed. Pascale winced sympathetically each time Jack's battered body was jarred by the movement. When Jack was no longer lying prone, he was able to feed himself. John Douglas shaved him, though, and Odelle brushed his hair, since he couldn't hold his arm up for long.

Pascale visited him, to relieve the staff, and most importantly John Douglas. Each time she saw him, he looked better. She ate some of her meals with him, telling him stories about her friends' escapades and her meetings with the strange people who hung about the fringe of the art world. Her father's adventures were always amusing. As when, two days after Jack had awakened, he happened upon Monsieur Nieuwerkerke, minister of fine arts, congratulating Renoir on those paintings of his that hung in the Salon. Though Papa had met the minister before, as recently as Princess Mathilde's party, the artist ignored the well-titled gentleman completely. When Renoir kindly reintroduced his old friend to the minister, Paul de Ravenault didn't recognize the name and said so. But he was kind enough to tell the minister of fine arts where to find the most interesting works in the exhibit.

As Pascale explained to Jack over a late second supper that same night, Papa's intentions were admirable. He had assumed, since Nieuwerkerke dressed in the latest fashion, and in the most expensive, that he was a man of taste and wealth. Therefore he could afford to buy his friends' works. In Papa's mind he was recommending a wise investment for the purchaser, and a nice sale for the artist. He could not understand the hilarity that greeted the story when Renoir repeated it at the café Guerbois that afternoon for Pascale's amusement. Jack appreciated it, though. He chuckled when told of the artist's naivete, and then grimaced at the pain in his side.

"Your father will be the ruin of you yet," he groaned.

Pascale bristled at that. "My father lacks some of the social graces, but he isn't intentionally rude. Unlike some I know. He blunders about, but he means well."

"Does he?" Devlin asked.

"Yes," she answered definitely. When Devlin said nothing more, she rose, unaccountably agitated by the exchange. She wandered across the room to the window. He was maddening, and unprincipled, to cast aspersions on her father's character, knowing she would not argue with him in his weakened state.

As though he read her mind, Jack said meekly, "I don't want to fight. Please sit."

Pascale took another turn about the room, but there was nothing else to do but to return to the little stool that sat beside his bed.

"I'm sorry," he said, when she was seated once again. "I think your loyalty to your father is admirable. I just don't think he needs you to protect him. *He* should be taking care of you."

His words did not soothe her. "I've been explaining this to you since we met. He is my only family. He may not be perfect, but he is everything to me."

"But you can only expect so much," Jack said. "You have pinned all your hopes on his work. You are supposed to be the practical one. You said he's like a child. You must have something else to fall back on. What if his paintings stop selling at some point?"

"Jack, you worry too much," she chided him. "Eat."

"Don't you see," he said earnestly, "you are devoted to a dream. Your father is talented. I have seen his work. But no painting is that important."

Pascale was not yet ready to discuss The Painting with him. He had lost it, and she could not quite forgive him. True, she no longer regarded the work as vehemently as she once had, but if he had returned it when she asked, it would at least have been preserved.

"Not to you, perhaps, but to us, to the de Ravenault family, it was very precious."

Jack sighed. "I wish there were something I could say to convince you—"

"It is probably better if we talk about something else," Pascale said quickly. In his ramblings, when he'd been delirious, he had made his feelings about the value of art quite clear. He didn't believe in its worth as she did. He had his own reasons, and they were good ones. But she knew they could never agree.

Pascale didn't want him to know that he had relived that

sad part of his youth while he'd been unconscious. She knew he would see through her understanding to the compassion that lay beneath it, and she was quite sure this was a man who would not tolerate pity. He was even surly when John Douglas tried to ease his pain. If he could not accept the sympathy of his long-suffering companion, Pascale had no hope of comforting him.

She adopted a brisk tone as she told him instead about the farm. "At home, I would recommend that you sit in the sun for an hour each day. The fresh country air aids in the healing process. You'd be up and about in no time, I've no doubt. The vineyard is only a short walk, and if that was too much for you, you could ride. The stables are not well stocked, but we have a gentle old mare who would be perfectly content to pull you in a gig. I think you could manage that, in a day or two. In a few weeks you could ride her. The lawns are quite smooth, and long enough for a good gallop, and the barn is just a few yards from the house."

By telling him about the farm, she hoped he would understand the de Ravenaults' circumstances in no way compared to those of him, his mother, and the mysterious Aunt Jane. She didn't know if her strategy had worked, but he sat back, watching her out of half-closed eyes, lids drooping as the medicine she'd given him began to take effect.

She kept talking. "The air here in Paris is laden with smoke, and the streets with garbage. Though I think Baron Haussmann is going to solve that little problem with his new sewers," she mused.

His lips tilted up in a half-smile as he said, "What a little optimist you are, Pascale. If anyone had told me the night we met that your ambitious soul masked such a soft heart, I wouldn't have believed them."

"I don't think I am any more optimistic than most people," Pascale retorted. "Nor do I think I am overly ambitious."

"For your father, you are," he said, his eyelids drifting fully shut.

The smile, which had formed on Pascale's lips in answer to his own, faded as she pondered his words. She had always thought herself too sensible to be an optimist—or indeed anything other than a devout realist. But Jack obviously saw something in her that Pascale could not. Her daily discussions with Jack always had the effect of making her question her own judgment, or wisdom. She didn't understand this strange power he yielded over her.

She watched him as he slept. She felt safe with the shadows of the moon cloaking the tiny room, content to watch the rise and fall of that broad nut-brown chest. John Douglas had washed Jack's hair earlier that day, and the soft black waves shone. He was beautiful, easily the prettiest man she had ever seen. And it was not just his body that drew her to him, it was his spirit also. She had learned a lot about him from his manservant. John Douglas was so proud of his success.

For herself, Pascale had found him to be unusually intelligent, and she was pleased even more by his articulation and knowledge of art, music, and literature. She would have thought they were well suited, if she'd met Jack under different circumstances.

It was his underlying aura of sensuality that most disturbed her. She remembered the feel of that well-formed mouth on her own, and the warmth of his hands at the nape of her neck. She had long since abandoned her shock when recalling the kisses they had shared. The memories of that embrace were as natural to her as breathing. Her heart's reaction to these lascivious thoughts still frightened her, though. She did not want to feel this strong pull toward him.

Pascale was certain that Jack was attracted to her, and he was clearly grateful for what she had done for him. But she sensed he still disapproved of her. He had once called her a shrew. She certainly bullied him these days; for his own good, of course. Perhaps that was how he still thought of her. Or did the expression in his eyes soften, as she imagined, when she faithfully arrived to attend to him at moonrise. She couldn't be sure.

This uncertainty was driving her mad. Worst of all, she didn't know how she would feel if he did care a little for her. She was afraid he might kiss her again, afraid of her own response. At the same time, she couldn't stop hoping that he would, so she could return his kiss. It was all very confusing, and well outside of her previous experience. There had been men who had been interested in her. There had even been one whose regard she'd returned. But there had never been anyone who had made her feel this way. No one had ever tempted her the way Jack did. And certainly no man had threatened to come between herself and her father. She had never contemplated marrying. That would entail leaving Papa. She planned to stay with him always.

She suspected that Jack Devlin didn't think much of Papa. He had made it clear, from the very first time they met, he didn't think the de Ravenaults, *père et fille,* had a proper relationship. His comment this evening had again shown that he didn't understand Pascale's ambition for her father. There was nothing wrong with it. It *was* her life. Let the captain scoff all he wanted. A man like Jack could never understand her motivations: love of Papa, but also love of the art itself.

She had never been able to explain that to other ordinary people. She was like them, so she understood that they couldn't see beyond the need for a comfortable living, a place to live, food to eat, a family. But she also understood artists, better sometimes than they did themselves. They, too, were human, and they, too, enjoyed fresh fruit, candles to provide light, firewood to provide warmth. But they were driven by some inner compulsion to spend their energies instead on producing their works of art. So, Pascale fulfilled these needs for them. She was able to do it. And her reward was not only seeing it done, but also participating, just a little bit, in the difficult work of nurturing and developing their talents. She took a little bit of credit for the artwork her father had created in the past, and would create in the future.

Jack would never understand, especially since deep down he was prejudiced against artists' behavior. But he could appreciate her business sense. She could cozen a fishmonger out of half a day's wares with a handful of coins and a smile. She could raise the price of a painting by fifty francs with a discreet nod and a cough. Those were talents that Jack Devlin could admire, if he cared to.

Pascale's gaze wandered again to his chest, rising and falling as he slept. He would not awaken again until the small hours. She brushed his hair off his forehead, then leaned over him, planning to kiss his forehead as she would a child she'd just tucked in. John Douglas entered the room, and Pascale swiftly straightened up and busied herself arranging the uneaten food to be returned to the kitchen in the morning.

"Sleeping like a baby," the manservant grunted.

"He needs his rest."

"Yes, he does, so if you two don't mind."

They both jumped at the sound of Jack's voice. Pascale couldn't hide her chagrin from John Douglas, who just smiled knowingly and tiptoed from the room. She looked at the wretch lying quietly in the bed, sure that he knew what she had almost done. Embarrassment and exasperation fought for dominance within her, and embarrassment won. She tucked her tail between her legs, and ran.

Fifteen

Jack woke with a start, to find Philippe standing over him. *"Bonjour, Capitaine.* I shave you?"

"Where the devil is John Douglas?" Jack asked. The Frenchman gave one of those Gallic shrugs that were so expressive. Philippe neither knew, nor cared, where Jack's valet had gone.

"I shave?"

Jack slowly and painfully inched his way up into a sitting position, growling at the footman-turned-barber, when he tried to help, "I can do it!"

Every morning that he woke up in this state, he despaired. The healing process was slow and painful, and he had no patience for it. He had to get back on his feet. He owed his life to Henry Bates and John Douglas, and he was grateful to them for saving him, and for all they had done since. They searched diligently for answers to the questions that plagued him, but he wanted to find out for himself what in blazes had happened.

He closed his eyes while Philippe honed his razor's blade. The footman hummed tunelessly as he worked, but Jack was too immersed in thought to pay any heed. Jack was sure that the bombing had something to do with that message he carried for the government of France to the ruler whom Napoleon had installed in Mexico. But, for the life of him, Jack couldn't think who could have wanted to stop the message of support from reaching Maximilian. Napoleon's stance was no secret. Could this really have been the work of forces in the government who wanted to undermine the power of Napoleon III?

Or was the traitor one of the Mexican émigrés who lived in Paris? He found it hard to believe that any of these sad homeless souls was an insurgent in disguise. Nor was it easy to picture a group of the émigrés secretly meeting to plan the overthrow of Maximilian. He had shown himself willing to restore—by force, if necessary—the power of the Catholic Church to all its former glory. But, Jack had to admit, Maximilian did not have the money, or the men, required to undertake that task. Perhaps his supporters had become his enemies.

John Douglas had no access to the Mexican émigrés, whereas Jack—a link to the country they had left behind—was always welcomed by them. He needed to gauge for himself the level of support that they had for Maximilian. They might also have among them someone who was using them to undermine Napoleon's power in his own country, or with the Pope, or even with his wife.

Jack also wanted to meet face-to-face with Richard Trenton. His supposed friend had gotten him involved in this intrigue in the first place. He needed to question the young politician about who could have known of the mission. He had already sent a message to Richard's office, but he hadn't received any reply. He hoped to arrange another clandestine meeting, like their first. So he'd requested that his friend arrange one, ostensibly with John Douglas, who had been instructed not only to be very much on his guard but to try and discover if any danger lurked about the person of Jack's old friend.

Jack chafed at sending others out to conduct these interviews, which he could more effectively handle. He worried that he was putting his friends' lives in jeopardy. The worst restriction of all, of course, was not being able to publicly divulge his whereabouts, which would be perilous to his new friends, the de Ravenaults. He appreciated their concern for his safety and well-being. He could only reciprocate by making sure that no one knew where he was. John Douglas and Henry Bates were the only ones, outside of the de Ravenault household, who knew he was alive. Until he was up and about again, and far from his hosts' care, he could not risk publicizing the fact that he had survived the "accident."

It was not only his conscience that dictated his behavior. The more time he spent with young Pascale, the more protective he felt toward her. Jack was insatiably curious about the little minx, who was such a contradiction: soft as a flower one moment, a tigress the next. He had learned a lot about the woman while he'd been forced to lie helpless in her footman's bedchamber. She was forthright and honest, strong and resilient. He had suspected as much before he left Paris; now he had seen the evidence of it with his own eyes. She took care of her father, his house, and now, Jack as well.

François and Guillaume's devotion to Pascale had been clear to see. They said she was brilliant, not only as her father's agent for his work, but also as the chatelaine of his estate, and overseer of his farm. According to Pierre, the butler, it was she who had saved the vineyards from financial ruin. It was clear the chit took her responsibilities seriously, and managed the burden she had taken on with incredible skill. There was little danger that this one would make the mistakes his aunt and mother had—even for the sake of her beloved art. Pascale might be as idealistic as his aunt Jane about the value of art, but there any resemblance ended.

She was more intelligent and sensible than any woman he had ever met. She pretended to be hard-hearted and totally self-sufficient, but he could see through the pose to the caring, sensitive woman beneath. Even her pensioners spoke of her always with affection and admiration. Jack had become quite adept at setting them to talking about their mistress. He found it took his mind off of the frustrating situation he found himself in.

As Philippe approached, having completed the preparations for the delicate operation of shaving him, Jack decided to try a new line of inquiry; into Pascale's past. Philippe had grown up in the de Ravenault's château in Beaune, where his father had been first footman before him and he and Pascale had played together as children.

"Pascale used to paint when she was a child, didn't she?" Jack asked in French.

"Pascale paint *très bien*," Philippe said in his halting English. The footman insisted that he wanted to learn to speak English while he had Jack to "practice" with, despite the fact that Jack's French was much better than his English.

"*Sa père*, her father, has many student, *mais* Pascale were different. Not whoosh . . ." His hands formed an explosion. "*Avec couleur.* Always she paint flowers, people, perfect. She were just so when she begin *a peinture.*" Philippe put his hand out between them at waist level, and Jack understood him to be demonstrating Pascale's height at the time.

The footman tended to wave his hands as he talked, and since he held the razor, Jack feared for his life with every sentence. But he was too curious to suggest Philippe concentrate on shaving him.

"You grew up with her, eh?"

"Grew?"

Jack used his good hand to illustrate. "Grew . . ." he said, holding his hand out at the side of the bed. ". . . up," he raised his hand to the level of his head.

Philippe nodded. "Ah. Yes. I begin working when I have twelve. Pascale working now, too. Not painting." He searched his mind for the words he wanted. "In house, with Louise. You know, Louise."

"The cook."

Philippe nodded. "Pascale and Louise, and Odelle. Also, she help make *vin.*"

"She worked in the vineyards."

Philippe nodded. "*Oui.* She is in field, tell mens what to do."

"And she painted, too."

"*Non.* Mademoiselle stop." He shook his head. "*Quel dommage.* So many *artistes en château. Tres mal.*" He shook his head, in disgust. "Paint faces. No eyes, no nose, no mouth." He covered his face with his hand, to illustrate. "But she . . ." He kissed his fingers. "I always say, *'Bien,* Pascale. *Merveilleux!'* But too much work, in house, in field. *Elle ne peinte pas.* She no paint, her."

From the one small sample that Jack had seen—the sketch she'd done as a pattern for her embroidery—he agreed with Philippe. She had talent. Philippe left him and Jack sat, staring into space, as an idea began to form in his mind. Pascale was clearly an artist at heart. François and Guillaume had made it clear that she'd been one of the most promising young artists they'd seen. She had dedication; she'd devoted her entire life to the pursuit of art, even if it was the work of her father and his friends and students. She'd mentioned once that she had tried to live the life of an artist and failed—but Jack believed she would have been a more successful artist than many of the others he'd met.

For the rest of the day, he mulled over the idea that Pascale might be a true *artiste* herself, but for some reason—despite her love of art—she denied it. Most telling was her blind devotion to her father. Her mission in life was protecting him: they'd argued about it ever since they met. But Jack thought the old man was quite capable of defending himself, or ignoring those hardships from which she tried so hard to shield him.

In Jack's experience, artists were a thick-skinned lot who saved their sensitivity for their work and who were able to withstand ridicule and rejection even more, not less, than ordinary men. Paul was a good example. The old man seemed a sly old fox to him, especially where his daughter was concerned. She was his glorified (and unpaid) housekeeper, his devoted wife and his admiring child, as well as his representative in the world of art—all for the price of an occasional kiss on the cheek.

He knew the old man loved her, but if de Ravenault had been a proper father, he'd have made arrangements for his daughter to have a fulfilling life of her own. She could be an artist, herself. Or she could do what other women did—marry and raise a family. She certainly deserved a husband who would love her as she needed to be loved: a man who could give her a house full of children to chase after and shower with the love she now bestowed upon her father and his cronies. She needed a man who would cherish and protect her.

Jack almost wished he could be the one to show her how beautiful and desirable she was. She was everything he could imagine wanting in a woman. But she was also out of his reach. Unfortunately, she was an innocent, not at all suited to a man like himself. A liaison between them could only bring her pain. This was not a seasoned courtier ripe for a tryst. Jack could recognize at a glance the hardened prostitute within the genteel lady of quality. On his first few visits to London, he had been seduced by women of that stamp—eager to "try" the young black sailor, whom they found to be surprisingly well educated, and well versed with the manners and morals of the upper classes.

The education he'd received from "Aunt" Jane until the age of twelve had made him a rarity in London society. His mother's employer had insisted that he received the same tutoring a son of her own might have expected. She'd even taught him herself, passing along her love of art, music, and literature to the little boy whom she'd adopted as her own. His lessons had been of the kind that only the nobility, or the very wealthy, could boast. For the past five years, his business had given him an introduction to the exclusive circles of the ton. He had not found much to interest him in it. He had not belonged there.

Nor could he take up residence in Pascale's world. She was, like himself, well educated, but, unlike Jack, she had the breeding to go with her upbringing. Pascale might not ever be a prominent member of upper-class society, but with her lineage she was not a commoner, either. He couldn't steal a lady's heart. He couldn't risk breaking something so rare and fine.

Still . . . he could not regret the kisses they had exchanged before he left Paris. Sometimes she looked at him, in such a way, as to seem she was remembering that night, and that look in her eyes made his resolve waver. But he was too practical to give in to his desire for her. They could not be together. She was not for him.

She belonged here, in Paris, enjoying the Society he had no patience for. She was passionate and exciting, the kind of woman a man dreamed of, but rarely found. Jack knew the right man could bring out the passion she now spent on her father and *his* art. She innocently displayed an innate sensuality in her gaze and in her touch when she admired *objets d'art*. She denied herself any release, though. He was tempted beyond measure to show her that the human anatomy was designed to delight the senses in many other ways, as well as by being captured in clay or on canvas.

Jack groaned. Immediately, John Douglas's sleepy voice sounded from the shadows at the foot of the bed.

"Are you all right, Captain?"

"Yes," Jack said impatiently.

"Arm hurt?"

"Only a little," Jack lied. "Go back to sleep, John."

He was careful not to move until he heard the snoring of his faithful companion, then he tried to ease into a more comfortable position. Between the pain in his chest and his tightly bound arm, Jack couldn't maneuver very well in the small bed, and eventually gave up. He was determined not to let John Douglas dose him with any more of Louise's home-brewed medicine, which made him groggier than the laudanum he'd taken when he'd been wounded in the Navy.

He was awake the rest of the night, his thoughts alternating between strategies to discover all he wanted to know about the explosion that had cost him the *Aurora,* and plans to liberate Pascale from her self-imposed isolation. By the time the house started to stir, he was in a foul mood.

Jack ate the gruel Louise sent up for his breakfast, instead of throwing it at Odelle. He suffered silently the painful man-handling by Philippe and John Douglas as they bathed him. He even managed to be civil, if curt, as he explained for the fourth time in as many days why he had no message for Paul de Ravenault to deliver to François and Guillaume. But when Pascale came to coax him out of the doldrums, he snapped.

He knew damn well that she'd been sent by John Douglas, with wishes of good luck and Godspeed from the other members of the household who'd come in contact with him that morning. It wasn't her patronizing, sympathetic greeting that caused his bad temper, although that didn't help. It was the way that they all took advantage of her that triggered the outburst. Couldn't anyone else see that this lovely young woman should be cherished, her kind heart guarded against the pain that could be inflicted by bastards like himself? Pascale could not help but respond to their appeals for comfort and protection. But those who placed this burden upon her were all, like himself, older and hardier than she.

"What is the matter with you?" he asked, unable to contain his spleen. "Can't you see that this is not noble? Your attention is not welcome. This self sacrifice is useless. I thought you were smarter than that."

He hated himself for lambasting her, but she bore the brunt of his irate diatribe, without once bowing her head, or even trying to defend herself. He'd seen this before, in men so used to their powerlessness that they could no longer imagine any other way of life. But Pascale did not respond to his sarcastic, hurtful remarks in the flat, defeated monotone of one who expected no more from themselves than to serve as an outlet for his hostility.

"What will it take to make you realize you're just throwing your life away on a bunch of bloody ingrates. Don't just stand there! Go away! Leave me alone and don't come back! That's all that I deserve."

Instead he just kept trying to goad her. "I had another talk with your father this morning," he said, knowing that criticism of her pater was the one thing that really got her goat. "I still cannot understand how someone so obtuse could have a daughter like yourself."

"He told me," she said, clearly determined not to argue with him, even if he insulted her beloved parent. "You really should not be surprised. Papa is not like you or me. It will never truly penetrate that thick skull of his that your presence here could bring danger down on us all."

Jack felt even guiltier at her matter-of-fact response. This made his ire grow. "But I've explained it to him half a dozen times, and each time it's like the first time. I'm lying in this bed in front of him. I know what I look like. You'd think that that, at least, would serve as a reminder of the perilous situation in which he has placed us all by bringing me here."

"Perhaps if you could tell us exactly who we are hiding you from, he would remember that," she suggested, calmly.

"You are safer if you don't know," Jack said.

"Well then, for an artist like my father—"

Jack interrupted the familiar litany with a heartfelt moan.

Pascale raised her eyebrows at him, but continued to speak without missing a beat. "For an artist like my father, your visit to us is not remarkable. You are just another guest. Artists who are truly dedicated to their work don't often have time to notice the world outside of their studios and their canvases."

"I notice that he has time and money enough to while away hour upon hour of fruitless gossiping at the café Guerbois."

"Ah, but you see . . ." Pascale's eyes twinkled at him, inviting him to share a private joke with her. "That's truly important."

Jack was still too annoyed to smile, though he could feel his anger subsiding under Pascale's deft touch. He couldn't figure out how she could appreciate the irony of her father's foolishness, and yet not see how he used her so badly.

"He is hopeless," Jack said, with less heat.

"Yes. But talented," Pascale reposted.

"You should give up on him, Pascale."

"That's funny. He said the same thing about you." He felt a reluctant tugging at the corners of his mouth.

"We're probably both right. You should find a man more worthy of you than either of us."

"Better than you?" She mockingly pretended incredulity at his statement. This time her quick wit forced a rueful smile out of him.

"There might be one or two," he said.

"Ah, but what would I do with him, Jack? I wouldn't know how to talk to a reasonable man. Come to think of it, I don't think I've ever met one."

"He's out there," he assured her. "I have it on the best authority." She slanted a look of inquiry at him. "My mother," he joked. "She swears I'm a foundling. She couldn't have given birth to someone so selfish and ungrateful."

"You are neither of those things," Pascale averred loyally. "And neither is my father."

"We are, Pascale," he said seriously. "And you are . . . not." Jack couldn't say more than that. He didn't think she would believe him if he told her she was the most delightful, unselfish, bewitching creature he had ever met.

"Who are you to judge? You have never done anything more important than pile up money and possessions," she lectured earnestly. "Admit it, Jack, you haven't had a thought in years that didn't revolve around becoming a success in business."

"And your father has?" he asked.

"Yes. There are more important things in life than money or even recognition. Papa learned that long ago. He creates beautiful works of art and that is enough for him. I think you could learn a lot from him."

"I'm sure I could," Jack said sardonically. Pascale looked up at him, a troubled expression in her eyes. "You don't have to take care of him, Pascale. He should be taking care of you."

She wavered for a moment, poised to challenge the remark. He wished that she would. But instead she took her leave of him.

She had done what she'd set out to do, he supposed. She had worked her magic, and assuaged his anger. She was remarkable. She was also, as far as he could see, totally unprepared for the day that was coming—the day when she realized her foolish papa was never going to live up to her ideals. Maybe, just maybe, he could help. Pascale would hate him for thinking it. But it was the least he could do.

Sixteen

Pascale might be uneasy around him, but the rest of the household was in awe of Captain Devlin's ferocious temper. It wasn't just that he roared so loudly, it was the cold expression in his eyes when he became displeased that proved frightening. So she tried to spend as much time with Jack as she could, just to relieve the staff of the duty, of course. As she returned home from another afternoon of business happily combined with the pleasure of seeing her friends, she thought of the party that evening at Madame Manet's house. That should provide interesting material for stories for Jack.

It amazed Pascale that she could go on with her life, as though nothing remarkable had happened, while Jack spent his days lying helpless in her footman's bedchamber. She wished that she could tell Guillaume, at least, about Jack's infirmity—he was such a sweet soul, she was sure he would have helped her to try and keep Jack in good spirits. But she realized that the knowledge might put her dear friend in danger. John Douglas grew more withdrawn and nervous with every passing day. She did not think his inquiries were proceeding as he, or Jack, had planned.

So she was not at all surprised when John Douglas greeted her with less than his usual aplomb. "He hasn't smiled since you left this morn," was his report. "Seemingly you're the only one who can do a thing for him."

Pascale sometimes wondered if John Douglas was not trying his hand at a bit of matchmaking, since he jealously guarded his friend from everyone but herself. If he was, she feared he was doomed to disappointment. Jack had been a perfect gentleman since his return.

"I'll run up and see him. But I do have an engagement this evening, so I won't be able to stay for long," she reminded him.

"I hadn't forgotten, miss. I'll come up in half an hour."

Pascale ran up the stairs, barely pausing in her room to throw the notes from today's meetings onto her desk. She arrived at Jack's door just in time to catch sight of him leaning precariously out of the bed to place his heavy tray on the floor. With only one good arm, he had to twist himself into an ungainly position, and she held her breath until he was upright again.

"You would never know you were once a man of sense," Pascale scolded, coming into the room.

"I only wanted to get that monstrosity off my lap," he defended himself. "My entire upper body is already incapacitated, I don't want to add my legs to the roster."

Pascale sincerely pitied him. She couldn't imagine how she would feel if she were confined to a sickbed. She was a remarkably healthy girl, and had rarely been laid low in her life. It would have been unbearably boring to be stuck in one place all day.

"I've brought you the newspapers," she said briskly, never daring to let him see how very much she felt for him. "Shall I read them to you?"

"I thought you had a soiree to attend this evening," Jack said.

"I do. But I have a few minutes, if you want some company." He shrugged.

She opened the newspaper to the first page and started to translate the French into English, but she was barely conscious of the words before her eyes. Pascale worried that she might not be able to keep Jack in this little bed, or even in their little house, for very much longer. He was growing so impatient.

She had been concerned, almost from the start, about what might happen to him if his whereabouts were discovered. As if his poor mangled body wasn't enough of a clue that he was in danger, his secretive arrival and subsequent behavior made her sure of it. She was afraid for him, should he decide to leave. She was afraid for herself if he stayed.

Sometimes, Jack looked at her so strangely. It was clear that he saw her somewhat differently now than he had before he left. What exactly comprised the difference—of that she wasn't sure. There had been a change in his attitude, and in his voice, when he spoke to her. He'd mocked her before, and he still tried to goad her to anger, but that seemed to be because he resented her care, and didn't want her pity.

She thought it might be gratitude that he felt toward her. That wasn't what she wanted. She'd had enough of that from Papa and all the other men she'd met in her life. The students and friends of her father, whose needs she'd catered to when they stayed at her home in Beaune, had more than once been inspired to think themselves in love with her because she took care of them. It had been a nuisance each time. She didn't think she could stand it if all he felt for her was gratitude.

There had been a boy once, who had loved her out of gratitude, and that had been terrible. She didn't want to be desired because she was capable and practical and resourceful. She wanted to be admired for the same reasons other women were admired, for her beauty, such as it was, and her charm and grace. Most of all, she wanted a man, just once, to look at her and see her as she was—and be attracted to everything that was in her, including her insensible passion for beauty, and the flaws she tried to hide; her rebellious desire to thumb her nose at society and live as she wished, and her selfish wish to please only herself just once.

She was reading mechanically and didn't notice anything amiss until Jack interrupted her, "What was that?"

Pascale had not really been attending to her reading—she'd

read the newspaper earlier, and this section was devoted to the city and its problems.

She looked back over the article she had just read. It was gruesome, the kind of story that she read with vague disbelief, as though the author invented it. "An unidentified man was found today in the marketplace at Les Halles. The body of the dead man was found stuffed into a barrel, of the kind generally used to transport potatoes, carrots, and other vegetables." Things like this weren't unusual in Paris. When she thought about them, they made her wish she were home in Beaune.

She looked up at Jack, who was listening intently. "When Monsieur Furan, an apple farmer from the Loire Valley, closed up his shop today, he noticed that he had one more container than he'd arrived with. On closer inspection, he discovered the remains of a gentleman of medium height, and weight, and brown hair and eyes. Police have released the following information about the murder victim: a part of his ear was missing. They have asked that anyone who has any information about this individual, or the crime, please come forward."

Pascale looked up at Jack who was clearly stunned by the news. "Did you know him?" she asked.

"Which part of his ear?"

She had not been able to translate the word into English, but when he pulled on his own earlobe she nodded. "This is not a common thing, is it?"

"I don't know. Do they say anything more?"

"No, but if you think you may know this man, perhaps I should contact the newspaper—"

"No!" He stopped her immediately. "I am sure we will know soon enough who it might be." He tried to pretend he was unconcerned but he was lying to her. Jack knew this man, and the news of his death had alarmed him.

Pascale was well aware that Jack and his stalwart companion John Douglas were trying to find information—perhaps they hoped for revenge for the loss of the *Aurora*. She knew it had been destroyed, not by lightning but by design. John Douglas had let that fact slip.

"I could say I thought I knew him. What is the name of your friend with the missing ear? Perhaps if the police had a name, they could find out if it's the same man. They wouldn't have to know about you." She would have liked to know more about the forces that had brought him here.

"Leave it, Pascale. It's not that important."

"A moment ago it was important."

"I don't want you involved in this."

"Why, because it's dangerous? What about this? Knowing about this?" She gave the paper a shake. "Is that dangerous?"

"My men will take care of it."

"I might be able to help." Pascale wished he trusted her. But she imagined that even if Jack did think she deserved his honesty, he would still not take her into his confidence if he thought it might put her in danger.

His next words confirmed it. "I don't want you to draw anyone's attention to you."

"Perhaps I'll do that anyway, in my ignorance."

He only shook his head, stubbornly. There was nothing she could do. She couldn't force him to divulge his secrets.

Still, she couldn't totally hide her pique as she said, "Good night, then. I must prepare for the Manets' party. Your valet will be here shortly."

"Ah yes, Madame Manet's Thursday evenings. Your father is looking forward to it, is he not?"

Pascal looked up at him suspiciously. "You sounded just then as though you were in charity with Papa again?"

"I am just trying to be civil, Pascale."

"Why?" she asked.

"My business with your father is between the two of us."

"I thought you two would stop playing these little games now that The Painting is gone." He held her gaze steadily and it was she who looked away first. She said with all the dignity she could muster, "No matter. You men may keep your clandestine rendezvous. As long as they don't involve me." She knew it sounded petty, but she was hurt that Jack and Papa continued to hide things from her.

"But everything Paul does concerns you, doesn't it? One way or another." He was so smug. She would have liked to wipe that self-assured expression from his face. But she would not deign to answer him. "You cannot let go of this ridiculous notion that you were born just to care for your father." He paused, probably waiting for an argument. They'd discussed this before. She wouldn't give him the satisfaction of getting a rise out of her. "It is supposed to be the other way around," he continued.

"I'm his daughter. And I understand him, which you never could. You have been alone, responsible for nothing and no one but your own happiness for too long," she said calmly.

Jack shook his head in disagreement, "No. I think it is you who have been alone for too long," he said.

"I? I am hardly ever alone."

"Aren't you?" The look he sent her was quizzical, and she averted her eyes. Pascale didn't know how to respond to his question. She couldn't honestly say no, but neither would it have been quite true to say yes.

Perhaps she had felt a little lonely at times, but Papa had been there when she needed him. And he'd raised her to be self-sufficient, independent, free spirited, and free thinking, so that she had always been able to depend on herself, if not on him. Pascale sighed. She had certainly had to accept some hard truths since she'd met this man. He challenged everything she believed in: art, her work, her relationship with her father. But she had to believe in Papa. He was all she had.

When The Painting had been lost, and Jack as well—the first and only man she had ever met whose smile alone could make her pulse race—she'd felt both lonely and frightened. Her father had seemed almost a stranger to her then. His lies about The Painting and about Jack had been hard to understand, but she had tried. And she'd put it behind her. But, in the end, she had felt very much alone.

When Papa rescued Jack from his predicament, he had, in effect, saved Pascale as well. Since their irascible patient had awakened, he'd constantly tried to create a wedge between herself and Papa. This time he'd hit a delicate nerve. As his question, and all it implied, slowly sank in, Pascale found herself resenting his insight. She couldn't blame her father for his nature—even if his thoughtlessness did sometimes hurt her. She could and did blame Jack for twisting the knife in an open wound, which he had done, so far as she could tell, purely out of meanness of spirit. She had done nothing to him that merited this treatment at his hands.

"This is not something I wish to discuss with you," she said, sharply.

"And yet, we always come back to this, don't we." He was infuriating.

"Yes because *you* can't seem to leave it alone. Why can't you just leave Papa out of this?" She did not want to hear any more derisive remarks about her father.

"I was thinking about that, too," Jack said. "And I think I've figured it out. It bothers me. He is a selfish old man, and you are a sweet young woman. He doesn't deserve the attention you lavish upon him. And that bothers me."

"Selfish? You of all people should know how generous he is. Why Papa brought you here even though you lost The Painting."

"I didn't lose it. I hid it. Here, in Paris. He wanted to know where it was."

Openmouthed, Pascale gaped at him.

"I sent him a message before I set sail, that I was not transporting it farther away, in case he changed his mind about showing it to you before he disposed of it. His motives in bringing me here were far from pure."

"What!" Pascale was astounded.

She had not many illusions left about Papa. He'd lied to her about finishing The Painting, then about hiring Jack to spirit it away, and finally he'd let her believe Jack was dead. She had been able to convince herself that he hadn't realized how badly he hurt her. But to have lied again, implying that The Painting was lost—after all they had been through—was too much for her to take in. For Devlin to aid him in his various deceptions—and then accuse him of being wrong—was outrageous.

She felt this latest betrayal to her soul. Jack watched her expectantly, during the long pregnant silence that followed his announcement. She felt her control start to slip away when her eyes met his.

"How dare you judge us," she said, steel voiced.

"I am not judging you or your father," he protested. "You seem to think that he is somehow exempt from the rules that govern other men's behavior. I disagree, as you know. I think he should treat you, at least, with a modicum of consideration and respect."

"He does." At Jack's disbelieving look, Pascale said defensively, "If Papa is a bit absentminded, a trifle thoughtless, it is only because his art consumes him."

"His art is first with him. It is not the same thing. You hide behind this idea that he serves a greater good, and through him you do as well. But you cannot hide behind his work forever. You have to face the truth about him, and about yourself."

At that moment she honestly hated him. "The truth? The truth is there is nothing, nowhere, for a talented artist to count on but the people who appreciate his work. No one else understands why one must continually dedicate oneself to the process of creation. The time needed, and the concentration, is intense. I know. I tried and I couldn't do it. I could not devote myself solely to it and cut myself off from other people."

"Who told you that? Him?"

She could have hit him. Instead she bit out the words, "No. He encouraged my studies, and helped me. I realized all on my own that I didn't have the right nature to be an artist. Few people do. Papa must."

It was Jack's turn to stare in disbelief. "Do you purposely choose to blind yourself to the truth. Your friends are all men and women who devote themselves to the same ideals that you do. But they do the thing. Your precious papa has allowed you to give up everything for him. Can't you see there's something wrong with that."

As she seethed with anger, Pascale was struck by the irony of the situation. She'd been worried that all Jack felt toward her was gratitude. With these remarks, he proved himself ungrateful indeed. He had lied to her, and now he threw it into her face.

"How dare *you* question my ideals. You are just an adventurer, a mercenary. You do not know a thing about Papa and me."

"I know that you think you've created a safe place to hide from the world. The father you worship is just an illusion to make you feel useful and loved. You don't need all of that. You certainly don't need to fawn all over your father this way. He loves you. You're his daughter."

"I know that. You are the one who keeps forgetting it."

"I don't forget. I just see that he doesn't treat you as he should. He should care more for you than he does for his own comfort, and I see no evidence of that."

Pascale snorted in disgust. "You think I should demand that Papa repay each act of love with an equal act which demonstrates his regard and affection. Love is not a business transaction. I pity you if that's what you think it is."

If the cruel remark fazed him, Jack didn't show it. "No, I don't. But I know what it isn't."

"Do you? I don't think you do." She continued to rant at him, goaded beyond endurance. "Everything to you is just commerce. This for that. I knew it from the moment I met you. You're just like every other merchant I ever met. Everything you do is to serve your own purposes."

"If that is so," he argued reasonably, "then what purpose do you suppose I have in saying all this to you?"

"To hurt me," she answered honestly. "Not consciously perhaps, but because you were angry, maybe even frightened, at the news of your friend's death. I do not know exactly what his death meant to you, but I do know you were more deeply affected than you want to admit by that article in the newspaper. And I think that made you angry. I am here, so you are angry at me."

"Do you really think I would ill-use you so?" Jack asked.

"Why ever not? What am I to you? Nothing more than an ill-mannered shrew with whom you've jousted twice daily during a visit to France. You would think no more of wounding my feelings than you would of flinging a diseased rat from your ship into the sea."

He started to protest, but apparently thought better of it and subsided without saying anything. Pascale waited, perfectly prepared to continue telling him what she thought of him.

"Well," she urged, "have you nothing to say?"

"You have confounded me with your reading of my character," he said. "I didn't realize you despised me so," he said coolly.

"B-but I . . . ," Pascale stammered, about to disabuse the gentleman of the notion that he was so loathsome to her, but she stopped herself. This was the perfect opportunity to end this torturous association forever. If she left him now, she would no longer have to suffer his unsettling presence. She would not be forced into constant contact with him. She would escape those compelling eyes; those tempting lips, which uttered such unfeeling words. If she just walked away, Pascale could return to some semblance of her normal self, and recapture the even tenor of her orderly, purposeful existence.

It was her pride that wouldn't let her do it. Pascale didn't want him to know that his criticism held enough truth to dent her armor in the slightest. She would not give him that much power over her. With that thought her common sense finally reasserted itself.

"Don't be ridiculous," she said, the composed facade she usually presented to the world slipping back into place. She lowered her eyes, further masking her emotions and said as lightly as she could, "I do not despise you."

"That is a great relief to me," Jack said wryly.

"Yes, well, I must go and prepare for my party." Pascale gave him a cursory smile, without meeting his eyes, and left the room.

Seventeen

The walk to her own bedchamber seemed unusually long. Just as she reached her door, she heard someone on the stairs. Pascale waited, her hand on the doorknob, until she saw John Douglas come into view. She walked back to meet him at the top of the stairs.

"John Douglas, you would tell me if Jack were in any real danger here, wouldn't you?"

He thought about her question for a moment before he answered. "I suppose so, miss. But it would be up to the captain, of course. . . ." His voice trailed off as he looked at her speculatively. Pascale supposed he was wondering whether he should tell her the truth.

"I am sure he will not tell me anything. But I think he is in grave danger. I was reading him the newspaper, and he seemed quite upset by an article about a man who was murdered." John Douglas's thick eyebrows lifted. From the stoic valet, this was a sign of some distress. "I want you to know that I want to be of help. The captain is not well, and I do not think he understands how that might . . ." She searched for the word she wanted, but couldn't think of the English. She had to settle for saying, ". . . slow him down more than he realizes."

"I see what you're saying, miss. He may be too stupid to see, but I do appreciate what you've done for us. I knew you were a right one from the start."

Pascale nodded her thanks for the compliment, and they

parted company. At least, she was on good terms with Jack's valet. She was able to hold on to her weary smile until she reached the haven of her bedroom. Once there, she felt the very life drain out of her. Her spirits fell, like a kite suddenly deserted by the breeze that held it aloft.

She couldn't seem to catch her breath. Pascale felt as though a heavy weight sat on her chest. She couldn't cry, the hurt went too deep for tears. She had never thought to ask whether The Painting had indeed been lost. She had thought The Portrait of the Lady forever beyond her grasp, and they had let her believe it. It was this last betrayal that caused her the most pain. How could they do that to her? How could Papa lie to her again, and again, and again? She did not know how she could face him.

He came to find her just as Pascale was dragging herself listlessly through the last steps of her toilette. Her reflection in the mirror showed her that she looked just as she always had. The brown-skinned woman in the emerald-green silk evening dress looked serene, and self-assured. Her black hair had been smoothed back with heated combs and scented oil, black curls had been pinned to her crown and they cascaded over her shoulders and down her back. Her eyes were bright. Only the most astute observer could have guessed that their sheen was caused by anything other than her excitement at the prospect of the party.

Papa didn't seem to notice anything amiss. "Come along, *chérie*. We don't want to be too late this evening."

"I'm not going," she said sadly. "I have the headache."

He started to turn away, but came back to stand behind her. Pascale could see the troubled expression on his face reflected in the mirror before her.

"Pascale?" he said tentatively.

"Yes, Papa," she answered.

"Is something wrong?"

"Why do you ask?" She decided at that moment not to tell him that Jack had told her about The Painting.

"Well, I thought, or rather I felt, I just thought maybe you were unhappy," he stammered. She didn't feel the slightest compunction at his discomfort. She would persuade the captain to give The Painting to her, or she would never see it—but she wouldn't beg her father for a privilege she'd already earned.

"What could be wrong?" she asked, hoping against hope that he would tell her the truth.

He sat looking at her for a moment. She met his gaze. He looked away. "Oh, well, if you say so," he said cravenly. Something in her expression must have alerted him to the fact that his answer hadn't satisfied her completely. "I love you, Pascale," he said.

It wasn't enough. She didn't believe him. She had to accept the truth. If he didn't trust her enough to tell her about The Painting, how could he say he loved her?

Pascale rose at once, surprising herself as much as her father. Jack's revelation had been a shock, but this . . . this was frightening. Her world was unraveling around her. Pascale could not stop remembering all of the treasured moments that she had shared with her father over the years. She felt, for a moment, almost nostalgic for the way things had been. However, she could not bring herself to act as though nothing had changed. She'd always been pleased and proud of Paul de Ravenault. But it would have disgusted her to—what had Jack called it—"fawn" all over Papa when he'd once again played her false.

"Papa, you should go." She was surprised that her voice was so steady.

"Pascale?"

"Leave me! Go to your party!" He recoiled.

"What is it, *ma fille*," he asked, reaching out a hand to her. "I can't leave you like this."

"Don't touch me," she managed to grate out. "Just go. There is nothing you can do for me right now."

He finally left her alone. Pascale sat down again at her dressing table, staring at her reflection. The woman in the mirror was still deceptively elegant and sophisticated while Pascale felt as though she was breaking into a million pieces. Tears threatened, but she swallowed hard, holding them inside. Her anger had settled into a hard knot in the pit of her stomach.

How had she come to this? How could she have been so wrong? She had thought she was on the right path. She had worked so hard; for Papa, and for herself. And yet, it had all proven to be for nothing. The Painting was hidden from her. Her father was not the man she thought him. And Jack Devlin, whom she had almost started to like, had been lying to her all along. Obviously he didn't care about her at all.

Pascale was thoroughly disgusted with herself. She had thought herself so strong—so invincible. But she had just been a foolish dupe all along. She stood and started to strip out of her clothes like a woman possessed. She needed a hot bath. She rang for Odelle to request heated water.

She wanted to submerge herself in liquid warmth until she melted the ice that was creeping through her veins, and then wrap herself in soft clean towels warmed by the fire. She wanted to sleep, and wake to find it had all been a terrible dream. She wished she could start her life over again.

Pascale sat on the edge of her bed, shivering. She tried to think, but only one thought kept running through her brain. What could she do now? She had had one dream for as long as she could remember and now it was gone. Even if she got The Painting back, she could never undo the harm that Devlin had caused with his callous words about her father.

She could never trust Papa again.

Paul de Ravenault said nothing the next morning about what had occurred the night before in Pascale's bedroom. At the breakfast table, he spoke of nothing but the party the night before. Apparently, there had been only one topic on everyone's lips. The party had been abuzz with one important bit of gossip. *L'Événement* had cancelled the second half of Émile Zola's series of six articles on the Parisian art scene. The first three articles, including the one Cezanne had passed about at the café Guerbois a few days before, had stirred up such a storm that his editor had ordered him to bring the project to a halt.

"They are afraid of fines, or perhaps even jail sentences. You know how the authorities like to control the newspapers," Papa was saying as Pascale finished her repast. He had been ignoring her lack of response throughout breakfast, and he continued speaking even as she left the table.

"I think I could sketch Captain Devlin now, don't you? He can't move much anyway."

"I don't know if that is a good idea, Papa. I don't think he'd appreciate having you painting his suffering."

"Why should he mind? It's the perfect opportunity to catch him while he can't move—and it will never occur again."

Pascale was about to argue with him further, but she recognized the look in his eyes and knew he wouldn't hear her. Let the two men fight. Perhaps it would drive the two men even farther apart and make it easier to convince one or the other of them to show her The Painting.

Pascale should have known that it wouldn't be that simple. She was summoned the same evening to soothe the tumult that resulted from Papa's attempt to sketch the invalid. That afternoon, she had attended an interview with Monsieur Durand-Ruel, one of Paris's most esteemed art dealers. His pleasant reception had restored some of her confidence. She was feeling a little more herself as she was ushered through the front door by Pierre.

The butler was always taciturn, but this evening his bearing was stiffer than ever.

"May I take your cloak, Pascale," he said, and she sighed. He only used her given name when he was quite upset. Something, or someone, had offended him.

When he said nothing more, Pascale reluctantly asked, "What happened?"

"Your father should probably . . ."

Pascale had no patience for his equivocating. "Yes, he

should, but you are here and he is not. Pierre, please, just tell me, what has occurred?"

Pierre sniffed. "There is no cause for alarm, now."

Pascale was beginning to worry. "Has someone been hurt?"

"Not hurt, exactly. Our guest chose to throw his dinner tray at the master."

She sighed. "Papa tried to sketch him, didn't he?"

Pierre sniffed again. "That does not seem to me sufficient provocation for bodily violence, but, yes, Monsieur did choose perhaps an inopportune moment to take advantage of our guest's . . . infirmity."

Philippe hurried up to them from the back hall and stood at attention, clearly awaiting a chance to speak.

Pascale thought she might as well hear the whole story at once. "Philippe, were you present when the altercation took place?"

"Yes, *mademoiselle,* I was there. I tried to stop it, but I couldn't."

Pierre snorted. "All that would have been necessary, I would think, was to remove certain objects from the captain's reach," the butler commented, disdainfully.

"I thought it better to remove his target," Philippe said, without looking at Pierre. Pascale could guess what had happened. Philippe and Pierre were at odds because Philippe had taken their guest's part, and Pierre stood, as always, with the master.

She hurried back to the kitchen to speak with Louise, who would only say that she could not be held responsible for the effects of this latest disturbance on Jack's health.

She found John Douglas in his room. The valet was up in arms over the stupidity of their host in insisting in sitting just out of reach of his reluctant subject and sketching him despite Jack's vociferous objections. If John Douglas could have thought of another safe place to hide his employer, he would have removed him from the premises that very day. Pascale did her best to soothe his ruffled feathers.

After this little contretemps, Pascale tried to recall the satisfaction she'd felt at obtaining the interview with Durand-Ruel as she made her way to Jack's room. He had been charmed by her. If her father did not appreciate her, at least she knew that she had achieved a great triumph on his behalf. Durand-Ruel could be a valuable ally to any artist, and now, because of her efforts, he was well disposed toward her father's work. Whatever Jack might say, she was not useless.

The sickroom was dark. Only one flickering candle had been lit. Their patient was lying with his eyes closed, sheets and covers flung haphazardly about him. The stool that usually sat by the head of the bed lay on the floor at its other end, bearing mute testimony to the forcible ejection of Paul de Ravenault from the room.

The storm had left some wreckage behind, but it appeared to have spent itself. Pascale hovered in the doorway for a moment. Despite everything that had happened, she was still torn between her desire to go to him, and an equally strong desire to flee. She turned to leave.

"Won't you come in?" The voice came from the darkness, soft and deep, like a rumble of thunder on a quiet summer night.

Eighteen

Jack could picture her face, could see in his mind's eye that little upturned chin that made her look so determined and assured, and the uncertainty in her eyes that belied that brave stance. No matter how hard Pascale was hit, she bounced back to her feet and faced the next blow head-on. Because of what had happened between them, she expected that next blow to come from him.

He would gladly have withdrawn every word that he'd said at their last encounter. Or, barring that, he wished that he could at least take back the information about The Painting. He still thought she was better off without the picture, but she shouldn't have learned of her father's deceit that way.

"I'm sorry about this afternoon," he said.

"Don't worry yourself," she said. "I was as much to blame as you were."

"No. I should not have spoken to you that way."

"Then you won't do it anymore," she said.

He couldn't bring himself to make that promise. He didn't know if he could keep it. He had to be honest with her. He didn't think he could live with himself if he let her bury herself in her father's household affairs again.

"I will try not to, but . . . ," He wanted to help her, to repay her in some small way for all she had done for him. "No matter how badly I behave, I really am grateful to you."

He sensed, rather than saw, the fluttering hands, the shake

of her head. "I didn't do it for you. Like Papa, my motives aren't pure."

Ah, yes, The Painting. He knew they would come back to this. "But The Painting doesn't belong to you. Your father has the right to do what he wants with it."

"I don't want to own it. I just want to see it." He could only guess at what that admission had cost her.

"Why? What do you hope to find in it?"

"I've explained . . . ," her voice trailed off. She started again, her voice almost a whisper. "I just want to see her."

"Who?" he asked.

"The woman in The Painting. Did you recognize her?"

It had never crossed Jack's mind that Pascale might not know that she was the subject of The Painting she sought. Perhaps she had guessed, and that was why she was so persistent. "You mentioned that you had seen sketches. I thought you knew who the subject was?"

"No." She moved away from the bed, away from him, and busied herself with straightening the disordered room. "I never saw her face."

"Couldn't you guess?" But he already knew, she had no idea who the subject of the portrait was.

She came back toward the bed, but her face was still in shadow. "No. I told you. Is it . . . ? Did you know who she was, then?" She began fixing the sheets and blankets that had been thrown into disarray during his earlier fight with her father.

"I couldn't say," he answered, slowly.

"Couldn't? Or won't?" Pascale asked, working her way slowly up to the head of the bed.

Jack wasn't sure why he didn't just tell Pascale the truth. He felt instinctively that it wouldn't help Pascale to know that Paul had hidden from her not only his masterwork, but also a portrait of her. He had already driven a wedge between father and daughter. He didn't want to drive them further apart. Part of him also didn't want to bring them together.

She leaned down to pick up a pillow that had fallen to the

floor next to the head of the bed. When she would have moved
away, he reached out and grasped her wrist. "I'm sorry," he
said, pulling her down toward him, so her face was lit by his
single candle. Pascale flinched at his words, but didn't pull
away from the steady pressure he exerted to bring her closer
to him. "If your father wanted you to know, he'd show you,
or tell you himself."

"Please tell me," she beseeched him. Her pride remained
intact, even as she begged. He had never met a woman like
this one.

Her eyes held his steadily. He felt as though he were drown-
ing in those deep black pools. "Who do you think she is?"
Jack hadn't consciously formed the question. Instinct alone
made him ask.

Pascale's eyes slid closed, but not before he saw the flash
of relief flicker through them. "My mother," she admitted.

It all fell into place. He finally held the key to the mystery.
He was stunned at how simple it was.

Pascale had given him no hint, not a clue, that it was this
knowledge she had hoped to gain. Jack would have bet his
life that no one else knew, either—not her father, nor her
friends, could have guessed that this haunted her. She pulled
her hand gently from his loose grasp and stood.

"So now will you tell me who the lady in the portrait is?"

She was trying to find her mother. He thought back over
all of the conversations he'd had about the de Ravenault family,
and realized, finally, that her mother had never once been mentioned. Father and daughter were so completely a family—a
unit. No one thought to miss the other parent. Pascale had
become the parent to her father. She was much more than his
daughter, she was his helpmate, his soul mate.

Their odd relationship had bothered Jack since the moment
he'd met the family, but he'd never thought of the missing
element. He'd wondered why Pascale seemed so alone—and
now he knew. There was no one to nurture and protect her.
Apparently there never had been. The fact that she'd been con-

ceived out of wedlock was well known. That had never been an impediment for them—blacks who lived on the edge of an all-white society. Those who came in contact with the family accepted their heritage as "African." No further question of lineage entered anyone's mind. If the family had lived less removed, circulated in Parisian Society more often, Pascale's suitability as a wife, a mother, might have been discussed. Her lineage would have been important, and her mother's identity well known. But the de Ravenaults were self-sufficient. François and Guillaume had told Jack that Paul had not visited Paris in almost twenty years when suddenly he and his daughter appeared.

And all those years, Pascale had wondered.

"The woman in The Painting is not your mother," he said, definitely.

"How can you be sure?" She stood looking down at him, erect and untouchable as ever.

"I know her."

"Can't you please tell me who she is?"

"I can't. I'm sorry," he answered. She looked away. "Hasn't your father ever spoken to you about your mother?"

"Papa?" She smiled, indulgently. "I asked once or twice, when I was quite young, but he didn't answer. When he doesn't like to talk about something, he just doesn't speak of it."

"Perhaps you should ask him again, now that you're older."

"Maybe I will," she said. But he didn't believe it. It was exasperating, the way Pascale let that old man get away with anything, no matter how much he hurt her. She'd sacrificed her art for him, focused all her ambition on his career, and he barely acknowledged it.

Jack kept his feelings about Paul to himself this time, he didn't want to push her away again. They seemed to have reached a new level in their friendship. It had been forced upon her, perhaps, but Pascale seemed to trust him, now. He was privy to her most closely guarded secret. He felt honored, and overwhelmed. He had nothing to offer in return. Or did he?

"Anyway, it all happened years ago. There are more urgent matters to deal with, certainly. Did John Douglas find out if the man with the missing ear was your friend?" She was trying to divert him. He let her.

"Pascale, I don't want you to worry about that. It was kind of you to take us in. I don't want our presence here to inconvenience you any further than it has already. As soon as I can stand on my own two feet, we'll be leaving." The dilemma he faced was none of hers. He didn't want her to suffer for helping him. But more than that, he wanted to help her.

"Don't be silly. You're not going anywhere for some time. I don't want you to think you have to protect me."

"Someone has to," Jack muttered. For once, he wanted to show her that there were people whom she could care for, without having to give all and taking nothing. He didn't think she'd had that experience often in her life.

"What did you say?" She was staring at him, and from the veiled expression in her eyes, he guessed he'd offended her again.

Silently cursing his unruly tongue, he tried to undo the damage. "I only meant that I . . . don't want you involved—"

"I am already involved," she interrupted.

He spoke over her argument, "I don't want you to get hurt because of me."

"If you are in danger—"

This time, he was the one to interrupt. "I'm not. I promise. Even if someone wanted to harm me—and there is no reason to think that is the case—no one even knows where I am." She didn't look satisfied. "I swear to you, Pascale"

If the wry look she threw in his direction was any indication, she didn't trust him yet to tell her the truth.

"Come closer," he said. She approached the bed, warily. "Here, where I can see you." When she stood beside the bed, he reached out for her hand. She let him take it, reluctantly.

"I owe you my life." He kissed her hand. "I will not let any harm come to you."

She looked unnerved for a moment, then the steely-eyed look of determination was back. "I can take care of myself, thank you. I do not need a knight-errant to defend me. I've always managed quite nicely on my own."

"Have you," he wondered aloud.

Her defiant eyes met his challenging gaze. "Yes," she said, her voice faltering. "Yes," she repeated, more firmly.

"I seem to remember one occasion when you were not quite so sure," he teased. He raised her hand to his lips again, but instead of kissing the soft skin on the back of her hand, he turned it and kissed the sensitive palm.

She gasped. "Please let go. I don't want to hurt you."

"It would be worth it," he said. He nipped the tender flesh at the base of her thumb with his teeth. She jumped, but didn't pull away.

"Your injuries," she said desperately.

"I'm feeling much better, right at this moment," Jack assured her.

"This can't be good for you," she said, weakly.

"You are very good for me." He kissed her wrist.

"I'm not," she said, on a sigh.

He slowly pulled her closer. "You are," he whispered.

Pascale yielded to the slight pressure he applied to her hand, and sat on the edge of the bed. He could feel the tension in her body as she sat stiffly, unsure of herself yet unwilling to call a halt to this interesting experiment. He was pleased to see in her eyes the bemused look of a woman who had experienced the heady excitement of lovemaking for the first time, and craved more.

She watched intently as he caressed her hand with his own, and waited breathlessly as he again raised it to his lips. He placed her open palm against his cheek. She was drawn closer still by the action. Less than a foot separated them. Her hand remained, resting lightly on his face, even after he released it.

He turned his head and kissed her fingertips. His one good hand went to her cheek, and he ran his thumb lightly over her soft lips.

She mirrored the motion. Her soft hand felt wonderful against his heated skin, his hungry mouth. Jack couldn't remember anything ever feeling this good. A faint voice within cautioned him not to let this go on. He had proven his point. Pascale de Ravenault was not invulnerable. But she tasted too sweet, and he couldn't stop. His fingers roamed from her forehead to her jaw, then slipped behind her head. Her eyes slid closed as he started to close the distance between them.

His bruised and broken ribs made themselves felt. He sank back again, bringing her with him. Pascale leaned forward, her free arm taking the weight of her body as she tilted toward him. Her lips met his, and the pain was forgotten. She had remembered the lesson he'd taught her, and her lips were slightly parted when they touched his. He held the back of her head in his hand, and hot and swift his tongue plunged in, tasting the insides of her cheeks. Her lips clung to his as if afraid to let go.

His left hand wandered over her shoulder, down her back to her waist. His mouth plundered hers, one kiss dissolving into the next. He hooked his forearm around her neck and overbalanced her, so that she fell onto the narrow bed beside him.

"No," she murmured. He cursed his bound right arm as she wriggled like a soft little kitten, accidentally catching him in the stomach with her elbow as she tried to pry her way loose.

"Mphg!" He muffled the sound in her shoulder. She became still.

"Did I hurt you?" They were both panting, nose to nose, as he waited for the fiery pain to subside. "Jack?"

"Wait," he said, through gritted teeth.

The agony passed, only a faint discomfort remained. When he opened his eyes, she was watching him with that same concerned stare Jack had awakened to only a few days ago.

"I told you this wasn't good for you," she said.

"Nag," he taunted.

"Idiot," she rejoined, laughing. Her relief was palpable. She relaxed back into the pillows and giggled. "Now, will you let me up?"

"This is the most comfortable I've been in days," he said.

"Liar," Pascale accused, but a lazy smile still played around her mouth.

"Just let me get my arm out from behind you," he said. He leaned over her to give himself the leverage he needed. Her eyes widened, then darkened with desire. Once he had worked his forearm free, he held her in place with a hand on her shoulder, but there was no need. She stared up at him like a moth caught in the light of a flame. He lowered his head and kissed her again, very gently.

"Jack?" He started to lower his head again. "I've got to go." He wanted to kiss her forever. But she caught his eye, and he knew she was right. She had to leave. All he could offer a lady like her was friendship. He fell back onto his pillows, still aflame with wanting her. He covered his eyes with his forearm. She had stopped him just in time. Sanity slowly descended.

She eased out of the bed, careful not to jar him. "I'm sorry. I shouldn't have let you do that. Whatever you may think of me, I am not interested in having an affair with you, or anyone else."

"You may not be interested in anyone else, but you sure as hell are interested in me, whether you want to admit it or not," he said, as mildly as he could.

"I'm attracted to you, but it would be ridiculous, and improper," she retorted. "Besides I don't think I like you very much."

"Now that," he said, uncovering his eyes and looking up at her, "is just not true."

"I don't want to like you, then," she said, resentfully.

"That I believe." He closed his eyes.

He waited until Pascale left the room before he opened them again. John Douglas came into the room a quarter of an hour later. He might just have come in, but Jack suspected he'd been waiting. His suspicions were confirmed within moments.

"That little miss is a godsend," John Douglas commented, after he'd made his employer comfortable.

"Oh, God," Jack groaned.

John Douglas's thoughts on the female half of the species were well known to his employer. He was an avid misogynist—convinced that women had only one real use, and not particularly happy about that one, either. For years he had steered Jack clear of any woman who might, as he said, "sink her hooks into him." Like all reformed characters, now that the valet had decided that Pascale was the right woman for his captain, he had launched into his campaign with the same energy he had formerly expended in keeping his employer out of the clutches of unscrupulous females.

"I told you she was a bit of all right," he said.

"Have you found anything new to report?" Jack asked irritably.

With one last wistful glance at the door, John Douglas became his usual competent self. "You were right, sir. It was your friend Richard Trenton that was killed. So what does that mean, then?"

"It confirms that someone did not want that message delivered. Richard probably knew who it was."

"Do you think he was killed so he couldn't talk to you?" John asked.

"If they think I'm alive, that's a definite possibility. But only a handful of men know that I am alive—even some of the men who are working for me don't know. He could have been killed so he couldn't talk to anybody," Jack said grimly.

John Douglas got right to the point. "That still doesn't explain who's behind this."

"It has to have something to do with Count Nieuwerkerke. His secretary Serratt arranged and attended the meeting, which took place in his lover's home. And Napoleon appointed him, so it makes sense the emperor would trust him with a secret communique."

"You think Nieuwerkerke scuttled the ship? But why?"

"I don't know. He might have done it for the émigrés. Mathilde is quite involved with them. Or he might not have had anything to do with sinking the *Aurora,* one of his enemies might be the culprit."

"We need to find out which side he's on," the valet concluded.

Jack smiled ruefully. "Unfortunately, we can't just accost the minister of fine arts and accuse him of treason. Even if we were certain he was guilty, which I'm not. I still think he had some reason for seeking Paul de Ravenault out at the Salon last week. I didn't think anything of it when Pascale told me they met, but Richard Trenton was killed the next day. I don't believe it can be a coincidence."

"Nor do I," John Douglas agreed.

"However, it still raises more questions than it answers," Jack pointed out. "That's what's been bothering me about Nieuwerkerke. Too many things point to him. He can't be that stupid. If Nieuwerkerke was planning to scuttle my ship, why meet at Princess Mathilde's ball? He must have known I'd suspect him."

"He thought you'd be dead, that's why."

"I just don't understand it. What could he hope to gain? Napoleon will just send another courier. It would make more sense if the Mexicans had a spy on his staff. They could be trying to undermine the relationship between Napoleon III and Maximilian. That makes more sense. But it's still baffling."

"You can't trust politicians. My vote is for Nieuwerkerke." John Douglas was convinced.

"I can't get over the feeling that we're being pointed that way. By someone else."

"Who?"

"Someone who is close enough to Nieuwerkerke to make

it look like he's the guilty party. Maybe the minister is in the same boat we are. He's trying to find answers, too. That would explain why he talked to Paul." It made sense, but Jack knew he had to be missing a piece of the puzzle.

"But if he doesn't know where you are, why talk to the old man?"

"I don't know. Maybe someone steered him toward the artist."

"That's a lot of maybes. I've got a few more for you, though. What if maybe he blew up the ship? Found out you're alive? Killed your friend to find out where you are. When that didn't work, he went looking for someone else who might tell him where ye be?"

"That would explain it, but I don't think it does. It's too easy. Has Bates found out anything more about Richard's murder?"

"We're all working on it, sir. We've found two more people who spoke to your friend that day. He went to the market for some champagne. Perhaps he was celebrating something. No one has a clue who might have killed him."

"I'm sure his death was connected with everything that's happened. I just don't know how," Jack mused aloud.

"Careful does it. At least until we find out more."

"I agree."

"Meanwhile, it looks like you'll have plenty of time to sort out the situation here." John Douglas harkened back to his tête-à-tête with Pascale.

"Let it alone, John. I'm not going to talk about it," Jack said. He didn't even want to think about the repercussions of this night.

As for Pascale, there was one thing he knew. She would hate herself in the morning.

Nineteen

Jack didn't see Pascale in the morning. She avoided him all day.

She finally visited him at ten o'clock at night. He surmised from her unbending stance that she had only come because she could no longer put it off.

"John Douglas did not know when he'd be back, so he asked me to look in on you tonight. Is there anything you think you'll need before I retire," she announced without preamble when she went to his room.

"As a valet, he may lack finesse, but he makes up for it with his brashness," Jack commented.

Pascale was not at all amused. "He is just trying to care for your needs."

"Yes. He attends to everything," Jack agreed.

"In that case . . ." Pascale took her leave of him. A moment later she stormed back into the room. "You didn't tell him?" she asked, horrified. The accusation irked him, but Jack tried not to take offense at the insult. It sprang from her embarrassment about the previous night, he was sure. He had known that upon reflection Pascale would be even less pleased about what had happened between them.

"No, I didn't. I suspect he was lurking in the hallway last night." Jack didn't regret that they had shared the intimacies they had, even if the result was that John Douglas was encouraged to play matchmaker. It had been worth it. He had enjoyed all of it, but nothing more than the moment when he'd felt they were in perfect sympathy—before they'd even touched each other. He wanted to reach that point again. Looking at Pascale's unhappy face, he knew that it would not be that simple.

It was clear from her expression that she was taken aback by John Douglas's interference. "Wonderful," she said.

He wanted to comfort her, but there was nothing he could say. She wouldn't believe the truth—that they had shared a moment of closeness, and it was only natural that their mutual attraction had gotten the better of them. He wasn't ashamed of it, and she shouldn't be, either. But she was young, and naive. She probably thought she'd committed some unpardonable sin.

"He'll be discreet. I promise you." He wanted to explain that he understood that she didn't want a lover, and he only wanted to be her friend, but he didn't think she'd believe him at this moment. As though she'd read his thoughts, she said bitterly, "Your promises mean nothing to me."

All that he could do was try to reassure her. "They should," he said seriously. Her eyes searched his for a moment. "My word, as they say, is my bond," he joked.

It was the wrong thing to have said.

Pascale's head snapped up again, her eyes narrowing. "I am only amazed that you didn't accept my offer to pay you twice what my father paid to hide The Painting."

Jack had thought that she had come to know him better. But she still thought him a moneygrubbing opportunistic cheat. How could she think such things about him now, after all they had shared?

"Pascale, I did not intend last night to happen, and I can assure you that it will not happen again."

"I forgot, you are a man of honor and integrity. Bah!" She snapped her fingers.

"You may not believe me right now, but you can trust me."

"Trust you?" A crack of laughter escaped her. "And your precious integrity, too, I suppose? I'd as soon trust a snake."

Jack knew she didn't mean it. She had trusted him enough to tell him her secret.

"Tell me, why did you really refuse to give me The Painting? Was it just an excuse to annoy me?"

"Perhaps to drive my price up?" Jack said, losing his patience. "I'm surprised you didn't think of that, Pascale."

She looked stunned. But she said, "So, that's it."

Her simple acceptance of the outrageous statement was a blow to his pride. He had not really believed she thought so little of him. "For all that you despise merchants, and shop-keepers, and all of the other ordinary people who don't live and breathe art as you do, you are not above lowering yourself to bargain with them. You would like me to believe that it is all in aid of the greater good that you serve, but I believe you enjoy it."

"I never said I didn't. But I could never be like you. I wouldn't sell myself."

If that was what she thought of him, how could she have made love with him? For a moment Jack was baffled, but suddenly it was clear to him. It was The Painting. That was what had made her lose her head. It hadn't been him at all.

He was disgusted with himself. He should have known she would do anything for her precious Portrait. He'd felt so sorry for her when he'd realized she was looking for her mother's face, he'd forgotten that ambition also drove her.

"Wouldn't you?" He let his gaze travel insolently over her. "The Painting is still available. How would you feel about sweetening the pot? You have much more to offer than mere coin to convince me to break my faith with your father."

"How dare you!"

Jack shrugged. "I am, as you said, a businessman, first and foremost. I handle cargo and commissions, which I am sworn to protect. I have cultivated a reputation for honesty and reli-ability—purely for the sake of business, of course. I couldn't jeopardize that just to double my money on this one commis-sion. I am in a very sensitive position. I could never be disloyal to a man with your father's connections for mere money. I would have to be convinced that your claim was greater than his."

"There is no point in talking to you!"

"Talking? Not much," he agreed.

Pascale stormed out of the room and down the stairs to her salon where she paced back and forth as she fumed. She couldn't give up now. Not with her father's greatest work in the hands of a commoner who could not even appreciate its beauty and true worth. She had to get it back. She just didn't know how. She had already tried everything she could think of, and that had been before she had known what Captain John Devlin could do to her. She had less to fight with than ever. He was the most exasperating man she'd ever met. Worse even than Papa.

She considered enlisting her father's aid, but quickly thought better of that scheme. He still had not noticed her coolness toward him since she'd learned of his latest deception. She had very little hope left that he would honor any pledge he made to her. She was afraid that if he secured The Painting, he still wouldn't share it with her.

She might not have the same reasons for wanting to find The Portrait of The Lady, since she had learned it wasn't her mother's face that Papa had painted. Still, even if it didn't hold the key to her past, it could be an important part of their future.

Most importantly, she felt driven to win. If Jack Devlin thought that he could keep her prize from her, he was mistaken. Pascale was determined to emerge the victor in their battle of wills. She was sure to prevail, she still had right on her side. That hadn't changed, even if everything else had. Her world might have been knocked off of its axis, but she would restore at least one small portion of her universe to its rightful place. She would retake control of her father's work.

For the next few days, Pascale set about conducting her business with renewed determination. She managed to complete the various transactions concerning the sales of her father's work by the end of the following week. She didn't see much of Jack at all. He was still confined to his bed, with John Douglas and her household staff in attendance. She was occasionally teased by the unwelcome thought that she was avoiding him out of cowardice, but she excused herself on the grounds that she truly was busier than ever, preparing to transport her household home again.

John Douglas entered her small salon one morning. She looked up from her work at his arrival.

"Miss?"

"Yes, *monsieur?*"

"You'll be needing a coachman for the journey home, I reckon. I've got a good man for ye."

Pascale hadn't expected this. "The stable where we rent the horses usually suggests a coachman to hire."

"Is there any reason you have to use their man?" he asked.

"No," Pascale said haltingly, wondering what had inspired his offer.

"Thomas Bowman is a friend of mine. He hasn't been hired on to another ship since the *Aurora* was lost. He could use the work."

"I see." Pascale did not want to offend him, but she was unaccountably wary of John Douglas's offer. She couldn't rid herself of the feeling that Jack was behind it, but that didn't seem a good enough reason to reject the idea out of hand. "I'll meet with him, then."

John Douglas nodded. "Would this afternoon be all right?"

"Fine," Pascale agreed.

Monsieur Bowman turned out to be a very large man. He was the size of an ox, and had a placid brown gaze that reminded her further of the large lumbering beasts.

He spoke very little French. "My English is not great," he said. "So I don't reckon I'll be able to learn another language on top of it."

"I'm sorry," Pascale lied, slightly relieved that he'd furnished her with this excuse to decline his services. "I think we need someone who speaks French." His bovine brown eyes met hers. His open expression didn't alter as she explained, "The countryside is quite different from Paris. No one speaks English. It would make your duties impossible to carry out."

He glanced briefly at John Douglas, then met her eyes again. "I'm right sorry, then." He didn't seem particularly dejected as he said, "Ta, miss."

Pascale wondered if the valet had embellished on Tom's sad-sounding story when he recommended she hire the sailor. Bowman didn't act as though he were desperate for work as he followed John Douglas out of the room.

The next morning, Thomas Bowman returned. Pierre came to the kitchen, where Pascale and Louise were trying to decide which food they could safely take back to Beaune with them.

"He's brought another fellow with him," Pierre said, as he led Pascale back out to meet them. The butler's expression left little doubt as to his distaste for their unexpected visitors.

When she saw the two men awaiting her, she immediately understood Pierre's reservations. Next to Thomas Bowman stood a swarthy pockmarked man, perhaps half the giant's size. Their uninvited guest was an unsavory-looking character. He had the face of a ferret, and, though tiny next to the huge Tom, he looked an agile fellow.

"This here's William Baptiste," Bowman introduced them. "He was on the crew of the *Aurora* with me and John Douglas. He knows how to drive a carriage, and he talks French 'cause his father was a Frenchie . . . begging your pardon, miss."

She could easily see this man climbing a ship's rigging, it was harder to imagine him atop a coach piled high with boxes. "You have experience driving a coach and four, *monsieur?*" she asked in her own tongue.

"I apprenticed in a stable, *mademoiselle*," he answered in unaccented French.

"It's a four-day drive, and with all this rain, the roads may not be in very good condition."

"Yes, *mademoiselle*. John Douglas told me."

Pascale did not like the look of the man, but between John Douglas's recommendation, and Thomas Bowman's expectant face, she couldn't refuse. "I suppose it would be all right," she said, reluctantly.

William Baptiste smiled, exposing a silver front tooth that gave him an even more frightening mien. He looked like a pirate.

Her travel arrangements were almost complete, when it suddenly occurred to her that she was running out of time. She would have to stop avoiding Jack if she was to recover The Painting. Still she hesitated to see him.

She conversed regularly with John Douglas about their "patient," and had gained, she thought, his complete confidence. However, she had ascertained that he had no clue as to the location of her property. She had failed in her attempts to intercept any message to Henry Bates, and to add a query of her own. She was going to have to confront the devil himself.

Pascale put it off for as long as she could. On Thursday night, when she and Papa returned from their last evening with the Manets, she finally made her way to Jack's room. She had only been able to think of one way to approach him. She would pretend that their argument had never taken place.

"You are looking much better," she offered, in lieu of a more formal greeting.

"You are looking lovely, as usual," Jack said. The pretty compliment did nothing to soothe her shattered nerves. It was accompanied by a searching glance at her face—which she tried to keep as expressionless as possible. Whatever Jack found there seemed to reassure him, for he relaxed back into his pillows, with a satisfied smile.

"Jack, I need to speak with you."

"You decided to try that again, then," he joked. She was not at all amused, but he added quickly, in a more conciliatory tone, "I'm glad. I've missed our little talks." Pascale couldn't quite believe that, but she returned his smile with a faint one of her own.

"Still and all, you've improved during my absence."

"I feel much better."

"John Douglas told me that you've been out of bed a few times. But he gave me the impression that that kind of exercise was hindering your progress." Truth to tell, Pascale had thought to see Jack in much worse form. He was recovering very quickly. The bruised and battered face he'd sported only a week ago was almost returned to its former beauty.

"He worries too much."

"Perhaps. But it is only out of concern for you."

Jack made a face at her. "God save me."

Pascale crossed herself superstitiously, and he looked at her askance. "From the way your man paces all day, and rushes out as soon as night falls, I'd say you have quite enough to worry about without tempting the fates with such talk."

"I haven't got a lot to lose."

"In my opinion you do." He looked stunned, and she quickly clarified her statement. "You are the only one who knows where my painting is. If something should happen to you . . ."

Jack's look of amazement disappeared. "And here I thought you were worried about losing me. We're back to this again."

She came around the foot of the bed to sit in the chair beside it. "I believe you are in danger. I do hope we can keep you safe," Pascale said, surprised at her own sincerity.

"That's kind of you," he said.

"We're doing our best. But I think you are looking forward to facing that danger. You welcome the risk. You will not sit quietly and let it pass you by. Therefore, I wanted to make sure that you had made some arrangement about The Painting. Does anyone know what you have done with it?"

It was so hypocritical—pretending her concern for The Painting was the same as her concern for him, but this was the only argument Pascale could think of. At least, she was honestly concerned about Jack's safety . . . even though she wished she were not. She might despise Jack Devlin, but she didn't want any harm to come to him. But, she told herself, she was only saying this now to find out where The Painting was.

It wasn't difficult for him to see through her. "Very clever," he said. "But I don't think I will tell you."

"But—"

"You are persistent, I will give you that. However, I don't want it on my conscience when you badger the poor man to death."

"So someone does know!" Pascale thought furiously. If François or Guillaume had The Painting, they would have told her by now. What man could it be that he didn't want to see badgered to death? Bates?

"Not yet. But if anything happens to me, he will." He waited for her to assimilate that tidbit before he said, "It will be up to your father to decide what to do with that damned painting. Sorry, princess, but you lose."

"As long as The Painting will not be lost, then I am happy," she lied.

He laughed. "You are not a very good liar, Pascale."

"I'm not lying. I . . ." He had seen through her completely. I'm desperate, she thought. Aloud she said, "I thought The Portrait of The Lady was lost once already."

He did not look contrite. "But it wasn't. And if I remember correctly, you weren't exactly overjoyed when I told you the news. Admit it, you'll only be happy when you are holding your precious painting in your own two hands."

She gave him a rueful smile. "Fine. But it is true that I am worried about you. What are you and John Douglas up to, eh?"

"I'm not going to tell you that, either. What devious plot have you concocted in that pretty little head of yours?"

To tell the truth, she had no idea, but it was pleasant to have put Jack a little off balance for a change. "I have more pressing concerns at this moment than your foolishness, Captain Devlin."

It had been so long since she had been this comfortable

with him. She tried to remember when they had last talked like this. It felt like ages, but she had only met Jack a few weeks ago. She had thought then that he was clever and amusing. She had also thought him impossible, perhaps even dangerous. So much had happened since. She had found him to be all those things. She hadn't been able to enjoy this kind of repartee, however. It was pleasant to flirt with him like this, from a safe distance.

He let out an exaggerated sigh of relief. "You will not have time to nag, then."

"I do not nag." Pascale had trouble getting her tongue around the ugly little English word.

"Ha!" Jack still wore that teasing smile. "You are the worst nag I ever met. Except perhaps for John Douglas."

Pascale shook her head, repressively. "He and I are just sensible. As you used to be."

Pascale hoped to appeal to his practical nature, even though it seemed to have disappeared along with his cargo when the *Aurora* sank to the bottom of the English Channel. She could have used a good dose of Jack's common sense to bolster her own. But his next words didn't bode well for her plans.

"You call it sensible, I call it bossy," he complained.

This was not a word she was familiar with. "What is that, *bossy?*"

He searched his mind. "Like Louise. Telling everyone what to do all the time."

"Ah, yes, Louise. But you know it is true, what she says, it is difficult always to be the one who is right."

"I never met two fussier women," he said.

"How could you? On your ship full of men."

"John Douglas is a man. And he was never like this on board ship. You've changed him."

"He *is* much better now." She gave him a satisfied smile.

"He likes you, too." That smile still played about the corners of his mouth.

"Of course he does. He is not pigheaded like you."

"Me?" His eyes darkened. "I like you, too."

She looked away. "Well, soon you will forget me."

"Never." His voice deepened, suddenly rough, and she knew that he was serious. They were treading on dangerous ground. He knew it as well. "That's the problem."

"There is no problem," she denied. "I will go home, and you will buy another ship and sail away."

"Pascale, look at me." She didn't want to face him. She was afraid. He was doing it again—confusing her and making her heart beat faster. How did he do that with only his voice? "Please," he said, and she felt compelled to bring her eyes up to his. "I have to go. But I will not forget you. You are the bravest, most beautiful, most intelligent woman I have ever met. I will never be the same again."

She couldn't look away. "Good," she said. "Neither will I."

She rose and turned to leave, but couldn't resist one more glance at Jack. He watched her through half-closed eyes, his expression unfathomable. He had said it himself. He had to go. He couldn't expect any more from her. He hadn't even offered her the consolation of The Painting. If he cared anything at all for her, wouldn't he at least have given her that? Her eyes suddenly filled with tears. Pascale rushed out of the room, straight into her father.

They stood in the narrow hallway, dark at this hour. His arms had come up to steady her when she'd stumbled into him, and he didn't take them away. After a moment she leaned into the comforting solidity of him. He had broken her heart, but she had never needed him as much as she did now.

"Pascale? I was looking for you. I thought I might find you here." He was patting her back, awkwardly. Despite their closeness, he hadn't held her like this since she was a child.

"I was just . . . saying goodbye, Papa," she said into his shirtfront.

"Perhaps that was premature," he said.

"I might not have the time, later." Her explanation sounded lame, even to her own ears, but he never noticed these things.

"That's not what I meant. I think we should take him with us to Beaune."

Pascale stepped back to look up at him. "What did you say?"

"Pascale, I think there is something I should tell you." He tucked her arm into his side and they walked together toward the stairway. "I did give Captain Devlin the Portrait of The Lady to take to Spain, as you guessed. But it was not lost in the wreck. He had hidden it somewhere here in Paris."

"Why are you telling me this now?"

"Because I think he was right. I should show it to you."

New tears, ones of happiness, burned Pascale's eyes. "Thank you, Papa." They had reached the second floor and made their way toward the studio.

"It is important that you see it."

"Why, Papa?" Despite Jack's assurances, Pascale still wondered if perhaps the subject of The Painting might have some special meaning to her father and herself—one that he couldn't divine. "Who is the lady in the portrait?"

"She is someone very special to me."

"My mother?" Pascale asked eagerly, thinking for a moment that perhaps Jack was mistaken.

Papa gaped at her in astonishment. "Felicity? She was a sweet woman, but I don't think I could remember what she looked like well enough to paint her after all of these years."

"Oh." Pascale moved away from him, and busied herself lighting the large candelabra that stood on the sideboard. She'd been laboring under a delusion all of these years.

When Jack told her the lady in the portrait wasn't her mother she'd been disappointed, but a small part of her had also been relieved. Jack's revelation had made it easier to hear the truth from Papa, but it didn't stop her from feeling an incredible sorrow. Felicity, that was her mother's name. If she had ever known it, she'd forgotten.

That was sad. But sadder still was her father's bald statement that he couldn't remember Felicity's face well enough to paint her.

Once again, he surprised her. "I do have a little portrait I painted of your mother once, long ago. It never occurred to me to show it to you. You never mentioned her."

"Neither did you. I thought the subject was too painful for you."

"Painful?" It was his turn to look surprised. "No. But it is in the past. Why would we talk about it?"

"But," Pascale stopped to swallow the lump that had formed in her throat. "It's not *just* the past. She is still my mother, now, in the present. And she always will be."

"She gave you to me. I cannot remember her with anything but gratitude for that."

She drew him onto the couch beside her. "Why did she leave?"

"A man cannot serve two mistresses," he quoted. "My art was my first love. Felicity did not want to be second in my heart, and I could not offer her more. We had been attracted to each other, but once the initial attraction waned, we both realized that I could not make her happy. She wanted someone who thought only of her. Who loved her the way I loved . . . painting. She deserved that, I think."

"Did she find it?" Somehow, talking about the woman she'd so often dreamed of, and wondered about, made her sorrow start to fade. It was replaced by an intense curiosity to know more about the woman she'd invented, who was turning, with each passing moment, into an ordinary woman of flesh and blood.

"I think she did. Her father had died when she was very young, during the Revolution. She married an older man, nothing at all like me. I was quite young and dashing then, you know. But I think Bernard was what she needed, someone to be the father she never had. He was a solid fellow. A farmer. They eventually moved to the Loire Valley." Pascale had always pictured her mother as a seductive, young free spirit. That picture faded and was replaced by one of a staid, middle-aged housewife.

"Why did she never write to me, or anything? Do you know?"

He shook his head. "I do not think she ever wanted him to find out about our affair. He adored her but he was very strait-laced. And she knew you were happy with me. She made sure of that before she left."

"She did?" The thought brought tears to her eyes again. She wiped them hastily with the corner of her sleeve.

"Yes, of course. We both did." Pascale sighed, and her father pulled her back with him into the comfortable cushions of the couch behind them, his arm around her shoulder. She could not remember ever feeling quite this close to him.

"I wish I had that picture of her here. But it is at home. I can show it to you there."

"I would like to see it," Pascale said. She reached up to kiss his pointy chin through his beard.

"I should not have kept my new painting from you. I have made a mess of things. I don't think Captain Devlin will give it back to me. You were right, I should not have tried to paint him."

"I am sure that all you need do is ask Jack for The Painting. It is yours, after all."

"That man of his won't let me near him anymore," Papa said resentfully.

"I think I can arrange a meeting," Pascale said confidently.

"I don't know." He was doubtful. "I think the captain might not talk to me. He's been very mysterious since we brought him here."

"That is not because of The Painting, Papa. I think there was foul play involved in the sinking of his ship. He cannot let anyone know where he is."

"Oh." He looked worried.

"You haven't told anyone, have you?" His guilty expression gave him away.

"Well, I thought that it was time to discuss the situation last night at the party with François and Guillaume. It was François that suggested that we take Jack back with us to Beaune."

"Well, I think it is safe for them to know. I will mention it to Jack to make sure."

"But I didn't notice that there were other people nearby. In fact, Guillaume seemed to think that I should definitely remove Jack from the city. I had not realized it was so terribly important to keep his whereabouts a secret."

There was no point in remonstrating with him. The damage—if damage had been done by his thoughtlessness—was done. Pascale had to speak with Jack at once. Guillaume was no idiot. If he had told Papa to take Jack out of Paris, then that was probably the safest course of action.

Twenty

Jack was incensed. "Why the devil couldn't your father keep his mouth shut!"

Papa tried to apologize when Pascale brought him to see Jack, and to pass along François and Guillaume's advice.

"Jack, it seems to Pascale and me that we should do as they say and take you home with us."

"How the hell—" Jack interrupted him. "This is intolerable. I can't leave Paris now. Why can't you keep your mouth shut, old man!"

"We were planning to leave in a day, anyway. You must come with us."

"It seems safer," Papa echoed. His English was not sufficient to understand every word Jack said, but he understood that he was objecting to leaving.

"Don't bother, Paul," Jack said, scathingly. "Your advice is the last thing I'd take."

Papa clearly didn't understand him. "What?" he asked Pascale.

"Never mind," she said, instead of translating, and turned him toward the door.

Jack called after him, in French, "Don't speak my name outside of this house again!"

The storm, which had begun when he'd been told of her father's indiscretion, raged unabated through the next morning. "I did not want to expose this family to danger," Jack railed.

"Well, you didn't. Papa did. So you can stop feeling guilty.

We need you to keep a clear head. I cannot think of any better plan. If they know you are here, we must remove you from the house at once. If they have not figured it out, since we were planning to leave, no one will think it at all odd if we left a day or two early."

He stared at Pascale as if she'd gone mad. "If they know I'm here, then they'll know I'm there."

"Not necessarily. It is easier to hide you at home than it is here in the city."

"But if they follow me—"

"If, if, if. If they are after you, and if they know you are here, and if they follow you, then we will be ready for them. A stranger from Paris will stand out in our little village like a sore thumb. We'll be able to spot anyone suspicious much more easily in the country. Meanwhile, I am not leaving you alone here just when you've begun to heal. *If* they do know you're here, it is certainly safer for Papa and me not to remain. Hopefully, with John Douglas's help, we can divert them. Make them think we've left, and you're still hiding in Paris." She smiled at the valet, who bowed his head in stoic acquiescence.

"I think she's right, Cap'n. I don't much like it myself, but I can't think of a better idea. Can you?"

"Yes. She leaves, along with her fool of a father, and you and Bates and the rest of the men wait here with me for them to come and get me."

"That's all very fine and well, sir, but I'm thinkin' we can do that without you—if that's the best course o' action. Not much help you'd be all trussed up in this bed 'ere. I'd rather you left with the lady, and I'll stay here and put it about that you're here."

Jack was suddenly calm. "You know I wouldn't let you do any such thing, John Douglas. What if they set another bomb here. What if one of my own men is in on this thing, and he leads you into an ambush."

"That doesn't make any sense, Jack. It's all right to set yourself up here as a target with all your friends about you, but not to let them take that same chance without you here." She searched his face. "To help them." She made a moue of disgust. "Wonderful," she said, her voice dripping with sarcasm. "You'd be a big help, I'm sure."

He shot a withering look at her. "I would not ask any man to do what I'm not willing to do."

"You're willing, you're just not able. And it still sounds stupid to me. What difference does it make if they are targets with you or without you?"

"The difference is that they can fight back. You and your family cannot."

"We might do better if we knew who 'they' are. Who's looking for you?" she asked.

"That's the problem. We're not sure ourselves," John Douglas answered when Jack remained silent.

"You must have some idea. These people put a bomb on Jack's ship, correct? What do they want?"

John Douglas shook his head.

"We don't know," Jack answered her. "That is why I must stay in Paris. To find out!"

"You do have your suspicions, though, don't you?"

"That's all they are, suspicions."

"Who was the man who died? Was he involved in this?"

"He was a friend. I've known Richard for over ten years. We don't know why he was killed."

"But it had something to do with what happened to you," Pascale pressed.

"I think so. Otherwise, it's just too coincidental."

"But you don't know why he got himself killed?"

"Not that I know of. He recommended me to his employer."

"Who is?"

"Strictly speaking," he paused. "Napoleon."

"My God. You think the emperor had a hand in your accident?"

"Not really, no," Jack said. "It might have been someone

else on his staff. Or one of his enemies. It could even be one of my competitors."

Pascale's mind was reeling. "But why? What are you doing?"

"I was doing what I was hired to do. Transporting an item from France to Mexico."

"What item? A bomb?"

"It was a letter. A confidential letter." He continued as she opened her mouth to speak, "And that is all that I can tell you. I honestly don't know anything more than that about the bombing." With that, Pascale had to be content. "It would be too dangerous for you and those around you if you knew anything more. All we have are vague suspicions anyway."

"Everything you say makes me more convinced that you should get out of this city," she insisted. "I should think that would be your aim as well. At least until your right arm has healed."

He groaned. "It will be months before the breaks heal. If you expect me to just lie around until then, you are sadly mistaken in your notions."

"Aye, miss. He can't just wait for them to find him. But, Captain, I think we should continue with our original plan. Let's find out who the bastards are . . . begging your pardon, miss . . . then we'll get after them. Otherwise, they may have us outmanned and outgunned afore we know it. I'm thinkin' it's wisest you keep out o' sight, for now. Till we know a bit more."

Pascale nodded. Jack was about to say more, but a knock at the door silenced all of them. Philippe had come up, sent by Pierre to tell them that François and Guillaume were waiting below.

Pascale brought them up to Jack's room, and after they had expressed their gratification at seeing their old friend alive, if somewhat the worse for wear, she solicited their opinions.

Guillaume pursed his lips and let out a long, slow whistle.

"Well, I'm afraid Paul was a bit too loud last night for me to feel there is any safety here."

"If he couldn't keep his mouth shut last night, what's to stop the old gentleman from telling the world?" John Douglas was disgusted.

Guillaume gave Pascale an apologetic look as he agreed. "I would not place any confidence in his ability to be discreet. He must be got out of Paris, no matter what!"

"But I could stay here," Jack said. "It's better than taking a chance on leading them right to the de Ravenaults."

François thought it over and shook his head. "I don't think so, *mon cher*. If the secret is not widespread, there is no better place for you to lay low than the de Ravenault estate. And if it is already known, then removing you will make it more difficult for them to come after you."

Guillaume added, "We will join you for the journey to Beaune. You will be most vulnerable on the roads. And you cannot afford to draw attention to yourselves by hiring armed guards."

"That isn't a problem," John Douglas said, definitely. While Pascale saw to it that her household was packed and ready to go, Jack was busy making some arrangements of his own, though he had yet to resign himself to their change in plans. Bates and some of the other men would be providing protection for the party, from a distance, he told Pascale. He didn't tell her that he had arranged for her to hire one of his men, William Baptiste, as her coachman before Jack had even known he would be traveling to Beaune with the family.

With the help of François, a meeting was arranged with his first mate. François changed clothing with Henry Bates one afternoon in order to sneak him into the de Ravenault's rented house.

Bates had little information for him. "I've checked the surviving crew members. I'm satisfied they're all loyal to you, Captain. One man, James Tate, remembers that one of the Mexicans disappeared for a few hours the night before we left—but they found him drunk in one of the taverns. He may have had something to do with it. But we'll never know. He didn't make it back to shore after the . . . accident."

"Are you sure? Perhaps he's in hiding."

"We're sure, Captain And the other Mexican, Juan Alcazar, says he doesn't think the dead man was a traitor. He might have been used to get on the ship, but that seems to be the end of that trail. But I'm sure there was a bomb, we were able to find the man who made it. He was killed the next day. Whoever is behind this is very thorough. They killed him, and your friend—every link, it seems, betwixt them and us. They don't leave any loose ends."

"They left one." Henry's face might have been set in stone, and Jack knew that his implacable expression mirrored his own.

"Happen they'll be sorry about that," Bates said, clearly relishing the thought of getting his hands on them.

"Oh, I'm quite sure they will," Jack agreed.

In all of the hustle and bustle of packing up, Pascale didn't have a chance to ask him about The Painting. But he knew she had thought of it. He had seen her darting a look at him at one point when he'd mentioned the possibility of John Douglas's buying some personal articles for him. She had refrained from voicing any idea she might have had about retrieving the work.

Paul de Ravenault had had the nerve to ask him to arrange for its return, as well as to explain that he'd undergone a change of heart—he now wanted Pascale to see his work, just as she'd predicted. Jack had barely been able to keep a civil tongue in his head as he'd explained that he couldn't recover the *objet d'art* at the moment. He was hindered by the obligation of pretending to be dead. His sarcasm was wasted on the artist, but he did bring Paul to the realization that his options were, currently, limited. There was nothing he could do. With that, Paul had to be satisfied. Jack assumed he'd passed the information on to his daughter. He only realized much later that he'd been wrong in that assumption. At the time, he thought the matter closed and moved on to other more important matters.

In order to give his men time to station themselves on the road to Beaune, the household had had to delay their leave-taking for a day. Paul decided to stop in one last time at the Salon, and Pascale, having prepared everything for their journey, had the day free as well, so she decided to accompany him. Again Monsieur de Ravenault just happened to meet Minister Nieuwerkerke.

Pascale saw the minister right away. He was a distinguished gentleman. It had not occurred to her before, but this was the third time that she and Papa had met Nieuwerkerke in less than a month. And he seemed again, like last time, to be seeking them out.

An absurd suspicion formed in her mind. Jack had said that he'd been hired to take a message from Napoleon to Mexico, presumably to the government that he'd installed there, perhaps even to Maximilian himself. Nieuwerkerke was a member of Napoleon's government, and his lover, Princess Mathilde, was good friends with the Empress Eugénie, one of Maximilian's most ardent supporters. Could the minister of fine arts have some reason to seek them out besides Papa's work?

"Good evening, *chérie*," he said, as she inched between him and her father, hoping to prevent an incident like the one that had occurred the last time the two men had met. "It is a pleasure to see you again."

"And we are honored, of course, Minister Nieuwerkerke, Monsieur Serratt," Pascale responded, quickly. She nodded at his secretary who trailed slightly behind the minister. "Papa?"

"It is a pleasure to see you again, Minister," Papa said, bowing slightly.

Pascale tried to forget her wild musings about the minister of fine arts. "The Salon is quite incredible. Every time we come, we are amazed at what is being done."

"The Salon changes more each year," the minister agreed.

Pascale was not sure from his tone of voice whether he approved of the changes. "I hope that one of these years we will see some of your father's work on these walls."

"Papa is working on some new commissions, and we are thinking about painting an outdoor scene here in Paris, maybe the café Guerbois. Or some of Baron Haussmann's new structures."

"It sounds like an interesting idea. I have purchased for the state's museum some wonderful landscapes. Why shouldn't we also enjoy 'cityscapes,' as it were."

"That's exactly what Papa said, isn't it?" Pascale turned to her father and gave him a little nod of encouragement.

"Yes, of course," Paul de Ravenault said.

"I thought you were leaving the metropolis," Serratt said.

"We are, but we'll be back next year, as always," Pascale said. She was pleased that her voice didn't shake. The fact that a man like Nieuwerkerke was aware of her movements, and Papa's, made her very nervous.

"You have finished all your business in Paris, then?" the minister asked Papa.

"There is so much to do here, but yes, I think Papa achieved all of his goals," Pascale answered for her father.

"Of course, the heart of the city is its people," said the statesman. "It is always a pleasure to see old friends. And to make new ones," he said gallantly. "I understand you met Captain Devlin at the princess's ball."

Shaken, Pascale lowered her eyes, pretending to remember. "Captain Devlin? Oh, yes. My father's friend Guillaume Pelotte was a business acquaintance of the captain's, and he introduced us. We were fortunate that we didn't take his advice and invest in the captain's last trip." She laughed.

"Well, so . . . you haven't heard anything about him since his ship went down?" the minister asked. She caught his eye, for a moment, then he looked away. But she had glimpsed something there that turned her blood cold.

"Guillaume has talked of little else," she said, allowing a

hint of curiosity into her voice. "He could ill afford that accident."

"So you haven't heard the rumors that Captain Devlin survived the wreck, then?"

Pascale hoped she did a credible job of looking surprised. "Guillaume would certainly have been contacted if the Captain had survived. He's coming with us to Beaune tomorrow, I'll have to ask him if he's heard any such rumor. But I'm sure it's just another one of those silly bits of improbable gossip that people love to pass on." Tired of this little game, she brazenly asked him, "Did you know the Captain, then?"

"I never had the pleasure."

The minister exchanged a glance with his secretary, who promptly said, "We have an appointment in just one half of an hour, Sir."

"It was delightful to see you again, Monsieur de Ravenault. Mademoiselle," he bowed at the waist and followed Serratt toward the door. Pascale released her breath in a long whoosh, and sagged back against her father.

"I think it's a good thing we're leaving tomorrow morning, Papa," she said. He looked after the minister and nodded.

"I think you're right, *ma fille*."

Luckily, Jack had assigned Henry Bates and a bruiser from his crew named Thomas Bowman to keep an eye on father and daughter, so the men were able to report that the encounter occurred. Neither man spoke much French, but Pascale came to relate the tale herself and to ask what it meant.

"Probably nothing at all," Jack said, reassuringly.

"It must mean something. Why would Count Nieuwerkerke seek Papa out not once, but twice? I didn't think it so odd the first time, but this time he was quite direct. All he wanted to know about was you."

"Don't worry," he said. "I've already got Henry Bates investigating him. So far, we haven't found anything suspicious."

"Maybe I could help if I knew what we were looking for?"

"I don't think so," said Jack. "Especially since we're leaving in the morning."

"Can't you just tell me—"

"No," he cut her off. "It's too dangerous."

"If I'd known the minister of fine arts was involved, I might have found something out for you."

"That's all right," Jack said.

"But I might have ruined everything," she cried.

"Not you," Jack said confidently. "Your father perhaps, but never you, my sweet."

Henry Bates and Thomas Bowman were equally impressed with Pascale's handling of the situation.

"That toff you told us to watch last week was just awaitin' for them there. I wouldn'ta noticed, but I recognized him from then, so I happened to be watchin' him when he saw our two. He rushed right over to 'em."

"We can only be thankful she's on our side," Jack said wryly.

Thomas concurred. "Sure and all. He was atryin' to find out something, and she led him a merry dance. She kept in between him and her da. It took me a few minutes to get close enough to hear what they were saying, and they were speaking French, but she looked as sweet and innocent as a kitten with those big brown eyes o' hers."

"I think we've got a traitor among us, Cap'n," was Bates's conclusion.

"So, do you think we've got 'im?" The impatient Thomas was dying to know.

"Not really. But it certainly seems that Nieuwerkerke knows something. Now we just need to find out what it is," Jack said. He told Bates to set two men to watching Nieuwerkerke's house, including one that spoke French fluently. "I am looking for a more direct connection to the emperor or to Empress Eugénie. Mathilde and she are not great friends, though publicly they make sure they are seen as such. Mathilde and Napoleon are much more friendly, but I am sure it is Eugénie who is involved in this intrigue. It is she who convinced the emperor to put Maximilian in power in Mexico, and it is she that counts among her intimate friends the most vocal of the Mexican emigres who now live in Paris."

Thomas needed clarification. "The ship was blown up by the queen of France for some Mexican friends of hers?"

Jack smiled. "No, Thomas, the *empress* or the emperor were using me to send a message to someone, or someone else was using me to send a message to them. In either case, the message that I was carrying was sent to Mexico. Now I'm trying to find out whether they sent it, or whether the agent who hired me acted without their knowledge."

"Can't we just find 'im and ask 'im?" Thomas was a man of action.

"One of the two men who gave me the message to carry is dead. The other was Serratt, Nieuwerkerke's secretary, and he may not be acting on his own. I wouldn't want to take him on unless I had proof he played me false. Besides, he didn't have to meet me. He *wanted* me to know who he was."

"So?"

"So he didn't have to risk exposure, he could have sent his letter with anyone. I don't see any reason for his attendance at the meeting if he wasn't in earnest about the message being delivered. It doesn't make sense."

"But if he thought you'd be dead, he wasn't risking nothing, was he?"

"Possibly not. But a man like this—if he wants you dead, you're dead."

Thomas nodded, but he still looked somewhat confused.

"We're looking for them to send another message with another shipping bloke," Henry explained, more simply. "You know those men we're watching. Most of 'em own ships."

"Ah," said Thomas. "But where does this Newkirk chappie fit in. He don't have no ships."

"It was his lover's house where I first was approached. His secretary attended the meeting. He is friends, of a kind, with the royals, and I think he might have been involved in this—at least in volunteering the house as a meeting place," Jack answered.

"The main reason we've been watching him is because he suddenly went lookin' for the old man whose house the captain's staying in. Maybe that's because he was looking for the captain."

"After today, I'd say he was," Thomas agreed, much struck by their reasoning.

Twenty-one

The next morning they left for Beaune. Jack snuck out of the house disguised as a footman in one of Philippe's uniforms. Jack, Pierre, and Odelle shared the servant's carriage with boxes and bags piled about them, and Philippe rolled up in a rug which had been dragged to the carriage, and none too gently, by the new coachman, William Baptiste. As a precaution, the footman stayed in his "disguise" on the floor of the carriage and was used as a footrest until they had left the outskirts of the city far behind. Then he took Jack's seat when the captain moved into the de Ravenaults' carriage with Pascale and Paul.

The carriage ride to Beaune usually took four to five days if the roads were not too bad. Luckily, despite the spring rains, the roads were passable. The muddy holes were drying quickly as the month of June drew nigh, but it was not a very comfortable journey. If Jack Devlin would have preferred to stay in Paris and wait for his enemies to attack, he didn't say anything more about it. He kept glancing out the window. Pascale thought he might be looking for signs from his men that she couldn't see. At least worrying gave him something to do, she thought. She was sure she could trust his well-developed instinct for self-preservation.

Papa almost immediately started one of his long rambling discourses on beauty and art which went on for an hour. As a child, she had loved listening to him talk, but the tension emanating from Jack's taut frame, combined with her own nervousness about the possibility that they were being followed, made this particular speech seem endless to her.

It was not hard to see that her father's conversation chafed at the captain's nerves. Pascale did sympathize with Jack's impatience, which was exacerbated by his injuries. Jack suffered intensely from the jolting caused by the swaying motion of the carriage, but he wouldn't admit it. Even bolstered with numerous pillows and dosed with Cook's soothing potions, every bump in the road forced him to grit his teeth.

"And then there's human anatomy." Pascale sighed. Papa was discussing the body; she, herself, was finding it quite difficult not to reveal how greatly Jack's nearness was affecting her; and Jack was gazing at her father in disbelief. Pascale was reminded forcibly of the night they had met Captain Jack Devlin. They had come full circle. "Though some people shy away from the subject, the human body is one of God's purest and most beautiful creation. He fit form with function, for the most part." Papa was unaware of anything but his own thoughts.

He turned to Jack. "Did you know that Michelangelo had to buy cadavers illegally in order to study and sketch the human body. In those days, a classical model of the body, quite inaccurate in many ways, was the only form he was allowed to draw. It is strange, but the ancient Greeks, like Praxiteles, sculpted more realistic statues than the Romans, the Saxons, the Gauls, or generations of artists who came after them. But Michelangelo wanted to draw the human body as it really is— in all its beauty. Many of his sketches, though illicit, have been preserved. They're remarkable, really."

Though Papa spoke in his old-fashioned way, Jack seemed to understand his French perfectly. When Papa paused to take a breath, he responded to the question. "No, sir, I did not know that. What happened to the bodies after he immortalized them in chalk?"

Since Papa's question had been rhetorical, he was completely taken aback by the unexpected response. "Uhhh," he stammered, "I really couldn't say."

Jack continued, mercilessly, "Why do you suppose it was illegal to study the human form, anyway?"

"It was considered immoral and unChristian to look upon a naked body," Pascale couldn't help but intervene on her father's behalf. Her father was so woefully ill equipped to defend himself. "And you know it."

"Perhaps a dose of that old-fashioned morality would be good for our society today? What do you think of that, Paul?"

Papa just shook his head, bemused. When Jack's gaze fell upon her, Pascale took up his verbal gauntlet. "Would you deny models the right to make a living at their chosen profession?" she asked, facetiously.

"I don't think it would tumble any governments if a few vain idiots were forced to keep their clothing on their bodies," Jack replied.

Pascale remembered again the night they had met, and his disapproving stares when the subject turned to anatomy. "I had forgotten what a prude you were, Captain Devlin."

Jack almost smiled, but Papa interposed, "Modelling isn't just a matter of taking one's clothes off. It's not nearly so simple as it may look."

"How do you know, Sir? Have you ever tried it?" Papa subsided, defeated, and fell into a silent, thoughtful mood that lasted for some time. When he again began to ramble, Jack's verbal game of cat and mouse was resumed. Pascale felt like a bone being tossed between her father and her recalcitrant patient.

If it hadn't been for Guillaume and François, Pascale would have despaired. Those two gentleman rode, at intervals, within the carriage, and alongside, secured food and lodging, and generally made the trip more pleasant.

On the morning of the second day, Pascale watched Jack as he climbed into the carriage and tried unsuccessfully to make himself comfortable. His injuries made any kind of movement painful, even sitting in their carriage was intolerable.

Pascale tried to take his mind off the pain by conversing. Of course, the subject most on her mind was the mystery that had brought Devlin back into her life. But she tried to distract him, first, with slightly less inflammatory discourse.

Papa was sleeping, so she spoke in English for Devlin's benefit. "Was that Thomas Bowman I saw you speaking with in the common room at the inn last night?"

"Yes," he admitted, reluctantly.

"You didn't really think to hide him from me, did you? He stands out even more here in the country than he did in Paris."

"He's gone back to the city. This morning. I had him guarding our backs for the first leg of the trip, but he'll be more useful to Henry Bates in Paris than to us. And, as you say, he's rather too big to try to conceal." He grinned ruefully.

"He still works for you, then?"

"Yes. I wanted to be sure you and your father arrived at home safely."

"And our new coachman, William Baptiste, is he still in your employ as well?" Jack nodded. Pascale's lips pursed. "So that's why he pays no attention to my orders."

"And the rest of your men?"

"Some are guarding this coach, a day here, and a day there. Henry Bates will be with us all the way to Beaune, then he'll go back. He doesn't like to be so far inland, anyway."

She nodded, sure that he'd taken sufficient measures to get them home without incident to their château in Beaune. "And when we arrive? Do you plan to have men guarding the house?"

"Just a few. The rest will be otherwise occupied."

"You are still determined to find out who sank the *Aurora*, even if it's the minister of fine arts, or the emperor himself." He didn't respond, just looked through the window at something only he could see.

"What difference could it possibly make? Why not just leave Paris, while you've still got your whole skin?"

"There are men who weren't as lucky as I was. I'm responsible for them. I want to find the man who did this."

"Nieuwerkerke?" she asked.

"I don't know," he said. "He certainly acts like he knows much more than he's saying, but it doesn't make sense. What would he gain?"

"Nieuwerkerke has always supported Maximilian who was Napoleon's choice for emperor of Mexico."

Jack nodded. "Undermining Napoleon's foreign expansion is not likely to win Nieuwerkerke more favor in the imperial palace. Although I suppose the sooner Napoleon is out of Mexico, the better off he'll be. Maximilian will be overthrown eventually. My bet is it will happen sooner rather than later," Jack mused.

"I've noticed," Pascale said, cynically. "What made you choose to go to Mexico in the first place?"

"It was a market that hadn't been exploited much by English merchants. The Spanish and the Dutch are there, of course, but they don't sell Irish lace."

"Wouldn't it be safer to export goods to an existing market?" Pascale asked.

"Perhaps, but the gamble paid well." He was so cocksure.

"Why take the risk?"

Jack smiled. "I could never resist a challenge." He winked at her.

Papa stirred, and Pascale found herself hoping he wouldn't awaken. The tone of their conversation changed when he was listening. She enjoyed Jack's dry English wit. Papa didn't understand it, and he certainly wouldn't understand Jack's winking at her. Pascale felt self-conscious when he caught them sharing a private smile at some subtle nuance in Jack's tone, or her own. And, although Jack acted the perfect gentleman, when Papa watched them, she became very aware that she was constantly touching, and being touched by, this man. Contact between them was inescapable in these close quarters, and her body's reaction was not something she could help. But when she stretched out her arm across Jack's shoulders to keep him from being jostled when the coach hit an obstruction in the road, her father's surprised expression made her feel as if she had done something wrong. Perhaps it was because, during the course of the past few weeks, there had been an almost imperceptible change in the tenor of their friendship. Sometimes she would have sworn they thought as one. Jack Devlin—for all that he had done to her—was someone she had come to like.

Papa woke up and ran a hand through his beard, and Pascale knew that the interlude was over.

"Is it time for luncheon yet?" her father asked.

"Not yet," Pascale and Jack said in unison. The two men were silent. Pascale looked back and forth between them and despaired.

Over the next few hours, there was little they could do but try and be patient as the view outside the small windows in the carriage doors changed. The roofs of the houses went from slate to tile, the towns to villages and hamlets, the fields from wheat and cattle to vineyards.

Jack and Papa didn't speak to each other for most of the journey. Of course, when they did, Jack constantly tried to goad Papa into an argument. After luncheon that afternoon, Papa launched into a discourse on skin tones, a topic which presumably he thought would forestall any argument, as they were united by their shared race.

"I have always thought it odd that white folks do not refer to their own skin tones as lighter, darker, redder or yellower, as they do with ours. Although you and I share a similar darkness, my skin is more a taupe, and you share that golden hue to your skin that I admire in Pascale's coloring."

"The reason that whites don't classify their skin is because the only classification that matters to them is white or black," Jack said dryly.

"That is not true of artists, my boy," Papa replied.

"I think it is because we are such a small minority of the population," Pascale inserted into the conversation. "Had you noticed, at some of the inns they have been uncertain what to do with our party."

"Really?" Papa said surprised.

"Well, only François, Guillaume and Pierre are white, while you, myself, Jack, Phillippe, Odelle and Louise are all black. It's rare to see a group in which we are the majority. I am accustomed to being one of two or three black faces in a crowd."

"I suppose that's so," Papa mused.

"It is generally true, both here and in London. And, of course, it becomes more obvious as you travel upward in Society," Jack commented. "Or outwards, into the country. I haven't seen above one or two blacks since we left Paris."

"Black families are spread out in the countryside," Pascale told him.

"I know."

"But everyone is spread out in the countryside."

"True," Pascale agreed.

"Do you know of any other black families in Beaune?" Before Papa could answer him, Devlin added, "Any other families that are in your position?"

"No," Papa said thinking.

"In the provence?"

"Burgundy? No, not that I know of. But what does it matter."

"In Paris there were black merchants, writers, people in every class. Don't you think that it would be good to know such people."

"We have met some. And we have known a number of artists of mixed heritage," Pascale said.

Jack spoke directly to Paul. "Don't you think Pascale should meet other people like herself?"

"I don't see what all the fuss is about," Papa answered.

Jack directed a look of scorn at the older man. "Pascale is your daughter, not your wife. She should meet people her own age. She shouldn't be mouldering away in the countryside."

Pascale put a calming hand on his arm. "In a few years, we'll be able to visit Paris more frequently, and for longer periods of time."

"I've lived in the country all my life, and I never had any problems."

"You barely pay attention to your surroundings. Pascale shouldn't have to live so removed from the rest of society."

"Don't, Jack," Pascale warned. "I like my life."

Pascale did agree with much of what Jack had said. In fact she found herself in sympathy with many of his views, and those that they disagreed on just added spice to their conversations. Though she didn't like the constant friction between Jack and her father, she did enjoy sparring with him herself. There was a rapport between them. But Papa neither understood nor shared it, and it was quite obvious that Devlin did not have the patience to develop any kind of rapport with Paul de Ravenault.

By the end of that third day, Pascale was almost convinced her father was right—Jack wouldn't return The Painting to its rightful owner unless some reparation was made for the liberties the artist had taken with his person while he'd been confined to his bed. As it turned out, however, Jack's antagonism ran much deeper than that incident in Paris. His remarks that night at dinner became more and more pointed, as Papa kept telling stories that showed himself in a less than flattering light.

François tried to steer the conversation to the inoffensive topic of the weather, saying, "I hope it doesn't rain tomorrow."

Papa thoughtlessly remarked, "We have never had so many able bodied men to dig us out of the mud, should we get mired down."

"Oh, for goodness sake!" Jack muttered under his breath, but Papa didn't hear him.

"Pascale, do you remember our first trip home from Paris?

We were travelling alone, just a hired coachman, and we got bogged down on that stretch of road, just before we reached the village."

"Papa, I don't think anyone wants to hear that story tonight," Pascale tried to divert him.

"It was really very funny," he said to the others. "We were covered in mud when we arrived at the château. Remember that hired coachman wouldn't help us dig. He wanted to wait for the rain to stop. Well, we managed all right by ourselves, but we were filthy."

"You had your daughter dig out your coach in the middle of a storm?" Jack asked, incredulously. "You selfish old fool!"

"Are you mad, Captain? What's the matter with you?" Papa asked, bewildered.

"How can you be so blind?" Jack ignored her and turned to her father. "You're the expert in human anatomy. Do you see her at all. Does she look like someone who should be digging up roads to you?"

"Why, Pascale is much stronger than she looks," Papa assured him.

"I'm aware of that. And it's a good thing she is, or you would have broken her long ago."

"Jack, stop this," Pascale demanded.

"Do you hear this?" Jack asked François and Guillaume.

"Yes, Jack. Now just calm down," Guillaume said. "I think it's time we go and find the innkeeper. Let's see if he has some brandy."

Jack threw his napkin onto the table and followed Guillaume from the room. Pascale didn't know what she would have done without their escort. François lent her a sympathetic ear for the relief of her frustration while Guillaume took Jack away.

"Why does he do that?" Pascale asked her old friend.

"It's been a long day, and we're all tired," François said.

"I think one of the captain's wounds must be infected," said Papa. "He's raving. Did you hear what he called me?"

"Yes, Paul, we did. He was not too pleased with you."

"Why?" the artist asked. "What did I say?"

"You should not let Pascale dig ditches."

"I don't see why not. If she wants to dig ditches that's her business, not his."

"Not in the rain," François tried once more.

"I'm sure she wouldn't dig ditches in the rain, would you, *ma petite?* She's a very sensible girl."

When Guillaume and Jack returned, François had taken Papa off to bed.

"Ah, good." Guillaume said. "All's clear. The enemy has retreated, Jack."

"Must you argue with him all the time?" Pascale asked.

"Let him get that brandy in him before you mount the attack, my dear girl," Guillaume counselled her. "I call for a truce."

They sat in silence, the men sipping their drinks while Pascale stared into the fire. François soon rejoined them.

"Are we all calm, now?" he joked.

"Just taking a breather before the next salvo is fired," Guillaume reported.

"I'm done," Jack assured them.

"Well, I'm not," Pascale said. "Why must you fight with him all the time?"

Guillaume went to Jack to refill his glass and whispered loudly, "You don't think you're going to get out of this that easily, do you? Pascale has barely even launched the defense."

"Don't tell me you're on his side, Guillaume? You saw what he did."

Guillaume raised his arms in surrender and retreated to a chair by the fire.

François turned to Jack. "I warn you. Do not think you will escape unscathed. You insulted Papa," he informed him.

"You don't think this is ridiculous?" Jack asked. "Why is she defending that . . . that?"

"He's my father!" Pascale exclaimed.

"I know," Jack said, wearily pressing his hand to his eyes.

"Are you all right?" she asked, noticing that he was looking extremely weary. "Perhaps you should go lie down?"

"I just want to finish my brandy," Jack agreed.

"If there aren't going to be any more fireworks, I'm going to toddle off to bed," Guillaume said.

"Me, too," François echoed.

When they had left the room, Pascale sat watching Jack. He looked exhausted. That was probably a large part of the reason that he had lost his temper. Still, she didn't like the way he spoke to her father. She knew Paul de Ravenault could be a heedless old man, but Jack had no right to criticize: that was a right reserved to those who loved her Papa.

She was lost in a reverie when Jack spoke again. "I think you are making the same mistake I did," he said. His voice was velvet soft, and warm as candlelight.

"What?" she asked.

"My mother was a maid, to a woman who adopted me and my mother as her family when her husband died. We all moved into the Dower house together, and everything was fine."

"You don't have to tell me this."

"Listen. Maybe you'll understand what I'm trying to say about you and your father."

"The new lord of the manor was a distant cousin. There wasn't much to inherit. The only thing that hadn't been gambled or sold away by our squire was the land the house stood on and his wife's art collection. Our art collection." He paused, but Pascale didn't say anything. "Those paintings and sculptures were as familiar to me as your father's works are to you. The woman who owned that collection raised me and educated me. I think I loved her precious paintings as much as she did." Pascale watched him as he leaned his head back and closed his eyes. "It's ironic," he said, a small smile lifting one corner of his mouth. "I met you because I was raised to adore art, too. That's why François and Guillaume took me to Princess Mathilde's ball. I wanted to meet some of the artists I admired."

"My father?" Pascale asked, a catch in her voice.

"Him, too," he said, ruefully.

"But art cannot save you, Pascale. That's the moral of this story. We lost everything, trying to hold onto Jane's collection."

"I know. You talked a little, in your delirium."

"Oh," he said.

"How did it happen." Pascale couldn't resist asking.

"Jane was a sweet old woman. She never asked for a lease when the new squire offered to let her live in the Dower cottage rent free. Unfortunately, that promise was made before the gentleman who made it found out that the art collection she had saved from her husband's excesses were the only objects of value in the estate. When he realized that, he changed his tone. I didn't understand it all at the time, I was too young.

"When I was older I found out that he later asked her to pay rent after all, she didn't suspect that his motives were anything more than they seemed—the desire of a young man to support his rapidly growing family. He hardly took any money, he said he could live on his expectations, as long as his creditor saw that he had a good tenant.

"It was only after their debts had mounted beyond anything she could possibly repay without selling her precious paintings, that they had realized what he had been up to. By then it had been too late. Jane had had to relinquish her collection and move in with her brother, a rector. The clergyman agreed to hire my mother but an overeducated black boy with no talent for domestic service was another story."

Jack told the story in a monotone, quite different from the panicked accents Pascale had heard when he had cried out in his delirium.

"What did you do?"

"Mama got me a job at a neighboring house, but in a few years, I ran away and joined the Navy."

"But I'm not a little girl, I'm a grown woman. You must see

that my position is different from what yours was. If my father and I have problems, we'll solve them. I couldn't just run away."

"I didn't just run away. I told myself it was for her own good—so she wouldn't lose her one chance at securing a roof over her head."

"You were probably right."

He opened his eyes at that, staring bleakly into the fire. "I'm not so sure. I think that I was as eager to escape that place as Mama was to stay there."

"It sounds like you did the right thing, for both of you, but that doesn't make it the right thing for me to do. You had to lead your own life. I'm sure your mother understands that."

"That's what I've been trying to tell you."

"The situation is entirely different. Papa couldn't manage without me. I couldn't desert him. You were a little boy; you couldn't help your mother, so you left to make it easier for her. I'm sure she's proud of you. She knows you love her."

"And you love your father. How is that different?"

"I want the same things my father wants. I helped to create our home. Now that we go to Paris each year, I'm quite satisfied."

"I don't believe you. From everything I've seen, you should be painting yourself, rather than helping him. Can't you picture yourself in a little atelier in Paris; painting, studying, and visiting with your friends."

Pascale thought about it. "Maybe," she said, doubtfully, "but who would take care of everything?"

"I'm sure Paul could manage. He's a grown man, after all. It would probably be good for him to live his own life, too."

Pascale could scarcely argue the point. She'd just made the same one herself. "It's an . . . interesting idea," she said. "But I tried to be an artist once, and I just didn't have the heart for it."

"You have the heart," he said, definitely. "You have more heart than most men I know."

Sometimes, when he looked at her, she thought he, too, was

thinking of those stolen moments in Paris, but then Jack would start talking about the most mundane subjects—as if he hadn't another thought in the world besides clean neckerchiefs or lumpy mattresses. It was infuriating. It also fueled her desire for him.

She knew that could not be his purpose. There had been an occasion or two when she had been alone with him, and he'd been a perfect gentleman, or, more often, the elegant swell whom she'd met at Princess Mathilde's soiree the first week of May. His behavior was above question, but his beauty and grace reminded her of a panther she'd once seen in the zoo. Though she'd seen him furious, and helpless, and in pain, she knew little more about him now than she had that first night. Oh she knew about his mother and Aunt Jane, and that he'd decided to protect her from their folly. Perhaps he even felt a little fondness for her, at times. But she didn't really know him any better than she had before. It was she who had been transformed. Her desire for his touch was so strong sometimes that she—she! Pascale de Ravenault—considered casting caution to the winds. It went completely against her stolid, sensible nature, but she was tempted, often, to kiss Jack Devlin again.

On the fifth evening of their seemingly endless journey through the provence of Burgundy, Pascale found herself alone again with Jack in the taproom of yet another inn. Pascale had stopped the coachman early again that day, because she didn't think it healthy for Jack to continue on without any rest. The long and frequent delays which she thought necessary for his safety had stretched from what might have been a four day trip into what would probably be a seven day oddysey. She didn't regret her actions, but she did feel sympathy for François and Guillaume who spent most of their time in a hard saddle.

She and Jack waited while the other three men arranged for their rooms. He lay resting on a chaise, his copper skin burnished by the glow of the gas light. Pascale felt an awareness of him as a man that brought an odd response in her heart and body. She thought him the most beautiful man she had ever seen, and she was tempted to tell him so.

Desperately, she catalogued the many reasons for restraint. There were, of course, the purely practical considerations: she couldn't afford to draw any attention to herself. In the eyes of society, her home was little better than a brothel; she and her father entertained guests of all stamps, and Pascale had to appear above reproach at all times in order to counteract any impression that they condoned, or encouraged the behavior of their notorious house guests.

There were other, more personal, consequences to be considered as well. Pascale had experimented once, briefly, with romance, and she had been left feeling quite cheated afterward. Dorian had been an artist—young, handsome, ambitious, and very bitter. Tall and blond, he could have been a model. She had not thought about him in years.

He had been one of her father's students. In all of the years she had studied with her father, there had been no differentiation between Paul de Ravenault's treatment of his other pupils and that of his daughter. Papa insisted that they all learn their craft, just as the masters had done in their ateliers, and he put a lot of emphasis on his students perfecting their draftsmanship. She was one of them, living and breathing her art, completely immersed in perfecting her craft. Dorian was the only one who had ever treated her differently.

Dorian seemed to resent her ability to draw; his own sketching was a little sloppy, a little bit lifeless. It was difficult for him. He had the vision, and the dedication, to paint well, but he was lazy about his technique. He was not the only artist Pascale had met who suffered from a lack of self discipline, but he was the first to make her feel guilty about having a natural ability to paint.

Dorian wanted everything she had: her father, her home, her friends, and her talent. His jealousy had baffled her. Pascale, when she had met him, had been fourteen and just beginning to realize that other girls her age rarely even spoke to boys, let alone spent hours with them—working, eating, playing, sometimes even competing with them. The knowledge would not have bothered her, had it not been for Dorian's subtle hints that Pascale was so lucky to escape the usual restrictions of being female, without suffering the obligations that men had to shoulder. He made her feel as though she was lacking in femininity, and unfairly advantaged in her battle to be accepted as an equal to her fellow students.

She couldn't help feeling guilty in the face of his oft-repeated litany, "You're so fortunate to have a father who understands. My father would never help me, no matter how talented I was."

She had an entire year trying to convince him that she was not to blame for her good fortune. It was the first time in her life that working hard at her art had not earned her approval and admiration. Dorian's disapproval was never openly stated, but his "constructive criticism" was constant. He praised her, however, for her other accomplishments. He appreciated it when she helped him prime a canvas for his own work, when she brought him candles to replace those flickering in the studio as he worked late at night, when she had Louise make a special dish to celebrate the completion of one of his paintings. Finally, on her fifteenth birthday, he'd rewarded her by becoming her lover. She had not been impressed with the one intimate encounter they'd shared. Soon after he was called home, and Pascale had said goodbye to him without much regret. After striving for so long for so little appreciation, she had finally come to her senses.

But despite her realization that Dorian, himself, hadn't been the right mate for her, she had noticed that it wasn't Dorian alone who had appreciated her "feminine" talents. Her father and his friends also enjoyed the homey touches she added to their rooms, their meals, the studio. She didn't know when it had happened that she started to think of herself as a woman, rather than an artist. It was clear, though, that the two were not compatible.

It was about that same time that she noticed there was a reason that women, other than her mother and herself, put the men in their lives before themselves. It was more productive. If she sold her father's work, she felt proud; her father was happy; and the servants were paid on time. No matter how hard she worked, it was doubtful that she, a woman, could ever earn the prices or commissions he was able to command. Therefore, it made sense to put his work before her own.

She decided after that first experience with love that she would never pledge her love or loyalty to any man other than her father. And she had never felt the lack of male companionship, until now. Ever since the night Jack had painted his vision for her of what her life could be in Paris, Pascale had been thinking the unthinkable. She had imagined what it would be like to leave the château, and Papa, and live with only the responsibility of taking care of herself; satisfying only her own desires without regard for anyone else. Whenever she thought of Jack's beckoning eyes and seductive voice describing this *otherlife,* she felt a tingle of pleasure throughout her body—as if he had stroked her from her head to her toes.

She had hoped he didn't notice the way her pulse pounded when she touched him, though she'd occasionally caught him looking at her speculatively. She'd done her best to hide all but the charitable emotions one might expect a woman to feel under the unusual circumstances in which they'd become so intimately acquainted.

"We'll be home soon," she said.

Pascale heaved a sigh of relief at the thought of escaping Jack's keen eyes and even sharper tongue in just a day or two.

"Poor Pascale." He mocked her, but his smile took the bite from his words. "You can't wait, can you?"

"It will be lovely, you'll see," she answered. "You'll feel better in no time, once we get to Beaune."

"I'll miss our lovely evenings," Jack said, teasingly.

"We all will, I'm sure," Pascale returned in kind.

He raised an eyebrow. "You viper. That sharp tongue will get you in trouble one day," he warned. But he was smiling.

"You know," she said. "I've been trying to fix that, since someone I know called me a shrew."

"Well," he said, consideringly. "You *have* been nicer to me since I had my . . . accident, than you were before."

Pascale didn't answer him right away. She felt self-conscious. Her feelings toward Jack had undergone a complete reversal when she'd thought she'd lost him.

"Anyone else would have done the same. In the same situation."

"Not anyone," Jack said seriously. "You." She felt her skin heat under his tender scrutiny. "You have done more for my recovery than ten of the best doctors could, I'm sure."

She was relieved when François and Guillaume joined them in the dimly lit room, ordered a bottle of wine and settled in for the long evening ahead of them.

"Paul has gone on to his room, to work, I think," François informed them.

"You'd think he'd be tired of sketching this damn country," Jack said mildly.

"Never," Pascale told him. She said the first thing she thought of in order to distract him from the physical discomfort he had to be feeling after the grueling day. "It is impossible to find the same scene twice."

Jack looked around the room. "This scene looks exactly the same to me as the one last night, and the night before, and the night before that—except that Paul isn't here drawing it."

"Oh, but it's not. Last night, the chandelier lit your face completely differently. Tonight, these lanterns send a flickering orange glow about the room. Each creates a unique effect. Your skin is burnt-almond tonight. Last night, it was the color of roasting chestnuts."

Guillaume poured their wine. "Tonight, we have red wine. Last night, it was white."

Pascale smiled, and Jack ruefully joined in.

François hurried out of the room and was back in a moment with some paper and charcoal, both red and gray. "Show us," he said.

Pascale looked doubtfully at the supplies he had brought her. "You should ask Papa tomorrow evening."

"We might be in Beaune tomorrow evening, packing our bags for the journey home. Please, will you do it now?"

Pascale picked up the chalk and looked at the men. Almost by its own volition, her hand swept across the paper, leaving a swath of color as it passed. She sketched the two scenes, the one from the previous evening, and then the current one. When she had done, she handed François and Guillaume the two sketches.

"Ah," said Guillaume. "Now I see."

Both sketches made their way to Jack. He looked at them for a very long while in silence, and finally commented, "I prefer these to anything I've seen your father do."

"You are prejudiced," Pascale said.

"I don't think so," Jack answered. "I am telling you the truth."

He chose that moment to look up at her. When he saw her shaking her head, his expression hardened. "I have no reason to lie to you."

"I don't think you're lying," she assured him. She had had plenty of time to think, and rethink, her feelings for him, and all that had passed between them. She had accused him of having no integrity, of having no honor. She hadn't believed it, but she had said it, and he thought she meant it. She owed him an apology, but she couldn't bring herself to make it. She settled for a half-truth. "I believe you."

He wouldn't let her get away with that. "What do you believe? That I'm telling you the truth?"

"I believe that you think these sketches are better than Papa's."

"But you don't believe that they are." He turned to François and Guillaume. "Help me," he said.

They shrugged. "Of course," they said as one.

"Now do you believe me?" Jack asked her.

Pascale tore her gaze from his frustrated face to look at François, who nodded; then to Guillaume, who said, "He is telling you the truth, Pascale."

Twenty-two

By the time they reached the rolling hills of Beaune, they had wearied of craning their necks to watch for the telltale signs of their progress south and west. It was only when the old city walls were spotted, the crumbling gray stone standing higher than the rooftops on the western edge of the village, that Pascale felt they'd finally arrived.

Unfortunately, when she finally passed beneath the portico of her own home, another battle raged. Some of Jack's men had outpaced them, and the household was in an uproar. Out-and-out war raged between Madame Francine Pitt and Mr. Henry Bates. Apparently, these two had found themselves at odds from the moment he presented himself at the door. Upon being refused admittance, he'd mounted a forceful and indefensible assault. If Pierre had been present to lend his lined countenance and years of experience as butler and premier guardian of the de Ravenaults' domain, the outcome might have been different. But Francine had been completely at a loss in the face of the unprecedented invasion. Her sharp tongue and all-for-nothing tactics had gained her only the right to be held prisoner within her own home once Bates gained entry to the château.

Pascale listened to both sides of the story. Pierre tried to calm the strife, which raged from attic to cellar. The servants had ranged themselves behind their temporary chatelaine, and the captain's men behind their unrepentant first mate, and each side was full of righteous indignation at the treatment they'd received.

Bates felt entirely justified in the extreme action he'd taken. "I knew you'd explain it as soon as you came home, miss, and that fishwife would be trumped good and proper."

Francine was not at all mollified by the knowledge that Henry Bates had been sent to them by the family—just as he'd told her. Nor was she apologetic about her part in the confrontation.

"How was I to know this ruffian truly was a friend of the master's? He barges in here like he owns the house, and then expects me to do nothing. Well, I'll tell you, I didn't hesitate to show him the error of his ways, and I'd do it again." From the martial light gleaming in her old governess's eye, Pascale could well imagine that she would, this very minute, if Pascale just gave the word.

"Of course you would, Francine," Pascale said. "I'm very proud of you." Henry's mouth dropped open in shock, while Francine preened under her mistress's praise. Madame Pitt could not resist shooting a look of triumph at her enemy. But that was too much for the sailor.

"Now look here, miss, you ain't agoin' to tell me that you think it's right for her to act like some flamin' banshee. I ain't never had no fight with a woman afore, and that's a fact, but no matter how many times I told her I couldn't hit her, her being the fairer sex and all, she just kept comin' at me. Look at me hands and face. She's gone and scratched me up somethin' terrible. It's a miracle me men got her to her room without more serious injury. She kicked poor Ansel down the stairway." Pascale felt for Jack's first mate. His face truly was a sight.

"You come with me right now and we'll put something on those welts," she soothed. To Francine she said, "Why don't you go help Pierre get things under control, now that this little misunderstanding has been ironed out."

Francine flounced off, Henry Bates staring after her in amazement. "Well, I never," he said.

"She was just trying to carry out her duty to the family."

"She nearly took out my eye," he said wonderingly. "I never thought a wrinkled old prune like that had it in her."

Pascale smiled at him. "She's younger than you are. And if I don't mistake, you've got a wrinkle or two yourself. But I think between the two of you, I'll feel safe enough in my own home."

He smiled ruefully at her and said, "That you can, miss, that you can."

The household finally calm, Pascale retired to her room and the first real privacy she'd had in a week. She needed a quiet retreat to reflect on the changes in her feelings for Jack. For the past week—spent almost entirely under the eyes of her father, her friends, and her servants—he had flirted with her, argued with her, and even teased her, but his half-mocking, friendly tone never altered. In his presence coils of tension knotted in her belly, while he seemed virtually unaffected.

From the first he had tempted her to touch. Now she was ruled by want. She wondered at the way his kisses had moved her. She was intrigued by the possibility that she could feel more of that same sweet pleasure.

She was sure that he would give her The Painting if he was seduced, particularly since Papa had told him he'd changed his mind and no longer objected to her seeing his masterwork. This added to the temptation. She fell asleep still trying to decide if she had the courage to approach him. A good night's sleep brought a cooler head and calmer counsel.

François and Guillaume were leaving straight away to get back to Paris.

"Be careful," Guillaume warned, kissing Pascale tenderly on the forehead. "Have your men keep watch for strangers in the village."

"Jack . . ." She caught the slip and hastily corrected it, "I mean, Captain Devlin . . . ," she faltered.

"I know," François said, smiling knowingly.

"He will take care of that."

"Good," Guillaume said.

She bid them goodbye and saw them off, then went back to the kitchen to see how Louise was faring. She was bustling about the kitchen preparing coffee and cakes for the servants' midmorning refreshment.

"It's market day," Pascale said, as she came into the room. She didn't, at first, see the two young men seated at the large kitchen table.

They looked toward her as she entered. Her father's newest protégés were as dissimilar in appearance as they were in temperament. They were, of course, white. Only twice in her life had Papa had black students apply to him, and one had been African. David was light complexioned, with rosy cheeks, and honey-brown hair that fell to his rounded shoulders. When he saw her, his smile widened. "Look, Pascale's here, Yves," he announced.

"Ah good, the family's all together again," said Yves, the habitual trace of cynicism in his voice. His complexion was sallow, his eyes and hair almost black, and his stark black coat emphasized the angularity of his frame.

Pascale hadn't expected the young artists to be awaiting the family's return. She didn't think they'd question Jack's arrival. Each was, in his own way, too self-absorbed to be curious about anyone else's affairs. David was a lovely boy, though hopelessly incapable of handling the simplest social exchange. He walked about with his head in the clouds. He reminded Pascale of her father. His painting, though, more than made up for these shortcomings. Yves, on the other hand, was only moderately talented, but he was as driven and ambitious as his counterpart was unworldly.

"Louise, we have missed you," Yves said sardonically, sipping from a steaming mug.

The cook ignored them and turned straight away to Pascale. "I need everything; meat, flour, lard, fruit, oh, and chocolate. Those sailors have eaten everything in the house. You may want to see how the garden is producing—we may need onions and tomatoes as well."

It was pretty much as Pascale had expected, and she went to the pantry to take stock for herself, mentally adding the two half-grown men in the kitchen to her tally of mouths to feed. David would forget about eating as soon as he and Papa were reunited, and if she invited him to take his meals with them, she would have to include Yves. Neither man would thank her, but she had made it her business to keep David healthy, despite himself, and Yves was too clever to refuse the amenities of the house, and accepted Pascale's care, and her father's constructive criticism, with equal relish.

Pascale would never have questioned any of the duties that she took on in order to take care of her father and his guests, but for John Devlin's mocking comments, which resurfaced in her mind as she mentally composed her grocery list.

It was not in her nature to rebel—it was far easier just to get on with it—but she did feel the need, suddenly, to give fair warning of impending change.

"I won't always be able to take care of you two, you know. You must learn to fend for yourselves." She threw an old withered apple she'd found in a basket on the larder floor to Yves. "Have you ever been to the market, for example?"

"Certainly, I have," Yves said. "But I hope to avoid ever returning. Smells bad."

"I don't remember if I've been. Perhaps I could go with you today," David said, apparently much struck by the idea.

"If you let him choose the food, we'll all of us be dead by tomorrow," Yves teased. David didn't take offense. He didn't seem to have heard the remark, but was staring vaguely in the direction of the pantry.

"You should consider coming, too," Pascale said. "I think it would do you a world of good to get out among the common people, Yves."

He made a moue of distaste. "Why in the world should I do that, when you so enjoy doing it for us."

"I only enjoy doing it, as you so charmingly put it, for certain people."

"But that's discriminatory. Anyway, I don't see why I shouldn't be mollycoddled like everyone else in this house," Yves protested. "Why should David here, who can barely be prevailed upon to tear himself from his latest portrait of his most recent inamorata, be accorded special treatment, when it is I who truly appreciate all that you do."

David apparently heard his name mentioned. "Did you say something to me, Yves? I wasn't attending."

"I rest my case," Yves said, triumphant.

"He doesn't behave badly on purpose as you do."

"I meant to listen. But I was just thinking that Lisette might enjoy our sessions more if she were to dress up in costumes. She does want to act, after all. Perhaps it would be good practice for her to pretend she was someone else while I paint her. What do you think?"

"I think you are an imbecile," Yves said. "Lisette is never going to pay any attention to you until, or unless, you make money. She will, however, model for you as long as you pay her that modeling fee she demands."

"You are so cynical," David said to his friend. Turning his attention to Pascale, he asked, "Did you want me for something?"

"No," Pascale said gently, smiling at him. "We don't need you."

"Fat lot of good it would do if we did," Yves pointed out, but David had already lapsed back into his reverie.

"You, on the other hand, could be helpful if you wished, which is the reason why I discriminate between you," Pascale said, only half in jest.

Ruefully, Yves admitted, "I am, probably, capable of taking care of myself. But when I see the warm attention you lavish on the hopelessly incompetent strays that you take in, I almost wish I weren't."

Pascale shrugged, unsympathetic. David was lovable and

sweet, and she was more than willing to volunteer her humble services to keep him working in the face of minor distractions like life, and, more recently, love—until some other woman took over that mission for her. Yves, on the other hand, was more like herself and would manage to see his bills paid and a decent meal put on his table, no matter what.

Yves finished his coffee, and stood up, and David unconsciously followed suit. The tall angular man looked down contemptuously at his rotund compatriot and rolled his eyes. "If it were not for women like you, Pascale, he would starve to death, and I would give up art for something more mundane— like tax collecting."

"Eh?" David said, waking from his stupor. Yves took this in with a sardonic grin.

"You should give up your 'beauty,' and focus your attention on Pascale: She can balance your artistic nature with her more practical one." David stood staring after him as he left the kitchen.

Then he turned to survey Pascale. Yves's comment stung, but Pascale wouldn't let it bother her. She was sensible, rather than beautiful, but that was important, too. She might regret it occasionally, but she wasn't ashamed of it.

David apologized for his distracted air. "I was thinking of Lisette. I am meeting her this afternoon," he said earnestly. "Shall I accompany you to the market?"

"Thank you, but I think I'd like to walk alone," Pascale declined his offer. He would be of no use to her and he'd hate it. Jack might enjoy the odd characters who worked in the marketplace in Beaune's main square, but David, like Papa, would undoubtedly fail to recognize the unique characters and their strange manners. Lost in contemplation of how Jack might enjoy a visit to town, Pascale was startled when David spoke again.

"I think Yves was joking, but by God he's hit on something! Don't know why I never thought of it before," David mused aloud. "Would you model for me, Pascale? I would very much like to paint you."

"I am honored, sir," she said, curtsying. "However, I think Lisette is more in the current mode. You had better concentrate on her."

He took her gentle refusal well. "I daresay it's best," he surprised her by saying. "You are quite beautiful, but I'm not sure I could capture your essence. So much of your charm comes from within."

David didn't even realize his blunder, making her despair of his ever succeeding in his avocation. No woman liked to be told that her inner beauty was more appealing than her outward appearance. Even Pascale herself was no exception to that rule.

Still she managed to smile as she accepted his compliment with a graceful, "Thank you, *mon cher.*"

Francine, too, offered to keep her company on the way to the market, but Pascale declined. She couldn't think with Madame Pitt chattering away.

She thought she might better have spent her time talking to Francine by the time she'd arrived. Her thoughts had been occupied with David's unthinking compliment. Pascale had no illusions about her beauty. Her reflection in the mirror told her it was decent enough, but nothing out of the ordinary. With her dark skin, she couldn't hope to compete with the acknowledged beauties of the day. She might have been admired as an exotic, but her round face precluded her from those exclusive ranks as well. Her high forehead and almond-shaped eyes gave her a look of distinction, she'd been told. Anyway, beauty wasn't nearly as important as talent—which was immortal—she reminded herself.

She was still ruminating about the sincere but less than flattering compliment when she went to visit Jack. After she returned from the market, Pascale made her way to Jack's room. She'd made it a practice during the past few weeks to collect stories with which to entertain their bored bedridden patient, and it had become an ingrained habit on their journey from Paris to the farm. Pascale was certain Jack would enjoy the tale of her excursion to the market, and her dealings with Madame Turain and her sons.

His quarters, one of the guest rooms, was much larger and more comfortable than the servant's room in which he'd stayed in the small rented house in Paris. She took in his new surroundings, and was satisfied that he would be quite comfortable. The walls had been done up in blue-and-white striped satin. The carpeting, a large chair, and a chaise were upholstered with light-blue and maroon satin, which complemented the cherry-wood desk, bureau, and smaller chairs. The large bed—laid with white-and-blue damask covers—was a much more suitable lodging for his tall manly form than the narrow pallet had been.

She took in the light streaming through the tall windows, and was sure his spirits must be positively affected by the abundant light allowed in by the south-facing apertures. They had been left open to catch the balmy spring breeze, and the curtains waved gently at Pascale as she closed the door behind her. Their guest had been installed by John Douglas, Henry Bates, and the other men the previous evening, and Pascale hadn't had the energy, or the courage, to visit before this. She was pleased to see that the pinched look, which had taken residence about his nose and mouth on the harrowing journey, had already disappeared.

If he did not smile at the sight of her, Jack greeted her appearance with every sign of equanimity.

"Ah ha, our chatelaine," he said to John Douglas, who looked up from the paper and quill with which he'd been laboring at the desk. That individual didn't interrupt himself, other than to nod briefly in her direction. Jack cleared his throat, in an oblique warning that wasn't lost on his visitor. "We'll finish those later," he said.

"Don't interrupt yourself on my account," Pascale said, slightly offended that her guest would make such a point of hiding his business from her. "I just came to see that you were settled in."

"I had hoped you'd stay and visit awhile," Jack said with a disarming smile. "I miss my charming companion of the coach. Here I haven't even the passing scenery to enliven the day."

She allowed herself to be coaxed into taking the large comfortable chair set near the end of the bed. John Douglas was dispatched to get some coffee for his master. They were, once again, alone.

Despite the fact that they were on Pascale's home ground, she was even less comfortable here than she had been attending to Jack in his little room in the house in the city. Perhaps it was because, she noted with some pleasure as well as a little unease, he looked much healthier now. His hair shone black as a crow's wing. He was vital and tempting. His almond-colored skin was smooth, and unblemished, his clean-shaven chin a determined block. His brown eyes glowed seductively. Painful as the past weeks had been for him, nature had nonetheless continued its work, and the bumps and bruises on his face had healed completely. If it hadn't been for the sling, which held his arm in place, she would have felt that she had invaded a gentleman's private boudoir.

She shrugged off the discomfort, and set about telling Jack of the adventures she'd had that morning. He appreciated them, as she had known he would, and by the time she was finished telling her tales, they were sitting companionably sipping their hot drinks and chuckling together.

"Would you like some more coffee, or more to eat?" Pascale had easily fallen into the role of hostess as Jack didn't seem to need a nurse anymore.

"All I do is lie here and eat," Jack said, his reluctant tone belied by the eager glance he threw at the tray of pastries. Pascale stood and picked up the dish bearing the selection of delectable *gâteaux,* and waved it before him.

"And, therefore, Louise takes full credit for your recovery.

Let's not offend the chef." Jack was clearly tempted. "She delights, now, in making your favorite dishes. We wouldn't want that to change, would we?"

Jack surveyed the ambrosial concoctions laid out for his savoring, and finally chose one filled with chocolate cream.

"You wretch. You are trying to make me fat," he accused.

"Not I, my captain," Pascale turned to put the tray back down on his bedside table. "You may lay that fault at Cook's door. She is only happy when her charges are pleasantly plump."

Pascale reached out automatically to rearrange the pillows behind his head and arm, as she had done so many times during the weeks she had helped to care for him. She was mildly surprised when he transferred the éclair to his injured right hand and caught her wrist with the left. He inspected her wrist, and then her forearm, carefully.

"I do not see any evidence of that," he said. His hand slid up her arm to her shoulder, which he squeezed gently. "There's not an ounce of excess flesh on you."

Pascale's throat closed, but she managed a small smile as she tried to answer in the same light tones. "Ah, but I've spent years learning how to avoid the things that are not good for me . . ." She stumbled over the last words as his eyes lit with an inner flame. "Without offending her," she finished, falteringly, as his hand wandered to her cheek.

"Perhaps this is how you have fooled her. She doesn't look beyond this soft roundness."

A thought flashed through her mind. This man didn't see her as a practical, sensible housekeeper, as everyone else did.

In fact, he protested such treatment. Much as she might disagree with Jack, and dislike his insistence that she was, in fact, a helpless, vulnerable creature, it was . . . interesting . . . to be treated like a desirable woman, rather than a very efficient machine. Certainly, at the moment, he seemed to have other things on his mind besides being fed and cared for like a spoiled tabby cat.

"Your pastry." She tried to divert him. She reached for the éclair with the intention of putting it back on the serving platter and moving away. "If you don't want this," she said, taking the pastry from him, "I'm sure someone else will." He slid his hand down her arm to her other wrist and subjected it to the same exploration that the first had suffered. Her voice faded as he placed her free hand against his chest, where she could feel his heart beating quite as rapidly as her own.

"Oh, but I do," he said.

Pascale, entranced by the novel sensation of feeling his smooth muscular breast move under her palm, didn't remove her hand when he let it go. He reached out with his uninjured arm again, and cupped her other hand with his own. He guided their two hands, and the pastry she held, toward his lips. Pascale swallowed, watching as he took a small bite and sucked gently at the cream-filled éclair. A drop of chocolate stained his upper lip, and she licked her own in response. He followed the movement with hungry eyes.

"Mmmm." The appreciative sound came from somewhere low in his throat. "Delicious," Jack said.

His injured hand drifted upward to cover the hand splayed over his heart.

"I should really go now," she spluttered, unable to pull away abruptly, for fear that she might do damage to the bones knitting in his arm. His coal-black eyes locked onto hers. His chin tilted slightly upward and his lips parted, indicating his readiness for another bite of the pastry she held. The lure was irresistible. She continued to feed him bite after bite.

She hadn't noticed when his injured hand had been removed from atop her own. When he took the last bite from her hand, she was sitting on the side of the bed, his other hand lying harmlessly beside her knee. He nibbled at the chocolate that stained her fingertips, and her bones dissolved completely. Her legs dangled over the side of the bed. When he loosened her fingers, her hand fell as far as his shoulder, and lit there.

He sighed, seemingly replete, and let his head fall back

against the headboard. Pascale was conscious only of a vague sense of disappointment. But, she consoled herself, this was the opportunity she'd been waiting for. They were alone; unlikely, at this time of day, to be interrupted. And they were once again in charity with one another, rather than bickering. Jack would never again be as pliable as he was now.

To business! she thought.

"You offered, once, to let me have The Painting," she murmured.

"Your father will show it to you," he said, smiling.

"He might change his mind again," she pointed out. "I could never be sure."

His smile started to fade. "That's his right."

She leaned forward, staring intently into his eyes. "Would you give it to me now? Papa has agreed to it."

"I don't have it with me." The contented expression he'd worn had been replaced with a familiar stubborn look.

Pascale continued, undaunted. "I know," she said impatiently. "But I could send someone to retrieve it from its hiding place."

"No." His countenance was grim.

"Why not?" She tried, unsuccessfully, to keep her exasperation out of her voice.

"It's too dangerous."

"When this is over, I'll send someone. Just tell me where The Painting is."

He looked at her measuringly, and her breath caught in her throat.

"I don't think so," Jack said.

Twenty-three

Pascale lay in her bed, gritty eyed and exhausted, but still wide awake in the small hours of the night. If she closed her eyes, she could still feel the whisper of his breath, his lips and his warm callused palms. The encounter this evening had whet her appetite for more. Her curiosity about what it would be like to be held by him knew no bounds. It was distracting her from her real goal. She had to make Jack trust her, to make him believe she wouldn't do anything that would put any of their lives at risk.

Jack had implied once that he would give her The Painting if she made it worth his while. She'd been offended then. She was tempted now. Allowing him to seduce her would make him sure that he could trust her, and it would allay any fears he might have about her loyalty or devotion. There, in her virginal bed, she decided she would not wait to find out what it might feel like to succumb to him. She would seduce him.

It was unseemly. It was totally improper. But Pascale wanted The Painting. More than that, she admitted to herself, she wanted to beat Captain John Devlin at his own game. To hell with propriety.

There was little risk to her reputation. No one would ever know. A shiver of anticipation ran through her. But there was a measure of fear in the tremor as well. She hadn't ever undertaken such a foolhardy venture. Pascale didn't understand the code of honor by which Jack lived, but she knew that he wouldn't condone her behavior. He'd made it clear long ago that he thought her altogether too forward. Perhaps this scheme would rekindle, even set ablaze, the flame of righteous indignation she'd seen in his eyes the night they met.

Pascale turned the outrageous idea over and over in her mind until, unable to worry about it any longer, she finally fell asleep.

Despite her misgivings she soon found an opportunity to put her plan into action. The following afternoon, her father took Yves and David with him to paint in the vineyards, where pale-green leaves topped the bushy burgundy grape plants clinging to their stakes. They would spend hours trying to capture on canvas spring's promise of a fruitful harvest later in the year.

Jack had sent John Douglas to the village on some mysterious errand. Pascale knew he wouldn't return until after dark. He'd left explicit instructions for Philippe on how to administer his employer's treatment at dusk. And Francine, who lurked about the door any time that Pascale visited Jack in his room, had gone on her monthly visit to the hospital to bring the family's offering of wine, cheese, and fresh vegetables to the sisters.

This left Pascale with little to do, except to shore up her courage and tell Cook she'd bring Jack the light snack Louise insisted on feeding him between luncheon and dinner each day. It was the perfect opportunity. But her hands shook as she picked up the serving tray. She was so nervous at what she was about to do. Seduction was not something she'd ever attempted before, and the closer she came to the crucial moment, the more her nerves jangled and buzzed under her coppery skin.

"Cook tells me you didn't eat all of your noon meal," Pascale scolded as she came into the room. The trembling that assaulted her threatened to give her away before she'd even begun. She tightened her grip on the silver tray she carried, so her shaking hands wouldn't betray her.

Jack looked at her mockingly from beneath half-closed eyelids. "So they sent you in to work your magic on me."

"They sent in the big guns—isn't that the naval term?" she tried to tease. Her smile felt stiff on her lips.

Pascale fussily rearranged the contents of the tray, which she had set down on the bedside table. Then she sat gingerly on the bed beside him. She felt the hard length of his thigh against her hip and only just managed to resist the urge to shift away from him.

"Do you really think you are the best candidate for the combined offices of jailer and nursery maid? I'd say you were a little on the small side for such a big job, myself," Jack said. Jack had made it clear long ago that he resented it when she allowed herself to be offered up to him, like a lamb to the slaughter, by the people who should, in his view, be protecting her. They had argued about it often in Paris. She had thought that once he met Francine he would forget about this strange obsession of his, but apparently, her old governess's constant clucking over her hadn't changed his view at all. Apparently, her eternally stuffy companion did not satisfy Jack as the protector of the daughter of the house.

Once again, she marveled at the way he alone saw her. He made her feel like she might really be the fragile porcelain doll he seemed to expect. It was, in its own way, a heady feeling. For once she appreciated his protectiveness. It bolstered her resolve. He wouldn't carp on it so if he wasn't concerned for her.

"Eat your nuncheon," she commanded. She was agitated, and uncertain of herself, her nerves stretched to a breaking point.

She nearly jumped out of her skin when he said, "Pascale?"

She answered, with a cautious glance at him, "Yes?"

He opened his mouth to speak, then hesitated. "Will you sup with me?" he finally asked.

"I *ate* my midday meal," Pascale answered. "I will have a glass of wine with you, though. Just to keep you company."

She walked over to the bellpull and rang for Philippe, who appeared in minutes. "Please bring us some wineglasses," she requested of the footman.

"Certainly, mademoiselle." He bowed and hurried off.

When he returned he asked, "Is there anything else I can do for you?"

"No," Pascale said, looking at Jack, who shook his head.

"These women keep trying to fatten me up, like a calf," he complained to Philippe.

"Worse things have happened," said the footman.

"I don't think we'll need anything more." Pascale dismissed him with a nod.

That done, she wandered over once again to Jack's bedside. He hadn't touched any of the dishes she'd brought. But he did pour out two glasses of wine.

"You must eat. You need to keep up your strength so you can heal," Pascale admonished.

"So I can retrieve your precious painting?" His voice was dry, but he still wore that lazy half-smile.

"Not just for that," Pascale protested. "I'd like to see you on your feet again."

"Really?" he asked, and she nodded. "Somehow I thought you liked me better this way," he teased. "Flat on my back, and trussed up like a monkey." He let out a chuckle.

She tilted her head, considering him. "Well . . . ," she drew the word out, "It is nice to have you at my mercy."

"I am helpless. Do with me what you will," Jack said. He lay back, challenging her with his dark gaze.

Her eyes dropped to his lips before she could force herself to look away. This was not exactly what she had intended. Well, it was . . . but not the way she'd planned it.

She took a deep breath. "In fact, I had thought . . . well once you seemed to imply that . . ." She ran her tongue over dry lips and tried again. "I had been thinking that you . . . wanted me."

"More than once, I think. And I didn't imply anything, I said it."

"One time, specifically, you said, I had something to offer that my father didn't. Something much more attractive than money. Am I correct in assuming you meant me?" There, she'd finally said it. Pascale waited for his answer, afraid to look at him.

"Yes. That's what I meant," he said.

She kept her gaze on his chin, too nervous to lift it any higher. This was the most important, most difficult business transaction Pascale had ever had to negotiate. She couldn't afford to make a mistake.

"Well, I . . . ummm . . . I'm willing to make you an offer."

"Which would be?" His chin was set in a stern line, his lips no longer curved in a smile.

"I offer myself, in exchange for The Portrait. You can do whatever you like to me, and you, I, we . . . I mean—"

"I know quite well what you mean," he said, his voice as hard as stone.

"If you agree, I promise not to do anything foolish, like trying to get The Painting now. I'll trust you, if you'll trust me."

"And?"

His tone was forbidding, but she continued, resolutely. "I thought I was in love once, and so"—she took a deep breath—"I let a boy make love to me." She waited, but Jack said nothing. "I'm not saying this to shock you, but because I don't want you to think you'd be taking advantage of me." She met his gaze head-on.

He searched her face, she thought he didn't believe her. "It's true," Pascale said. "His name was Dorian."

"I see." His jaw had relaxed. Pascale sighed in relief. The hardest part was over. She let her gaze drop to his full lips again. All she had to do now was wait for his answer. "Did Dorian respond well to this rather cold-blooded approach to love?" he asked.

"Dorian? I don't know. We never talked about it. It only happened once."

"Did you seduce him, too?" Jack asked. Pascale searched his face for any sign of resentment, but she didn't see it there. The question did not seem to be facetious. She considered carefully and answered, "No, I guess he seduced me, but I think I like this better. . . . And I wouldn't describe it as cold-blooded." Pascale thought about it for a moment more. "I suppose you might say it's a practical approach," she added. "Everyone says I'm very practical by nature." She chanced a look up at him, but his eyes were unreadable. "I believe you find me desirable." Jack didn't confirm or deny the statement. She lowered her eyes and continued. "Since you have The Painting, and I want it, I thought it made sense to explore this mutual attraction that exists between us and come to some understanding."

"If I did consider your proposition, I would want you to do one thing for me," Jack said.

"What?" Pascale held her breath.

"We are making a bargain, aren't we?"

"I hope so."

"I understood that to be the reason for this entire outlandish conversation," he said.

"It is," Pascale agreed at once.

"You want the location of your painting, and I'd like something as well."

"That sounds fair." She'd meant to sound completely accommodating, but her voice was faint. She cleared her throat and said more loudly, "W-what do you want?"

"Come here," he said. Pascale felt compelled to obey the command. She walked slowly to the foot of the bed. "Here," he ordered. He raised his hand, palm up, and held it out to her. She came around the bed and stood a foot away from him, but didn't take his hand. He urged her closer, his outstretched arm going to her waist. "Look at me."

Pascale raised her eyes slowly. Jack waited, his face inscrutable, eyes hooded.

"You are the strangest girl. You are so busy all the time, attending to your father, your friends, your business. I wonder if you could be still, not on your way to some destination, or to take care of someone, but content just to enjoy yourself."

"There are quiet times here at home. Our annual trip to Paris is only a month long, so I have a full schedule while we're there. But, now that we're back in the country, you will soon see I am not nearly as busy."

"It sounds to me as if running this household is constant work. I thought that was why you said you gave up painting. Because you didn't have time for it."

"Not just time, but . . . It's hard to explain."

"I think I understand. There's never time enough for you to sit quietly, at peace. Look at you now."

His all-seeing eyes took in her hands, fidgeting with the folds of her skirt. "I'm nervous," Pascale admitted.

"Don't be." He got that speculative look in his eye again. "I accept your offer. On one condition. That you promise to relax."

Pascale didn't hesitate. "I will."

"It's not that easy," Jack said. "You're wound as tight as a clock. If I touched you now, I think you'd jump a foot in the air."

"No, I . . ." Pascale caught her lip in her teeth and worried it until she realized that was probably the very thing Jack was talking about. She stopped, self-consciously, then released her skirt and let her hands dangle loosely at her side. She summoned up the courage to say, "I want you to touch me. Really."

Jack raised an eyebrow in obvious disbelief and studied her rigid, straight-backed stance.

"Really?" His voice, full of doubt, challenged her. "Then, kiss me," he said.

Pascale leaned over the side of the bed and placed her lips

against his. She took a quick taste, just enough to whet her appetite for more. Then she straightened up again.

"Okay?" she asked.

"It's a start," he said. "Not bad . . . for a nun. Try again," he suggested. "Put your hands on my shoulders. Don't worry. I won't break," he reassured her as her hands fluttered in the air between them.

She was determined to prove she could do better than that first chaste caress. This time she darted her tongue between his parted lips into the enticing cavern beyond.

He nodded as she lifted her head. "Better," Jack said. "Again," he urged.

So she was smiling as her mouth settled lightly on his. She lingered over the exploration of his firm, moist lips, and her arms wound around his neck. All thought flew out of her mind as he wrapped his one good arm around her waist and pulled her to him. Her euphoric mood was replaced by a deeper satisfaction as he took control of the kiss with the same mastery that he had demonstrated on previous occasions.

He found the secret crevices of her mouth. His tongue dueled with hers and dared her to follow his lead. It was a challenge she was eager to meet. The inside of his mouth was hot and soft. Her heart beat so riotously she thought it would burst out of her chest. She strained even closer, resting one knee on the bed so she wouldn't overbalance as she leaned into him.

Jack sank into the pillows behind him, and Pascale's other knee rose onto the bed. She knelt over him, trying to keep her weight off of his broken ribs. It finally came to her that he'd slipped his injured arm out of his sling so that he could hold her with both arms and she started to pull away, saying, "Your arm."

"It's all right," he said, trying to recapture her mouth with his own, and settling on her chin when she lifted her head out of his reach. "Relax," Jack said as she craned her head to try and see his injured arm.

His lips blazed a fiery trail down her jaw to her neck, and

then feathered over the sensitive skin that covered her collarbone. She gave up on her effort to check that he wasn't straining his bad arm. There wasn't a trace of pain on his face, and
it took little effort to ignore her fading conscience and sink
again into a mindless state.

Her last vestige of resistance melted before the onslaught
of his questing lips. They skimmed across the gentle swell of
her breasts, which felt full and heavy as she knelt above him.
Her hands were buried in the pillows on either side of his
head, and she braced her elbows as his mouth moved downward. He nuzzled the skin exposed by her gaping bodice. His
uninjured arm came up and pushed the material down so that
her breasts were bared.

Pascale squeezed her eyes closed, embarrassed *and* excited
by the shamefulness of exposing herself to a man. His hand
cupped one pendulous breast, and he urged her to shift her
weight forward so he could kiss her there, too. His thumb
swept back and forth across one hardened peak, while his
mouth captured the other, matching the teasing caress with his
tongue. A shiver of delight rippled through her.

He released her. "Look at me," Jack said. He waited for her
to open her eyes. "It's my turn." He undid the buttons of his
shirt and pushed it to the sides. His chest was smooth and
brown as a hazelnut shell. Pascale eagerly reached out to touch
him. Her hands slid over his firm skin and traced the shape
of the muscles beneath. She leaned down to suckle his nipples,
and they pebbled into hard kernels in her mouth. A thrill of
pleasure surged through her at her power to move him as he
moved her. She raised her head.

"Enough?" she asked.

"For now," he answered, pulling her head down to plant a
wet, openmouthed kiss on her smiling lips. His hand went to
her bosom again, and he started to play idly with one red-
brown areola. He traced the contours of each breast with one
fingernail.

"Let's try something," he mused aloud, leaving her in a fever of curiosity as he tugged her over till she straddled him.

It was deliciously improper, kneeling astride a man. Her skirts and his blankets separated their bodies, but a tremor of anticipation traveled from her head to her toes as she sat in that compromising position. She could feel the blood coursing through her veins. She was aware of every inch of her body in a way she never had been before.

Jack seemed to recall himself and regarded her intently. She offered him a tremulous smile.

"It feels good, doesn't it . . . to relax?" he asked.

Pascale could only nod. She could never have imagined that relinquishing the iron control she maintained over herself could be so freeing. She felt a strange combination of heady exhilaration and almost frightening vulnerability. She couldn't wait to explore these new feelings.

Jack said, "Kiss me again."

Pascale complied. Her inhibitions gone, she fulfilled his request with relish, taking her time to plunder his mouth. His hand was at her breast again, and she arched her back in silent encouragement of his caresses, like a cat stretching out in a patch of sunlight.

She missed him instantly when he took his hand away. Her disappointment grew as his hand slipped beneath her skirt.

It was over, then, she thought. The glorious rush of excitement, the building passion, the new and wonderful sensations he had inspired in her were about to end. She bit her lip to keep a groan from escaping. Her first "lover" had been less skilled than Jack, and from him she had learned that the culmination of the kissing and the sighs was a few minutes of frantic fumbling beneath her skirts, exactly like the hasty couplings of the animals on the farm.

She tore her mouth reluctantly from his. "Do you need help?" she asked, mindful that with only one hand he might find it difficult to open the fastenings of their undergarments.

"A kind offer, Pascale." He deftly untied the ribbon that

held closed her cotton drawers, and skimmed them down to her thighs as he spoke. "Tempting, but, I think, unnecessary. We have plenty of time."

He cupped her female center in his palm, and she jumped. It felt both wicked and wonderful to have his long strong fingers hold her like that—much like the sinful delight of his mouth on her breast. A rush of liquid desire swept from her breastbone down to the juncture of her thighs, causing her to try and wriggle away. When she moved, two of his fingers slipped around a nub of flesh that stood stiffly at the entrance of her most secret place.

"Oh," she said. Surprised and slightly uncomfortable at the unexpected intrusion, she wanted to close her legs, but his thighs were between hers.

"Stop wriggling," Jack said, between clenched teeth.

Pascale stilled. Her legs seemed to turn to rubber, and she had to brace her arms on the bed behind her to hold herself upright. This forced her breasts to jut forward even more. She barely had time to steal a glance at Jack's face and to discover his eyes were, thankfully, closed, when Jack began to slide his fingers back and forth around the sensitive little button of flesh between her thighs.

She jolted upward, but his hand followed, never ceasing in the maddening caress.

"Stop," she gasped, unable to catch her breath, or to still the involuntary movement of her lower body, which seemed to pulse in time with her wildly beating heart. Jack's only response was to lean forward to capture one erect nipple between his lips.

"Jack?" Pascale moaned as a wave of heat coursed through her. "What are you doing?"

"Teaching you a lesson, my little shrew," he answered against her breast. He was breathing as hard as she was. Pascale strained forward into his hand, and one finger slipped inside her. Her breath hissed out between her teeth as she moved frantically against his hand and mouth. Her head fell back. Her eyes closed. All she could feel was Jack, and the pressure building deep within her.

That mischievous finger slipped in and out of her again, and then, a heartbeat later, two fingers. She felt herself stretching, opening to pull him deeper inside of her, and he seemed to feel it, too, as he said, "You are so soft and tight inside."

She felt herself contract at the smooth slow slide of his withdrawal. "Please," she said, panting.

His hand stopped moving. He took his mouth from her heated flesh. "Please what?" he asked. She moved jerkily against him, now that he no longer set that graceful, natural pace.

"Please," she said. "Don't stop."

He slipped his fingers inside her again and flexed them, once and then again. Pascale rocked back on her heels. A wave of sensation washed through her. Then another.

"I want you," she heard herself say.

"No," Jack said. She stared at him, uncomprehending. The one harsh word had doused some of the fire flowing through her veins. He released her and quickly pulled her drawers up and retied them.

"What?"

"The lesson is over." He pulled her bodice up, covering her breasts.

"What's happened?" she asked, uncomprehendingly. He lay back in the bed, awkwardly attempting to put his sling back over his bandaged arm.

"I changed my mind. I think I'd rather stick with my original plan. I'll deliver The Painting to your father when all of this is over." He managed to pull the sling back into place.

You can't, Pascale thought, but she couldn't get the words out. She was afraid that if she spoke she'd start to cry with frustration—not because of The Portrait, but because she was still atremble with desire for him.

It hit her suddenly. He'd planned this all along! She was

sure of it. She swallowed convulsively, until the knot in her throat began to subside.

Finally she managed to speak. "How dare you!" She climbed over him out of his bed.

"How dare I?" Jack laughed, humorlessly. "You are the one who suggested this."

"Only because of what you said."

"Because of that? Or because you wanted your painting and you didn't trust me to deliver it as I was hired to do."

"I do trust you. Or I did," Pascale retorted. "Even though I knew you didn't really understand how important it was to me, I trusted you enough to let *this* happen."

"I don't believe you. I think you were trying to regain control over your father and crawl back into that hidey hole you made for yourself rather than face the truth."

Her shocked expression seemed to give him pause for a moment; long enough for Pascale to interject, "That's not true. And even if it were, what difference does it make to you?"

"All the difference in the world. Whatever you may think of me, I'm not interested in this kind of a "deal." I cannot be a party to this illusion you've created."

"What illusion? I just want The Painting back."

"To tell you the truth, Pascale, I don't think you know what you want. And I didn't hear you admit you want me."

He covered his eyes with his good arm, effectively shutting her out.

"You—!" Pascale turned on her heel and started for the door. Before she reached it, though, she'd turned and retraced her steps. "You are an arrogant, heartless, ungrateful fool!"

He lowered his arm and Pascale recoiled at the anger in his eyes. "Arrogant? You are not one to say anything on that score. Who was supposed to be so honored by the noble sacrifice of your precious virtue that I would finally prostrate myself at her feet? Heartless? Look to yourself, Pascale."

"What are you talking about?" Pascale was growing more confused with every word he uttered. "You were the one who suggested this in the first place. Why are you so angry that I took your advice? You have no right—"

"I have every right to keep you from trying to seduce me. You don't even know what you're doing."

"Stop treating me like a child," Pascale raged. "All you had to do was say no."

"That is harder than you might think," Jack muttered.

"What?" She could not have heard him aright.

"Forget it," he said. "Forget all of this and remember only one thing. I will return your painting when I am good and ready to do so. Nothing will change that, despite anything I might have said in the past. If you come near me again, I will not be responsible for what might happen."

"Don't worry," Pascale said bitterly. "I won't be bothering you again."

"Just be careful," Jack warned. "You are playing with fire."

"Not anymore, I'm not." Pascale turned with as much dignity as she could muster, and left the room.

Twenty-four

Jack waited for the door to close behind her and then gave in to the urge to curse, long and loud. He had not intended to let things go so far. Pascale's "offer" had taken him by surprise. He had known she was curious—even eager—to discover more about the passion that seemed always to erupt between them. He should have guessed her agile mind would come up with this bizarre scheme to seduce The Painting's hiding place out of him. Pascale was nothing if not tenacious.

What had truly shocked him had been his own loss of control. He knew she didn't think much of him—but he hadn't thought she could take seriously the proposition he'd made to frighten her away. The comment had been outrageous, he knew, but he hadn't been in earnest. The fact that she had taken the jest at face value had been insulting.

He'd wanted to punish her for that offense, unintentional as it was. But he had only meant to frighten, or enrage her. He hadn't thought she would meet his challenge. He couldn't possibly have imagined that she would meet it so enthusiastically. Her response had nearly undone him. It was only when Pascale begged for satisfaction that he'd finally come to his senses.

Captain John Devlin had crossed the line for the first time since he'd left his boyhood behind. He had walked arrogantly into a situation well beyond his control—and made it an impossible one. What a fool he was! He still wanted her. More than he had wanted anything in a long time. But he had no right to even think about making love to that beautiful young girl. His very presence in her house might be putting her in danger.

John Douglas had passed along some very bad news in his latest report. One of Jack's men had been killed in Paris. Though the barroom brawl that had resulted in the sailor's death might have been just another drunken wrangle, Jack was inclined to think it a tad too coincidental. Unfortunately, the man who had died was one of the men Henry Bates had assigned to protect the de Ravenaults on their journey to Beaune, so he was afraid that he'd been murdered after letting slip Jack's location.

John Douglas was meeting with Henry Bates and the men at a little town halfway between Paris and Beaune in order to find out who the man had last spoken with, and whether he'd said anything that might explain why he'd been singled out for this seeming assassination. Jack wished that he could have gone with his valet to that meeting. There had to be some clue as to the identity of the assassin—and he might be the only person who could recognize a description of the killer, just as he might have been the real target.

Even if his current situation hadn't been so dire, Jack knew full well that he was no fit match for a woman like Pascale de Ravenault. She had the bearing and assurance of a noble, while he had spent his entire life among rough men in rougher places. Half an hour in Society chafed at his nerves.

Jack was, above all, a man of the sea. That rough life suited him. It was all he knew. He had felt a vague longing, occasionally, for a home where he could rest, with a woman waiting for him, and children for whom he would build the shipping empire he dreamed of. But when he got the nagging feeling that something might be missing in his life, he took on a new cargo and shipped off for some foreign and exotic port of call.

The grueling work of commanding a ship across treacherous, unfathomable seas, was sufficient to occupy his mind as well as his spirit. There was no time for fanciful daydreams on the high seas—they faded into obscurity in the face of real battles, with life and death in the balance.

With difficulty he maneuvered himself back into a sitting position and swung his legs over the side of the bed. A loud groan escaped him as his chest and stomach protested the strenuous activity. He tried to be quiet. It was rare that he was without his nursemaids for long enough to get any exercise at all. Jack wasn't accustomed to this enforced inactivity. It couldn't be good for him, no matter what Louise, or Pascale, John Douglas, or Philippe said. He needed to get back on his feet as quickly as possible. He was careful to lean heavily on the bedside table as he rose. He didn't want to be found sprawled on the floor by . . . anyone.

Jack made his way, slowly and painfully, to the window. He stood looking out at the well-tended lawns and gardens below. The cultivated fields stretched, far out in the distance, to a small mountain range. The vines, in uniform rows, marched across the undulating land to the horizon.

Pascale had certainly created a haven, of beauty and peace, on the de Ravenault estate. Jack could well understand the lure of the château for the artists who were drawn back here, year after year. It was more than pleasant, it was an oasis. Even a man like himself could appreciate the charm of the old house, the efficient staff, and his unconventional hosts.

He again felt a pang of guilt as he thought of Pascale. She was a most remarkable woman. One might have expected her to be jaded, infected with the same loose bohemian ideals as her father and his friends. But somehow she had developed her own sense of what was proper and correct, and it had evolved into a strict personal code of honor: the first tenet of which was to devote herself to her father's well-being.

If only . . . he let his thoughts drift. If only she were not so burdened by the responsibilities she'd chosen to shoulder. If only her mother had not abandoned her. After her mother's desertion, it made perfect sense that she had devoted herself to creating the perfect home for her father. Her home was a haven for any artist; comfortable for them to work in, and a simple setting for conversation and communion. She provided artists, young and old, famous and unknown, with everything they needed to create. In return they gave her the opportunity to use her innate ability to cushion those frailer than herself from the drudgery of daily life. She arranged for her charges to live, eat and sleep in comfort. Now he, himself, had come under her protection. She had more reason to leave him to fend for himself, than to take him in, and yet she cared for him.

Perhaps, if her mother had stayed to insure she had the happy carefree childhood that suited her station, she would not have given up painting. She would not, then, have had to work so hard to find her place in the world. Maybe she would not be trying to earn the love of her father. If her mother hadn't left her, perhaps she wouldn't be so afraid of losing her Papa. Then Jack could have indulged himself in a harmless flirtation, even perhaps an affair, with that delightful, unusual, woman without fear that she'd be hurt beyond repair.

But Pascale was, for all her strength, too fragile for a man like himself. She might fall in love with him.

Worse, he might fall in love with her.

It would be too tempting to stay and prove to her how easy she was to love. Such a course was not for him. He was the kind of man who left women behind easily, without regrets or remorse. That was what he had always been. Of course, none of the women he had known were anything like Pascale. She was truly an original.

He could feel the bemused smile on his lips, and cursed himself again for indulging in this dangerous train of thought. His aching ribs begged for relief, and he made his clumsy, faltering way back to the accursed bed, which had become his prison. He had to escape the damnable circumstances he found himself in. Otherwise, he might be persuaded by a certain childlike Venus to forget the lessons he'd learned in his hard life, and throw his natural caution to the winds. His well-honed sense of self-preservation foundered before the force of her smile and her sparkling eyes, like a ship buffeted by the rocks and shoals of an uncharted harbor.

John Douglas didn't return until early the next morning. He'd been riding all night, he said, to bring back the little news he'd been able to uncover.

"We've nothing that leads directly to the minister, sir, but that other queer fish you wanted watched, his secretary, he tipped his hand a couple of days ago."

"The minister is not definitely involved, John, as I told you. My money's riding on your 'queer fish.' There is no doubt he's involved."

"The man, and not his master? That's hard to believe. Alike as two peas in a pod, they are, if you was to ask me. But that's politicians for ye. The government seems to like 'em."

"Go on, man." Jack knew his show of impatience was likely to encourage John Douglas to torture him further, but he couldn't restrain himself.

"The chappie was at your friend's funeral. And then the next day he met with that ship's captain, the one who tried to outbid us on that cargo of Chinese silks."

"Germain Forêt?"

"That's the one. They had another meeting, too. Day before yesterday, it was. Thomas and Gustave were on watch, so Gustave could translate. And the captain, he started shouting how threats don't mean a thing to him and he'll sail when he's good and ready to go. Happen he don't want to tell the old man when his boat's asettin' out to sea. Mebbe because of what happened to the *Aurora*. Anyway, the old gent said, clear as a bell, havin' to talk over that Frenchie's yellin', 'You don't want to have an accident like your old rival, Devlin, do you?' "

"I don't know," Jack said. "It's not a lot to go on."

"There's more, Cap'n. The Frenchie went white as a sheet, old Thomas told me. He was watching them closely since he couldn't make out what they was saying. Forêt argued some more, and then the secretary chappie said, 'It can be arranged. I've done it before, as you know.' "

Jack pursed his lips in a silent whistle of amazement. John Douglas nodded. "He as much as admitted what he done, I'm thinkin'."

"I think we need to set up an appointment with Captain Forêt. It sounds like he might just hold the key to all this."

"Bates thought you might say that, so we sent one of the men to follow him and find out where he lived. It just so happens he's in the process of hiring some men for his next voyage, and two of our fellas have hired on with 'im."

"Perfect." Jack had confronted Forêt when the Chinese silk had been at issue. The man was a coward and a cheat, and Jack would feel no compunction at beating the truth out of him. "I'll return with you to Paris tomorrow."

"No, sir, that you won't do. That arm-bone is just starting to set nicely, and heaven knows how those ribs of yours are faring. You can't take a trip like that one again so soon."

"I want to see the look on that bastard's face when he finds out I'm not dead yet. I've got to talk to him."

"Then we'll bring him to you," John Douglas said. "Henry and I figured you'd want to talk to 'im. We thought we'd bring him down the Saône River on a barge. Bates has probably got him by now. We'll bring him downriver to you."

"Not here. We can't take a chance on someone discovering this family is involved. After he is taken from the barge, he'll have no idea where he is. If you leave tomorrow morning and ride to the closest town to the Saône, you can meet Henry and tell him to wait there for me—then send the men to tell me where you were. It's only a day's ride by coach, but it should throw anyone who's following the scent."

John Douglas nodded his understanding.

"How long do you think it will take?" Jack was roughly aware of the distance, but his valet had just ridden over the road.

"In a couple of days, three maybe. When I find them, I'll send a man here to tell you."

Jack didn't think Forêt would hold out on him. As soon as he got his hands on the bastard, he'd have the name of the man who'd scuttled his ship.

He was determined to be standing on his own two feet when he saw Forêt. The next morning, he insisted on going downstairs to sit outside. At first he met only objections, but eventually it was agreed that the sun, which was shining brightly, might do him some good. He was supported by John Douglas on one side, and Philippe on the other, but he managed to walk. That small triumph didn't exactly fill him with elation, but he felt better than he had in some time.

He didn't see anything of Pascale at first, and he was torn between disappointment and relief at the reprieve. He had decided he had to apologize for the shabby way he'd treated her the day before. He hadn't deserved her insults, but neither had she deserved the treatment she'd received from him. He couldn't leave her house with her anguished look of betrayal on his conscience. He hoped to put an end to the war of wills going on between them.

He suspected she'd avoid him unless he actually summoned her. Even then, he wasn't sure she would give him the opportunity to make his peace before he said goodbye.

It was from two strange young men, whom he quickly learned were also guests at the château, that he discovered how deeply Pascale had been affected by their disastrous encounter.

"She's painting again," said Yves, a young pale-skinned buck of sartorial elegance, who commandeered Jack's midmorning coffee and cakes without so much as a "May I?"

"We saw her taking an easel down the garden path," David said. He was a pudgy youth with a vacant expression in his eyes that reminded Jack of Paul de Ravenault. "We asked her where she was going and she said she was going down to the stream to draw. I couldn't believe my ears, really!"

"Shocking," Yves said, sarcastically.

"I think I know the spot she's headed for. Right down by a little copse of trees, near the bridge. I tried to paint the bridge last fall, but the weather was terrible, windy and gray. It's much more charming at this time of the year." A thought struck him, apparently, and he blinked. "Maybe I'll try again."

"I think Pascale probably wants to be alone," Yves said. "She didn't seem to want to tell us where she was going, remember?"

Clearly the absentminded young artist didn't remember, even after his friend reminded him. "It would be fun to paint with Pascale. She's so sweet."

Yves turned to Jack. "Now I suppose I'll have to find some way to distract him. He may look and sound an idiot, but once he gets an idea in his head, he's almost unstoppable."

"She could teach herself, after all these years with her father." David was still clearly intrigued by the idea of painting with Pascale. "Some of the old guys say she was quite talented when she was younger," the young whelp said.

"That's easy enough to believe," Yves said, still lounging nonchalantly in his lawn chair. "Have you ever known Pascale not to succeed at anything she does?"

David was clearly in awe of the lady's talents. "No, by Jove, I haven't."

Yves exchanged a speaking look with Jack, and hauled himself to his feet. "I'll ask Louise to bring you some more coffee. I seem to have finished it." For someone so thin, he had certainly managed to denude the table of everything edible, and quite quickly. David pulled himself up more slowly. After saying goodbye he jogged after his graceful friend, bringing to Jack's mind the picture of an exuberant young puppy trotting along faithfully behind his world-weary parent.

Jack mulled over Pascale's choosing to respond to his cruel lesson by taking up painting again. Perhaps his visit here wouldn't end in complete disaster.

He smiled. Perhaps he had repaid his hostess in some small

way for the many kindnesses she'd shown him. It was nice to think he wasn't totally without redeeming qualities.

Jack was well on his way to thinking he'd actually retained the upper hand in the battle that raged between him and this unique woman, when she came to him in a fury about his unexpected departure.

"Do you really expect me to let you leave this house in your condition? Heaven knows what might be awaiting you back in Paris! This is so stupid. Just because your manly ego was offended by my inept advances on your virtue—"

"Pascale . . . ," he tried to interrupt, but he couldn't stop her tirade.

"You have nothing to fear from me, *Monsieur Capitaine,* I already learned my lesson. In case you hadn't realized it, your methods are quite effective."

"I'm not leaving because of that." He nearly had to shout to get her attention.

"Then, why?" Her arms folded across her chest, her foot tapped impatiently on the ground as she waited for his answer.

He chose instead to try and placate her. "I wanted to apologize for my behavior yesterday. I never intended to let it go so far."

"It?" she said angrily. "Me, you mean. You have no need to worry about a repeat of the incident. After your exemplary behavior in the face of my untoward advances, I am convinced you are truly the consummate gentleman." She made the word sound like a curse.

"I was wrong," he said simply. Pascale stood staring at him for a moment.

"Then you're not leaving?"

He shook his head. "I have to go, but it is *not* because of you."

He could tell that she didn't believe him, even before the closed, mutinous expression descended upon that lovely face. "Thank you, kind sir. Those words mean everything to me, coming, as they do, from your lips."

"Pascale. I don't want to leave with this between us. I would rather anything than that."

Jack thought he detected a softening in her expression, but Pascale just shook her head in denial and walked away.

Twenty-five

Pascale's anger faded as she walked away from Jack. She didn't want this barrier between them, either, especially not when he was leaving. She didn't want anything to come between them. Despite everything, she still ached for his touch.

She tried to hate him, but she couldn't. She felt ashamed when she thought of what she had done, but she also remembered the rush of exhilaration that had come when she'd molded her lips to his. She couldn't regret that passion that had ignited between them.

She would have liked to have parted as friends. More than that, she wished they had completed their act of love. She had no doubt that it would have been very different from the first time. Jack had absolutely nothing in common with Dorian. The young art student had been jealous and self-serving; a spoiled boy. His lovemaking had been clumsy and selfish. Jack was a man, and his hands had the power to bring out a sensuality in Pascale that she hadn't even known she had had. Moreover, he seemed to delight in her response. He might block her at every turn, and challenge her constantly to examine her life and her beliefs, but in the end it wasn't his own desires he wanted to satisfy. He wanted her to be the selfish one. She suspected that if she made love with him, he'd want her to wring every ounce of pleasure from the encounter for herself.

Though she had always repressed the yearning before, for the first time in five years, she actually took out her sketchbook and let herself be drawn into that half-conscious state of awareness that was necessary to create. Soon she found herself going to the studio to collect supplies and heading for the stream at the bottom of the garden path. It had been so simple to lose herself in The Painting.

The morning had been a revelation. It had felt so right to release the frustration and unhappiness of the night before onto a blank canvas. The stream's music had calmed her. The sunlight dancing in the leaves above had soothed her battered soul; and the rocks and reeds on the stream's bank had intrigued her, and been the willing subjects of her sketch.

She had felt almost peaceful. It was only when she'd come back to the house to learn that Jack was planning to leave that the agony that had plagued her through the night had come rushing back. She didn't feel any less indignant after talking with him. He might be out of danger now, and capable of taking care of himself, but he was not ready to leave. He was foolishly going to risk reinjuring himself. He should not ignore the telltale signs of pain that warned the broken and infirm that they needed to rest and heal. But she was certain he would.

She would never forgive him for that. She stormed into the house and brushed past Pierre and her father without saying a word; eager to reach the sanctuary of her boudoir.

"Pascale?" The concern in Papa's voice stopped her.

"Yes?"

"What's wrong?" he asked.

She nearly broke down. She couldn't believe that he would choose this precise moment to emerge from his cocoon and suddenly become sensitive to her feelings. Pascale was afraid to look him in the eye, for fear she would start to cry.

"Is there anything I can do?"

"No, but thank you, Papa," Pascale sniffed.

"Is it because Captain Devlin is leaving?" A tear rolled down her cheek. She nodded. "It's probably better that he leave now, before you get too attached to him," he advised.

"Probably," she agreed. But it was already too late. Her

father's eyes were finally opened, but his warning came too late. He seemed to sense that his words were not enough. He came closer, and patted her on the shoulder. Then he ran up the stairs. Pascale stared after him, openmouthed. Pierre had been studiously ignoring the two of them, but when Pascale went past him to the staircase, he smiled at her stupefied expression.

Pascale made her way upstairs slowly, her anger largely abated by the strange encounter, her mind furiously working to assimilate the knowledge that her father was aware of how she felt about Jack. She didn't know how she'd given herself away. Perhaps he had just guessed. She hoped that however he'd figured it out, it wasn't apparent to everyone else in the house. The situation was already mortifying enough.

Jack had rejected her in the most humiliating manner and held The Painting hostage, and yet that didn't stop her from wanting him. He had beaten her at every turn, and still she couldn't stand to watch him walk away. It was ironic. He had rejected her and yet she was going to apologize to him.

The de Ravenaults kept country hours while at home, so Jack's supper was served later than theirs. He took dinner with John Douglas most evenings. Pascale timed her arrival at Jack's room carefully, to coincide with the evening meal shared by valet and master. She was afraid to be alone with him, afraid of what she might say. John Douglas was, as she had hoped, partaking of a hearty meal when Pascale entered the room. He rose, but she waved him back down into his seat.

"I am glad you are both here," Pascale said with heartfelt sincerity.

"I didn't think you would forgive my behavior," Jack said, ignoring his servant's presence. John Douglas didn't seem to hear. He kept eating, his eyes on his plate.

"It is I who should apologize," Pascale confessed. "And I really mean it. So won't you please stay?" She turned to John Douglas to enlist his aid in persuading his employer, but the dour manservant was shaking his head.

"We can't, Pascale," Jack said. "I swear it's beyond my control. I would like to stay longer, honestly. But we can't. We will be leaving in a day or two."

"Where are you going?" she asked suspiciously. "Back to Paris?"

"No, we are going somewhere safer."

"You are safe here," she pointed out. "You are surrounded by your friends."

"Maybe. But we don't want to wait to find out for certain. By the time we know we're wrong, it will be too late."

"Your mind is made up?"

"We have no choice, Pascale," Jack answered.

"But we'll be back, miss," John Douglas promised.

"That's right. I've a promise to keep. I have a piece of precious cargo to deliver to you," Jack added.

"I think you know you'll always be welcome," Pascale said, dejectedly. She didn't want to leave that room. She wanted to stay, but there was nothing left to say. She was tempted to tell Jack she'd started painting again. And that her father was looking for a picture of her mother. She was tempted to thank him, and to reveal that she wanted him—*just him,* and not The Painting at all.

But she couldn't say anything of the kind, of course. She could almost imagine the look of shock on John Douglas's face if he had been privy to her thoughts. She was glad she had had the foresight to come and visit Jack while he was present. The stolid, watchful servant was the only thing that kept her from making a complete fool of herself. Her pride and her self-respect seemed to have utterly deserted her.

Pascale moved through the rest of the evening in a haze of confusion. When she finally went to bed that night, she fell into a deep sleep the moment her head hit the pillow. But she awakened a few hours later, wide-eyed and completely alert. She lay listening to the silent household, her mind clear for the first time in weeks.

An hour later, the course she had chosen seemed the only

one. Jack had come to mean a lot to her. He tempted her in a way no man ever had. And he'd given her back her art. She would go to him. She rose out of bed, and stretched. The full moon shone brightly through the window. She padded silently over to look out across the silvered lawn and to listen to the wind rustle through the leaves of the trees. The moment of peace seemed to confirm the rightness of what she was about to do.

She made her way silently to Jack's room. John Douglas slept right next door, but after his long journey the day before, she assumed he would sleep deeply tonight. Even if she did happen to meet him, patrolling the halls as he was wont to do, she was sure he wouldn't try to stop her.

She stepped into Jack's darkened room and stood just inside the door, listening to his deep, even breathing. She had thought, somehow, that he'd be waiting for her. She hadn't anticipated having to awaken him and she hesitated, but Pascale couldn't resist the lure of his still form in the big bed. She crossed the room, her bare feet moving soundlessly over the rugs on the floor, and stood looking down at him as he slept. The shadows lent a wicked cast to his thick black eyebrows, but his long black eyelashes and smooth jaw gave him the look of an angel.

She reached out a hand to caress his cheek, and his eyes opened.

"Hello," she said. "I couldn't sleep."

He glanced about the room, took in the long shadows of the night, and the full moon shining high above the horizon, and then looked back at her, seemingly unsurprised.

"Is it okay?" she asked, her voice quavering. She thought nervousness was making her voice shake, but then realized her teeth were chattering.

"You're trembling," he said. "Are you all right?"

"I think so," Pascale said. She leaned down to kiss him. Against his forehead she breathed, "I need you," then lifted her head to look down into his eyes.

He lifted his light blanket in invitation, and she slipped beneath it to press herself to his side. His warmth enveloped her, and Pascale felt welcome as she never had anyplace else.

She kissed his chin, her hand slipping over the smooth planes of his chest beneath the open cotton nightshirt that he wore. He pulled her close with an arm about her shoulders, and she pressed her face to his chest and wrapped herself around him, arms and legs embracing as much of him as she could reach. Even so, she was careful not to touch the bandages wrapped around his torso.

Jack nuzzled her hair; his lips found her forehead, then her eyes, feathered over the bridge of her nose, and finally came to rest at the corner of her mouth. She turned her head and slanted her lips under his, and they kissed, hungrily, voraciously.

He turned until he lay on his side, facing her. "Are you sure?" he asked, only awaiting her emphatic nod before plundering her mouth again. She met his ardor with equal passion; her hands on his back skimming over the thin cloth that separated flesh from flesh. He dipped his head to find her breasts, and suckled her through her white cotton nightdress.

In spite of his injuries, it took them very little time to divest themselves of their clothing, each helping the other to unfasten their nightgowns and push the white fabric out from between them, while their lips found each bit of skin as it was exposed.

She twined about him, lithe and agile as a cat, while he explored the range of motion permitted by his partially healed ribs. His left arm was virtually useless, but he didn't seem to be impaired. With his free hand and his mouth, he caressed every inch of her body. His toes tickled the backs of her calves, his hands slid down her buttocks to her thighs.

This time, he didn't stop. He fit her body to his, until she felt him fully up and down the length of her. He guided one of her legs up around his waist. She felt the length of him, smooth and hard, slip just inside her. He slowly slid deeper into the slick passage, until she held all of him within her.

He filled her perfectly. She felt the walls inside her stretch and grasp at him, trying to hold on as he slipped away. But he didn't leave her. He filled her again, deeper, and then again, until she thought she couldn't stand it any longer. She was aware that the long smooth strokes were taking their toll on Jack as well. Sweat beaded on his forehead as he drove into her, faster and harder, while she met each surge with a thrust of her own hips. He groaned.

"Jack," she gasped, "don't hurt yourself. We can s-stop whenever you want."

"That's what you think, my sweet," he whispered. He lowered his head to her breast and sucked one engorged nipple into his mouth. Pascale felt a spasm pass through her, causing muscles deep inside her to constrict. She felt the slide of him through the tight passage and bucked wildly. A sound escaped her lips, like the coo of a dove, and she buried her face in his shoulder.

His right hand moved down between them to find that secret button between her legs, and he stroked it with his thumb while his lips danced from one breast to the other. The spasm racked her again, but this time it didn't stop, but traveled through her in wave upon wave. It gathered low in the pit of her stomach, and broke on the hot pulsing point under his thumb and through the walls of the passage that he filled.

She felt him tremble, too, and her heart threatened to burst out of her chest. Her hips ground into his. Her teeth clenched on his shoulder, and her body was racked by one final aftereffect of that internal explosion.

"I knew you couldn't last any longer than me," Pascale said, satisfied, and he chuckled and rolled gingerly onto his back. Pascale leaned up on her elbows, remembering how she had bitten him in that heart-stopping moment of ecstasy. She found the telltale mark on his shoulder.

"Uh-oh. John Douglas will know."

Jack's eyes slid closed. "You're not going to sleep now, are you?" she asked, aghast.

"You woke me up," he mumbled. "And then you tired me out."

"But . . . you can't," she said. "Jack, wake up."

"What?" He was caught unaware by another huge yawn. "I need to rest."

She was tired, too, but watched him sleep for a while before finally slipping out of his bed and into her nightgown. She kissed him tenderly and went back to her own room, and fell soundly asleep the moment she climbed into bed for the second time that night.

Twenty-six

Pascale and Jack sat together in the sunny garden the next morning. They spoke desultorily of nothing and everything, while she sketched him. The previous night wasn't mentioned.

She watched his face change. His eyes were half closed while he rested, content. His jaw clenched when their eyes met, his gaze ran over her, touching her like a caress. He looked away when she mentioned her father.

These telltale signs were the key to Jack Devlin—and she cataloged them not only in her mind, but with her deft fingers on paper. The charcoal in her hand grew smooth and worn, and still she kept capturing bits and pieces of him hitherto unseen; the angle of his cheekbone as he turned his face to the sun, the tiny scar under his lip, the shadows under his eyes that deepened when he was concerned about something.

"I want to see what you're doing." He leaned forward, as though he might get a glimpse at her sketchbook.

"Wait," Pascale ordered, as she put the finishing touches on his profile. She glanced at her work critically and turned the page. "It's not quite right. Let me try again."

"Just show me," Jack urged.

"It takes me a little while to decide how I want to paint a subject."

"I just want to know what you see when you look at me."

Her hand hovered over the blank page for a moment, then she relented. "All right, but this is just a sketch."

"Don't worry," he said. "I'm not a critic."

"Everyone's a critic." Pascale grimaced, but gave him the sketches. He leafed through them, slowly, then pursed his lips in a silent whistle of admiration.

"This is fantastic."

Pascale couldn't help but be pleased by the compliment, but she smiled knowingly as she joked, "It's a good thing you're not vain."

"I think you've caught something here, in my expression, that I've never been able to actually see in the mirror."

"Is that your polite way of saying it doesn't look at all like you?"

"No, just the opposite. It is me. How did you learn to do this?"

"When I was a baby, Papa and all of his friends encouraged me to draw. It kept me out of the way, at first. Whenever I cried, he gave me a paper and pencil." She laughed. "Then he couldn't get rid of me. We were together all of the time. He tied a cord around my waist so I wouldn't wander away when he was concentrating. He tied the other end to his easel. Everyone used to laugh about it."

"You had no nurse?"

"Not until I was eleven. Papa hired Francine to tutor me; he was terrible at math and I liked it."

"Francine didn't approve of your painting."

"No one who met Francine could mistake her prejudices against artists, and more particularly towards Papa. Francine was very nice in her notions of what a gentleman or a gentlewoman was. She had striven to instill the same values in her young charge. To a certain degree, she had succeeded.

"Francine thought a young lady should have a rudimentary knowledge of sketching, perhaps a little practice with watercolors. Anything beyond that wasn't quite the thing. She came from the household of the Duke of Bourgogne, and our way of living seemed terrible to her."

"I'm surprised she stayed."

"She took it as a personal challenge. I fell in love with her on first sight. She was so . . . so fussy and strange. I suppose I was a bit of a hellion. And I needed some kind of order in my life. She was the first person I ever met who didn't take my father or his work seriously. She actually yelled at him. I'd never seen anyone do that before. He's not an easy man to fight with. He just wanders away in the middle of the argument."

"I've noticed."

"Francine taught me to apply myself to my studies; to love books and music and other things besides painting. We all appreciated the little changes she managed to make. Regular meals, clean rooms, except the studio. She couldn't go in there. But for the first time in my life, there was always wood for the fireplaces. She hired a real housekeeper and some maids who weren't always modeling. The whole house was clean all the time, more attractive."

"That sour-faced creature decorated this barn?"

"Well"—Pascale laughed—"she tried. But she was very parsimonious. A preacher's daughter. The food came regularly to the table, but we were as like as not to eat chicken stew night after night. And she got rid of the dust, but she didn't see why she should replace a perfectly good chair with another one, just because it was more comfortable. She has wonderful taste, though, and she guided me when I started to decorate."

"I see."

Pascale had the uncomfortable feeling that he could indeed imagine what had happened. She defended herself. "Well, it made perfect sense that I would take over, after a while. Francine wasn't able to do much with Papa. I, on the other hand, had no such scruples and I could get him to pay for improvements, and luxuries that she wouldn't have dreamed of." Pascale leaned toward him and whispered conspiratorially, "You might not believe this, but I was quite headstrong back then."

"No!" Jack exclaimed with feigned amazement.

"Yes." Pascale chuckled. "I wanted what I wanted, and I

went after it. Just like Papa. There's a lot of him in me. Really. He encouraged me always to go after what I wanted."

"And what you wanted was . . ."

"In the beginning, I wanted to paint, but I wanted to eat chocolates every day, too. We were shockingly poor then. Poor Papa was not a very good estate manager."

"So you took over."

"I wanted to help." A shadow passed over his face, but in a moment, it cleared. He looked down at the sketch in his hand.

"You are a remarkable woman," Jack said.

"Thank you, kind sir."

"These are wonderful." He handed her the sketches.

"I think now I could enjoy painting again. Perhaps not every minute of the day, but here and there."

"I'm glad," he said sincerely.

"Me too." Her smile was almost shy as she looked away. "It's largely due to you that I decided to try it again. I had no idea how much I missed this." She wanted to kiss him, but since they were sitting outdoors in plain view of anyone who passed by, she started to draw his mouth, instead. "Thank you," she said, under her breath.

"You're welcome," he answered. She looked up into his laughing eyes, and smiled at the smugness she saw there. "I'll take my reward later, in my room," he said.

She would have delivered the set-down he deserved for his arrogance, but she saw Francine approaching with a tea tray. It was fitting that her chaperone unknowingly delivered his punishment; more food.

"The captain's tea," Francine announced, depositing a heavily laden tray on the table.

Jack groaned, while Pascale tried not to snicker aloud. Manfully, Jack put a flaky crescent roll on his dish. Pascale watched him, amused.

Francine gave her a look that Pascale recognized: She wanted to speak privately. Pascale rose, bidding Jack adieu.

She put her arm around her old governess's waist as they walked toward the château together.

"You seem to have grown quite comfortable with that young man," her former teacher said. Francine didn't hold a high opinion of sailors, though she'd been somewhat mollified when Jack had taken her side over Henry Bates in their dispute. Pascale had not seen much of Madame Pitt since her return from Paris. With last night very much on her conscience, Pascale wished she could have avoided her companion for another day or two—until after Jack left.

"I don't know if comfortable is the word I'd have chosen. I've grown accustomed to him, though," Pascale said carefully.

"That is quite understandable, in the course of things. The servants have told me that you quite brought him back from the dead."

"I had a lot of help."

"Well, I'm sure no one would leave a young, innocent girl alone with a man like that. It's a good thing you had Odelle and Philippe with you." Luckily, Francine didn't look at Pascale as she spoke, for Pascale was sure she looked quite guilty. "But you've got to be careful of this kind of man. They have no more notion of propriety than . . . than that set your father runs about with. I've no need to tell you, I'm sure. And yet . . . I notice that you are on terms of great familiarity with the fellow."

"He is shockingly familiar, it's true. But, as you said, I'm well used to that."

"I've no worries about you, my girl. Never think it. But I am a little surprised that he is not more respectful, more grateful after all you have done for him. His man, Monsieur Douglas, is always singing your praises. Not that I approve of the captain's valet." Francine's forbearance in even mentioning Jack's valet was due to the fact that, in the battle between Bates and Pitt, Douglas had declined to take sides. He would, generally, have joined with Bates in any argument with a female, but John Douglas blamed Bates for their poor reception at the mansion.

"I think perhaps, now that he's recovering so well, you should not spend too much time with that man."

Pascale couldn't bring herself to agree. But she soothed Francine's fears by saying, "Well, they should be leaving in a day or so." She felt a pang of sorrow at the thought of Jack's departure, but knew it was for the best since he not at all the kind of man whom she was accustomed to dealing with. Even though she felt he was her soul mate in many ways, his world was far removed from hers. Her rekindled dreams of artistic achievement and her quiet sensible life would bore him stiff—he was a man of action, a lion of the seas. If they had little in common, he and her father had even less. She could not imagine a life with Jack in it. Sadly, neither could she imagine her life without him.

That night, she went to him again. He, too, was subdued as he wrapped his right arm around her. She wondered if he was thinking, as she was, that these precious moments would be their last together.

"I've been waiting all day for my reward," he said as she came into the room at moonrise.

"Don't be so smug." She laughed, then leaned over the bed and kissed him on the nose. "You would think you'd completed the labors of Hercules."

"Changing a woman's mind is a greater feat," he boasted.

"Oh, is it?" She climbed onto the bed, atop him.

"Yes." He sat up suddenly, catching her by surprise.

"Careful," she said before his lips met hers.

"I'm feeling much better." He proceeded to demonstrate, and soon she was lying beneath him.

"Are you sure this isn't hurting your ribs?" she asked nervously.

"Just don't make any sudden moves," he warned, his lips feathering down her jaw to her collarbone. She was so sweet to touch and to taste.

She shivered as his mouth moved lower. "I'll try." She had to modify her answer as he took one dark-tipped mound of flesh into his mouth. She arched into him, and he was consumed with pleasure as she clutched his head to her breast.

Jack didn't plan to repeat last night's mistake. It was unforgivable that he had been unable to stop himself once before. Tonight, he planned to send her back to her room, satisfied, but without anything more to regret. And he wanted to know that she would not go back to the half life she'd been living before he came. He wanted to talk to her, almost as much as he wanted to touch her. Almost. He wanted only to please her this last time. He knew he was playing with fire as his tongue dipped into her navel, but he was determined to show Pascale this one final pleasure before he left her. He slowly lowered his hand to find the soft warm flesh of her buttocks.

"I am claiming my reward," he spoke into the smooth brown concavity of her stomach. She sucked in her breath, and his lips followed the movement. Her hands on his hair tried to tug him upward but he resisted the gentle pressure. "Tell me why you stopped painting," he demanded. He could feel the tension in her body as he stroked her thighs. They resisted the gentle pressure of his hand as he tried to part them and find the hot moist place that had held him so sweetly the night before.

"You asked me that already."

"But you didn't answer me."

"I was too busy."

"That's no reason."

His hand slipped between her thighs, and they closed around him. She was slick and ready for him, but her hands went to his shoulders and he stopped, waiting for her. "Why?" he asked.

"What are you doing?"

"Don't worry, I would never hurt you."

She held her legs tightly together. "I want to kiss you," she said.

He raised his head to look up into her eyes. "Tell me why, first."

She was scared, not of his hands and his mouth, but of his

questions. He could see it in her eyes, hear it in her voice as she said, "Kiss me, please."

He shook his head. Still holding her eyes with his own, he sank down and kissed the underside of her left breast. Her body shook beneath him. "Tell me why you gave up your art." He licked one nipple, then the other.

"I don't know," she cried. With that capitulation, he felt the muscles in her legs relax as well. He stroked her there, gently. "I always loved it. My grandmother told my father that we had art in our blood. In Africa, his grandfather had been a great sculptor. But I think I just wanted to be with him. All those years, we were so close, Papa and I. I thought we would paint together forever. Back then, I was very serious about my work. I thought I'd be just like Papa. But I wasn't. There was more that I wanted to do than just paint." His tongue made wet circles on her flesh. His fingers, below, circled the tiny point of flesh that begged for his attention. Her legs opened fractionally wider. She threw one hand across her eyes, and kept talking.

"I didn't even realize how much of my time it was taking, running the house, inviting guests down from Paris and then playing hostess. Then I started to have to choose between painting and all the rest. By then I had come to know that I really liked all the rest. I wasn't like Papa at all. He wouldn't have allowed little things like his household finances to interfere with his work. He was dedicated only to art. I liked talking to people, about everything. Paint and canvas and clay are inanimate. They can't . . . talk to you. I needed people. I enjoyed the people in the marketplace in town, the artists and students who visited us. We had all sorts of people here."

Jack's tongue circled her navel, moved lower. With the pad of his thumb, he pressed into her center. Pascale gasped. Her hips came up off the bed. His hand stilled. He waited for her to settle back down, then continued his teasing caresses. She started to move in a rhythm as old as time, but she kept talking, low and fast.

"It was much easier to create the perfect dinner for twenty people than to try and capture a sunset that changed with every minute." She gasped, then stilled, but he didn't stop his caresses, and soon her hips were moving again. She groaned.

"Go on," he urged.

"Papa was proud of me, but he was not an easy teacher. He expected me to be as good as he was. Better." Jack's head slid lower, he hooked his good arm around her thigh and ran a fingernail down the back of it. He kissed the tiny button at the apex of her thighs, and felt her shiver. At first he didn't notice she'd stopped talking, so intent was he on her body's reaction to his ministrations.

"And . . . ," he prompted, raising his head to look up at her.

Her eyes were closed. She bit her lip. "I c-can't talk anymore. Please . . ." Her hands dug into the sheets at her side.

He relented. His lips came down voraciously on her. She was near the edge, so close. He fastened his mouth on her, holding her in place with his strong arm. Her knee collided with his useless arm, but he barely felt it. She arched into him, muscles clenching, once, then again. He kissed her down there once more, then slowly raised his head. She was staring down at him, dazed astonishment filling her eyes.

"That was *your* reward?" she asked, incredulous.

"I enjoyed it," he said with a wide grin.

She smiled back at him weakly. Then she turned her head away. "Why do you want to know all this?" her voice was barely above a whisper; he nearly missed the question.

"I need to know. Why would you give yourself to me for a painting you've never even seen?"

"But I told you."

"You told me all your reasons, but you never told me why. I still don't understand. You're beautiful, and you're certainly no fool. Why do you bury yourself out here, in your father's house, away from the people whom you most enjoy? Why did you give up the art you so clearly love? Why are you so convinced that this is all there is for you? You could have anything you wanted, any man, any life? Why do you settle for so little?" She looked confused and uncertain, but Jack couldn't help himself. He had to know. He couldn't ask the one question that most tormented him: *"Why would she choose him?"* Instead he asked, "Why can't you see that your father is a selfish old fool who doesn't even realize what he's done to you?"

She pulled him up to her, kissed his cheek. "I do see it, now. I didn't feel like I was missing anything before, but I know now that I was."

"Don't let Paul change your mind."

"I won't. I couldn't." When Jack didn't look convinced, she added, "There was a man, one of my father's students, who made me feel . . . like my talent wasn't important, only my name counted. He made me feel like I was nothing. Papa, for all his faults, makes me feel like something special."

"But he let you give up painting."

"I announced that I had made up my mind it wasn't for me. I explained to him that I didn't think I had the dedication necessary to pursue it, and he didn't try to make me continue. I think he was trying to do the right thing."

"But that wasn't what you really wanted? Didn't he see that?"

"I had my chocolate every day. The farm was doing better, and students were coming to live here more, and paying better. I don't think it occurred to him to miss his painting partner. It's not something that you really do together anyway, you know. Painting is an intensely personal thing. You can talk about it, and try to learn from others, but in the end, it's your eye, your hand, your mind and heart. And we could still talk about it. And then, by that time, I was selling his work for him, so money was coming in. It was the most comfortable we ever were. We've been perfectly happy ever since. Until you came along." She kissed his chin. "I needed you to make me think about what I had given up. I didn't want my world turned upside down, but I needed it, and I'll never regret it.

I'm painting again, aren't I?" She kissed his shoulder. "You've taught me a lot about myself." She smiled mischievously at him. "One way or another."

Jack tried to return her smile, but it was an effort. He had thought to end it, here tonight, and walk away without any regret or remorse. He had believed that he could change everything. But in the end, he'd disappear, and Pascale would be left alone again. He was just like all of the others. Somehow he knew she'd continue believing that she could not be loved like other women. And this time it would be his fault.

There was only one thing he could think to do. It was not enough, but perhaps if he could achieve this one thing before he walked out of her life, he wouldn't continue to hate himself. He had to return The Portrait of The Lady before he walked out of her life forever.

Twenty-seven

The next day, the captain's men arrived. Jack was sitting in the studio, watching her paint, when John Douglas came up to give them the news. Pascale didn't hear any more of the conversation. She was overwhelmed by the sudden realization that he was truly leaving her, possibly to die.

Pascale didn't turn away from her canvas until well after John Douglas left. The silence seemed to mock her, but she couldn't bare to break it when all they had left to say was goodbye. She had a sudden premonition that this heavy silence would be all she had to look forward to after Jack left.

Finally, when she thought she could maintain her equilibrium, she turned to face him. Jack's eyes searched hers, and she hoped that the sorrow she felt was not written too plainly there. She didn't want to lose him.

"You will finally have your answers," she said, pleased that she sounded so calm.

"Yes," he agreed.

"So, this is goodbye." She went over to him and reached up to kiss his chin.

"Are you so eager to be rid of me?" He tried to joke, but his voice sounded strained. Or perhaps that was just what she hoped to hear. Pascale didn't know anymore.

"No," she answered honestly, turning her head into his chest. "I don't want you to go," she said, her voice finally breaking, but safely muffled against him. "You're going to get yourself killed."

"I'm not," Jack said.

"You won't let them undo all the hard work we've done here?"

"Nothing will happen to me. I swear it." He kissed the top of her head. "I have a painting to deliver."

"That's all I needed to know," Pascale lied. She pulled his head down to hers and kissed him hungrily, thinking, *This is the last time.* She would have to hide her feelings when they left this room. There would be no more Jack to talk to, and no one else would understand.

She had always known he would leave. But she hadn't realized that it would hurt quite so much to let him go. She had not guarded her heart strictly enough. He would be leaving with a large part of it.

Pascale tried to be sensible. If it hurt this much after only one month, maybe it was better that he leave before she could fall completely in love with him.

But the thought brought no comfort. He had given her so much. He had even given her back her art. She should be grateful. She had never thought to meet anyone who would make her feel as he had. Now she knew that it was possible. He had shown her that anything was possible.

But the slight hope that she had harbored, against her will— that Jack might change his mind and choose to stay—finally died as she stood with Philippe, Pierre, Francine and Papa and waved Jack's carriage out of sight.

All that day Pascale felt isolated from the life of the château. It flowed around her, but could not pass through the barrier that separated her. A fight between Pierre and Louise concerning the care and feeding of their two remaining guests brought Francine rushing to the kitchen, but Pascale could not persuade herself to follow. When Francine and Papa fought at dinner about whether the resolution of the disagreement was fair, Pascale was removed.

She was finally dragged into the conflict by the combined pleas of both her father and her friend. They convened in the library with snifters of brandy. Pascale played with her drink, focusing on the amber liquid as she swirled it gently in the bottom of the deep glass.

"Pascale, it's unreasonable for your Papa to expect Louise to cook for him and those two boys when they frequently miss their meals. If they are going to be painting through lunch—as usual—and even through dinner, then the food, and her work, is wasted." Francine put forth her side of the debate quite reasonably, but her voice shook with the force of her emotions. "I just suggested that Yves and David inform Louise when they are going to want their meals. That's fair, don't you think?"

"It sounds fair," Pascale said. She couldn't summon any enthusiasm for the role of moderator today. She still felt as though she were engulfed in a cloud of cotton that shielded her from the sharper edges of the world, including Francine's resentment and her father's indignation.

"But, *ma fille,* the boys do not always know when or even if they will want lunch, or will be able to stop for dinner. You know that when one is caught up in the work, it is impossible to keep a time schedule."

"True," she agreed, noncommittally.

"Well, they'll have to try," Francine doggedly insisted.

"It's impossible I tell you!" Papa argued.

"May I suggest that Cook make up a cold plate for the boys if they aren't sure whether they'll be able to join us for regular meals, Francine?" Pascale offered.

Papa seemed satisfied with the solution. He nodded. Francine could not find fault with the suggestion, and she agreed reluctantly. "I'll ask Louise," she said. With one last withering look at the master of the house, she scuttled out of the room.

"Papa, you'll tell David and Yves, won't you?" Pascale asked.

"Yes, *ma cherie,* I will tell them tomorrow."

"Good." She was, once again, his chatelaine. It was not the same though. Jack had changed her. She felt no pleasure at the successful negotiation of the truce. Surprisingly, she felt no bitterness. It seemed natural to resume her duties, just as it felt natural to paint again. Pascale left the library and went to her room. Her sketchbook lay open on her desk. Jack's devilish smile greeted her when she glanced at it. She felt nothing at the sight. She stared at her drawing, emotionlessly cataloguing its strengths and weaknesses. She noted, listlessly, that it had no more power to move her than anything else.

She welcomed the strange sense of seclusion. Nothing could hurt her, nor make a dent in the calm passionless state she had entered. Only painting felt right. She moved through other activities, such as dressing, eating, and talking, with a vague sense that she had left something unfinished. Her chores seemed a nuisance, easy to handle, yet never ending. When she immersed herself in her art, the lack of passion didn't seem to matter. Before, painting had been for her an expression of her deepest emotions, and had been accompanied by intensely felt emotion that shut her off from everything around her. Now that she felt nothing, her artistic vision seemed clearer than ever. It was odd.

That first night after Devlin left, the first crack appeared in the rockhard shell that seemed to have formed around her heart. Pascale was working on a painting in the studio when Papa, David and Yves came back from another day spent painting in the vineyards. She ignored them at first, which was easily done as her attention was totally focussed on 'finishing' her painting of the barn, the distant mountains a backdrop to the rural scene. But gradually the men's voices penetrated.

"David, you fool, you've no talent with people, and less with letters. How can you even consider becoming a clerk." Yves's annoyance with his witless companion was more pronounced than ever.

"I've got to earn some money. My allowance is barely enough for supplies, and Lisette insists on being paid."

"Find another model, *mon fils,* there are many who will work for much less," said Papa.

"But I want Lisette," David insisted.

Yves snorted. "And well she knows it. I guarantee you, if you just have one sitting with another wench, Lisette will be back—and willing to model for much less than you're paying her now."

"It sounds like trickery," David said, his voice full of doubt.

"It won't be, if you really mean to use the other girl," Papa said. "David, I can't believe you're even thinking about giving up your freedom for a clerk's position. You are much too talented! Maybe the girl will come back to you, or maybe she'll move on, but at least you won't have thrown your talent away."

Pascale felt something inside her shift at hearing those words from her father's lips. Suddenly she was fifteen years old again and telling her beloved Papa that she was going to give up painting altogether, forever. She clearly remembered his baffled expression, but she couldn't remember him saying to her what he was saying to David. Because he had never uttered those words to her.

"You cannot waste the talent God gave you," Papa said to David.

"I'll keep painting, sir," David vowed. "I can't help myself."

"I said the same thing. But it was only pure chance that I was able to resume my painting career."

"Chance?" Pascale said, under her breath. It had not been luck, it had been her. She had made it possible for Paul de Ravenault to go back to his painting. And she'd done it gladly, in return for a little attention and less gratitude.

"You must continue to paint," Papa said emphatically.

The voice of the fifteen-year-old Pascale cried out in her mind, "Why didn't you say that to me," so loud that she thought she might have actually spoken it. But she could not have done so. The three men continued to argue, ignoring her presence in the room.

"But, Monsieur, I love Lisette," David said.

"This is not love, *mon ami,*" Yves interjected. "This is infatuation. And she loves you not at all, or she'd model for you for free."

As David began to defend his love, Papa said, "It is not relevant. All that matters is—"

Pascale finished the statement for him, "You must keep painting, David. If you decide to waste such talent, you should do it for some better reason."

David nodded. Pascale barely noticed. She was still busy puzzling over her father's behavior. He had persuaded David to continue painting, but had hardly voiced a word when she'd told him she planned to give it up. Why?

The depth of her jealousy was a shock after the last couple of days. Her anger was slow to rise, and she tried to hold it inside. She swallowed, repeatedly, until she felt that she would choke if she didn't speak.

"Why didn't you argue with me, Papa? You always said I was talented. Were you lying all those years?"

"What are you talking about?"

"When I told you I was going to give up painting, you hardly said a word." Her voice was hard, cold and flat, but her heart ached.

"But you said you couldn't enjoy it any more. For two years, you said, you'd been trying to paint and have a life, and you couldn't do both. What was I supposed to say?" he asked, bewildered.

"Paint!" The word exploded out of her. "All you had to say was that I should keep painting. Forget cleaning up after you and your friends, running the farm and selling your work, and paint!"

"But you said—" he began.

"I was fifteen, Papa. Just fifteen years old."

"You knew your own mind when you were five. I never could tell you what to do."

"I thought you knew me better than that," Pascale said sadly. "Even if you didn't think it would make a difference, why didn't you tell *me* I had too much talent to waste? I'm your daughter, your own flesh and blood. Why didn't you fight for me?"

"I didn't know that was what you wanted to hear," he said.

Pascale could only stare at him, feeling betrayed once again. Finally she summoned the courage to ask, "But wasn't it true?"

"Yes." His response was swift, and sincere. "It was true. But you know that. You were born knowing that."

"No one knows that," Pascale protested. "Why did you hide The Painting from me? Your own daughter? Because you, a full grown man, didn't even trust his own talent. And you've proven yourself as a professional artist."

"That's different," Papa said. "I've worked on that portrait all of my adult life."

"I was painting almost before I walked. That's all I ever knew, all I ever did!" Pascale shouted.

"How can you compare the two?" her father demanded, his anger rising to meet her own.

"It's the same thing. You're the one person in the world I'd have expected to understand that! To understand me. Oh, it's no use talking to you, it's like talking to a wall."

"I'm here." Papa raised his voice so its volume matched hers. "I'm here," he said, again, taking her by the shoulders. "And I'm listening." Pascale crumbled at his touch.

"But you don't see," she said into his chest. "You let me waste my life taking care of you and your needs, and you didn't say anything, or do anything. Why couldn't you once have said I was wasting my talent?"

"I didn't want to hurt you," he said. "I swear, Pascale, *ma petite,* that's all it was. I'm sorry."

"You didn't want to hurt me?" Pascale echoed in disbelief.

"I didn't realize . . . ," he started to say, but she couldn't stand to hear him say it again. His apology meant little to her. God help her, she still wanted to hear him say it. She pushed away from him and ran.

Once the floodgates had opened, she couldn't stop the tide

of pain that came pouring through. The night was a waking nightmare. Every hurtful memory came back to haunt her. Pascale suffered again through the years of doubt about her absent mother, Francine's disapproval, Dorian's biting sarcasm, her father's betrayal, and lastly, the battles with Jack.

She couldn't help but realize that she'd been foolish, gullible and naive. Jack had been right all along. She should have been painting. And she shouldn't have tried to force him, or seduce him, into giving her The Portrait of The Lady. She had been trying to live through Papa. She should have let him go; just as she had to let Jack go. She couldn't depend on these men.

Pascale finally fell asleep, determined to change those things in her life that were not as she wanted them. She planned to begin by forgetting about Captain John Devlin.

Twenty-eight

Monsieur Baptiste rode up to the house early the next morning. She hadn't expected him, and invited him and his partner into the house before she'd taken a look at his becloaked companion. When Pierre took the garbed man's hat, she was surprised, to say the least, to see Nieuwerkerke's secretary, Monsieur Serratt, with one of Jack's men.

"William Baptiste, *mademoiselle.*"

Pascale nodded. "I remember you."

"Captain Devlin sent me for you." He darted a quick look at Serratt, who nodded. Then she did wonder what was amiss.

"Where is he?" she asked, trying to think of some way to signal Pierre, who was about to leave the room.

"In Paris."

Pascale shot another glance at the butler, who was looking at Baptiste with an arrested expression. He slowly turned his head toward her and met her eyes. She tried to telegraph her concern to him without giving herself away to the other two men. He nodded, almost imperceptibly, and started toward the door.

"Wait!" Serratt ordered.

Pierre stopped walking, but did not turn around. "I will ask Cook to prepare some refreshment for you. You have traveled a long distance."

"No, thank you. Just have a maid pack a few things for your mistress. We must leave as soon as possible," the man ordered.

Pierre nodded and began again toward the back of the house saying, "Certainly, and I'll have the coach brought round."

William Baptiste, at some covert signal from Serratt, drew a long dagger from his belt and stepped closer to her. She instinctively shied away from him, but not quickly enough. He caught her hand and pulled her into the crook of his arm, holding the knife against her throat. It all happened so quickly that Pascale didn't have a chance to warn Pierre.

"I suggest you stop where you are, *monsieur,*" Serratt said to Pierre.

After a slight hesitation, her butler stopped and slowly turned. When he saw the evil-looking knife at Pascale's throat, his eyes widened.

"Bring the others in here." When Pascale and Pierre turned to look at him, a gun had appeared in Serratt's hand.

William Baptiste knew everything about the house. He had become very familiar with the château and her staff on his first visit to the estate, when he'd acted the coachman. Apparently, he had briefed Serratt. They quickly had all the servants brought into the front hall and shepherded them and Paul de Ravenault into the room beneath the cellars, where the older wines were stored.

They were wary and on guard, and Baptiste's blade was never more than an inch from her throat. He hauled her about with him from place to place, occasionally knicking her skin with the tip of his knife. Though Pascale knew that most of the servants would have given their lives for hers, they were never given the chance. Less than an hour after the two men had ridden up to the house, Pascale was thrown up onto William Baptiste's horse like a sack of potatoes. She held on to the saddle for dear life as they galloped down the drive.

The two men set a grueling pace. They traveled north on the road to Paris. She saw a couple of farmers' carts, and a coach, but each time she considered shouting for help, Pascale felt Monsieur Serratt's eyes on her, and saw his hand go to his gun. She couldn't risk it. She didn't want to cause anyone to get hurt. She doubted that the farmers could protect her from her abductors, and it was unlikely that the gentlefolk in this quiet countryside would arm themselves for a jaunt in the vicinity of their homes. Frightened as she was, she had to work to keep her wits about her.

Jack would come for her. He must already have discovered Baptiste's treachery in the course of his investigation. He'd find out about Serratt, too. He would come. She held on to that thought. He was probably closing the distance between them with every passing moment.

The men stopped to water the horses at a brook, after a few hours. They refreshed themselves with wine and water, and refilled the flasks they carried. Both men were leery of every movement Pascale made as they waited for the horses to cool down. Pascale was careful to move slowly as she looked around, searching in vain for an escape route. The country was too open, she could see for miles. She stood, testing the limits they'd allow her.

"Sit down," Baptiste snarled.

"May I have some water?"

William Baptiste just snorted his disdain at her question. She feared bodily harm from him. When his eyes wandered to her, she could barely keep from running. But the other man was undoubtedly the one in charge, and she kept her eyes on him while he considered her request. His cold glare was even more frightening than Baptiste's heated gaze. He acted as though the whole fantastic situation was commonplace. Serratt's calm demeanor suggested to Pascale that he'd think no more of watching Baptiste slit her throat than he would of casually shooting any stranger to whom she might turn for help. However, she didn't think he planned to hurt her. . . . Not yet. He had some other aim in mind. He brought her his water flask and waited while she drank. Then he offered her Baptiste's wine flask.

Pascale shook her head. While she had his attention, she thought she would try to find out what they wanted. She started with the most obvious question. "Why are you doing this?"

Monsieur Serratt was eager enough to talk.

"Your friend, Devlin, has been enough of a nuisance. Kidnapping Captain Forêt was the last straw. We've decided to use you to control him." He was clearly pleased with his own cleverness.

One of the puzzle pieces fell into place for Pascale. So that was why he had to leave so abruptly. He'd located one of the conspirators.

"What makes you think he'd do anything for me?"

Baptiste answered the question by leering at her. Pascale couldn't help flinching under his repulsive gaze.

"Captain Devlin has made his interest in you quite plain. At least to those among his crew with whom he entrusted your care," Serratt said.

Pascale shot a furious glance at Baptiste, who only laughed and taunted her. "The graveyards are full of people who trusted people they should not have."

"Will I be one of them?" she asked.

Serratt smiled. "Perhaps. We don't really need you, after all. All we need to keep Devlin out of our hair is a dress your family can identify. But we don't want to kill you—too many people have died already, and we'd rather not make anyone suspicious if we can help it. If you are cooperative, I think we can release you, after a certain ship leaves our shores." He was lying. She could smell it. They would kill her, after they got what they wanted. She still didn't know what that was.

Since Serratt hadn't objected to her first question, she pressed on, "But weren't you the one who blew up Jack's ship? Why are you so concerned now about this other ship?"

"Jack was carrying a message from the emperor. The new messenger is more amenable to a change in destination than Devlin would have been."

"Why change its destination? Where is this message going?"

"The same place as the first, almost. Mexico."

"No, I meant to whom? Maximilian?"

"Very clever. She is as bright as she is beautiful, William. You never mentioned that."

"Didn't notice, myself," was Baptiste's unabashed reply.

"Any message Napoleon sent had to be a pledge of support."

"I can see why Devlin admires you, *ma petite*," he said, looking her up and down.

Pascale hid a shudder of revulsion. "That doesn't answer my question. Why, then, are you arranging to send your employer's message again."

"This time, I've chosen my own man for the job. Nieuwerkerke had no choice but to use the man I suggested. Captain Forêt's ship is the only one leaving for Mexico at this time."

"Forêt? The man Jack kidnapped? He's working for you?"

"Very good, *mademoiselle*. It really would be a shame if something had to happen to you."

"So where will Forêt deliver this missive, if not to Maximilian?" Pascale asked. She wanted to keep Serratt talking. He was eager enough to comply.

"Unfortunately, the emperor's message will end up in the hands of the Americans. Accidentally, of course."

"To what purpose? The Americans already know that Napoleon supports him. Our emperor installed him on his throne."

"Maximilian," Baptiste growled. "That pig." He spat on the ground.

"I'm just buying time for my . . . employers. They believe the Americans will convince our emperor to withdraw the army. They don't approve of our foreign rule, or the invasion. When they get Napoleon's pledge of support for Maximilian, we think they'll start to put pressure on our emperor to withdraw it. We won't need to lift a finger."

"But you've already killed and maimed all those men. And

now you're kidnapping me so you can trap Jack and murder him. I'd say you're doing your share of the dirty work."

He looked slightly taken aback, and then smiled. "Perhaps you're right, *mademoiselle*." He turned to his cohort. "She's brilliant, Baptiste! How could you have missed it?"

The sailor shrugged. Pascale's blood ran cold when he didn't deny her accusation that he planned to kill Jack. She had suspected as much since they'd abducted her. If all they wanted was for Jack to release this Captain Forêt, it would have been far simpler just to send a message to Jack that they would kill her if he didn't do as they said. They were keeping her as bait. It made sense. Jack probably knew too much about them, if he'd found their cohort.

Her first real opportunity for escape came at the posting house, where a change of horses was clearly a necessity. Their horses were suffering from the grueling pace set by the madman Serratt, and she hoped that while they were exchanged for new mounts, she might have a chance to slip away. But Serratt had already bespoke the new horses, and they were ready and waiting as the three of them rode up to the inn. The ostler was quick to change the saddles, and they were up and off again before Pascale had any chance to look for help.

She balked at getting back up onto her mount, but Serratt grasped her wrist, and, after a quick look around to see that no one was watching them, he brought his gun to her back.

"Mademoiselle," he said, jabbing his gun into the small of her back. "I could kill you right now. It doesn't matter to me." Her blood ran cold. Bait or not, he *would* kill her. "Will you get back on that horse, or would you rather die?"

Pascale mounted, slowly and carefully. She didn't want to die. Another thought occurred to her. Even her death wouldn't necessarily stop this madman. He could hide her body and convince Jack he still held her. If the murderer intended to use her as a lure, he might keep her alive long enough for Pascale to think of some way to escape. It was her only chance.

Twenty-nine

Jack couldn't close his eyes without seeing Pascale's sweet face in his mind's eye. He'd said farewell to women in ports all over the world, but this was different. John Douglas had even gone so far as to allow Pascale to embrace him. Even the stolid, woman-hating valet had been touched by her.

In the coach and pair, it was impossible to travel the sixty miles to the village where Henry Bates waited at the foot of the Saône River in under fifteen hours. If Jack had been able to ride, it would only have taken five or six hours. Frustrated at their slow pace, Jack snapped at John Douglas, "Can't they spring the damn horses!"

"They're going as fast as they can," his man answered unruffled.

They had to stop when night fell. His men tried to make him comfortable, but Jack fretted over the time lost.

John Douglas was maddeningly calm. "It will do Forêt good to cool his heels. What little nerve he's got will be gone by the time we arrive," his valet pointed out.

He climbed out of the carriage. A brilliant canopy of stars and a nearly full moon above shed enough light for him to perceive his men, sleeping not far from the carriage.

The horses didn't even raise their heads when he gave the pair a cursory examination. They weren't exactly prime horseflesh, but seemed to be pretty evenly matched.

"We haven't too much farther to go now," John Douglas

said, following him. "We'll be off betimes, and shouldn't arrive much past nine o' the clock in the morn."

Jack had healed enough to almost enjoy his second ride through the wine country, but he was too impatient to really appreciate the beauty of the vineyards as they set out again the next morning. As the sun rose, it turned golden the dewy vines, thick with leaves and small clusters of ripening grapes.

He wondered if Pascale was taking in the same breathtaking view, and whether perhaps she would be inspired to paint it. The vague longing he felt to have her still by his side he attributed to their last enchanted nights together. This unfamiliar sensation would fade in time, he was sure.

The carriage finally came to a halt outside a tiny inn located in the center of a small hamlet of no more than four or five houses. Henry Bates met John Douglas and himself at the door, and directed Jack to the cellar beneath the small structure where they were holding their prisoner. Jack went down to see Forêt straightaway.

It was satisfyingly dank and musty in the wine cellar. The atmosphere created by the sodden walls and heavily webbed bottles couldn't have been better if Jack had planned it. In striking contrast to the dirty surroundings, his men had created a comfortable, even luxurious, living space for their captive. The cot had been made up with clean sheets and a colorful quilt, the table was set with simple country crockery and shining silver, and still held evidence of the simple but hearty remains from the prisoner's most recent meal. His captive appeared to have been in good appetite.

"Forêt," he greeted the pasty-faced little Frenchman. "It has been a while."

Forêt had turned white as a ghost at his entrance, and could only stutter, "I—I th-thought you were d-dead, Devlin?"

Jack smiled sardonically at his hapless prisoner. "As you can see, Captain, I am not."

"Wh-what do you w-want from m-m-me?"

"The name of your current employer," Jack said lightly.

"Why, but . . . I don't understand."

Jack was happy to explain. "The man who commissioned you, recently, to carry a message to Emperor Maximilian in Mexico requested that I play courier for him right before my ship suffered its untimely demise. I think you may be next."

Forêt tried to laugh, but his sad effort came as something between a choking cough and a desperate cry. "I don't know what you mean, Captain."

"Perhaps your grasp of English is at fault."

"To prevent any further misunderstanding, I will speak your language." He repeated the question in Forêt's native tongue. He almost regretted it, as Forêt spewed forth a torrent of French, most of which Jack guessed to be obscene. The gist of his tirade was quite clear. The captain didn't know whom Jack was talking about, all of his contacts were totally above-board, and, most importantly, Jack hadn't needed to coerce him into giving up information. They were both the masters of seagoing vessels, and as such, entitled to any tales of their opponent's misfortune so as to avoid falling into similar pit-falls.

Jack was still smiling, struck by the similarity between Forêt's complaints and to his own reasoned statement.

"But that's exactly my point, Captain Forêt. You may win my argument for me," Jack said facetiously. "I'll wait."

He hooked his foot around the leg of a chair and pulled it closer before he sat on it—careful not to give any signs of the pain the simple maneuver cost him.

When Forêt didn't respond, he added, "We have plenty of time."

"I cannot supply the name you require, because I do not know it. This I swear, as one ship's captain to another."

"Your pledge is no good here." Jack's certainty of the other man's guilt grew with each word. The telltale flickering of the man's eyes as he searched out the small guarded entry to his "cell" was all the confirmation he needed. "There is only one way for you to leave this room alive. Tell me what I want to know." Jack hoped Forêt recognized the menace in his tone. He was losing patience with the man, and he hadn't had a lot to begin with.

"If I give you the names of the men whose cargo I've bought or carry on consignment, will that be enough for you?"

"If you include the name I want, it may be."

"You know already who you are looking for?" Forêt asked, puzzled.

"I am asking the questions here. When I am interested in answering your questions, I'll let you know."

"But if you know who it is . . . ?"

Jack erupted out of his seat. It was not difficult to ignore the pain to his ribs, now that he was so close to his goal. He had crossed the few feet that separated him from the ratlike Forêt, and pulled him across the table in seconds. "Speak!" Jack held him in a purposeful grip, but loosely enough that Forêt could answer him.

"He'll kill me," he choked out.

"If you don't tell me, I'll kill you. I swear it."

Jack could see the beads of sweat on the man's forehead, but he didn't relent. He couldn't even feel any pity for his rival, the spineless little runt. Jack and Forêt had had a run-in over the illegal cargo carried by the Frenchman to New Orleans right before the War Between the States. Forêt had been involved in the slave trade, boasting of the profits derived from his human cargo.

Jack was an Englishman. He believed in the highest ideals of the country of his birth, though he knew that those ideals weren't always upheld. He'd fought in the Navy, and even been wounded, alongside men who had given their lives for those ideals. The importation of slaves had been outlawed in England in 1760, and slavery declared illegal in 1772. Although slavery had not been outlawed throughout the Empire until two decades ago, the evils of the institution were well known to Jack's countrymen— and all men of good heart. Though he'd suffered the prejudices of men who would never accept a black man as their leader, he'd also seen them stand tall defending the freedom of the blacks they despised. There was no black and white in Jack's mind, only shades of gray. Forêt was not evil, only small-minded and afraid. The man who had hired him, though, was the lowest of the low. Jack hated him to the depths of his soul, and he needed confirmation of his identity.

Captain Devlin slowly regained control of his temper, and released the mouse who trembled beneath him.

"As I said, Captain Forêt, I have all the time in the world."

He strode to the door, ignoring Forêt, who called after him, "Wait! Devlin! You've got to let me go."

Let him sweat out another night in the cellar. He'd talk soon enough. Jack could be patient.

By the next morning, as Jack had expected, his prisoner was ready to divulge the information they needed. His enemy's name was revealed.

"Monsieur Serratt hired me." Forêt was nearly sobbing.

"Nieuwerkerke's secretary? Not the minister of fine arts himself?"

Forêt was so surprised by the question, Jack couldn't doubt the sincerity of his answer. "Nieuwerkerke isn't involved in this, is he?"

"Isn't he?" But Jack only asked because he wanted Forêt to be afraid that he'd revealed more than he knew. He was satisfied that if the minister had been involved, Forêt would have known of it.

"I don't think so. Serratt told me Baptiste had scuttled the ship in order to stop the message from being delivered. The minister has much more efficient assassins at his disposal. Men who would have made sure you were dead, if that was their intention. Why would he use an amateur like Baptiste?"

"Baptiste? William Baptiste?"

Suddenly it all clicked into place. Serratt had been paid by someone, who could have been a Mexican émigré or a supporter of Juarez, to stop Napoleon's message from reaching Maximilian, in order to undermine the new government in

Mexico. Serratt had probably approached the Mexicans on Jack's crew to discover if their loyalties lay with their countries first elected government. That would explain the mysterious death of his crew member. Serratt must have killed him to cover his tracks. Until the moment when Forêt mentioned his name, Jack had forgotten that William Baptiste was half Mexican. The sailor despised his mother so much, that he'd changed his name from Guillermo to William. But Serratt must have discovered his mother was half Mexican and approached him anyway.

William Baptiste would never have joined up with him out of loyalty to "his" country. His loyalty was strictly for sale. Jack had thought he had purchased it when he signed on, but Baptiste was a traitor. Jack ran from the room, barely hearing Forêt's startled yell, "Devlin! I've told you what you wanted to know—"

John Douglas awaited him outside the door. "We heard. Henry went to find out where William is now."

The news wasn't very promising. "He was one of the men stationed in Paris. He was assigned to watch Serratt's house with Tom Bowman. I don't remember how he pulled that duty—perhaps he volunteered," Henry reported.

"Has a man been sent to Paris?" Jack asked, a premonition overwhelming him as he looked into Bates's knowing eyes.

"No. The last time I spoke to Thomas, when we were leaving Paris, he mentioned Will hadn't shown up to take his shift, watching the house. I told Thomas to send a man to rouse him from whatever barmaid's bed he'd fallen into, but told him not to worry overmuch—we'd be watching Serratt until we finished questioning Forêt, but we wouldn't be moving against him for at least the next couple of days. I've just spoken with Gustave who went to find Baptiste. He says he never discovered the man's whereabouts, but when he told Bowman, Tom just repeated what I had said, so Gustave assumed everything was all right."

"Damn!" Jack swore.

John Douglas was shaking his head. "He is fiery-tempered, but he's not stupid. He knows you'll be looking for him."

Jack mulled it over, a growing feeling of alarm overwhelming him. Baptiste was a survivor. Jack didn't think he'd live in hope that he'd be able to hide from his captain and his crew. He'd want insurance of some kind. And Serratt must have discovered by now that Captain Forêt was missing. The two men would try, at the least, to cover their tracks.

The thought of Pascale leaped to Jack's mind. Baptiste knew Jack felt responsible for the de Ravenault family. He might even have guessed how Jack felt about her. He could guess that Jack would not want the family hurt, which was why they had gone through an elaborate charade in order to secure him the position of coachman.

Jack felt in his bones that William Baptiste would retreat to Beaune, to cower like a trapped dog somewhere in the little town. He'd use Pascale's life as a bargaining chip to negotiate for his own life. Serratt was the enigma. Had Baptiste been informed that Forêt was in danger of being abducted before Henry Bates had even finished the operation? Or had he been involved in something altogether different, and only disappeared later when he arrived at his post and Thomas told him about Forêt's kidnapping?

There were too many intangibles, but at most they had a day on him. More likely, William Baptiste was already in Beaune. A chill ran down Jack's spine.

"We've got to go back to Beaune." Jack couldn't restrain his impatience.

"I've already got the men preparing the carriage," Henry Bates said.

"I can ride."

"Captain—" John Douglas started to remonstrate.

"It will take half the time. I'm fine!"

"What do we do with him?" Henry tossed his head toward the cellar door.

"Let him go."

Jack ran up the stairs and out of the inn, directly to the stables. He bypassed the men hitching up the carriage and went directly inside. He took a moment to choose a horse among those stabled there, and then saw a gray thoroughbred, who seemed both restive and eager to go. That was just what Jack was looking for.

Jack slung a saddle on him, one handed, and started to cinch up the straps. Thomas appeared.

"Captain?" His open, trusting face was riddled with guilt, but Jack couldn't spare the time to reassure him.

"Finish this up for me, Thomas, will you?" Thomas eagerly complied, but said, "Captain, I don't rightly remember whose horse this is."

Jack's voice cut the air like a whip. "It doesn't matter." The moment Thomas Bowman heard the tone, he led the horse into the yard. "Have everyone follow me as soon as they can settle up here and get mounted."

"Captain!" Devlin heard someone shout out behind him.

He swung up onto the horse, not without a little difficulty, and was off before anyone could stop him.

That bone-wrenching ride to the de Ravenaults was the longest five hours of his life. He and the gray were both lathered by the time they reached the estate. The grounds looked serene when he cantered up to the door. The house was quiet when he ran inside. Pierre was nowhere in sight. The silence was eerie.

Jack made his way to the kitchen. Louise was also missing. He forced himself to remain calm. There could be any number of explanations for the deadly quiet.

By the time he had searched the entire house, he was frantic—and murderously angry. He stood at the library windows, searching for any sign of movement, when he heard a distant thud. He cocked his head, straining to hear, but there was no other sound. Until he heard the pounding of galloping hooves outside.

Henry Bates and the other men would not have been far behind. He strode toward the library doors to go and greet them out front. That was when he thought of the cellars—where Bates had imprisoned Francine Pitt when he'd been here before. He marched to the front door and pulled it open with such force that the heavy oak panels shook in their ornate frames.

"I can't find anyone. I haven't checked the cellar yet."

Bates and the four men with him followed. The clattering of their boot heels on the marble floor made a mockery of Jack's earlier attempts at stealth. But Jack's rage had far outstripped his reason. He felt only grim satisfaction that William Baptiste might be listening to the menacing sound of his approach.

The deadly fury that gripped him was not assuaged as two of the men broke through the door that led down to the bowels of the mansion. Candles lit the steep wooden stair. But when they reached the floor below, they found nothing out of place.

"I heard something, right before you arrived," Jack said, frustrated. He searched the dark corners of the room for some sign that the thud had originated there.

Bates strode to the far wall. "There's an entrance somewhere down here to the storage area for the wines." All the men fanned out, searching for the door. "I went down through the storage house, but we came out through here. It's a big arched door, about a foot thick. The wood is solid. Like these walls. They're too big to hide. It's got to be here somewhere," he insisted.

Jack stood in the middle of the room, torn between continuing the search at this end, or running back upstairs and outside to the entrance above ground.

"Here!" Bates exclaimed as he slipped behind a pyramid of wine barrels stacked one above the other to the ceiling.

Jack ran forward, hearing a hinge creak shrilly as Bates pushed part of the wide curved door open.

Paul de Ravenault and his servants sat bound and gagged in the middle of the floor. An up-ended table was evidence of the group's attempt to pull themselves to their feet.

Pascale wasn't there.

Jack and the others started to untie them.

"They took Pascale," Francine said, as soon as Henry removed the kerchief from her mouth. "Early this morning. One threatened to cut her with his knife if we didn't do just what he said."

"I can draw his face," Paul volunteered.

"We know the man," Jack said. "Do you have any idea where they were planning to take her?"

"Paris," Philippe answered. "I heard the older man say they'd be riding all day and half the night to get there."

Thirty

It felt as if she'd been on this road forever, but Pascale guessed by the sun that it was only the middle of the afternoon. They hadn't passed anyone else in a long time. If any of the people they had seen had thought them an odd sight, a black woman in morning dress, with two white men, in traveling clothes, Pascale had seen no indication of it. She could not expect help unless Devlin arrived.

The two men had relaxed their guard a little. They were on guard again as soon as a farm was spotted, but there were several long stretches of road where all that could be seen were the vines, spreading in their straight rows as far as the eye could see.

Pascale thought that soon they'd be leaving the wine country and entering an area where wheat fields dominated. But she knew many of the vintners in the area and those she didn't were sure to know the de Ravenault name. It was convenient that she was a black woman. Most everyone in this part of the world knew that the de Ravenaults were people of color. Pascale wouldn't have any difficulty persuading anyone that she was who she said she was. If she could find a protector who could defend her and himself from these men's weapons.

She was puzzling over the problem when the men slowed as the road climbed up a small hill. When they topped the rise, all three of them breathed a sigh of relief at the view that spread out before them. The men relaxed because there wasn't a house in sight, only the tall thin spire of a distant church steeple. A stand of old trees offered the only contrast to the fields. Grapevines covered acres of gently rolling earth in all directions. Far in the distance the road forked. Pascale took in the scene with the eye of a general preparing for battle. Halfway down the slope she pretended to lose her balance and sent her captor's horse sidling away from Serratt and his mount. As they skidded to the bottom of the decline, Baptiste turned back to look over his shoulder at Serratt, who shouted, "Careful, you fool!"

William relaxed again as his tired stallion slowed to a walk and he turned back to face the road. Pascale was waiting for that moment and she swung around putting all her weight behind her shoulder as she rammed it into his right side. She had only meant to keep him from holding on to her, or slashing out with his knife, but the force of the blow knocked him sideways, nearly unseating him and making it possible for her to grab the reins out of his hand. She took advantage of his stunned disbelief, wheeling the horse abruptly to the left. She kicked her heels into the animal's side and he jumped forward into a gallop, and Baptiste toppled off of the horse. One of his feet caught in the stirrups and Pascale almost slowed when she realized she was dragging him, but she heard Serratt's shout behind her and urged the horse on. She had to get to the cover of the trees. Serratt had a gun, and no good reason to let her live.

Just as she reached the side of the road, Pascale heard the report of the gun going off. Then she was in the shade provided by the little wood. A bullet pinged against the trunk of an oak and she leaned low in the saddle, letting the horse find its own way into the center of the small copse. A moment later she half slid, half jumped, from the stallion's back and gave it a swat on the rump to speed it on its way, then she ducked down in the undergrowth.

She listened carefully, but couldn't hear any sound of Serratt approaching. Then she heard the gun spit again—not from behind, but from the left. Nieuwerkerke's secretary had decided not to follow her into the woods, but to circle it. He was skirting the northern side, and so she made her way to the southern edge of the woods and then carefully peeked out. The grape-vines ran back up the hill that they had just ridden down. Pascale thought she could lose herself in the bushy leaves of the plants, which were well over three feet tall already.

"Pascale!" She heard Serratt cry out, and that told her all she needed to know. He was still on the far side of the trees. She didn't look back as she ran to the nearest row of grape-vines. A cornfield would have been easier to hide in, but the wheat fields wouldn't offer as good a hiding place as the vine-yards. She needed to get to the top of the hill before he com-pleted his circuit of the woods, so that she could watch Serratt, without him spotting her.

She started up the incline, bent low. When she had gotten halfway up the hill, she glanced back and saw "her" stallion, wander out of the trees. He no longer dragged Baptiste, and she wondered how badly the sailor had suffered from the run—but she couldn't think about that now. She could only hope that looking for his colleague would slow Serratt a bit, and keep going. She scrambled up the hillside, imagining herself a part of the earth and the grapevines, and finally crested it. She looked back over the rise and saw Serratt ride around the far edge of the trees.

She ducked down even further and held her skirts out of the way as she started down the far side of the rise. The run down was faster than the crawl upwards had been, it pulled her down-wards, her skirts hampering her movement. She stood and quickly took her bearings. The grapevines were thick and bushy, up to her shoulders, but there was of course, the empty space in each row where the pickers worked. A little narrow for a man and a horse, but she didn't suppose that would stop the madman who searched for her. Her best hope was to get as far as possible from where he had last seen her. She'd hide in the endless fields, and hope that he wouldn't find her before help arrived.

Pascale decided to take a chance on the open space between the rows, and run for it. She was still, she was sure, visible from the top of the rise, and she needed to put more distance between herself and her pursuer. She started to run, casting a look over her shoulder every few seconds, though she knew that if she saw him, she was dead. The effort was grueling. The sun was high, the ground beneath her feet soft and dusty making it difficult to find purchase. She almost slipped several times, and her heart pounded in fear and desperation as she finally ducked down again to rest.

She looked back to see how far she'd come. Serratt rode over the top of the hill. He was just a black silhouette against the sky to her. But his eye scanned the slope and came to rest directly on her hiding place. She looked down. She was hidden. Just then, the breeze blew her hair ribbon across her face. She'd forgotten about that.

He dismounted and tied his horse to a tree branch with slow deliberate movements that made her blood run cold. She watched through the leaves as he walked slowly up the hill, his gun trained directly at her. Pascale prayed silently that Jack would appear, magically, now, as Serratt came closer.

"Mademoiselle, please stand up." Pascale rose, afraid that he would shoot her right then. But he only gestured down the hill with the gun. She started walking, giving him a narrow berth. When she had passed him, he followed a few feet behind.

"What did you think you would achieve?" he asked.

She couldn't help herself. "Your partner is dead, isn't he?" Her voice was too shaky to sound truly triumphant.

"That fool. It's a loss to no one, I assure you," Serratt said. "In fact, it's more for me," he chuckled.

"According to you, everyone is a fool."

"Not everyone. I thought I had made it clear that I admired your . . . mind . . . enormously," he said.

"This may surprise you, but your opinion does not mean very much to me. You are just a mercenary—at the beck and call of the highest bidder."

"So that's what you think, eh?" Surprisingly, he didn't take umbrage at her insult, he only smiled smugly. Pascale was tired of this game. Her body and her mind were both worn out. As they approached his horse, she concentrated on keeping him talking.

Exhausted, she wasn't sure which questions would be safe to ask, or even useful, but she kept on. "Who hired you?"

He fairly cackled with glee. "The Mexicans themselves. They can't abide young Maximilian. Certainly not as their lord and master. They pretend to support him—they are obliged to do so because it was they who pestered the emperor until he deposed Juarez—but they know the count is not in a position to do what must be done. The country is too big, the population too large, and he can barely support his soldiers. They hired me to undermine his relationship with Napoleon—I think they hope to have one of their own put in his place."

Serratt thought this such a good joke, he was still laughing when Jack shouted from the tree line, "Release her, Monsieur Serratt."

Pascale nearly fainted as Jack stepped out of the woods, just thirty feet away. She veered toward him immediately.

"I will shoot her, Devlin," Serratt threatened, and Pascale faltered, but her feet took her steadily closer to Jack.

"No you won't. She's the only reason you're still alive, as you well know. If she survives, you have a remote chance of walking away from this on your own two feet."

Pascale did not look back. She concentrated on putting one foot in front of the other; closing the distance between Jack and herself.

"Drop that gun." He was completely focussed on Serratt, his gun at the ready. "I could shoot you right now, Monsieur," Jack said. "Another step and I will."

As Pascale came to within a few yards of him, she chanced a glance behind her. Serratt had lowered his pistol and stood staring at Jack.

"You win, Devlin. I give up."

"Behind me, Pascale," Jack ordered as she reached him.

"But he'll kill you. He hates you."

"He wouldn't take the chance. He knows the only reason I haven't pulled this trigger is because I wouldn't kill him in cold blood, no matter what he is. Although I was tempted when I saw him holding that gun at your back. And no decent man would blame me."

Serratt smiled. Even from this distance, Pascale thought she could feel the evil emanating from the man. "What now, Captain? You know I won't offer you any resistance. Are you really going to let me just walk away?"

"Do you think you can? What did you plan to do after your little adventure was over? Could you return to your old life of sorting through another man's correspondence and arranging his calendar? Didn't you think you might be bored?"

"Boredom is not a big problem when one has money, I've found. And even if I should get a trifle dull in Nieuwerkerke's employ, there are always people willing to pay for the services of one who has access to the kind of contacts which I do."

"Assuming Nieuwerkerke hasn't found out about you."

"There's not much danger of that."

"And the de Ravenaults? They're not exactly unconnected themselves. Nor am I for that matter. You can be sure we won't let this go unreported. The authorities should be quite interested."

Serratt shrugged. "You have no evidence. It is your word against mine. If worst came to worst, I could silence her quite easily. I could even arrange another little accident for you."

"I don't think so."

"You can't stop me," he said confidently. "Unless you're willing to pull that trigger."

A gun went off, and Pascale screamed. For a moment she thought Jack had fired, but as the secretary clapped his hand to his stomach, Jack grabbed her and pulled her with him to the ground. His eyes searched the woods around them.

"Baptiste!" Pascale exclaimed.

"It must be," Jack agreed. "My men will get him, never fear."

They waited silently, but there was no further sound or movement except the rasp of Pascale's breathing and the rise and fall of Jack's chest.

His hand went to her forehead, then her cheek, and Pascale felt a slight stinging where his fingers brushed her skin. The cuts Baptiste had made with his knife. "Did he hurt you?"

"I don't think so. I don't remember. I was so scared."

"My poor little heroine. Everything will be fine, now," he said soothingly, and somehow, even lying there in the dirt, with Jack's gaze darting from tree to tree and a lethal weapon in his hand, she believed him. Pascale rolled over and looked up at the sky through the leaves of the trees. She felt as though she'd been wrapped in layers of gauze. Every move, every word, everything that happened seemed dreamlike and fraught with meaning.

Jack pointed and she turned her head to see his men approach with William Baptiste in tow. But even as Jack took her hand and helped her up, it still didn't feel real. John Douglas appeared, as if from nowhere, at her side, and caught her gaze with his. The cobwebs seemed to dissipate a little.

"Do you think you can stand to ride a ways, miss? I bespoke us rooms at an inn a few miles from here."

"I want to go home," she said. The words slurred together and reverberated in her brain.

"It is a four hour ride to Beaune, at top speed. We wouldn't arrive before dark," John Douglas said.

Pascale wanted to be in her own house, as soon as possible, but John Douglas's concerned glances were not only for her, but for Jack as well. The sea captain looked exhausted and his ribs were clearly paining him.

"You're right. I wasn't thinking. I need to rest. We'd better go to your inn, John Douglas. Thank you."

They mounted up. Pascale rode with Jack. The late afternoon sun streamed down on them, but her teeth were chattering. Jack wrapped his arm around her.

Pascale barely registered their arrival at the inn. She was soon tucked into bed with a warm rock at her feet. Some time during the night, Jack slipped into the bed with her and she nestled into his chest, welcoming the warmth of his encircling arms. Then, she slept dreamlessly.

Pascale awoke alone in her bed. She felt surprisingly refreshed. The previous day's events came flooding back to her, and she was able to think of all of it, the shock and the terror and the miraculous rescue, with only a deep feeling of thankfulness that the nightmare was truly over. Now she could let Jack go.

Pascale had slept in, which wasn't surprising considering how weary she'd been in mind and spirit when she'd gone to bed the night before. Everything was prepared for their departure by the time she'd breakfasted.

She rode in a saddle of her own this time, and so was able to ride beside each man for a time and thank him. John Douglas was uncomfortable at her expression of gratitude, and she was easily able to turn the conversation to his employer's plans.

"Jack already met a bloke who has a ship for sale. He was thinking of buying a second boat before we lost the *Aurora*, he went to see her before we left Paris."

"That's wonderful," Pascale tried to summon up some enthusiasm for his good fortune.

"He didn't want 'er. He wanted another clipper. Course they stopped building them years ago, but he could refit another one, like we done before."

"The *Aurora*?" she asked.

"Yes." His dour face softened. Pascale didn't understand this attachment these men had for their vessels. But she thought it adorable. "She were a sleek beauty. The new four- and five-masted ships might have more cargo space, but they just don't have her lines. And they can't match her speed."

"Methinks he doth protest too much," she borrowed from the Bard. She smiled indulgently at John Douglas's catalogue of the clipper's attributes.

"Eh," he said, suddenly very dignified and aloof.

Pascale couldn't help teasing him a little bit more, hoping to bring the old seaman out again from behind that stoic facade. His arrogant British demeanor offered a challenge she couldn't refuse to take up. "The larger ships lack the grace and beauty of the clipper ship, don't they?" she asked.

He considered the question and answered solemnly, "I'd be lying if I said no."

"But as a businessman, Jack would never let so mundane a consideration as 'beauty' influence such an important decision."

Finally, a smile appeared at the corner of the valet's mouth. "Not much," he stated emphatically. But his eyes gave him away even before he chuckled, saying, "You little harpy. Don't you dare tell the cap'n that I told you none o' this. You don't know nothin' about clipper ships, do you?"

"I do now," she said. "I know it is less than sensible for Jack to buy one." He shook his head, but he was still smiling. "Even if it is the fastest."

"There are times when speed is of the essence," he continued to defend his and Jack's sentimentality. His words, however, brought to mind yesterday's misadventure, and her fear that help wouldn't come in time. Pascale sobered.

John Douglas noticed the change in her right away. "I'm just glad you're all right, miss." Even that slight display of emotion was too much for the crusty old sailor. Pascale deftly changed the subject once again.

"So, do you think you'll be going up to Paris right away, now that this is all over?" she asked.

"I don't know, miss." Pascale smiled and nodded and tried to ignore the compassion in his steady gaze. She was ashamed of herself for giving him reason to pity her, but she found she didn't feel as embarrassed as she ought that she was curious about Jack's plans. She wanted to spend as much time as she could with him—regardless of the fact that he was leaving and that he'd never pledged himself to her. She didn't care if the de Ravenaults had always been respectable. Even though her father was quite unusual, they had always been firmly anchored by her practical nature to the humdrum, unexciting rules of propriety that precluded them from ever belonging to the ranks of the more colorful artists of their acquaintance.

Perhaps she'd been wrong all this time. Her father's loosely held belief, and her firm conviction, that goodness and morality should be dictated from within rather than from without might just be a license, of sorts, to behave however they pleased. She couldn't believe the intimacies she'd shared with Jack were wrong. But neither could she deny that she'd allowed her baser instincts to guide her, rather than paying heed to her inner voice's sensible objections. She should probably feel guilt, or shame, or at least a modicum of remorse. Instead, she felt only joy at the thought of being with Jack Devlin—even if it was only for one more night.

He rode by her side for most of the trek, but they spoke little.

Papa, and the rest of the staff were waiting when they rode up to the château. She had bruises all over from Baptiste's rough treatment. She hadn't felt the pain of Baptiste's handiwork until now, she'd been too afraid. Papa placed a solicitous hand on her shoulder, and led her back toward the sofa.

"Quel bete. Let me call Cookie." She stared after him in shock as he strode out of the room with an air of purpose.

Jack let out a shout of laughter. "Paul!" Papa stuck his head back in the doorway. "I think that's the first sensible thing I've ever heard you say, sir. But you stay with Pascale. John Douglas is already taking care of everything." Paul de Ravenault came back to the sofa and sank down at Pascale's side with a sigh of relief.

Pascale was reeling with fatigue, but Papa's hand on hers gave her the energy to ask how he fared.

"Never felt better," he said. "I was able to convince Captain Devlin to promise to give you The Portrait if we found you . . . in time." Pascale shivered at the implications of this innocuous speech, but he didn't seem to notice. "It's my way of apologizing for everything."

"Thank you, Papa." She reached over and embraced him. When his arms came around her, tears filled her eyes. She had lived through a nightmare, without ever outwardly losing her composure. But those three simple heartfelt words caused the tears to brim over.

Paul de Ravenault took in the unusual sight of his ironwilled daughter with tears streaming down her face, and blanched. "I never should have hidden it in the first place. I knew that all along, but today—when we were riding after you—it was as if a bolt of lightning struck me. I never should have tried to get around you. I don't know why I thought I could handle this painting on my own. Look what a mess I got into the only time I ignored your advice."

Pascale didn't bother to set him straight about their part in this messy affair. In Paul de Ravenault's world, everything revolved around himself and his work. Pascale knew it was an extremely selfish attitude, but it was hard not to feel complimented that he included her in the small group of people who populated his universe.

That night, Jack came, for the first time, to her bedroom—her private sanctuary. It seemed somehow more wicked to lie with him there than when she had gone to his bed. Pascale felt, when he first appeared in her doorway, like an innocent maid about to be seduced by a worldly, devilish rogue. It was as if she suddenly stepped into the pages of a play, but it was real, too.

The lure of the forbidden enhanced her pleasure. Her nerves were stretched taut before he'd even touched her. So much for her practical, sensible nature, she thought. It was her heart, rather than her head, that had her cross the room and lead him to her bed.

They kissed, as though they'd been apart for years, rather

than just a few days. Pascale gloried in the shuddering sigh that he released as his hand found her breast. The feel of his rippling muscles under his nightshirt was not enough. She pulled the garment up and over his head quickly and eagerly and tumbled with him onto her bed. He divested her of her nightclothes more slowly, methodically, touching her all over as he unfastened her buttons and laid the gown open about her shoulders. It was not long before she welcomed the slick length of him inside her.

When she felt him deep within her, all she could think was, this cannot be sinful. Then she could no longer think as Jack brought her to the height of pleasure with his caresses.

For a long time after they lay still, holding each other. Pascale had said goodbye to him the last time they made love—but not aloud. This time she didn't say it at all. This wasn't the last of Jack Devlin. Now that his enemies had been brought to light and vanquished, he could visit Paris whenever he wished. She would see him again.

This time, when he left, he'd be whole and healthy. "A hard man to kill," Serratt had called him. Thank God. The thought was also a prayer. Jack had come to her rescue, just as she'd prayed, and she could only wish him happy. Her near brush with death had nullified any regrets she'd felt about the intimacies they'd shared. When she thought she was going to die, she'd been able to believe in Jack. She loved him. And she'd go on loving him even after he left her.

"Will you be staying in Paris long?" she whispered.

"I doubt it. I saw a ship before I left Paris that I wanted to purchase."

"A clipper?" she asked.

She felt his smile before she saw the flash of white teeth.

"Yes," he admitted. "She needs repairs, but by the time I get my new cargo, she'll be better than ever. At least I hope so."

"That's nice," Pascale said, nuzzling his neck. She ran her hand over his chest to his stomach, and then followed the same path with her mouth. "It's always good to hope for things."

She dared to hope he might even come back to her.

Thirty-one

Jack said goodbye to Pascale silently, not wanting to awaken her. She slept peacefully in her bed, her beauty unspoiled by the ordeal she'd suffered less than forty-eight hours before. He kissed one soft, smooth cheek, warm and golden brown in the dawn's gentle light. She looked as innocent as a babe. He should have cursed himself for taking advantage of that innocence, but he could no longer look on her without remembering the passionate wanton creature, who gave him more pleasure than any woman he had ever known.

She might look a delicate flower, but there was steel in her, and abundant courage, and a fire that burned deep.

He loved her. He felt the pull at his heartstrings, stretching thin between them like a golden chain, as he left her room and walked down the hallway. Paul emerged from his room just as Devlin was passing his bedroom door.

The old fellow hailed him with a hearty, "Good morning," as though the sight of a man in his nightclothes coming out of his daughter's bedroom was an everyday occurrence.

"Paul," Jack nodded, trying to stem the tide of guilt that washed over him at being thus discovered.

"So, I suppose you'll be able to make some arrangement to return The Painting now?" the artist asked.

"Of course," Jack said, through clenched teeth. Did the old man care nothing for his daughter at all? He should have been threatening to kill Devlin for having compromised her virtue. It wasn't natural for him to stand chitchatting idly in this situation.

"I really want to give it to Pascale. She'll need something to cheer her up when you're gone."

Jack's indignation was replaced by amazement. Paul de Ravenault had said exactly what Jack had been thinking only moments ago. Had Paul suddenly had a moment of rare insight, or could this mean he was, himself, as obtuse as Pascale's father.

"She . . . will be pleased, I'm sure," Jack responded.

"She would probably rather have you, instead," Paul mused. "But of course I can't give you to her." He wandered off down the hallway, leaving Jack standing staring after him, openmouthed.

Jack dressed hurriedly, and went to meet Henry Bates at their host's stables. Tom Bowman was waiting there with Henry, as was John Douglas. Jack's mind was still occupied with Paul's surprising comment and he only grunted in response to their greetings.

"Henry, I have a different errand for you today than the one we discussed. I want you, personally, to retrieve that package for me from Rouen. John Douglas can accompany me to my bank in Paris."

"Aye, Cap'n." Henry didn't blink an eye at the change in plans.

Jack gave his first mate his instructions and sent him on his way. He squashed the voice within which nagged that he should have handled this all important task himself rather than entrusting it to Bates. Jack had no choice. He was running out of time and he had an appointment to keep with his new bankers in Paris.

Henry would handle the thing, just as he always did. He had saved Jack's life, more than once. He could be trusted to complete this simple commission. Jack tried to put it out of his mind and concentrate on the business at hand. His leavetaking was rushed, but Jack could only be pleased that he was back in control again. He barely had time to say goodbye to Pascale, but he planned to bring her The Painting himself and knew he'd have a chance then to thank her properly for all she'd done for him.

Once back in Paris, Jack worked like a madman. He'd had the *Aurora* insured against loss, and the telegram he'd received from the London firm that held the policy had been reassuring. Though he wouldn't recover the full value of the ship and its cargo, he had not lost everything when his ship had gone down.

That communique had boosted his credit even further with his bankers. The future was starting to look brighter.

He hired some new men. He secured new cargo, forced for the first time in several years to carry other merchants' goods rather than buying and reselling his own, but he still managed to gain a contract in which he would share in the profits, if they were as high as he expected them to be.

Jack made some personal arrangements as well. While the last of the rebuilding was being carried out on the new clipper, he gave some of his men a week's leave—Henry Bates and John Douglas among them. He'd been pushing his crew nearly as hard as he'd done himself, and hadn't expected anything but a joyful "Hurrah" at this unexpected reward. Henry Bates, however, was not so easily distracted.

"What have you got up your sleeve, Cap'n?" asked his second in command. "I've never seen you so . . . high-strung. You're frazzled as a priest in a whorehouse. Are you agoin' to take some time off yourself, or are you agoin' to keep runnin' yourself ragged?"

"I'm fine, Henry. Everything's shipshape," Devlin assured him.

"I've seen you cooler under fire than you are now. What's in your mind? Or should I hazard a guess?"

Jack avoided his knowing eyes. "Just leave it be, Bates."

John Douglas flatly refused to leave Jack's side. "Where e'er you're going, I'm bound as well," he insisted.

"I don't want you, John Douglas. Why don't you go carousing with the other men and enjoy yourself. Forget about work for a few days. Forget about me."

"I canna do it, and it's breath you're wasting if you try and say me nay. I'll just follow ye."

"For heaven's sake, man!" Jack couldn't hold on to his already strained temper any longer. His valet's impertinence was the final straw. "I'm not a child to be cosseted and fussed over, though I understand why you've been so concerned. I order you out of my sight. I'm tired of looking at your face, and worrying about you worrying about me!"

He couldn't hold on to his anger, though, and John Douglas

knew him too well to be fazed. He waited Jack out and then continued to pack their things.

"I can't say I don't think it's a mistake you're makin' because I do, but that woman is better nor any I've seen yet, and if you've got to have one, she'd be my choice for ye. So let's bring her that package you've got hid in the back of the wardrobe, and get this embarrassin' business over with." And with that, Jack had to be content.

Despite his earlier impatience, the journey to Beaune was not hurried. The further he went the more slowly he found himself going. The carriage ride was not quite as excruciatingly painful as it had been on his first trip to the provence of Burgundy, and as the river valleys gave way to the rolling hills of the wine country, Jack found himself feeling like he was going home. Still he didn't spring the horses, or speed on his way. The closer he came to his goal, the more slowly he progressed. They stopped for lunch at a posting house on the third day, only four hours from their destination, and he found himself tarrying over his ale.

After making a hearty repast, he suggested to John Douglas, "Maybe we should stay the night here and time our arrival for the morning. I sent no message to inform anyone that we were coming. They won't expect us."

"They don't stand on no ceremony at that house, no one will care nor we came an hour after dark. The door will still be unbolted at midnight, as well you know. That old man's like as not to be wandrin' around in his nightshirt looking for sleeping people to paint. Get a hold of yourself, Cap'n and bite the bullet."

His only hope for delay at an end, Jack had the horses put to and climbed atop the box with his servant beside him. The horses followed the road at a sedate pace as his mind wandered. He didn't really wonder at the reception he'd receive. Paul was nothing if not a congenial host.

He just didn't know what he could say to Pascale to let her know how much she had come to mean to him. He loved her, but he didn't think that he could say that to the most maddening, most independent woman of his acquaintance. He felt like a boy again, trying to figure out how to say what was in his heart. Worst of all, he had no idea how she'd respond. Had Paul de Ravenault been right when he said he thought Pascale preferred him to her precious painting? The thought had haunted him for days.

He had thought Paul wrong at first, because Paul was always wrong. Jack was not an artist, or anyone fine—he was just an ordinary man, perhaps a bit wilder than some, and certainly less attractive a prospect than many he could think of. But as he thought back over all that had passed between them he had come to see it differently. If Pascale cared about him half as much as he cared about her, she would want him in her life, just as he wanted her in his future.

He was certain she cared about him, and yet . . . she didn't believe in her own father's love. How could he convince her she had his heart?

The carriage turned into the de Ravenaults' drive just after dusk. Men working in sight of the road raised their heads and shaded their eyes to see who was coming to call. The carriage was rented, so they wouldn't know at first sight who it belonged to. He saw a lad run across the lawns to the house after spying them coming.

Pierre was waiting at the open door when he brought the horses to a stop in front of the entrance. "Ah, hello, Sir. It's a pleasure to see you again," he said without any visible sign of surprise. He sent the boy who hovered behind him to the stable, for a man to come and take the horses around back.

"Thank you, Pierre. I don't have much with me, but will you have my things sent to my room without delay?"

"Certainly, Sir. I'll take care of it right away."

Jack and John Douglas climbed down from their seats and followed the stolid butler into the house.

"Are they in?" Jack asked impatiently as he entered the library.

"The master is up in his studio and left orders that he wasn't to be disturbed before dinner time, which is fast approaching.

Mademoiselle is down by the river. She should be in soon as the light is fading."

He gestured toward the tall windows that looked out over the lawns, to the woods beyond, where Jack knew a stream ran through the property. The evening light was almost gone, and he could see the moon rising over the trees.

"May I offer you gentlemen some refreshment?" Pierre asked.

"No, thank you," Jack said. He strode to the window and stepped through it, suddenly eager to get the business over with. "Unless you'd like something John Douglas?" He tossed over his shoulder without turning around, as he stepped through the portico.

He checked as he heard John Douglas emit a crack of laughter behind him, and turned in time to see his stalwart valet pound the dignified old butler once on the back before saying, "Can we find a proper cuppa tea in this house?"

Shaking his head, he walked briskly down the garden path, a smile forming on his lips as he caught a glimpse of water shining through the trees ahead of him. The sky was deep blue, and the rays of the moon reflected off of the water as he rounded a bend in the path and came to a bridge across the little stream. He spotted Pascale a few yards from the water's edge, standing in front of her easel, cleaning her brushes, her delicate silhouette framed by the sky which had darkened to deepest blue. She hadn't heard him come, and he had time to admire the pretty picture she presented. Her black hair was in thick braids which she had coiled up and curled around her head to nestle at the nape of her neck, the chocolatey skin there was set off by her simple white dress which shone in the twilight.

She jumped as a twig snapped beneath his feet and whirled around, a hand at her throat. Her eyes grew wide as he approached.

"You frightened me."

She seemed suspended in time, staring at him as he loomed closer. "What are you doing here?" she finally managed to ask.

"Looking for you," He said, stopping an arm's length away. He turned to look at her painting. "That's beautiful."

"You should see it in the light," she said, unable to disguise her pleasure in his compliment. "I still don't understand. Why are you here?"

"I brought you something. It's up at the house. Come on." She still stood, frozen. "Don't you want to see?"

He imagined she could guess what it was, so he was surprised when Pascale turned away from him and began packing the paintbrushes she'd been cleaning in a small box. "We said goodbye in Paris. I don't want to do it again."

"I said *au revoir*," he said. "As you know that doesn't mean goodbye, it means until I see you again."

She covered the painting with a piece of muslin and leaned it against a tree as she collapsed the easel. "But you have to go." It was a simple statement, but it rang in his ears like a death knell.

She gathered up the easel, paint box and canvas and started toward the path.

"I don't want to leave you," he said, taking her hand. She resisted at first, but then gave in. He stopped walking and waited for her to turn to him. Then he raised her paintstained fingers to his lips.

Pascale watched him kiss her hand, caught between laughter and tears. He knew she was confused. He should have said something before he left, instead of waiting. Now, perhaps it was too late.

He thought, finally, of the right words, the words that would convince her.

"Marry me, Pascale," he said, his voice rough.

She stared at him, her expression unreadable, then gently disengaged her hand and started walking toward the house. He trotted after her.

"You want to marry me?" She was clearly stunned. "Why?" she finally asked.

Jack almost smiled. "For the usual reasons. I love you. The question remains . . . do you love me?" he asked.

Slowly comprehension dawned, and along with it, uncertainty. "What about Papa?" she asked.

"I think your father could get along without you. Now that

he's completed his masterpiece." They had reached the house and he steered her toward the library where he strode over to the couch. There a framed canvas rested.

He uncovered the painting. She came to stand next to him to examine it. It was a portrait of Pascale, herself. Her father had caught her painting, her eyes looking out beyond the half-finished canvas at some vision that only she could see. This was not the practical, sensible housekeeper she had become. There was a mischievous quality to her expression, like that of a child. It was her as the artist she had once been—the artist she hoped to be again.

She finally looked up at Devlin. "I never cry," she said, through her tears. "It's just that I didn't expect . . . I never thought . . ." She turned her head into Jack's shoulder and his strong arm came around her back, pulling her closer.

"He knows you, Pascale. And he loves you. That will never change. I promise you."

Some dam within finally broke open, and she clung to him, glorying in the wash of tears and the release of the pain she'd held on to for so long. Not only had he given her himself, but he had freed her from the loneliness she'd known for so long.

"I love you," she said. "I love you so much."

"Thank heaven," he said, kissing her wet cheeks and then her trembling lips. When at last the kiss ended, they turned as one to look again at The Painting.

"It's really me," Pascale said, "I can't believe my father painted this."

"He adores you, you have only to see this portrait to know it." He nodded at the painting. "But you didn't believe it."

"I wanted to believe," Pascale said. "But I just couldn't. I was too busy trying to prove it to myself."

"I know," Jack murmured. "He should have just shown you this. He'd have saved us all a lot of trouble."

"Now he agrees with me," Pascale said in tones of mock indignation.

About the Author

Roberta Gayle is the pseudonym for a New York City Literary agent. She is the author of SUNSHINE AND SHADOWS, praised by critics as "an insightful, great reading experience." She is busy writing her next romance.

[handwritten at top: usually will Receive 1st wk of said month]

Look for these upcoming Arabesque titles:

June 1996
SUDDENLY by Sandra Kitt
HOME SWEET HOME by Rochelle Alers
AFTER HOURS by Anna Larence

[handwritten: 4½G, 4, 4 beside the June titles]
[handwritten: Will Receive @ 3 Jun 96]

July 1996
DECEPTION by Donna Hill
INDISCRETION by Margie Walker
AFFAIR OF THE HEART by Janice Sims

[handwritten: @ 3 Jul 96]

August 1996
WHITE DIAMONDS by Shirley Hailstock
SEDUCTION by Felicia Mason
AT FIRST SIGHT by Cheryl Faye

[handwritten: @ 96 3 Aug]